Ye:

Yesterday's Tomorrow
© 2011 Mark A. Roeder

Cover Design: Ken Clark

ISBN-13: 978-1460930465

ISBN-10: 1460930460

Acknowledgements

I'd like to thank Ken Clark, Kathy Staley, and James Adkinson for all the work they put in proof-reading this book. I'd further like to thank Ken for designing the cover and James for all his efforts in formatting this book.

Dedication

To Daniel Farmer—thanks for inspiring this book.

To Hunter—thanks for introducing me to Soma and showing me new sights in Bloomington.

Other Novels by Mark A. Roeder

Also look for audiobook versions on Amazon.com and Audible.com

Blackford Gay Youth Chronicles:

Outfield Menace

Snow Angel

The Nudo Twins

The Very Troublesome Ghoulish Bizarre Boy

Phantom World

Second Star to the Right

The Perfect Boy

Verona Gay Youth Chronicles:

Dark Angel

Ugly

Beautiful

The Soccer Field Is Empty

Someone Is Killing the Gay Boys of Verona

Keeper of Secrets

Masked Destiny

Do You Know That I Love You

Altered Realities

Dead Het Boys

Dead Boys of Verona

This Time Around

The Graymoor Mansion Bed and Breakfast

Tadzio – A Death in Verona

Shadows of Darkness

Heart of Graymoor

Come Back to Me

Skye & Colin

Marshall Mulgrew's Supernatural Mysteries

Christmas in Graymoor Mansion

The Fat Kid

Brendan & Casper: Older & Better

Light in the Darkness

Transitions

Three Months

Dream Lives

Farm Boys

Wicked Intent

The Ghost in My Closet

The Not So Secret Garden

*Second Chances**

There and Back Again: An Adventurous Boys Holiday

Big Brothers

The Worst Swap Ever

Lost in Tydannon: The Battle for Holbytlaton

Bloomington Gay Youth Chronicles

A Triumph of Will

*Temptation University**

The Picture of Dorian Gray

*Second Chances**

*Crossover novels that fit into two series

Adam Bluestone Novels:

Teen Idol Secrets

Falling Star

Take Two

Suddenly Real

Other Novels:

Nikias

Cadets of Culver

Lake Maxinkuckee Summer

Benji & Clyde

Fierce Competition

The Vampire's Heart

For more information on current and upcoming novels go to markroeder.com.

Bloomington, Indiana
Wednesday, June 17, 2009

I set the cardboard box down on the antique work table and took a moment to look upon my new home. After years of wandering about, I'd returned to the comfortable and familiar: my old hometown of Bloomington, Indiana. I nodded with approval as I walked through the small home. The movers had placed the furniture where it belonged and had stacked the packing boxes in the living room as instructed. The small brick home was built in the 1850s. It had two bedrooms, one of which I'd use as a guest room, a large kitchen, a nice-sized living room, a bathroom, and best of all a wraparound porch. I remembered walking past this very house when I was a kid, dreaming about owning it someday. I'd taken the long way around, but here I was.

I made a couple trips out to my Shay roadster to haul in the remaining boxes. Each was packed with possessions too valued or fragile to entrust to strangers. The task was soon finished. I'd learned over the years to cut down on my possessions, especially when it came to moving. After my last move, I'd sworn the next time I relocated I'd sell everything and walk out of the house with only a backpack filled with clothes. I hadn't kept my promise to myself, but I *had* dumped a lot of excess junk.

I stood looking at the stack of boxes. I'd narrowed things down as much as possible, but I still had too much stuff. I guess I hadn't done half bad, considering I was a collector.

A light rap on the glass of the door pulled my attention from the stack of boxes in the living room. I stepped to the door, opened it, and promptly froze. With great effort, I kept my mouth from dropping open.

"Hi. I saw the moving truck earlier. I...are you okay, mister?"

I pulled my thoughts together, attempting some semblance of control.

"Yes. Sorry. I have a lot going on today."

"Well, I don't want to bother you, but I wondered if you were interested in taking *The Herald*. It's the local paper. I deliver it."

"Um, sure."

"Great. Would you like the daily, the Sunday, or both?"

"Um, both, I guess."

"Great. Here's the info. You can let me know the length of subscription you'd like when I deliver the paper. What's your name? I'll put you down in my book."

"Spock. Percy D. Spock."

The boy paused for a long moment, gazing at me.

"Are you a writer?"

"Yes. Why?"

"I read your books!"

"Oh, you're the one," I said, smiling.

"Come on. You're famous."

"Mark Twain is famous. I'm just a writer and not a particularly well-known one."

The boy laughed.

"You're well known to me. I can't believe you live in Bloomington! No one interesting ever moves here, but I should let you go. You're busy unpacking. I'll deliver your first paper next Wednesday. It was nice meeting you, Mr. Spock."

I almost held my breath for the inevitable *Star Trek* comment, but it did not come. Percy DeForest Spock was my penname, chosen partially because I'd long been a big *Star Trek* fan. I'd taken to using the name when I started writing several years before. My real name was Tyler Perseus.

"It's nice to meet you..."

"Tyler," the boy said.

I very nearly raised an eyebrow, just like my namesake from Vulcan, but stopped myself in time.

"Tyler, call me Percy."

"Cool, although I like Mr. Spock. It makes me feel like I'm on the bridge of the Enterprise." Tyler laughed. "Bye."

I guess the *Star Trek* comment was inevitable after all.

"Bye."

That voice...that face...that hair...I shook my head as I closed door. I walked across the room and sank into a nearby chair. I rubbed my eyes. For a moment there, I'd thought...but no. The boy who'd just come to my door was twenty years too young. I was remembering the ghosts of my youth.

I leaned up, pulled out my wallet, and slid out the photo I'd carried with me since my senior year in high school. There was the eighteen-year-old me smiling back at me. I wasn't a bad-looking kid back then—dark hair and eyes and a nice smile. I was seated so closely beside a shorter boy with reddish-brown hair that our shoulders were almost touching. Daniel. It had been twenty years, but Daniel was always with me. You don't forget your first love.

I smiled. It wasn't love at first sight. In fact, I all but ignored him the day we met...

Northern Indiana—Camp Neeswaugee
Saturday, June 17, 1989

"I'm Daniel."

"Huh?"

I turned to the boy standing near me. My attention had been so focused elsewhere I didn't even know anyone was standing near.

Smooth move, Perseus, why don't you just tell everyone you're a fag.

"Oh, sorry. I'm Tyler. Hey."

"Hey."

Daniel grinned. Did he know I'd just been checking out the hunky blond counselor across the room?

God, please no. The last thing I need is to be pegged as the homo counselor. Yeah, that would go over great with the kids and their parents.

"So... we're supposed to introduce ourselves. I'm Daniel Keegan. I'm a counselor in Division 6."

"I'm in Division 4."

I kept stealing glances of the blond hottie, but far more carefully now that Daniel had latched onto me. I was hoping he'd just go away.

In case you're wondering about the division stuff, the summer camp where I'd signed on as a counselor was part of the Blackford Military Academy. The camp had a military framework with ranks both for counselors and the kids, marching, parades, and all that. It was mostly just a summer camp or I wouldn't be here. I'm not the military type, unless watching M*A*S*H counts and I don't think it does.

"Ah, the enemy," said Daniel with a grin. "My division will be competing against yours and Division 3 for the athletic and marching banners. First summer?"

"Yeah."

"Me, too. So what do you think of orientation so far?"

"Well, I like meeting new people."

"Very diplomatic of you. It is a little boring, isn't it?"

"Yeah, a little." I smiled.

I heaved a quiet sigh of relief. Daniel gave no further indication he'd noticed me checking out the blond hunk. I had to be more careful. I'd made it all the way through my junior year at North High School in Bloomington without being found out. I couldn't let my guard down just because this was camp.

"Now, switch," said Mrs. Tripp, the Program Director.

We were supposed to be introducing ourselves to the other counselors. I'd actually forgotten all about that, but then bulging biceps tend to distract me. We were involved in a "get to know the staff" exercise. I was tempted to zero in on the heartthrob I'd been checking out, but I'd learned my lesson. Instead, I turned toward a girl standing near me.

"Hi, I'm Tyler."

"I'm Amy."

Soon, we all took our seats in the Dining Hall again. My mind drifted as I sat at the round table and tried to listen to Mrs. Tripp. I have an attention span of about fifteen seconds, so it wasn't easy to stay with her, even though I was trying. I didn't know squat about being a camp counselor so I needed all the help I could get.

The Dining Hall was huge. There were two serving lines and probably thirty or forty large round tables. Six counselors sat at my table and there was room for at least a couple more. The Dining Hall had a shallow U shape and was built like an A frame. The point of the roof soared thirty feet or more above our heads. The windows were screens, not glass, which made sense for a building only used during the summer months.

My attention was drawn back to Mrs. Tripp as she handed out our class assignments. Like everyone else, I'd checked off what classes I wanted to teach during the instructional periods. I prayed I'd get one of my choices.

Please, no sports. No sports.

I'm not all that athletic; well, I'm not athletic at all. I'd make a complete fool of myself if I had to teach basketball or soccer.

Yes! Indian Crafts!

I smiled as I walked back to my seat. Let others sweat it out in the hot sun. For the first two weeks at least, I'd be spending my days with beads, paint, and yarn.

The rest of the meeting was just too boring for words. At least there was a nice cool breeze coming up off distant Lake Potawatomi. I always tried to find something good in every situation.

One very good situation indeed occurred later in the afternoon. At least I thought it was a good situation at the time. I walked into the staff latrine (latrine is what they call the rest room/shower area at Neeswaugee. Military academy, remember?) and almost ground to a halt when I spotted the blond hunk wearing nothing but a towel. If I'd been five seconds earlier, I might have seen *everything*. He'd obviously just finished his shower.

"Hey," he said.

"Hey."

It took a colossal effort not to stare. I'd been attracted to his good looks half-way across the Dining Hall, but up close and half naked...damn! He was sooo handsome. I'd say cute, but he was too masculine to be cute. He had this wavy blond hair and pale blue eyes. His body—yum! Rivulets of water traveled down his muscular pecs and over the ridges of his abdomen. There was a bulge in his towel that hinted at what he had down there, too. I cursed myself for not coming to the latrine a few seconds sooner!

"I'm Tyler, Division 4."

"Ah, you're with the cubbies. I'm Brand. I'm with the D&B."

Cubbies means cubs as in wolf cubs, the 9 to 11 year olds. Divisions 3, 4, and 6 were the Cub Divisions. The older boys in camp, 11 to 13, were called Beavers. No, I don't know why. Neeswaugee had been going since 1912, so a lot of stuff was lost in time, at least to a new guy like me. The Beaver Divisions were 1, 5, and 7, and then there was the D&B, which is short for the Drum & Bugle Corp. Before you ask, no, I don't know why there is no Division 2. There's a rumor they were lost in a war, but that's just ridiculous.

"This your first summer?" I asked, mainly because I didn't know what else to say and I didn't want Brand to leave just yet.

"Second. You?"

"It's my first."

"Kind of overwhelming, isn't it?"

"Yeah."

"Just remember, everyone was new at some point."

"Thanks."

"See ya."

"Yeah, see ya."

I checked Brand out as he opened the screen door. He had a wide muscular back and, even though it was covered with a towel, I could tell he had a nice ass. I wanted Brand so bad I could hardly stand it.

I looked at myself in the mirror.

Give it up, Tyler. There is no way you'll hook up with Brand. Don't even try. There is no way he's gay and even if he was, he could get guys ten times better looking than you. You've got to keep your homo thoughts under wraps. You're here to be a counselor, not check out other counselors.

I nodded to myself, but was I strong enough to listen?

Bloomington, Indiana
Wednesday, June 17, 2009

I grinned as I remembered that long ago encounter with Brand Elwolf. What a name and what a body! I had never met a guy with such perfectly sculpted pecs, abs, and biceps outside the pages of a magazine. (I still haven't.) It's little wonder I barely even noticed Daniel. If I knew then what I knew now...but then hindsight is 20/20. When I was seventeen, Brand seemed like nothing less than a god.

I was amazed by the memories that had returned to me, not the memories of Brand and Daniel, but all the little details of camp. In my mind, I could picture exactly how the Dining Hall looked back then, the humidity of the latrine, and even the damp-wood scent of the cabins. Of course, some of my memories were far from twenty years old. I'd stopped working summers at Neeswaugee, what, four or five years ago? I'd been a counselor for years, then the Division Commander of Division 6, my old enemy. I wondered what the seventeen-year-old me would have thought about that? In my final years, I was the Indian Crafts Director. Along the way I was the Military Officer for Division 4, the Camp Military Officer, and a counselor and Senior Counselor in the Specialty Camp that came after the six-week session. Back in 1989, it was all in front of me, though, and I doubt I could have imagined I'd stick with Camp Neeswaugee all those years and do all those different jobs. Sometimes, I still couldn't believe I'd been a Division Commander and held the rank of Major.

Tyler. I couldn't get the boy who shared my name and had just come to my door out of my thoughts. He looked so much like my first love I'd actually thought it *was* him for a split second. If reality had been kept at bay a few moments more, I would have hugged him. It's a good thing I realized inside a second that the boy before me couldn't possibly be Daniel Keegan. He'd be thirty-seven now, just like me. I wondered briefly where Daniel was now and what had become of him, but it was no more use than it had been through all the long years. I'd even searched for him on the internet, but had never found him. I just hoped he was happy.

I'd spent enough time reminiscing for the moment. I got up and put myself to work. The house needed to be made livable. My first task was to get the kitchen in some sort of order so I wouldn't starve to death.

When I walked into the kitchen, it looked as if a trip to Hardee's or Arby's would be in order later. I had a lot of cleaning to do before I could even begin to unpack the boxes marked "kitchen." I immediately wished I'd asked Tyler if he wanted to make a few extra bucks by helping me move in. It was too late for that now. I'd just have to tackle the job myself.

The kitchen in my "new" home was unlike most kitchens because it had no built-in cabinets. This had been a selling point for me because I liked to use antique kitchen furnishings instead of the bland built-in cabinets found in most homes. The lack of built-in cabinets saved me the time and expense of ripping them out. I loved the bank of large windows that made up most of one wall, looking out into the small back yard filled with roses, lilac, and snowball bushes. More windows were located around the door that led out onto the wraparound porch, and still more were located on the opposite wall. The result was a large kitchen with plenty of natural light. The original builder really knew what he was doing. Of course, the home was built at a time when electric light had yet to be invented.

My large, cherry step-back cupboard, a Hoosier cupboard, my great-grandmother's pie safe, and an oak kitchen cupboard had all been set in place by the movers, as had my oak kitchen table with lion's paw feet and the set of four slat-back chairs that were as old as the house.

I'd cleaned the old, wide plank, wooden floor before the movers had brought in my furniture, but it needed cleaning again. The windows needed washing, inside and out, all the furniture needed dusting, and the old soapstone farmhouse sink needed a good scrubbing.

As I worked, the scent of the pine cleaner pulled my mind back to twenty years before, when I was cleaning Cabin 34 in anticipation of the opening day of summer camp...

Camp Neeswaugee
Tuesday, June 20, 1989

The cabins were supposedly cleaned before our arrival, but one of the first things I'd done was drive into town for cleaning supplies. After cleaning my own small room, I wiped down all the center bins, athletic bins, closets, and the rails of the bunk beds. The scent of damp wood and Pinesol filled the air.

I had a lot of time to think as I cleaned. I hadn't counted on being attracted to other guys at camp. I'd thought of Neeswaugee as a sort of vacation from the torment of high school, where I was surrounded by guys I wanted but couldn't have. Okay, that makes me sound like a total slut. I don't mean I wanted *all* the guys around me. I probably only lusted after one in ten. Well, maybe two in ten, but you get my meaning. I hadn't even been with a guy yet, if you know what I mean. Okay, I'll say it. I'm a seventeen-year-old virgin. Kind of embarrassing I guess, but then it's not easy to find someone when you're a boy who likes boys. Things aren't especially violent at my high school, but checking out the wrong guy could earn me a fist in the face. I'm getting off the topic again, but I do that a lot so you'll have to get used to it. My point is that I thought that this summer I'd be away from guys who made my pants dance. When I thought about summer camp, I thought about being around kids. I'd totally forgotten that those kids would have counselors, male counselors my age and older, counselors who could look like Brand. It was high school all over again, but even worse.

I had to be even more careful at Neeswaugee than I was in school. At my high school, I was just another student. Here, I was a counselor, working with *boys*. If the boys in my cabin or their parents found out I was gay, they'd probably freak out and think I was some kind of child molester or AIDS carrier. Some people thought that about gays. It was total bullshit, but let's face it, a lot of people will believe anything they're told. That's why X-ray glasses, miracle weight-less pills, and penis enlargement drugs sell so well. I didn't have the slightest sexual interest in boys. I thought some boys were cute, yeah, but I also thought puppies, kittens, and baby chicks were cute, too. Even if my campers were my age, which would just be stupid of course, there is a thing called self-control. I had a couple friends at school who were totally hot, but I didn't think of them *in that way* because we were friends. Not that I think it's bad for friends to mess around. I just didn't want to risk those friendships because I didn't know if those guys were gay or not. Plus, I didn't want to change things between us even if they were gay. I wanted sex, yeah. I needed it! But, I needed friends, too.

Despite my lack of forethought, there were some hot counselors at camp. I was just going to have to keep myself reined in. It was kind of unfair really. I'd already seen some of the guy counselors flirting with the female counselors who stayed just across the soccer fields. *That* wasn't considered unprofessional. Our situations weren't quite the same, though. The hetero guys wouldn't be showering with the girls across the field, although I bet they would have paid their entire summer's salary to do so. I, on the other hand, would be showering with the other male counselors. Chances are I'd see most of them naked. If I was a straight guy, I don't know how I'd feel about a gay guy checking me out. I might be flattered or I might be uncomfortable. I didn't know how these hetero guys thought. They were kind of a bizarre species. Of course, I had no interest at all in most of the other counselors. There were only a select few I wanted to see naked.

I tried not to check out Brand when our paths crossed. Really! It was almost impossible, though. His face alone was so achingly handsome the mere sight of him made me sigh. Brand made our staff shirts look sooo sexy. His chest looked ready to rip right through the Neeswaugee Staff logo and his biceps stretched the sleeves to the ripping point.

Despite the torment of Brand, camp was a blast! At least so far, and this was only orientation. The kids hadn't even arrived yet. I enjoyed hanging out with the other counselors, though, and some things I'd learned helped set me at ease. I'd been kind of concerned about the whole military aspect, but each division had a military officer to handle most of that, and our M.O. wasn't me! Captain Fitch would handle teaching the boys how to march and he'd get them ready for parades. There was a whole leadership program at Neeswaugee so the boys appointed as division leader, guideon-bearer, and such, would be taking care of the military aspect under the supervision of the counselors.

The military element of Neeswaugee was a rather small part of it anyway. It was basically just a summer camp, even though it was the largest summer camp in the whole U.S.! There were around 200 staff members alone and when the kids arrived, the camp population would rise much higher! I really only had to worry about the ten to twelve boys who would be in my cabin and the 60 boys in my division, plus the kids in my Indian Crafts classes. It was only in my cabin that I was on my own. Everywhere else there were other counselors to help.

The counselors mostly stuck with the guys in their own division. Orientation was kind of bonding time. We did hang out with guys from other divisions and, of course, a lot of the guys flirted with their female counterparts and vice versa.

I was running late to lunch on Wednesday so I ended up sitting alone after the other D4 guys took off. I was perfectly content to be alone with my own thoughts for a while, especially when I saw Brand chatting up one of the female counselors. He was leaning up against the wall with his hand braced above her head, his bicep flexing. He was obviously hitting on her and after just a bit, they left together. I frowned.

"Having a rough time?"

"Huh? Oh. I dunno."

"Mind if I sit here or are you not allowed to sit with the enemy?" Daniel asked.

"No, sit down. I've been abandoned by my division so it will serve them right if I consort with the enemy."

Daniel laughed. I remembered him from that first orientation meeting that now seemed so long ago.

"The kids start arriving on Friday," Daniel said. "I'm excited, but a little nervous. I don't know if I can handle ten-year-olds."

"Yeah."

"You seem distracted."

"Huh? Oh, sorry."

Quit thinking about Brand. You'll only drive yourself insane.

"So, how do you like the counselors in Division 6?" I asked.

"They're cool, mostly, but they're a little too much like the jocks at my high school. I think they're going to be obsessed with winning."

"So you're not the athletic type, huh?" I asked.

"No."

"Me either. I just know I'm going to suck at coaching softball and soccer. I am not looking forward to cabin games."

Daniel laughed.

"I still haven't gotten the whole off-sides thing figured out in soccer," Daniel said.

"That's so confusing! My major said we'll get a lot of boys from Mexico and a lot of them are killer soccer players. My plan is to pick out one of the boys who looks like he knows what he's doing and put him in charge of the team."

"You'll make a great coach then."

"What makes you say that?" I asked.

"Because you're smart enough to know that you don't know what you're doing. I think I'm going to steal your idea."

"Uh-oh. I'm aiding and abetting the enemy."

"I won't tell if you won't."

"Deal."

Daniel and I talked and laughed all through lunch. That's one thing I loved about camp, there was always someone to be with. Most everyone was friendly and you could pretty much sit down at any table and feel welcome. The Neeswaugee Dining Hall was so different from my high school cafeteria. There were no territories here. There was no jock table, no auto shop table, and no burnout table. We all wore the same white shirts with same Camp Neeswaugee logo and the same khaki or hunter green shorts.

I spotted Brand again just before I finished lunch. He was alone. He'd only been gone with that girl about fifteen minutes, but that was plenty of time to do a lot. I guess it didn't matter. Brand was obviously interested in girls. I wasn't surprised, but I was disappointed.

Yeah, like that stud would want you even if he was gay.

"Are you sure you're okay?" Daniel asked.

"Huh? Yeah, I'm okay."

I stole another glance at Brand as he walked out of the Dining Hall with an apple. I turned back to Daniel. He was watching me.

"Well, I have to run!" I said.

I wasn't in a hurry, but I could feel my face growing red and I didn't want Daniel to see.

"Later," said Daniel.

"Yeah, later."

I stepped out of the main entrance of the Dining Hall and looked out across the soccer fields. Sunlight glinted off the surface of Lake Potawatomi in the distance. One of our orientation meetings had been held on the bleachers in front of the crew shed down on the shore of the lake. I'd read that Lake Potawatomi was big; one-and-a-half miles wide and two-and-a-half miles long, but that didn't prepare me for the vast expanse of crystal clear blue water that seemed to stretch out forever. It wasn't difficult to see most of the east and west shores from the academy, which was located on the north shore. The south shore was nothing more than a hazy line in the distance. Sailboats, jet-skis, and fishing boats cruised along the surface at all hours of the day and night. Even from the Dining Hall I could see sailboats sailing along the north shore.

I turned to the left and walked up the steep hill into the boy's area. I passed through Division 3, one of the enemy divisions, and then entered Division 4 territory. Soon, I was back at Cabin 34, my home for the entire summer. All was relatively quiet now, but the boys would soon arrive.

Bloomington, Indiana
Tuesday, June 23, 2009

"How about the books?" Tyler asked.

"Try to arrange them by subject. Arrange the history books by time period if you can. The *Star Trek* novels are numbered on the covers."

When Tyler had returned a couple of days after our initial meeting, I'd asked if he was interested in a part-time job helping me to get moved in. He'd jumped at the opportunity. Now, we were in the living room, trying to establish some semblance of order.

"Can I be nosy?" Tyler asked.

"What do you mean?"

"Well...I'm wondering what you're working on now."

"I have a few projects going, but right now I'm focused on a book of Christmas stories."

"Christmas stories? In June?"

I laughed.

"If I want the book to be ready by Christmas, I can't wait until the holidays to start writing. Actually, I hope to have it out by early-November."

"How do you write Christmas stories in the summer?"

"I'm actually not writing Christmas stories, I'm rewriting them. For several years, during the holidays, I've written Christmas tales. I finally have enough for a book, so I'm polishing them up to get them ready for publication."

Tyler continued filling my shelves.

"You have a lot of books on ghosts."

"I like to read 'true' ghost stories."

"You think they are true?"

"Some of them. I imagine a lot of them are made up but others are real. I read ghost stories every fall, from about mid-September to All Saints' Day."

"All Saints' Day?"

"November 1st, the day after Halloween. Once November hits, I switch over to reading Christmas stories and writing them, too."

"Dang! There's a whole box of *Star Trek* novels!"

"You should have seen my collection before I sold all the copies I'd already read."

"Yeah?"

"There were two or three hundred more."

"Whoa! Are you sure you aren't a Trekkie?"

"Not full-fledged, I just like watching the shows and reading the novels. It's a great escape because it's so different from my life. The characters and settings are so familiar that it's easy reading."

"Don't take this the wrong way, but it seems kind of strange that you like *Star Trek* when your house is kind of like a museum. I mean, you've got all this old, old stuff and then you've got these books about the future."

I laughed.

"Perhaps my unusual perception of time has something to do with it."

"What do you mean?"

"To me, the past, present, and future aren't separate. Most people think of the past as something that is over and done with and the future as something yet to come. They only live in the present."

"Um, isn't that how things are?"

"Not for me. To me, the past, present, and future are all what most people consider the present."

I laughed at the strange look Tyler gave me.

"I should warn you—writers tend to be very strange people."

"Hmm, maybe we should hide these away. I think you've had enough," Tyler said, pretending to take my *Star Trek* novels.

I laughed.

Tyler looked so much like Daniel it was scary. In all my years at Camp Neeswaugee, I'd noticed that there were certain types of looks—facial features and such. Time and again, I'd seen a boy who looked very much like another boy who had been in camp some years earlier. Sometimes, it was a younger brother, but often it was someone completely unrelated. Tyler looked exactly as I remembered Daniel. Such a striking resemblance was rare but not impossible. When I was somewhat younger than Tyler, I'd spotted my own twin while on vacation in Kentucky. He wasn't really my twin. I had only one brother who was ten years older than me and we looked nothing alike. The boy I saw looked so much like me, though, that I think we could have switched places without anyone ever catching on. My mom actually thought he was me when she caught a glimpse of him. I wished I'd gone over and talked to him, but I was too shy then and I don't think he even saw me.

"You sure have a lot of stuff," Tyler said.

"This is the scaled down version. You should have seen all the junk I had a few years ago before I started selling it off."

"You had *more*?"

"A lot more. I blame my parents. They took me to auctions with them when I was a kid, by the time I was eight years old I was buying stuff. When I was your age I already had as much junk as I have now."

"No way!"

"Yeah, I've narrowed things down a lot. I keep only what I like the best."

"You do have some cool things. Most of it looks really old."

"Most of it isn't that old, only a hundred years or so."

"You don't call that *old*?"

I laughed.

"Here," I said, digging through a box I was unpacking. "I'll show you something old."

I pulled out a flint spear point about four inches long and handed it to Tyler.

"This is called a Clovis point. The Native Americans used spears with points like this one to hunt Mammoths and Mastodons."

"You're putting me on, right?"

"No."

"Just how old is this?"

"At least a hundred centuries."

Tyler's mouth fell open.

"This is 10,000 years old?"

"At least. It may be a good deal older."

"Whoa. Take it back. I'm afraid to hold it."

I grinned, took the point back, and placed it with a few other artifacts I was placing in an antique cabinet.

"So you see, a hundred years isn't that old when you compare it to 10,000 years. I guess I'm so accustomed to using antiques that I don't think of them as antiques. To me, anything made after 1900 is new."

"You're not like anyone else I've ever met."

"I told you, writers are *very* strange people."

"More like interesting."

We continued setting the living room in order until the mid-afternoon. I invited Tyler into the kitchen where I put on a tea kettle.

"I never thought to ask—do you like tea?" I asked. "I have soft drinks in the refrigerator if you'd prefer. I plan to buy a coffee maker and some coffee for guests, but I haven't gotten around to that yet."

"Tea will be great. My dad got me to drinking it. I think he's a teaoholic. He's got me hooked."

"What kind do you like? I have Scottish Breakfast, Irish Breakfast..."

"Oh, Irish Breakfast! That's my favorite."

"Hmm, that's one of my favorites, too. So, tell me about yourself, Tyler. I guess you live with your parents?"

"Just my dad. My mom died when I was little. I don't remember her."

"I'm sorry."

"I don't miss her much because I was so young when she died. I wish I could have known her, but maybe it's easier that she died when I was little. I couldn't handle my dad dying. I'd miss him so much."

"So, did you grow up in Bloomington?"

"Yeah. It's a cool place, mainly because Indiana University is here. It would probably be boring without the university. Most of the little shops and unusual restaurants wouldn't exist if IU wasn't here."

"I know what you mean. I moved back because there's so much to do here—museums, theatre, cool restaurants, and shops. Bloomington has things that are usually only found in much larger cities, and I don't care for large cities."

"You lived here before?" Daniel asked.

"Yes. I grew up here. I went to North High School."

"No way! I go to North High School! I had no idea you were from Bloomington."

I smiled wistfully as I turned to the steaming tea kettle and took it off the stove. I poured the near-boiling water over the tea bags in our Blue Willow cups and placed it back on the burner.

We sat there, talked, and sipped hot tea. I thoroughly enjoyed Tyler's company. If I'd been twenty years younger...but then I wondered if I was really thinking about Tyler or about the boy from my youth who looked so very much like him. I suppose it didn't matter, but I was glad I'd found someone so companionable to help me get settled in.

We returned to work in the living room. There were a few more boxes to unpack, but we spent most of the time rearranging the furniture to get it just right. All the furniture was antique, of course, except for two reproduction wing back chairs and a love-seat, all in dark burgundy leather. As much as I loved antiques, some of the chairs and sofas from days gone by weren't all that comfortable. The chairs and love-seat matched the older pieces so well I doubt anyone would notice they weren't antique.

The one other non-antique item was a large screen TV. This was my home, not a museum after all. Of course, the TV sat on a low worktable that dated to about 1830. I'd purchased the table for $40 at an auction when I was only fifteen. I'd kept it all these years mainly because it retained its original red paint and because I suspected it was Shaker.

Tyler and I placed a large braided rug in front of the TV and arranged the love-seat and wing-back chairs around it to create a room within a room. The rug was dark red, black, gray, and blue, with some lighter red and rose thrown in. It matched beautifully with the red of the table and the dark burgundy of the other pieces.

"This piece scares me just a little," Tyler said as he helped me move a large wooden trunk in behind the love-seat.

"Why is that?"

"It looks like a coffin."

I laughed, then stood back to try to see the chest as Tyler might.

"I suppose it does, but I always thought it looked more like an oversized treasure chest."

"Hmm, now that you mention it...I like thinking of it as a treasure chest better anyway."

"I did see a coffin sell at an auction once. I thought about buying it because it was so unusual, but what would I do with a coffin?"

"A coffin? Really?"

"Yes, it was an old wooden one. I guess it was used as a display piece by a coffin maker way back. I'm sure it was never used. Unlike other items, used coffins don't turn up at auctions, for obvious reasons."

Tyler grinned. He was incredibly cute. When he smiled like that, it was if Daniel was in the room with me. I wouldn't let myself linger on such thoughts, however.

"So, what is this thing?" Tyler asked, still looking at the chest.

"It's an immigrant's trunk. When people came to the U.S. from other countries, they packed all their possessions in a trunk like this one. Mainly it would be filled with clothing, quilts, and family heirlooms. This one is dated 1843 on the front if you look closely. It probably came over on a clipper ship or perhaps a steamer. Do you know why it has a domed top instead of a flat one?"

"Um, because it looks cooler?"

"No, because the hold of the ship might have dozens and dozens of trunks in it. Those with rounded tops like this one had to be placed on top, because another trunk won't sit on it. Therefore, it was less likely to be damaged. If the hull leaked a little, it was also less likely to get wet."

"It's really cool to think this came all the way across the ocean way back then. Do you know where it came from?"

"No, but the name on the front is German, so it's likely from Germany or at least a Germanic country."

"I think I can see why you like old stuff. There's a story with every piece, isn't there?"

"Yes. I just wish I knew the stories behind all these pieces. Come over here and I'll show you my favorite piece."

I led Tyler to a small wooden chest, not quite two feet wide and less than a foot tall. The wood was very dark and it was decorated with metal-work that looked as if it might be brass. Two stylized peacocks faced each other on the front.

"What is it?" Tyler asked.

"I've never been able to figure that out. It's a chest, obviously, but it's quite unusual. Try to open one of the three little drawers at the bottom."

Tyler tugged, but the drawer wouldn't budge.

"It's stuck."

"Actually, it's locked."

"But there's no key hole."

"Watch this," I said.

I opened the lid and lifted up a small metal rod that ran down inside the front of the chest, then I pulled the drawer open.

32

"That's really cool," Tyler said.

"There was a hasp on the front of the chest so the lid could be padlocked. When the lid is down, the drawers can't be opened. My guess is that it's some kind of spice or tea chest. There is the lingering scent of some spice inside, but I've never been able to figure out the scent."

"How old is it?"

"I found it in an antique mall. The dealer believed it was from the 18th century. I think it may be far older. I bought it because it was so unusual and because it looks Narnian."

"Narnian?"

"Haven't you ever read the *Chronicles of Narnia* by C. S. Lewis?"

"Um, no."

"I'm buying you copies then. You'll love it."

Tyler just smiled.

In another hour, we had the living room in shape.

"I'm starving," I said when we'd finished. "I'm also far too lazy to cook. How about I take you out for supper?"

"Really?"

"Sure. Why don't you go home, get cleaned up, and come back? I need a shower and a change of clothes before I go anywhere."

"Yeah, me too. Definitely. The guy I work for is a slave driver!"

I laughed.

"Get going and I'll see you back here in a few."

As I was putting on some cologne after my shower, I stopped and gazed at myself in the mirror. I was far more excited about taking Tyler out to eat than I should have been.

It's been way too long since you've had a date.

I didn't even want to think about getting back into the dating game. I just wanted to enjoy my life for a while with no entanglements and no commitments. Tyler fit the bill quite nicely. I enjoyed spending time with him, but since he was young enough to be my son I could go out with him without any expectations. Taking him out to eat was just that and nothing more. I could relax and not be concerned about what he thought of me. Then again, I was never overly concerned with what anyone thought of me. With me it's pretty much what you see is what you get, at least it's been that way since my college years.

Tyler came back looking very sharp in jeans and a dark green polo shirt. I had dressed in khakis and a dark purple shirt I'd bought at the Aeropostale outlet store in Edinburgh—Edinburgh, Indiana that is, not Edinburgh, Scotland. I'd always loved purple.

"I'm ready for our date," Tyler said and then grinned.

I was mostly sure his choice of words was a joke, but what if he was one of those young guys who were attracted to older men?

Yeah, like you're such a prize.

I was reasonably attractive and in much better shape than most guys my age. Still... Besides, I was worrying about nothing.

I led Tyler out to my car. He slowed, then stopped.

"This is yours?" Tyler asked. "I saw it parked here, but...this is so cool. It's a Model A, right?"

"Yes and no. It is Model A, but it's not as old as you think. It's a Shay. A few of these were made back in 1980. It was advertised as the last Model A. It looks like an antique car, but it has a modern engine and can go much faster than an original. It's actually far more rare than a Model A built in the late 1920s or early '30s. About 4.5 million were made back there. There are less than 5,000 of the newer versions."

I stood back and admired the car with Tyler. I'd always loved antique cars, but they weren't terribly practical. The Model A convertible with a rumble seat was a classic. I loved the spoke-wheels, the spares on the running boards, and the old fashioned round headlights. My Shay was dark gray with black fenders. Right now, I had the top down.

We hopped in.

"Where to?" I asked. "You can choose. Just make it someplace that's not a chain restaurant. I love Texas Roadhouse, O'Charley's, and all those places, but I want to try something new."

"How about the Trojan Horse?"

"Is it still open? I remember eating there while I was still in high school."

"We can go somewhere else," Tyler said. "If you've been there before, it won't exactly be new to you."

"I haven't been there for years. The Trojan Horse sounds perfect."

I didn't need directions. The Trojan Horse was on the square. I pulled away from the house and headed downtown.

"How fast can this car go?" Tyler asked.

"If it had modern tires, it could go over 100 mph. With these narrow original tires the car begins to shake if I push it much past 40 mph. I mostly drive it in town. I have another car for longer trips. This is my toy."

"This is so cool. I might have guessed a writer would have an unusual car. This has so much more character than a Corvette or a BMW."

"As you already know, I like old things. Even though this wasn't built in 1929, it is a Model A."

I blew the horn and the distinctive ah-ooh-ga sounded. Tyler grinned and sat back, letting the wind run through his hair.

I found a parking spot on Kirkwood, across from the courthouse, and we used the crosswalk at Walnut Street to get to the restaurant.

The old place was much as I remembered it, even down to the Trojan Horse shield on the side of the restaurant and the round window in the door. When we walked inside, the interior was the same too. The restaurant was narrow with small booths. A larger bar area was located up the stairs in the back. As I sat down in a booth facing the door, I noticed something else was the same, too. The interior was so dimly lit that the light coming through the window in the door seemed unusually bright. I was glad it wasn't lunchtime. The light would have been almost blinding then.

The waitress came for our drink orders and then departed. Looking across the table at Tyler, I could almost believe I was twenty years in the past. Where had all the years gone?

We browsed the menus and were ready to order by the time our waitress returned with our Cokes, mine diet. Tyler ordered

Souvlaki, which the menu described as marinated pork loin, skewer broiled, served on pita with tzatziki, fresh sliced onions and tomatoes. It sounded great, but I opted for a chicken gyro, which was grilled chicken wrapped in a pita and topped with fresh onions, tomatoes and tzatziki sauce. Gyros are traditionally lamb, but I could never make myself eat baby animals. I felt guilty enough eating chicken.

"So, you used to eat here?"

"Yeah, The Trojan Horse was something of a Bloomington landmark even then. Of course, it hadn't been around quite so long."

"What other places were here when you were in high school?"

"I'm not sure. I haven't had much of a chance to look around and see what's still here. I assume Nick's English Hut is still around. I think it opened in the late 1920s."

"Wow, that place is old! I've never been there."

"I'll take you sometime. I haven't been there for ages either."

"How about Cracker Barrel?" Tyler asked.

"That's a new addition. It's over on the west side, right? I think I passed it on the way to Hardee's."

"I guess things have changed a lot since you lived here before."

"A lot has changed. A lot has remained the same." I laughed. "Just call me Mr. Obvious."

Tyler grinned.

"I like being places I've been before," I said. "Perhaps that's why I returned to Bloomington. I have a lot of memories of this place."

"Good memories?" Tyler asked.

"Some sad, some unhappy, some even painful, but mostly good. That's to be expected. Life is filled with a variety of experiences and one can't expect them all to be enjoyable."

"Like, you can't always expect to be happy?"

"Exactly. Happiness, like all emotional states, is temporary. That's why there is no living happily ever after. No one is happy all the time. Some people are happy most of the time, a good many perhaps, but they aren't happy every minute of every day."

"Do you think it's possible?"

"Possible? Yes. All things are possible. It's just very unlikely. What if you were happy for hour after hour and day after day? Happiness would be your expected emotional state. What happens when you get a bad grade, or when you discover someone you love is suffering, or that someone you have a crush on doesn't like you back? Wouldn't those things make you unhappy? If you were always happy, chances are that the smallest of unpleasant events would make you unhappy simply because you're accustomed to always being happy."

"Yeah, I think I get what you're saying."

"I don't think unhappiness is a bad thing. I think it makes happiness that much more enjoyable. Cloudy days make one appreciate sunny days. Cold rain pelting against the window makes one feel all the more cozy snuggled in a blanket inside, and working or going to school makes one appreciate free time."

"So contrast is important."

"I believe so, and I think I'm happier for that belief."

"Why?" asked Tyler.

"It allows me to appreciate a wider variety of experiences than most. I love bright, sunny days, but I love rainy days and snowy days and cold days just as much. I love having nothing more to do than sit down with a good book, but I love working, too. I enjoy the company of others, but I also enjoy solitude."

"It sounds like you like everything."

"No, but I have gained the ability to find enjoyment in most things. There was a time when there wasn't much joy in my life. I learned then to find happiness in things most others ignore."

"Like what?"

"The warmth of the sun, the cozy feeling that comes from walking in the rain under an umbrella, the colors of everyday objects, the beauty of a leaf, the softness of a towel. When you start looking for things that make life enjoyable, you find those things.   Think about the fact that you can walk into your bathroom, turn a knob, and have hot water come out of the wall. How cool is that? Yet, most people take a shower without even thinking about it. They don't notice the luxurious warmth of the water, except in its absence. They don't pay attention to the color, scent, and feel of the soap and shampoo. Most people just mechanically take a shower, failing to notice what a wonderful experience it is. To me, a shower is a trip to a spa."

"I've noticed how wonderful hot water feels in the shower and I like the smell of my shampoo, but I haven't really thought of most of the stuff you just mentioned."

"These are just examples. All of life is like that. There are a lot of wonderful things and experiences in life, but one has to take the time to notice them or they go by undetected."

"I knew hanging out with a writer would be different."

"I warned you. Writers are strange, strange people."

"I wouldn't say strange, just different."

"You're very diplomatic."

"No. I like how you're different. You talk about more interesting things than most people."

"Some would say I talk about more boring things, but then everyone has their own interests, their own likes and dislikes. I think what's important is to be in touch with what makes you happy.   Some like reading great literature, others enjoy demolition derbies. One is just as valid as the other in terms of happiness.   There are, of course, those who like both great literature and demolition derbies."

"Do you?"

"I've never been too excited about either. I've often found classic literature a disappointment.   Many books that are considered great literary works just don't stack up against works that are considered more mundane.   I've never been to a demolition derby so I don't know if I'd enjoy one or not, but all things considered I'd rather stay home and watch *Frasier* or *Star Trek*."

"*Star Trek*—there's a big surprise, Mr. Spock," Tyler teased.

"What I'm saying is that each of us likes what we like. It doesn't matter if anyone agrees with our tastes."

"Damn, can you come talk at my school? If you're not wearing the right clothes and shoes, not listening to the right music, and not hanging out with the right people, you are not cool."

"It was the same when I was there. I'll tell you a secret. That's basically a high school thing. It only works in a small community. In the larger world, all that falls apart. Many people expend great energy in trying to make the world one big high school, but it's never worked."

"That's good news."

"I'll tell you something else about high school. When you're there, it's your world unless you find a way to escape. Once you graduate, that entire world becomes meaningless. The social hierarchy crumbles, the cliques disappear, people who seemed important or powerful become insignificant."

"I never thought of it like that. I'm so used to going to school that I almost can't imagine life after high school," Tyler said.

"For now, it's your world. Later, you'll live in a different world and that old world won't mean much. It's kind of like moving from one town to another. All of a sudden, you're hanging out with a different group, going to different places, and experiencing different things. Some things may be similar, but it's never the same. Leaving high school is even a bigger change."

"Is college like high school?"

"No. It's a different world. There are cliques in college as there are in high school. There are still jocks, there are still those who dress in the latest 'in' fashions, but college is a larger world. It isn't possible for a small group to rule. Some will try, but it won't work. There's too much diversity, too much independent thinking, and there is more focus on succeeding. Most of those who attend college are serious about getting their degree, even if they party as much as humanly possible."

"Wow. Do you know everything?"

"I occasionally claim to, but it's a lie."

Our food arrived and we stopped talking for a while. My chicken gyro was tasty, but I would have liked it a bit spicier. I hoped I wasn't boring Tyler with my philosophical talk, but he appeared interested. He seemed mature for his age, but then again perhaps I was just buying into the stereotype of immaturity in the young. In many ways, the younger generation seemed wiser than the older.

After we ate, we walked across the street to aptly named Book Corner, a bookstore located on the corner of Walnut and Kirkwood and right across the street from The Trojan Horse. While I liked big chain bookstores like Barnes & Noble and Borders, there was something appealing about a privately owned bookstore. I also thought it important to patronize such shops whenever possible to help insure their continued existence.

The selection in the Book Corner wasn't as large as what one would find in a large chain, but the smaller number of books allowed one to focus. I'd found more than a few treasures over the years by browsing in such shops. Today, my task was simple. I bought Tyler a set of Narnia books.

"You really didn't have to get me these," he said as we waited at the light to go back across Kirkwood.

"Of course, I didn't. I wanted to get them for you. Maybe it's the writer in me, but I love to share my favorite books. If you like these, I'll get you Tolkien's books. They're incredible. If you don't like them, you can just give them away to someone you think might."

"Thanks. I really appreciate it."

"Kirkwood is as busy as always," I noted.

"As long as IU is here, I don't think that will ever change."

Kirkwood led directly to the official entrance to IU. Along the street were found the Monroe County Public Library, various restaurants, and shops. Its proximity to campus explained in part the crowded nature of the street, as did the allure of the unique eating establishments and quaint shops. Many came from quite a distance to visit Kirkwood.

"Want me to drop you off at your house?" I asked as we climbed back in the roadster.

"Sure. It's not too far from your place but I am kind of tired."

I drove Tyler home. He lived within easy walking distance of my place, but we'd had quite a day of unpacking and organizing. I was rather beat myself. Tyler thanked me again for the books as he climbed out of the car.

I'd had an enjoyable evening. I'd worried about nothing when Tyler had called our time together a date. We talked and laughed and had a great time, but Tyler never gave me the impression that he was interested in me beyond friendship. I was relieved. I wasn't quite sure what I would have done had he flirted with me. I did like younger guys, but seventeen was just too young. I also liked things just as they were with Tyler. I hadn't known him long, but I loved his youthful enthusiasm. I liked how excited he became when I showed him new things. He almost made me wish I'd had kids of my own. My feelings for him were paternal, not romantic.

It was still only 8 p.m. and not dark out. Oh, how I loved the summer! As I pulled up in front of my house and got out of the car, two shirtless IU boys ran by. They were both rather good looking, but the blond one really caught my eye. He was extremely handsome and very well-built, with a chiseled chest, and defined abs. He was also a good deal older than seventeen. He grinned when he caught me checking him out. He reminded me a great deal of Brand from my first summer at Camp Neeswaugee.

Camp Neeswaugee
Thursday, June 22, 1989

I was soothed by the gentle lapping of the waves as I walked along the north shore of Lake Potawatomi. As twilight deepened, running lights appeared on the pleasure craft plying the gentle waves. Lights also appeared in the old brick academy buildings that sat back from the shore. Some of the barracks dated all the way back to 1895. It was in the barracks that kids resided who were too old for Camp Neeswaugee. I was glad I was with the younger group across the road and not with the thirteen to sixteen year olds. I was only a year older than some of them!

I stopped by the pier near the Naval building and gazed out at the lake. A light breeze rocked the sailboats docked by the pier, causing the rigging to clang like gentle bells as it rapped against the masts. Lights twinkled from the cottages on the shores.

"Skipping the movie, too, huh?"

I turned. It was *him*! My heart beat faster and I took a moment to rein in my excitement before I spoke.

"Yeah. I didn't think I could sit through *Beetlejuice*. I'm a little stressed about tomorrow."

"Stressed, huh?" Brand said. "I know something than can help with that. Follow me."

Brand walked back toward camp without checking to see if I followed. He was self-assured to the point of being cocky. I found him irresistible. I caught up with him and walked by his side. Brand was wearing a white tank top and black Umbros. The tank top accented the defined muscles of his arms and torso. I wanted to reach out and touch him so bad I almost couldn't bear it.

Brand turned to the right just before we reached the boat shed. We stayed close to the lake and soon we were on the narrow path the led down to the swimming pier. He led me out onto the pier, stopped, and pulled off his shirt. Even in the failing light his chest was magnificent.

Brand kicked off his sandals and pushed down his Umbros. He wasn't wearing anything underneath! I couldn't help but steal a look.

"Come on," he said and dove into the water.

"What if someone sees us?" I asked, my voice pitched a little higher than normal.

"No one is going to see and so what if they do? Come on. It feels great!"

I kicked off my shoes and socks and pulled off my shirt. I was thankful for the dim light. I didn't look too bad without a shirt, but I was no Brand. I unzipped my khaki shorts and let them drop to the pier. I pulled down my boxers and dove into the lake.

The water was a lot warmer than I'd expected. I'd never skinny dipped before. I felt like I was being touched in places I'd never been touched.

Brand disappeared under the water and popped up again only two feet away. Water cascaded down over his face and neck. If he'd come closer and brushed against me, he would've found out just how sexy I found him, if you know what I mean. Being so near that seductive, naked boy was a delicious torment. Oh God, how I wanted him, but he was obviously into girls. He likely had his own harem.

Brand moved a little closer.

"Doesn't this feel incredible?"

"Yeah," I said.

"It's great for relaxing your muscles. I love to swim after a workout."

"You were working out?"

"Yeah, I was over in the gym. You should check it out. The academy has some great equipment."

The thought of Brand working out turned me on like mad. I would have given just about anything to watch him pumping out bench presses, especially if he was shirtless.

Brand grinned, then in one swift movement he was on me. I thought he was going to dunk me, but I received the shock of my life. He kissed me! Lieutenant Brand Elwolf, the star of my less-than-innocent fantasies, kissed me! When he pulled his lips from mine, I gawked at him in shock.

"I...you...how did you know?"

Brand laughed.

"Dude, you're obvious. You've been checking me out since day one. You practically drooled when you walked in after I'd showered. I thought you were going to drop to your knees and blow me."

I was so stunned I was speechless. I thought I'd been so careful. If Brand noticed, had everyone else?

"It's okay. I wanted to kiss you since I saw you staring at me during that first orientation meeting."

"*Me*? *You* wanted to kiss *me*?"

Way to sound like a moron, Tyler.

Brand didn't answer. He just grabbed me, *down there*. He pulled me to him and kissed me again. This time, he opened his mouth and slid his tongue between my lips. I didn't resist. I was powerless. I'd never so much as kissed another guy before and this incredible hunk was all over me!

Brand and I made out as the water lapped against us. I forgot all about the possibility of someone seeing us. Brand didn't take his hand off me, *down there*, and it drove me insane. I moaned into his mouth. I couldn't stop touching his shoulders, his biceps, and his pecs. His soft skin was such a contrast to his hard body. Brand's tongue was so silky and sexy. I'd fantasized a lot about sex, but I'd never realized that making out could be so freaking hot!

I ran my hands around behind Brand and gripped his butt. I couldn't believe I had the balls to do it, but damn! There was no part of him that wasn't firm and sexy. We kissed almost savagely, especially Brand. There was a violence to his kissing but an erotic violence. Nothing happened that I didn't want, but the thought that Brand might not stop if I wanted him to only excited me more.

I felt up Brand's pecs again and then ran my hands down over the hard ridges of his stomach. I trembled as I ran my hands lower. I groped him, *there*, and then began to touch him as he was touching me.

Brand kissed me harder. Our hands moved faster and we panted and moaned into each others' mouths. Brand locked his mouth over mine as I cried out in passion; otherwise I think I would have moaned loud enough to be heard all over the lake. Brand moaned into my mouth, too. I swear my eyes rolled back into my head.

I seriously think I would have drowned if Brand hadn't held me tightly in his strong arms. I went completely limp after we'd both...you know. Brand held me and kissed me again, more gently this time. He was so intense and incredible. I think I was in love.

Brand pulled away and swam to the pier. He lifted himself from the water effortlessly, then leaned over to give me a hand up. He pulled me up with ease.

Water cascaded off our bodies. The night air felt cool after the warmth of the water and goose bumps appeared on my skin. We dressed as waves lapped against the peer and the shores of the lake.

"Feel better?" Brand asked.

"I've never felt this good in my entire life," I said.

"I told you I knew how to get rid of stress. Come on, I'll walk you back to camp."

I was in a daze. Brand had completely swept me off my feet. In the darkness of the tunnel under the road, he pulled me to him and kissed me deeply again. I returned his kiss with passion. We walked on up the hill into the silent camp. Worries about tomorrow had completely left my mind. I felt so mellow and relaxed.

"I'll see you tomorrow," Brand said when we reached the fork in the path.

"Yeah," I said, grinning. "Thanks for tonight."

Brand laughed and headed up the hill into Beaver territory. I cut off the path and walked to Cabin 34, my head in the clouds, my heart soaring.

***

My "old" boys, those who had been to Camp Neeswaugee before, arrived on Friday. Rod's parents dropped him off first. They lived right in the little town of Kulver, which was within walking distance. Rod was polite and got right to work folding his blue Division Four shirts and all of his other clothing. Jeremy arrived about half an hour later, followed by Caleb. They talked and laughed like old friends, which they were. All of them were Gold "Cs" which meant this was their third year in camp and they were working toward a Gold C pin. More importantly to me, it meant they were experienced and could help me show the newer kids the ropes.

I introduced myself as the boys arrived and tried to help them settle in, but the truth was they knew more about the Neeswaugee way of folding clothes and making beds than I did, which made me feel a little foolish. I was the new guy and I sensed immediately that it was going to cause me some problems.

By lunch, Cody and Greg had also moved in. Armando, Fernando, Diego, and Günter wouldn't arrive until Saturday because they were coming in by air. Some people in Indiana didn't even know Camp Neeswaugee existed, but it was known the world over. Campers from other countries, especially Mexico, were not at all rare. Shane, Steve, and Tripp also wouldn't arrive until the next day because they were new boys.

A whistle blew four times and the boys rushed from the cabin. I followed them up the hill and stood back and watched while the division formed up. One of the Gold "Cs" acted as Division Leader. He gave out commands just like they did in the real military. I don't think I could have handled that when I was eleven. The boys marched through the camp and down to the Dining Hall. I felt vaguely out of place, but I figured I'd catch onto the Camp Neeswaugee way soon enough.

I ate with my boys at lunch and we got on well. I spotted Brand with his older boys. He arched his eyebrows at me and I grinned. Cody gave me a funny look and luckily, I had the presence of mind not to panic. The kid didn't know anything.

"Inside joke," I said.

Cody shrugged and went back to talking to his friends.

There wasn't much to do since most of the kids hadn't shown up yet. Once their things were put away, my boys ran out and played ping pong and tetherball. I wasn't the sporting type, but I walked around and supervised, which was my job. I talked with some of the other counselors. I even played ping pong with Greg. He was delighted when he kicked my butt.

After supper, the Division Commander, Maj. Wilder, gathered the division together for an "old boys" talk, which was mainly about leadership and providing a good example for the newer boys. After the talk, we went to the big field on the other side of Division 6 and joined our rivals in a game of Capture the Flag.

I have to admit I had a blast playing Capture the Flag. I loved taunting the D6 kids. Sometimes, I let one get close and then took off with a burst of speed. My longer legs were a great advantage. Still, I had to keep my guard up at all times. Counselors were always tempting targets. By the end, I was panting and my heart was racing, but I hadn't had so much fun in a long time.

The counselors were faster and stronger, but the kids could change direction with lightening speed. I felt a little like a battle ship surrounded by speed boats. I managed to tag ten boys before a Division 6 kid got me. The other side just about lost it cheering, as they did when any of the counselors were taken down. Daniel was taken out by one of our boys about the same time as me. We passed each other as we walked back to the "jails." Daniel smiled and shook his head.

The boys talked quietly after lights out and laughed sometimes, but they didn't make too much noise so I didn't get onto them. I was so tired myself I was unconscious less than five minutes after my head hit the pillow.

The next day, Fernando, Diego, and Armando arrived by air from Mexico. Günter flew in from Geneva and Shane, Steve, and Tripp were dropped off by their parents. The cabin was a beehive of activity.

This was the first true day of camp. It was also the day when my life at camp began to fall apart. Ten-year-old boys are not naturally interested in making beds, folding, and putting away clothes, especially when everything has to go in a specific location. By noon, I was ready to pull my hair out. By the mid-afternoon, I just wanted to hide in my quarters. Fernando announced that making beds was work for maids. Shane informed me that his parents didn't pay hundreds of dollars for him to learn how to fold shirts. Steve didn't complain. He just mooned me. No, it was not a good day! Even with the older boys helping it, the situation was out-of-control.

"Guys! The cabin has to be in order by 5 p.m. The major is coming around then to look things over!" I shouted at last.

That at least partially got their attention.

"If we want to have a chance at honor cabin, this place has got to be perfect," said Rod, one of my Gold "Cs."

"Why should we care about honor cabin?" Shane asked.

"Because we get to hang the honor cabin plaque on the side of the cabin for a whole week if we earn it."

"Big whoop," Steve said.

"And I'll buy you guys pizza if you get it," I said.

Silence fell for a moment.

"Real pizza?" Steve asked.

"No, plastic pizza," I said. "Of course, real pizza. I hear Papa's in town is awesome. You guys win honor cabin and I'll buy pizza and Cokes for everyone."

"I'm in!" Steven said.

"Fu... I mean heck, yeah!" said Cody.

"It's not worth it," Shane said. "Keep this place cleaned up for a whole week?"

"It's easy if we keep it picked up," Caleb said. "The hard part is getting it fixed up at first. Once that's done we just have to not throw our junk around."

Shane didn't look convinced, but peer pressure won out in the end and my boys actually started putting their stuff away. Yeah, bribery is good.

Bedtime was a fiasco. I could not get my boys quiet. I'd no sooner than get one of them to shut up when another would mouth off or laugh. I was about to lose it, but I tried my best not to go ballistic. The little monsters enjoyed defying me. Steve even flipped me off.

"In bed and quiet, now!" thundered a voice as footsteps pounded up my stairs.

Captain Fitch strode in. The boys who'd been out of bed scrambled for their bunks and absolute silence fell.

"If I hear any more noise out of this cabin tonight, you'll be outside practicing drills. Is that clear?"

"Yes, sir!" said a couple of the Gold "Cs." The rest quickly followed. I wasn't surprised. Captain Fitch even scared me a little. He was as intimidating as hell. He always looked as if he was on the verge of ripping someone's head off.

The captain nodded to me and left. My kids remained quiet and I walked into my quarters, totally humiliated. Another counselor had to come into my cabin because I couldn't control my kids. I was a complete failure as a counselor. This wasn't how I'd imagined camp. My boys had no respect for me, they wouldn't listen unless I resorted to bribery, and half of them were openly defiant. I was a joke. I lay down in my bed and felt like crying. At that moment, I just wanted to leave.

***

I got an eyeful of Brand coming out of the shower the next morning, dripping wet and, of course, naked. There was no one else around so I wasn't shy about checking him out. After all, I'd touched his magnificent body, I'd kissed his lips, and I'd...well, you know. Brand grinned at me. Another counselor entered and Brand wrapped his towel around his waist and departed. It was a fleeting encounter, but it erased any notions I might have had about bailing on Camp Neeswaugee. I didn't want to quit just because things had gotten rough, but to be perfectly honest, I wasn't about to give up the opportunity to be with Brand again. I'd dreamed about him the night before and well....let's just say I had *very* pleasant dreams.

After my shower, I returned to my quarters in Cabin 34. My quarters were small, perhaps eight feet wide and fifteen long, but it was my own private space, my sanctuary. I guess I should say semi-private. There was no ceiling, other than the sloped roof fifteen or twenty feet above. The walls only went up about ten feet, so sound traveled freely between my quarters and the rest of the cabin. I guess that was a good thing. I could keep an ear out for trouble. At the moment, all was quiet but then it was about 6:30 a.m.

I had only a small bed, with a single mattress on top of squeaky metal bars and springs. There was a very large wardrobe, which was no doubt an Academy cast off. There were all kinds of little compartments in it as well as a place to hang clothes. There was even a holder for a rifle, which I wouldn't be using, of course. There was an old wooden desk and a Windsor chair. I loved the chair. It was at least a hundred years old and I collected antiques. I'd made bookshelves out of plastic milk crates "borrowed" from the Dining Hall. My books and a couple of rugs on the floor added a personal touch. The rugs were a great luxury. The soil outside was sandy and tracked in easily. Without the rugs I'd have been walking on grit. I had to shake out the rugs every couple of days or I'd have been walking on gritty rugs. I also had a mini-fridge, another great luxury, where I kept Diet Cokes and cold water.

Reveille was coming up fast so I didn't have much time to spare after I'd dressed. My uniform consisted of green athletic shorts and a white tee-shirt that read "Neeswaugee Staff" on the left breast. I stole a few moments to read from a *Star Trek* novel. The familiar characters of Kirk, Spock, McCoy, and the others set me at ease. All too soon it was 6:50 a.m. The large bell down the hill rang out and one of the D&B boys played reveille.

Some of the boys did not want to get out of bed, but the noise level quickly increased so that sleep was impossible. I harassed and annoyed those who tried to stay in bed until remaining in their bunks just wasn't worth it. After only a few minutes the boys were moving about, getting dressed, and making their way to the latrine.

Things went a little more smoothly during the morning. When I crossed paths with Captain Fitch, he didn't say anything about the night before. He was a Neeswaugee veteran at twenty-three and had no doubt seen his share of green counselors losing control of their boys. I still felt like an inept fool and was embarrassed about losing control of my cabin, but I was determined to stick it out at least a little longer.

I hid my feelings of inadequacy from the boys. I knew what boys were like. They would walk all over me if they sensed they could get away with it. I might fail in the end, but I was going to go down swinging. I was determined to act more authoritative, even if I didn't feel it. This was a military academy, after all, and I was a lieutenant.

Camp truly got going on Monday when classes started. I was relieved to leave my cabin behind and head for Indian Crafts. During orientation, Major Burrows, the Indian Crafts Director, taught Lieutenant Cody and me how to make ojos. It was one of the easier projects. Just notch a couple of sticks, glue them together to form a cross, and wrap on yarn. Okay, it's a little harder than that, but that's basically it.

Lt. Cody and I ended up with eight kids, while others inside the large tent did bead work, painted shields, and made masks. Lt. Cody convinced the kids I had a college degree in ojo making, which I found hilarious. I guess kids will believe pretty much anything.

Some of the kids caught on fast and made some really cool ojos. Others had more trouble. Lt. Cody kept things interesting.

"That looks like a pre-21st Century Hopi design," said Lt. Cody as he examined an ojo I was helping a Division 6 boy make.

"Uh, Lieutenant, *everything* is pre-21st Century," I pointed out.

"See? I'm right! Aren't I?"

"I guess I can't argue with that, although I'm not so sure it's a Hopi design."

Lt. Cody laughed. I could tell he was going to be a lot of fun. He was kind of cute, too.

There were five class periods in the day, each forty-five minutes, with a ten minute break in between. None of the classes were very crowded. Major Burroughs told us to enjoy it while we could. Indian Crafts always became very popular when the kids found out what was made there. Apparently, we could expect the Indian Crafts tent to be bursting at the seams the second and third trimesters. For the first two weeks, however, things would be more laid back.

I enjoyed teaching Indian Crafts. The tent was located on the edge of little woods and was shaded and reasonably cool. The kids wanted to be there, so they didn't cause trouble. Lt. Cody and I could act as goofy as we wanted without losing control of the campers. The kids were plenty goofy, too. I spent a lot of time laughing. Things weren't going smoothly in my cabin, but at least I didn't have to get stressed out about Indian Crafts.

***

I began to grow more at ease with the whole camp counselor thing, but I wasn't looking forward to lights out. While the kids were off swimming during the afternoon, I sought out Maj. T. T was short for Thomas, but almost no one called him that. He was Maj. T to everyone, perhaps because he called everyone by their last initial. He'd been a counselor for years and years before taking over the Indian Lore department. There was a rumor he'd been present at the founding of Camp Neeswaugee in 1912, but there was no way he was *that* old. Some of the kids believed it, but then they believed I had a college degree in ojos.

Maj. T wasn't in the Indian Lore cabin when I hunted him down, but it wasn't locked up so I figured he hadn't headed out to the Council Ring yet. The Indian Lore cabin was a real log cabin from back in the 1800s, which I thought was really cool. While I waited for him to return, I looked at the Indian Crafts, Indian Dance, Top-Notch, and Master Dancer patches on display among other Native American pieces in the glass display case. These were the patches the kids could earn to have sewn on the dress jackets they wore in Sunday parades and when they went out on permit.

The Master Dancer patch was especially attractive. It was an eagle dancer on a red background. This was the most sought after patch in all of Camp Neeswaugee. Only the best of the Indian dancers even had a chance at it. No more than twelve boys could become a Master Dancer each summer. The Indian staff voted on candidates and a single "no" vote would blackball a potential Master Dancer. Even after candidates were selected, they had to go for an entire day without speaking a word. Then, there was some kind of secret initiation during the night. I didn't know what it was, of course, but I'd heard rumors about the boys having to swim Beaver Pond and pass all kinds of tests of strength and courage. The Master Dancer Society was serious business. It was the only secret society on campus.

"Hey, Lt. P," said Maj. T as he entered the cabin.

"I've got a problem with my cabin. Can we talk?"

Maj. T invited me into the Indian Lore office, the only air conditioned location in camp other than the nurse's office. I took in the signs on the walls. One read, "He who hoots with the owls at midnight cannot soar with the eagles at dawn." My favorites were mere photocopied pages. One had the word "whining" with a circle drawn around it and a bar diagonally cutting across "whining." The other had a drawing of an angry Calvin from the *Calvin and Hobbes* comic. At the top it read, "Every day of my life I have to add someone to the list of people who can just kiss my ass." Below were columns for "Today's List" and "Permanent List." I'd laughed the first time I saw it. The only person on the permanent list was Maj. Kinder, the athletic director. He was widely known, behind his back, as "The Tool" and the athletic cabin was known as "The Tool Shed."

"So, what's the problem?" T asked, leaning back in his chair behind his desk.

"I can't control the kids in my cabin. Sometimes I do okay with them, but at others I can't get them to listen. Taps is the worst. I can't get them quiet. They just keep egging each other on. Capt. Fitch had to come in and quiet them down for me. I was so embarrassed."

"Welcome to the life of the cabin counselor," said T. "I was about your age when I had my first cabin. It's hard to believe, I know, but true. My boys weren't big on listening either and gave me a lot of trouble. I tried yelling at them, but the problem with yelling is that they quickly grow used to it. It's just noise after a while. I learned that one of the best ways to get them quiet wasn't to yell, but to talk more softly and quietly than normal. I'd start in a slightly raised voice, tell them to get quiet, and then get quiet myself. They couldn't hear what I was saying if they talked. In fact, they had to strain to hear what I was saying. Sometimes talking more quietly is enough to get the boys quiet.

"Taps is a difficult time. The boys are often wound up and don't want to sleep. I learned a little trick, however, and I think it will work for you."

Maj. T shared his secret with me. I smiled. It was a great solution. There's definitely something to be said about experience.

I left the Indian Lore cabin feeling much better. I had some ideas to use, but even more than that, just knowing that Maj. T once had experienced similar difficulties made me feel less like a loser. T was a Neeswaugee legend and if he had trouble with his boys at the beginning, maybe there was hope for me too.

***

"All right. Lights out! Everyone in bed!" I said as the D&B bugler began to play Taps at 9 p.m.

Some of my boys did as they were told right away; others were slow to move. Steve, of course, felt free to just ignore me.

"Now!" I said, putting some authority into my voice as Maj. T suggested. "I want everyone in bed and quiet before I start reading."

"Reading?" Greg asked.

"Yes, I'm going to read you guys *The Hobbit*, but you've got to keep quiet. I'm not going to try to read over you talking."

Even Steve climbed into bed. I'd chosen *The Hobbit* partially because it was one of the books I'd brought with me, but also because Steve had a copy of *Prince Caspian* on his center bin, so I figured he was into fantasy books. If I could keep him quiet, the others would be easy.

There was some more talking and I just stood there.

"Okay, when you guys are ready to shut up, I can start reading."

"Quiet, guys! Will ya?" Shane said.

"Okay, when I turn out the lights, no talking. If you talk, I stop reading. If you're quiet, I'll read a whole chapter. If you stay quiet after I'd done, I'll read again tomorrow night.

I flipped off the lights. Silence. I pulled out a chair, sat down, and turned on my flashlight.

"In a hole in the ground there lived a hobbit..."

***

The next morning, I dropped in on Maj. T in the Indian Lore cabin before my first class.

"Thank you so much," I said. "Reading to them worked. I had a couple of boys talk while I was reading, but I did just what you said. I stopped reading and they stopped talking. They were even quiet after I'd finished. Of course, most of them were asleep by then."

"It's a little trick I learned years ago," Maj. T said.

"It worked. They almost drove me crazy at taps the first night of camp. I don't think Capt. Fitch will have to come in and quiet them down again. I was so embarrassed by that."

"Don't worry about it. It's tough in the beginning for everyone. I've been here a long time but I haven't forgotten what it's like to be a new cabin counselor. It takes a while to learn what works. Handling a cabin is something only experience can teach."

"At least one problem is solved. Now, if I can get used to being on my feet most of the day, I might survive. My feet were killing me last night."

"Try changing into a different pair of shoes a couple times during the day."

"Yeah?"

"It helps a lot. I usually change shoes at lunch and again at supper. It's another little trick I learned."

"You should write a book on tips for counselors."

"Maybe a pamphlet."

I laughed. Maj. T. was awesome.

My morning classes sailed by. I enjoyed Indian Crafts, but I must admit 4th period was my favorite, because that was my period off. I had 45 minutes all to myself, ideally at least. I usually tried to sleep 4th period, but someone or something always disturbed me. If it wasn't Maj. Wilder coming through to do his A.I. (the daily Anytime Inspection which counted towards honor cabin), it was a kid skipping class or the service department deciding that 4th period was the ideal time to mow around my cabin. Still, it was time when I could rest. It was also the best period to have off since it was right before lunch.

I stopped by Main Headquarters to check my mail box before heading to my cabin. My mail was being forwarded for the summer and there was always some note, memo, or schedule waiting on me. Sometimes, there was even a letter from home. Most of the memos had nothing to do with me and I tended to read my mail right over the trash can so I could dump all the crap.

As expected, three memos were waiting on me, one that concerned only water front staff, another about laundry pickup, and a memo about who was in charge of deciding whether or not the boys were to wear their dress coats in the Chapel. Some of the memos I'd received so far this summer were so ridiculous I wondered if they had just been made up. I paused. My mischievous side awakened.

When I returned to my cabin, I pulled out a notebook and began to write. By the end of my free period, I was finished. That night, after Taps and after my boys were asleep, I walked down to Main HQ and made use of one of the typewriters and the photocopy machine. I stuffed a copy of my fake memo into each mailbox, including my own.

I said goodnight to the O.C. (the Officer in Charge) and walked back to my cabin with a grin on my face.

***

I was so busy the next morning I'd all but forgotten my illicit activities of the night before until I was reminded at breakfast. A D6 counselor at the neighboring table laughed out loud and stopped Daniel and Lt. Cody who were on their way to other tables.

"Did you guys read this?" he asked.

They looked at him confused.

"Listen to this."

The D6 lieutenant read my memo to his fellow counselors.

Memo on Memos

By Order Of: Maj. P, Director W.S.A.
(Neeswaugee Security Agency)

A vast array of memos is necessary for the smooth operation of Camp Neeswaugee. In the interest of conservation and general cheapness, we would like to cut down on our use of paper. While it is impossible to lessen the number of memos, we think we have come up with a plan that will save both trees and money.

As you're well aware, the same memos are used year after year with no significant alteration. Therefore, effective immediately, all staff members are instructed to retain a copy of each memo delivered to their mailbox. All staff will take the memos home at the end of the summer and bring them back next year. Next summer each staff member will be responsible for supplying himself or herself with the appropriate memos. For example, on July 12, each staff member will place the July 12 memo from the previous summer into his or her mailbox so that it may be picked up at his or her convenience later in the day. Occasionally, it will be necessary for certain memos to be delivered on a date later than that indicated on the memo. In the event of such an occasion, a memo memo will be issued instructing each staff member to place the appropriate memo in their mail box on that day. For example, a typical memo memo might read "Please place the June 24 memo in your mailbox on July 11." As you can see, this will save a great deal of paper.

New staff will, of course, not have a folder of memos from the previous summer. New staff will receive memos as usual but will be asked to retain a copy of each for use during subsequent summers. If any returning staff member has lost a particular memo, there will be memo request forms available at the Neeswaugee Security Agency Office, which is conveniently located in the cabin next to yours. On the request form, merely write in the date of the memo you wish to receive. If you cannot remember the date of the memo, please borrow a copy of the memo from another staff member and write down the entire text of the memo on the request form. You will receive a copy of the memo, a.s.a.p., usually in 3-5 days. In the event that the date of the memo has passed, you will also receive a memo memo advising you to place the memo into your mailbox immediately so that you may pick it up and obtain the necessary information as quickly as possible.

Twice each week you will receive a weekly summary memo that includes the full text of each memo and memo memo that pertains to that week. By placing all the memos into one memo the cause of conservation of paper will be further implemented. In the interest of simplicity, each staff member will receive a 340 page instruction manual summarizing the new memo policy. We hope this will be of use to all staff members in our efforts to conserve paper and streamline the memo system.

The counselor reading the memo could barely keep from laughing as read. Lt. Cody burst out laughing. Daniel grabbed the memo and looked at it.

"This has to be a fake."

"Duh! Of course, it's a fake. I wonder who put it out. There's one in every mailbox."

I smiled to myself. Caleb, one of the boys in my cabin, caught me. I merely raised an eyebrow. He laughed and went back to his cereal.

When I headed to Main HQ later to check my mailbox, I heard several counselors talking about what was now called the Memo Memo. I pulled my copy from my mailbox and pretended to read it. I didn't want anyone to know I was the culprit. I planned for this fake memo to be only the first of many.

Bloomington, Indiana
Tuesday, June 23, 2009

I experienced a sense of happy sadness as I thought of my summer camp days. I suppose "happy sadness" needs a bit of an explanation as the one emotion seems to negate the other. It is not so, however, for I've felt both happy and sad simultaneously many times in my life. At the moment, my old summer camp memories brought me happiness. Thinking about Maj. T, the boys in my very first cabin, the memo memo, and my fellow counselors from all those years ago made those days live again in my mind. The sadness came from the knowledge that those days were over and that I couldn't go back, except in memory. Sometimes, I still wished I could spend my summers at Camp Neeswaugee, but I knew deep down I didn't really want to go back. For one thing, I was no longer up to the task of keeping up with a dozen nine to eleven year old boys. It was hard enough when I was seventeen. At my age...well, I just didn't want to go there. No, summer camp was best left in the past. I had photos. I had memories. Now, I'd moved on to other things and I'd have to say I'm as happy now as I was back then. Besides, my Neeswaugee days were very much still alive in my mind. Within my memories, summer camp was still going on. For me, the past and the present were much the same thing.

Of course, not all my memories of camp were happy. There was that first night when I wanted to quit. There was the practical joke that went wrong. I don't even want to think about *that* one and I'm definitely not telling anyone about it. And then, there was Brand...how could I have been so naïve? Then again, I had no idea back then I was dealing with a master of manipulation.

I walked over to the bookshelves and pulled out an old photo album. I flipped through the pages and there he was, Lieutenant Brand Elwolf. Brand was as gorgeous in the photo as he had been in real life. It's no wonder I'd fallen for him, no wonder I'd been so easily seduced.

I looked at the photo—at Brand's broad shoulders, bulging biceps, muscular chest, and defined abs. I gazed into his pale blue eyes, still so seductive. If I didn't know what I knew about Brand, I could have fallen for him all over again. I was no fool when I was seventeen. I have the feeling Brand could have seduced anyone. I just didn't know what was hidden behind that beautiful facade...

Camp Neeswaugee
Wednesday, June 27, 1989

"Are you on duty tonight?" Brand asked as I was walking back to my cabin after lunch.

"No."

"Want to slip off while the kids are over at Eppley and mess around?"

I swear I began breathing harder right then and there. My mind raced back to skinny-dipping in the lake with Brand, his hard muscles, his silky tongue, and his big, hard...

"Definitely."

"Good. I really *need* it. I've been so busy I haven't even been able to jerk off."

If Brand kept talking like that, I wasn't going to be able to walk. I wanted to kiss him so bad I couldn't stand it, but we were in view of several campers and counselors. No one could hear us talking, but they could see us.

"I'll stop by your cabin when the divisions have moved out," Brand said.

"I'll be waiting."

The hours could not pass fast enough for me. I didn't even mind coaching my first cabin softball game. Luckily, most of my kids more or less knew what they were doing. Most, but not all...

Armando didn't have a clue about softball. I guess they didn't play it much in Mexico. He didn't speak much English so I couldn't help him all that much. Let's face it—I couldn't have helped him if I spoke Spanish because I was definitely not fluent in softball. I had played when forced to do so in gym classes, but I'd never been that talented. Fernando and Diego came to the rescue by shouting out directions in Spanish. Armando didn't know the game, but he was a natural athlete. He smacked the ball and sent it sailing. The kid darted around the bases like a bolt of lightning, his long brown hair flying, and actually scored a home run. I was shocked. Armando didn't look big enough to hit a ball past first base.

I was smart enough to keep my mouth shut during most of the game. I did occasionally tell a boy to run back to his base or run onto the next. I didn't know much about the game but I wasn't an idiot. Mostly, I just shouted words of encouragement and urged my boys on when they were racing around the bases. I was also able to help the most inept boys, such as those who hacked down at the ball as if they were chopping wood. Even I knew enough to keep a swing level and I didn't know much. I was patient with those who lacked athletic talent because I lacked it myself. Sometimes, being without talent can be an asset.

Oh, we lost the game 11-6. A win would've been great. Perhaps my boys could've won if they had a better coach. I pretty much sucked as far as sports knowledge was concerned so I wasn't much help. The counselors also had to officiate, so I was calling balls and strikes while my kids were in the outfield, and watching the bases when they were up bat. I tried to be fair and in that, at least, I did a good job. I also let my boys know that losing was no big deal. I'd seen some other counselors scream at their kids for losing and I thought that was very uncool. My boys played well and didn't bicker among themselves too much. We just had some bad luck and the other team was exceptionally good. At the end of the game, we shook hands with the other team, gave them a cheer, and headed back to Cabin 34.

I took a shower in the officer's latrine while the boys were taking theirs in the camper shower area. I got into the shower as fast as possible because I knew the hot water might run out and I hate cold showers. I might have benefited from one. Thinking about hooking up with Brand later that night really worked me up.

I caught sight of Brand later during supper while I sat eating with my boys. A couple of female counselors were fluttering around him. Even some of the older female campers were vying for Brand's attention as he carried his tray toward his own table filled with D&B boys. Lieutenant Elwolf was the stud among the male staff. All the females wanted him. All the males wanted to be him. I grinned as I watched the girls pursue him.

Tough luck, ladies. He's mine!

I laughed out loud.

"What?" Jeremy asked.

"I was just thinking funny things," I said.

"You're very, very strange," Rod said, eyeing me and smiling.

"You would be too if you had to deal with eleven little monsters," I said.

"Angels," Shane said.

"Monsters!" said Maj. T as he passed.

I laughed.

"I hear Maj. T has been here for like...fifty years!" Günter said. "Is that true?"

"Well, he does go home in the winter. It's not like he lives here, but yes. He was a cabin counselor for years. He's been the Indian Lore Director since before I was born."

"Wow!" said Stephen, which was kind of amazing since Stephen rarely spoke.

I knew all this about Maj. T because I'd been hanging out in the Indian Lore cabin during my free time between classes. The cabin was the hang-out place for the Indian Dance instructors and the Indian Crafts staff. I'll be honest, while I liked talking to T and the other counselors, I was mainly in there because Brand taught Indian Dancing and just seeing him for a few moments was a thrill. Every time I spotted him I couldn't believe I'd actually *been* with him.

After supper, I stood in Division 4 HQ and watched as the nearly sixty boys of the division formed up to go to Eppley Auditorium to watch *The Princess Bride*. I wasn't on duty, so the kids were someone else's responsibility until lights out. I just had to be back in time to put the boys to bed and read to them. I had planned to go see the film myself, but there was no way I was passing up an evening with Brand!

Our eleven-year-old division leader took the report from the platoon leaders. I was quickly growing accustomed to the military aspects of camp: platoons, formations, marching, and orders such as "about face", "left face", "report", "forward, march", and "division, halt." Most of the kids got into the marching a lot more than you'd think. Some of the kids could not keep in step with the beat of a cadence, but I didn't see how they could keep from it. Whenever I was on duty or just going along with the division I found it almost impossible not to be in step and I wasn't even trying.

A gentle breeze wafted through the screens that served as windows in our HQ just as they did in the cabins. The headquarters cabin for each division was almost exactly the same as all the other cabins, except with eight small rooms and a center hallway instead of one large room for kids and one smaller room for the cabin counselor. I didn't envy our junior counselor or our Division Commander. The rooms in HQ weren't quite half the size of mine and my quarters weren't exactly big.

The division pulled out. The sound of sneakers hitting the asphalt grew more and more distant as the boys marched away. The counselors not on duty took off, leaving me alone in the division. Now that the coast was clear, I went to my quarters and put on a little cologne. If my boys had smelled cologne on me, they would have asked what was up. They never missed *anything*. I sure couldn't tell them I had a date with Lieutenant Elwolf, their Indian Dance instructor. I could just imagine their reaction to that. They'd probably be shouting, "Our counselor is a homo!"

I heard footsteps coming up the stairs to the counselor's entrance to the cabin and the screen door opened. Moments later, Brand poked his head in the open door to my quarters.

"Ready?"

"Oh, yeah."

"Let's go."

I wanted to kiss Brand right then and there, but it would be just my luck for some counselor or stray kid to walk in and catch us making out. We weren't supposed to talk about anything of the least sexual nature around the kids and getting caught making out would be a disaster. Girls and female counselors weren't even allowed on the boy's side of camp and the girl's side was a no man's land. That's where Brand and I had a definite advantage, but we still couldn't take chances.

It was still light out when we left the cabin, so I was sure we weren't heading to the lake to skinny dip again. I didn't know where we were going, but I didn't care. I was with Brand and that's all that mattered. The merest glance at his hard body was enough to set me on fire with lust. It was all I could do to keep from jumping on him.

Brand led me down the hill, past the bell, and across the soccer fields toward the girl's side of camp. He was headed for Cardinal Bridge, which crossed a small creek and led to the academy grounds. We crossed the old wooden bridge, then the highway that stood between Camp Neeswaugee and the Academy proper. We took a right after we passed through the opening in the wooden fence and walked past Oliver Field (the football field and track) and then past the tennis courts.

I was beginning to get a feel for our destination. Brand led me down through the tunnel that dipped under Highway 10. When we emerged on the other side, we were on the winding path that led through the woods and towards the Council Ring. The ring was where Indian dance programs were performed every Saturday night. We'd been in camp less than a week, so I had yet to see one, but we'd had an orientation meeting at the ring so I'd been inside the small, wooden amphitheatre.

It was darker among the trees, but by no means dark. A sense of anticipation filled the air as Brand led me up the winding path. I trembled slightly with nervousness and excitement. Neither of us spoke. We just kept on walking. We crossed a small bridge over a stream and then walked up a small hill. The Council Ring loomed before us. I thought maybe this was our destination, but Brand passed it by. We followed an old gravel road that led us east and then walked along a beaten path that crossed a large field until it entered the forest once more.

The path through the forest was narrower and obviously used less often than the path which led to the Council Ring. My sense of anticipation grew as we walked deeper into the woods. Brand led me off the path and into the cover of the trees. We found a small hollow on the top of a rise which all but hid us from view. We were well away from camp now and out of sight of prying eyes. Brand turned to me, pushed me up against a tree, and kissed me savagely. Something instinctual awakened inside me. I kissed him back passionately. It was if a dam had burst.

Brand and I tore at each others' clothing. Brand's tongue invaded my mouth. Skinny dipping and messing around in the lake had felt like a love scene in a movie, but now I felt as if I was in an action film. Brand was extremely aggressive and I surprised myself with my own aggression. I ripped Brand's shirt over his head and ran my hands over his hard muscles. He tore at my belt and jerked my shorts open. It was as if we'd been waiting on each other forever and couldn't wait a moment more.

Brand pressed down on my shoulders. I kissed his chest and licked at his nipples. He pushed me to my knees. I knew what he wanted. My desire was even greater than his own. I leaned in and Brand moaned.

Brand was rough with me, but that was okay because it's what I wanted just then. I wondered briefly if sex between a guy and a girl ever had such an edge of violence or if it was only something that happened between two guys. It was almost as if Brand and I were struggling for domination, but yet that wasn't it. Neither of us was a submissive partner. I was as aggressive as Brand. Well, almost.

Despite our roughness, we took our time. Neither of us was in a hurry to reach the end. My body cried out for release, but I wanted our time together to last. Being with Brand, touching him and being touched was something I not only wanted but needed. I'd needed it for as long as I could remember and had too long been denied it. I felt like a poor wretch lost in the desert who had at last found water. I intended to drink my fill.

I lost control of myself. Something primeval was at work within me. Conscious thought left me as Brand and I shared our bodies. Nothing else mattered but Brand's hard muscles, his lips, his penis, his tongue. Brand became ever more aggressive, but I was too lost in the moment the care. He guided me with his actions communicating what he wanted without words.

Brand became animalistic. He took control. Some part of me was aroused by his dominance and I submitted to his desires. I had never experienced anything so intense before. Still, I should have stopped Brand when he turned me around and pushed my face up against a large tree. I should have protested when I felt his hard penis rubbing against my butt. I knew I shouldn't let it happened, but at the moment I didn't care. I both wanted and needed it.

When Brand entered me, I cried out in pain. I'd never dreamed it would hurt so much. The pain was blinding. I felt as if my ass was on fire. With the pain came clarity and reason. We weren't even using protection!

"Stop! It hurts!"

I pushed away from the tree, but Brand held me in place. He was too strong for me.

"Easy, easy," he said as if he was talking to a skittish horse. "It only hurts at first."

"No," I said. "Stop."

Brand held me up against the tree, even as he pushed himself in deeper.

"You know you want this," he whispered in my ear.

"It hurts, Brand."

"It will feel much better soon."

Brand's breath on my ear drove me crazy. He chewed on my ear lobe for a moment, then nibbled at my neck, and bit my shoulder. The sensations made me want to give in to him and give him anything he wanted, but common sense fought for control.

"No. Stop. We're not even using protection."

"You're a virgin, aren't you, Tyler? I've never done this with a guy and I always use protection with a girl. There's no risk."

Brand pushed harder against me. I cried out in pain again. Tears streamed from my eyes.

"You'll dream about this later," he whispered into my ear.

I was confused. I struggled against what was happening, but at the same time part of me wanted it to happen. Brand held me in place and he forced himself inside me. He kept whispering to me, reassuring me, telling me he knew I wanted it, that I'd been asking for it all along.

I cried out again as he buried himself completely inside me.

"Take it out! It hurts!"

"Do you really want me to stop, Tyler? I'll stop if you want me to, but I know you want it. It hurts now, but it's going to feel better than anything you've ever experienced in your life. No one can make you feel like I can. You've taken the pain. Do you really want to miss out on the pleasure? You've never felt anything like it, Tyler. If you want me to stop, say the word, but there are no second chances. It's now or never."

I let Brand seduce me. I let him have what he wanted. Brand bit my shoulder again and then he gripped my hips and began to work himself in and out. It hurt so bad I couldn't stand it and yet it felt better than anything. Brand was right. The pain lessened and the pleasure increased. As I relaxed, the pain lessened still further. Sensing my receptiveness, Brand went at it harder. He was like some wild thing, totally lost in the act of coupling. Brand went at it harder and harder until he shoved himself completely inside me again and groaned.

My mind was swimming. Brand pulled out, turned me around, and kissed me deeply. His hand sought out my equipment and he brought me almost more pleasure than I could bear. I moaned into his mouth as I finished. Brand had to hold me up as I experienced the most intense orgasm of my life. He grinned at me when I was done.

"You're so sexy," he said. I melted under his gaze and his words.

We dressed, then smoothed out our clothing and walked back toward camp. The darkness had deepened. There was barely enough light for us to make our way down the forest path, but it was a good deal lighter when we walked out from the shelter of the trees. We didn't speak as we walked. Brand seemed completely satisfied with himself. When our eyes met, he smiled at me and raised his eyebrows. I smiled back uncertainly. Things were different now, but I didn't know how. I couldn't put a name to the emotions I experienced.

Brand walked me to my cabin, but I didn't stay there. Instead, I set out alone for a walk along the lake. Had I wanted what had happened or had Brand forced me? That's the question that bothered me. He was so attractive and so seductive. I didn't know he was going to do *that* to me when I followed him into the woods. I knew we'd mess around, but...I hadn't planned to do *that* for a long time. Brand had obviously planned to take me. Why else would he have taken me to a place so secluded? It's not like he'd forced me, or had he? I could have resisted a whole lot more. He'd given me a chance to stop, but I'd let him continue. I must have wanted it or I wouldn't have given it up.

Would Brand have stopped if I told him to? He'd ignored me before when I'd told him to stop. He'd just held me in place and told me I wanted it. He had given me that final chance, but was it a real choice? If I'd told him to stop would he have stopped or would he have just told me that he knew I wanted it and kept going? I hadn't told him to stop, so I'd never know for sure.

When he finished, he hadn't forgotten about me. He'd kissed me and held me and he'd gotten me off. There was a little part of me that felt used, but hadn't we gone out into the woods to have sex? To satisfy our mutual needs? I felt satisfied. My body was relaxed and all the built up sexual tension was gone. I had gotten what I'd gone into the woods for and so had Brand. Was there anything wrong in that?

I almost couldn't believe he'd done that to me, but he was so nice to me after. He'd told me I was sexy. I knew I was lucky to be with a guy like him. He was so hot he could have anyone, but he'd chosen me. The mere fact he wanted me made me feel good about myself.

We shouldn't have done it without a rubber. What was I thinking? *Stupid, stupid, stupid!* Brand was right. I was a virgin. I was his first guy. He'd always used protection with girls. There were still risks, though. I didn't like to think about it, but what if Brand was lying to me? How did he know it would start to feel good for me if he'd never done it with a guy before? Had someone told him? Had he read it somewhere? Some guys lied to get sex. What if I wasn't his first guy and what if he did it without protection with others, too? If other guys did it with Brand without protection, how many guys had each of them done without wearing a condom? I might as well have been gang banged by a whole football team.

Now you're just being paranoid, Tyler. Brand didn't lie to you.

I felt so stupid. I'd promised myself never to do it without protection and I'd let the first guy who came along do it to me without a rubber in the woods. I felt slutty.

Doing it with one guy does not make you slutty, Tyler.

Okay, I wasn't slutty, but I had done something stupid. I couldn't blame it on Brand either. I could have insisted we didn't do *that* until we got some protection. I hadn't insisted, though. I'd let him talk me into it. I'd been thinking with my penis and now I'd just have to worry about it. I knew I'd be worrying. "What if" was going to haunt me. It would be there in the back of my mind the next time I wasn't feeling so good. If I felt a chill or came down with a cold or just felt unusually tired, I'd wonder if I hadn't caught something bad from Brand. He looked plenty healthy, but HIV and the clap doesn't always show for a long time, does it? I knew I should get tested. Maybe I would. I didn't think I could deal with knowing I had something, though. Maybe not knowing was better. What a mess. I really was young and stupid. The question was, would I let it happen again? No. At the very least, I was going to go buy some condoms and keep one in my pocket when I went anywhere with Brand. Even if he didn't want to wear it, I was willing to bet I could get him to do so. He'd do it so he could have me, and I wanted him to have me again.

The waves gently lapped along the shore. The moon reflected off the surface of Lake Potawatomi. There was supposed to be a song called "Potawatomi Moon." I wondered how it went. I could see how the lake inspired a song. I'd read a little of the history of the area. Quite a few writers and songwriters had lived on the shores of the lake, or at least visited. Kurt Vonnegut had a cottage here. Cole Porter had visited in his youth and used to sneak onto the steamboats and play the piano until he was spotted. Then, he'd dive off the boat and swim to shore.

Brand. When I thought about guys, it was more along the lines of having a boyfriend, but I'd lusted after guys like Brand for as long as I could remember. I didn't know when I first started thinking about guys *in that way*, but I couldn't remember a time when I didn't. I'd worked through a lot of fantasies in my head. The reality of it was quite different. Doing it with Brand had been exciting, intense, painful, pleasurable, and thrilling. Part of me felt ashamed I'd let him do *that* to me and part of me was proud that he wanted me that bad. Brand, the hottest hunk in camp, wanted *me*.

I walked slowly along the north shore of Lake Potawatomi, listening to the waves, feeling the cool breeze, smelling the scent of the spring-fed lake. It was quiet and peaceful. I let the lake calm me and slow my thoughts.

By the time I'd walked back to my cabin I was feeling better. Yes, I'd made a stupid mistake, but that was my fault and I just had to deal with the consequences. Hopefully, those consequences would only be worry and uncertainty. If I really did get something...I guess I'd just have to deal with it. God, why did I do it? Because I'm a horny teenage boy who was thinking with his dick instead of his brain, that's why. I would not make that mistake again.

As for Brand, he had seduced me, but I let him. The truth was, I would let him again. Yeah, Brand was cocky and full of himself, but that was part of what made him so sexy. Out of all the guys in camp, he'd chosen me. Yeah, my interest in him had been pretty obvious, but there had to be other guys who wanted him too. He'd picked me. I never dreamed a hunk like Brand would actually want me. I found myself wishing I could take him back to Bloomington with me at the end of the summer. That would never happen, but a summer fling wasn't such a bad thing.

On Friday, I walked down the hill to Cabin 34 after my morning shower. Only the gentle cawing of crows and the occasional sound of a screen door creaking disturbed the silence at this hour of the day.

I quietly entered the cabin, then my own quarters. I closed the door, put my robe on a hanger in the wardrobe, and dressed. I liked this quiet time just before reveille at 6:50 a.m. My boys were still sleeping, as usual, and I had a little time all to myself. I looked in the mirror and combed my hair. Our uniforms weren't bad. They were a lot sharper than the dorky clothes actors were forced to wear in summer camp movies. Our dress uniform, worn at parades, chapel, and other formal occasions, consisted of khaki slacks and a white polo shirt with the logo on the breast. Some of the older counselors told horror stories of dark green polyester dress pants that pulled out leg hairs as one walked and felt like they were melting on hot days. I was glad I'd missed out on those particular tortures. Further back in time, uniforms had been made of wool. So much for the "good old days."

I made my bed with the proper military folds. I kept my quarters organized and neat, even going so far as to fold my clothes like the boys did. I was an organized person and liked things neat, but my real purpose was to show the boys that I practiced what I preached. It was a good thing too, for Steve had already called me on it. During a P.I. (the morning Personal Inspection where the counselor checks to make sure each boy has his bunk made properly, his clothes put away, and etc., Steven had said something along the lines of "Why do we have to make our beds and keep our things neat when *you* don't?" I stopped and took all the boys into my quarters, where they were normally not allowed. There, my bed was made up just like theirs, my clothes were folded, and all my stuff was organized in neat rows. Nothing was out of place. From that moment, my kids knew I wasn't asking them to do anything I wasn't doing myself. That's not to say they all made their beds and kept their stuff picked up like little angels. Getting them to keep the cabin neat was a daily, sometimes hourly struggle, but at least I set a good example and frustrated Steve. The latter was more enjoyable than the former.

My quarters were small, but I had my own semi-private space. My single bed was shoved up against the wall opposite the door. I used the wardrobe as a room divider so I could sit on my bed and read without being visible every time someone walked by the door. Near the door were my desk and chair. The coolest feature of my quarters were the screen windows. The entire upper half of east side of my room was made up of six large screen windows. Four more windows gave me a great view to the north. I kept the bottom windows on the east side closed for privacy, but as my cabin was on the side of a hill, the north side was so far off the ground I could keep all the those windows open. It was kind of like living in a screened in porch, perfect for the summer months.

Some rag rugs on the floor, a piece of antique stoneware from my collection, and a small group of history books and *Star Trek* novels gave my quarters a personal touch.

Reveille was coming up fast. I picked up my current *Star Trek* novel and read a few pages. I loved camp, but sometimes I liked to rest my mind by spending a few minutes on the Enterprise with Kirk, Spock, Scotty, and McCoy. I think Doctor McCoy was my favorite. I loved how he got into it with Mr. Spock. Scotty was really cool too. I'd actually met him, Jimmy Doohan that is, the actor who plays Scotty. I even had a picture of us together on my desk. One of the kids saw it and said, "You know Scotty!" I explained that I didn't know him. I'd just met him. It's not like we went out for dinner and hung out together. Anyway, I didn't have much time to read at camp, but reading even just a couple of pages allowed me to step into that other world for a while. It also allowed me to carry that world with me and turn Neeswaugee itself into a starship. A little crazy, perhaps, but crazy is fun.

The bell just down the hill rang and one of the D&B boys played reveille. I walked out into the boy's area of the cabin and threatened them with death if they didn't get up. Okay, not really, but I did threaten to get out my super soaker, load it up with water from my little refrigerator, and give anyone who tried to stay in his bunk a rude awakening. Yeah, I became a counselor because I enjoy being mean to kids. Okay, not really, but that's what I told my boys.

A few minutes later, Division 4 formed up for breakfast. I was glad I wasn't on duty. I didn't mind being full or part duty, but it was nice not to be in charge.

I ate breakfast with my kids, as always. Daniel smiled and said "hey" when he spotted me. Daniel was cute. A lot of the counselors were cute! I was glad I had something going with Brand because otherwise I'd spend way too much time drooling over hot guys. I was determined to be professional so drooling was definitely out. Brand and I played it cool whenever someone else was around. Sometimes, he played it too cool, like he barely knew me, but we couldn't risk anyone finding out about us.

Speak of the devil. There was Brand, flirting with one of the female counselors again. The sight created a knot in my stomach. It was necessary to keep our relationship secret, but flirting with girls was going a little too far. Of course, I'd never out and out asked Brand if he was gay. Perhaps he was bi. Straight was definitely out. A straight guy might experiment and do what Brand and I had done in the lake, but I doubted it. He kissed me after all. There is no way a straight guy would do what Brand had done to me on Wednesday night. Then again, what did I know? No, Brand wasn't straight; bi maybe, but not straight. I didn't like him flirting with girls in any case. I considered him mine.

Jealous, Tyler?

Okay, I'm jealous. Shoot me. Brand and I had experienced something intimate. I'd given him my virginity. To me that meant something and I didn't like to see him flirting with anyone else, male or female. We hadn't said we were dating, but it was kind of implied. Then again, I was pretty clueless when it came to a relationship with another guy. Why hadn't someone written a guidebook about this?

"Is the milk supposed to have chunks?" Stephen asked quietly.

"Huh? No!" I said. "Don't drink that."

"Oh, chunky milk," Lt. Baer said, pausing as he was heading for his own table of Division 4 boys. "I hear it's new. It's called Hurl and it's found in the non-refrigerated section, in the green carton."

I laughed, as did most of the boys.

"Chunky milk alert!" Lt. Baer called out.

I shook my head. I liked Lt. Baer a lot. No, not like that! I mean I enjoyed his quirky sense of humor.

After breakfast, I returned to Cabin 34 where my boys were preparing for their P.I. I tried to perform the inspection as fast as possible because ten-year-old boys are not known for their ability to stand at parade rest. They were fidgety at best and disruptive at worst. To be honest, I wasn't a stern enough counselor to make my boys take the morning inspections as seriously as they should have. I was a nice guy and my kids knew it, no matter how I tried to pretend I was a bad ass. It made for some not-so-successful inspections and yet I think I was a better counselor because my boys knew that I cared. Some of the boys had been homesick and there were the inevitable problems with conflicting personalities and hurt feelings. My boys knew they could come to me with their problems.

The kids headed for class after P.I. and I wasn't far behind. I had truly lucked out by landing a job in Indian Crafts. Most of the kids who took the class were laid back and genuinely interested in making ojos, beadwork, and shields. The instructors talked and laughed with each other and the kids. Camp was very tiring and I loved the calm and mostly restful atmosphere of the Indian Crafts tent.

The proximity to Brand was a nice fringe benefit, too. The Indian Dance classes met at the top of hill not far from our tent. Throughout the day I could hear the rhythmic thump of the drum. Of course, what I liked best was catching sight of Brand. I checked out his legs as he walked up the hill. He had such sexy calves. My view was often blocked by admiring campers who flocked to Brand. The girls adored him and the boys idolized him. Why wouldn't they? I still almost couldn't believe we'd...well, you know.

Near the end of the third class period, Maj. T approached the Indian Crafts tent, which was rare. He usually worked in the Indian Lore cabin or out at the Council Ring. I figured he was coming to see Maj. Burrows, but he headed straight for me.

"Lieutenant P, this is for you," he said, handing me a thin sheaf of papers. "Your part is highlighted."

"My part?"

"For the Council Fire on Saturday. Practice is tonight. You should have plenty of time to memorize your lines."

I gulped.

"I..."

"Don't worry. There is a soundtrack. You only have to mouth the words, but try to memorize the dialogue if you can. We really need you for this first Council Fire. We usually get a lot of volunteers for the acting roles after the first week, but I'd really appreciate it if you could help us out."

I found myself agreeing to do just that. How could I say no to T? Panic mixed with excitement flooded me as Maj. T walked away. I wasn't an actor! How could I memorize lines? I wasn't even sure I could remember what I'd eaten for breakfast. What if I made a complete fool out of myself in front of the entire camp? Worse, Brand would be right there to witness it. As an Indian Dance instructor, he'd be in the Council Fire for sure. I suddenly felt like Linus in *A Charlie Brown Christmas*. I was doomed.

In between classes, I looked through the script. The title was *Sacred Fire* and it was eight pages long. My character didn't appear until page 3. I was to play the part of the messenger of the Great Spirit. I had a whole paragraph of dialogue on page 3, but I didn't appear again until page 7 and had only one smaller paragraph of dialogue. I began to relax a little. I didn't know how I'd handle appearing in front of a few hundred people, but at least I wouldn't be in the spotlight for very long. I had a cool part, too. I'd kind of thought of trying out for a play at school, but I'd never had the courage. This was summer camp. It was my chance to try something new. If I did make a complete fool of myself I could console myself with the knowledge that camp would end in only five weeks and I'd probably never seen any of these people again.

Bloomington, Indiana
Wednesday, June 29, 2009

Did wisdom only come with age or would I make the same mistakes now? If I had my life to live over, I'd avoid Brand completely or at the very least stay away from him after the night we went skinny-dipping. If things had been left as they were at that point, Brand would have been a pleasant memory. I didn't have the benefit of hindsight when I was seventeen. I didn't know what was going to happen. Would I have avoided Brand if I knew he was going to take my virginity in the woods? I like to think I would, but then I was a typical teenage boy in a lot of ways—horny and desperate for sex. I might very well have followed Brand into the woods even if I'd known what he was going to do to me. Ah, the stupidity of youth. Hopefully, I was wise enough to spot players like Brand now. A hot young guy could still turn my head, but I hoped I had enough brains to know when I was being manipulated.

A knock at the door interrupted my thoughts. I smiled. It was Tyler.

"Hey, I've been reading the Narnia books. I finished the first two. You were right. They're great."

"Come in and tell me about them. I'll make some tea."

I put on the kettle and prepared a tea pot while Tyler began to tell me about *The Magician's Nephew* and *The Lion, The Witch, and The Wardrobe*. It had been a while since I'd read the books, but as he spoke about what he loved in the stories, they came back to me as if I'd read the tales yesterday.

"You know, J.R.R. Tolkien, who wrote *The Lord of the Rings,* tried to convince C.S. Lewis not to publish the Narnia series," I said.

"Really? Why?"

"He thought they were too short, too much children's tales, and I believe he objected to the religious aspects. It's been quite a while since I read about it, so I'd want to check my facts before saying so for sure."

"There does seem to be a lot of religion in the Narnia books, even though it's never stated outright."

"Yeah, which is interesting, because C.S. Lewis was an atheist for at least two long periods in his life."

"I would never have guessed that."

"There are usually stories behind the stories."

"I've been wondering...is it hard for you to write? I mean, is it work or does it come easy?"

"Sometimes it's work. Sometimes it's almost effortless. I have a very short attention span so I can only write for a few minutes before I'm off onto something else."

"How can you get a whole book written then?"

"I write for a few minutes, go and check my email or make some tea, then I go back to writing. Speaking of tea..."

I got up, took the kettle off the stove, and poured the near boiling water over the Yorkshire tea bags.

"I really want to be a writer."

"Then you should."

"That's what Dad says. He says I should be realistic. He says being a writer is like being an actor, a musician, or an artist. It's hard to make it, but it's important to do what you love."

"Your dad sounds wise."

"You'd like him I'm sure. He's very supportive of whatever I want to try, like my disastrous flirtation with the keyboard. I never could learn how to play that thing."

I laughed.

"I tangled with the keyboard myself. I quickly learned to stick with the one attached to my computer and avoid the musical variety."

"Yeah. He probably knew I couldn't hack it, but he let me try away."

"It sounds like he thought you deserved a chance. You never know what you'll be good at until you give it a shot. The only real failure is not trying."

I poured steaming tea in Blue Willow cups for Tyler and myself.

"Trying new things is important, although things don't always work out. My experiment with pepper tea is a good example of something that was less than successful," I said.

"Pepper tea?"

"Yes, made with black pepper and it's just as vile as it sounds."

Tyler laughed.

"You're starting to get this place into shape," Tyler said.

"Thanks to your help. If it wasn't for you, most of my stuff would still be packed in boxes. There's no way I could move most of this furniture around by myself either."

"Oh, no. You're not rearranging *again*, are you?

Tyler grinned. The movers had set everything just where I'd indicated, but I'd been moving things around to try to get just the right flow and look. Tyler had helped me move some of the same pieces as many as three times.

"Just a little. Think of it as job security."

"This is great tea."

"I was a little surprised when I discovered you liked tea. Most of the younger generation is more into Starbucks."

"Blah. I hate coffee. Of course, I only tried it a couple of times, but it's so bitter. I tried it once with lots of sugar and cream, but by the time I got rid of most of the bitterness there was more sugar and cream than coffee."

I smiled.

"In England, they often drink tea with quite a bit of milk, depending on the tea, of course. I like mine a bit stronger. Did you watch *The DaVinci Code*?" I asked.

"Yes."

"Remember when they were trying to get into the Englishman's estate in France and he asked them that question about tea? It was something like; 'Do you take your tea with milk or lemon'?"

"Oh, yes, and the answer is 'That would depend on the tea.' It's quite true of course, Earl Gray with milk would be ghastly," Tyler said.

I truly liked this boy. I would never have thought a teenager would have any interest in sitting and discussing tea with me. If he was a decade or so older...

"I'm glad I came to hit you up for a subscription."

"I am too. You've been so much help and I enjoy your company."

"I like hanging out with you, too. You're so interesting."

"What have you been drinking, Tyler?"

"Really! I mean it. I can't believe you're actually a writer."

"There are millions of writers, Tyler."

"But you've been published."

"That means nothing, although I do enjoy the royalty checks. Plenty of appalling books get published while thousands of incredible books do not."

"I *really* want to be a writer," Tyler said.

"Are you writing?"

"Yes. I've tried my hand at a few short stories and I'm even working on a novel."

"Then you are a writer."

"I've never had anything published."

"That doesn't matter. Being a writer is a state of mind. If you write and you think you're a writer, you are one."

"Yes, but what if no one likes my stuff?"

"That doesn't matter. Some won't like what you write—you can bet on it. I don't know who said it, but long ago I ran across a quote that said something like 'No matter what you do, a third of the people will hate it, a third will love it, and a third won't care one way or another.' It's quite true. I haven't read a review of one of my books in years because I know that some will hate what I write, some will love it, and some just won't care. Back when I did read the reviews I noticed that what one reviewer hated, another would praise as brilliant. It's all just opinion. Have you ever noticed how many types of cereal are available at the grocery?"

"Um, I'm completely lost now. Cereal? Weren't we talking about writing?"

"Yes, but have you noticed?"

"Sure."

"Well, there are scores of different kinds of cereal because no one can agree on which is best. Different people have different tastes. If we can't agree on cereal, why should we expect to agree on books?"

Tyler laughed.

"You're just a little odd."

"Oh. I'm more than just a little odd. I'm quite odd. Most writers are."

"Hmm, maybe I am a writer then because I'm definitely odd."

"There you go then. You've reached your goal of becoming a writer. Now, all you have to do is keeping writing so you'll become a better writer."

"I don't know if I'll improve."

"Of course you will! You should see the first book I tried to write. It was horrible. I cringe when I go back and read my first books. I can't believe I could write anything so terrible. It's depressing, but then I realize that I only think my early books are horrible because I've improved so much over the years. If you keep writing, you'll be a far better writer in a few years than you are now."

"You know," Tyler said, "I really should be getting to work. I'm supposed to mow your yard today, right?"

"I suppose I have bored you enough for now."

"Oh, I'm not bored at all. Will you teach me? To be a better writer I mean?"

"I don't really know if that can be taught, but I'll let you in on the secrets I've learned. Most of it has to come from inside. I can show you how to improve your work, so yes, I'll teach you what I can."

"Thanks! Now I'd better get to the lawn. If the grass gets any higher, we'll have to bale it instead of mow it."

"Come in when you're finished, Tyler. I'm sure you'll need something cool to drink by then."

Tyler walked out the back door. I felt a bit guilty for having him mow my lawn on this horribly muggy day. It was 90 or so out, but the humidity is what made it truly uncomfortable. I didn't mind hot, but I hated it when my shirt stuck to my body. I didn't feel too guilty because I was paying Tyler and he was young. He could stand the heat better than a guy my age. I almost laughed. I was thinking as if I was in my 70s rather than my 30s. Still, I was considerably older than Tyler and the years made a difference.

I heard the push mower start up as I busied myself in the kitchen. There was something comforting about kitchens. It's little wonder I spent so much time in my own. I was pleased by the atmosphere I'd been able to create. Blue and white spongeware and stoneware, Blue Willow, antique china, old baskets, and kitchen antiques gave the kitchen a nostalgic touch. This wasn't a museum, however. I couldn't live without a microwave or a dishwasher. I might have nostalgic thoughts about the past, but I didn't want to live there!

I looked out the window as Tyler walked by. He'd taken off his shirt and his slim torso glistened in the sunlight. I experienced an instinctual attraction to this smooth, sculpted body.

You're old enough to be his father, pervert.

I really didn't think age was a relevant factor, at least not when it came to the relationships of others. There was a fifteen year age difference between my brother and his wife. I knew other couples who were more than twenty years apart. When it came to me, however, I was more cautious.

I forced myself to stop watching Tyler. I didn't want to think about him in that way. He most likely wasn't gay and even if he was, I was already falling into the role of mentor. I liked Tyler. He reminded me of myself at his age. Besides, at my age I could surely control my hormones. I wasn't seventeen anymore. Thank God for that! A lot of people longed for their teenaged years, but I was far happier as an adult. Perhaps I just had a better memory of what those years were like than most. I think most people tended to remember the good and forget about the bad. Perhaps I'd be like that too if some of the events of my young life hadn't left such strong impressions. I'm not saying I dwelled on the negatives. On the contrary, I tried to let go of the pain, embarrassment, and heartache of my youth, but I acknowledged them. When I looked back I thought mostly of my joys and not my sorrows, but I also didn't let myself forget that youth is a difficult time for all.

As Tyler mowed the lawn, I pulled out a stoneware pitcher from my collection, colonial blue in color with a grape and trellis pattern, and proceeded to make lemonade. I had only two lemons, but I kept a bottle of ReaLemon for use in tea. It had been ages since I'd made lemonade, but my grandmother had taught me how to make it long ago. I started with a cup of sugar and a little hot water in which to dissolve it. Next, I added cold water from the refrigerator and a few splashes of ReaLemon juice. I sliced the lemons and added them to the pitcher, rind and all. Now, it was merely a matter of balancing the sour taste of the lemon juice with the sweetness of the sugar. It took a few minutes, but at last I pronounced it excellent.

I smiled at myself. I was quite content making lemonade for Tyler. I felt nearly paternal toward him and yet there was another emotional attachment at work quite different in nature. Tyler reminded me so much of Daniel, the lost love of my youth, that I had to remind myself that many years had passed and the boy who had recently entered my life was not the boy I'd fallen for so many years ago.

I set the pitcher in the refrigerator to chill and pulled out a couple of my cobalt blue tumblers. Unlike most of what I used, the tumblers weren't antique. I'd purchased them new years before, when I'd purchased my first home. They were the perfect color and size. I'd bought twelve of them so I'd still have plenty as I inevitably broke one now and then. Surprisingly, I had yet to break a single tumbler.

Tyler came through the back door a half an hour or so later, his shirt hanging from his shorts. His hair was plastered to his forehead and his bare torso slick with sweat. At that moment, I was so powerfully attracted to him that I wanted nothing more than to take him in my arms and slip my tongue into his mouth. With considerable effort, I looked away from his sleek, glistening, teenage body and headed for the refrigerator.

"Would you like some lemonade? I made some while you were working."

"That would be great!" Tyler said.

I intentionally kept my eyes off him while I added ice to the tumblers and poured us both glasses of lemonade. I didn't look at him again until I was seated across the table from him. I was still drawn to him, but I'd managed to get myself under control.

"It must be terribly uncomfortable out there," I said, stating the obvious.

"It's so humid outside! It's even kind of hard to breathe. It's like being underwater."

"I hate humid weather. That's one reason I hired you to mow my lawn. I'd rather pay you to suffer than do it myself."

I grinned.

"Oh, I see. This is like a sweat shop."

"Today, for sure."

"I don't mind sweating. It feels good, but with the humidity, it makes me feel sticky. Yuck."

"You can use the shower if you'd like."

"I'd take you up on that, but I'd better get home soon. I promised Dad I'd mow our lawn today. There's not much use in showering since I'll just get all sticky again."

"I hope your yard isn't too large."

"A little bigger than yours, but not by much. Oh, it feels so good in here!"

"Yeah, I think I'll be hanging out inside today. I'm itching for a walk, but I'm going to wait until this evening when it cools off.

Tyler and I sat, drank lemonade, and talked. A feeling of sadness descended upon me when he departed several minutes later. I thoroughly enjoyed his company, but I wondered if I liked him a little too much. Was I setting myself up to get hurt?

I shook my head and laughed at myself. I was thinking as if I was going to be dating Tyler, which was not the case. It was doubtful he'd find an older man of interest even if he was attracted to males. Besides, as I'd thought to myself more than once before, I liked the nice, comfortable relationship that had developed between us. I also liked having someone I could trust to hire for odd jobs.

The last was particularly valuable today. I gazed out the window at the freshly mowed lawn and the deceptively beautiful weather. The lilacs swayed in a gentle breeze. The sunlight bathed the red, pink, and white roses that grew in abundance. No doubt the roses perfumed the air with their sweet scent, but this was a wonderful day to stay inside. Thanks to Tyler, I could do just that. I poured myself another glass of lemonade, carried it into the living room, and sat down to relax. Yeah, being older had its advantages.

As I sat there sipping my lemonade, my mind traveled back through the years to my first summer at Camp Neeswaugee—the summer I met Daniel.

Camp Neeswaugee
Friday, June 29, 1989

My courage began to wane as Council Fire practice neared. All the Indian dancers met in front of Main Headquarters right after supper. When I approached the bleachers, there was already a large group of kids there, including Steve, Greg, and Caleb from my own cabin. My kids were surprised and excited to discover that I was going to be in the Council Fire, too. I was excited myself, but growing more and more nervous. I sort of had my lines down, but I seriously doubted the wisdom of getting in front of a large group of people.

Do not wuss out, P. Just do it!

"Hey."

I turned around. It was Daniel.

"Hey."

"Have a part in the Council Fire?" Daniel asked.

"Yeah, Maj. T waylaid me this morning. You?"

"The same, except I volunteered. It sounded like it might be fun. So what's your part?"

"I'm the messenger from the Great Spirit."

"Oh, you're the enemy then. I'm playing the bad guy—the evil shaman. I don't come in until near the end."

"My part isn't very big, but that suits me just fine. I'm not so sure about this."

"It will be a good time. Just have fun!"

Daniel's enthusiasm was contagious. I found myself growing a little less nervous.

Brand walked by just then looking so sexy in his khaki shorts. Damn, he had a nice ass. Brand had nice everything. I glanced at Daniel for a moment. He was watching Brand too, but he was frowning. Daniel realized I was watching him and quickly looked away from Brand. His frown disappeared.

"So how is Indian Crafts?"

Had I told him I worked in Indian Crafts? I couldn't remember.

"I like it. I've mainly been helping with ojos, but I'm getting into the painted shields some. Maj. Burrows is going to get me started on beadwork soon so I can help out with that too. I guess he thinks I'm crafty."

"I'm doing leatherwork in Arts & Crafts. The Gold Cs are making these cool billfolds. Some of them have great designs punched into them."

We didn't have time to talk more because Brand called for everyone to be quiet and then called roll. Lt. Elwolf was only a year older, but he was so confident and strong I felt like a boy compared to him. I smiled as I sat there, remembering skinny-dipping in the lake and sex in the woods. I had mixed feelings about what happened in the forest and yet part of me wanted to do it all over again.

Brand's eyes met mine for a moment and he gave me a cocky grin. The smug, mischievous expression on his face made me want to jump on him. I noticed Daniel looking at me and I quickly looked away from Brand. No one could even suspect we were lovers.

Once roll was called, the Indian dancers headed out on the trek to the Council Ring. Daniel and I trailed along behind. Daniel had grown quiet, but I didn't mind. I had a lot to think about. At the moment, I was thinking about slipping off with Brand after taps. I'd gone into town on my period off and purchased some condoms at the Revco. Thankfully, a young guy was working the checkout counter. I'm not sure why, but it would have been really embarrassing if a woman, especially one my mom's age or older, was working the cash register. It was much easier with a guy. I don't know if I was expecting a knowing grin or what, but I was kind of surprised that he acted as if my purchase of a box of condoms was no more significant than buying a tube of toothpaste. Then again, why should he care if some guy he didn't know was getting laid? What was a significant event in my life didn't mean anything to him.

I fingered the condom in my pocket. I was prepared, but I wasn't sure if repeating the woodsy sex scene was such a wise idea. Brand and I had gone too far in the heat of the moment. I shouldn't have let him do that to me, especially without a condom. Still, a part of me wanted to do it again. The condom was insurance. If we did do it again, at least this time it wouldn't be so unsafe.

Just thinking about Brand... Damn, when did I become obsessed with sex?

Hmm. When you were thirteen, Tyler?

The little voice in my head thought it was funny sometimes. It was usually wrong.

At the Council Ring, or simply the Ring as Maj. T called it, everyone sat on the wooden bleachers except for those who would be in the very beginning of the *Sacred Fire*. Maj. Burrows pressed play on an old tape recorder and a narrator with a sonorous voice began the tale. The basic story was that the sacred fire in the medicine lodge of a band of Potawatomi had gone out because it was not properly tended and had to be relit as soon as possible so as not to anger the gods further. Apparently, the gods were already kind of ticked off because the Potawatomi had let the fire go out in the first place. The fire had to be lit in a special way with magic kindling from one place and special black liquid from a remote spring. Black Wolf, played by Brand, was chosen to go on the dangerous quest to obtain the kindling and black liquid.

I watched as Maj. T guided the actors to their marks and then observed them lip synching their lines to the taped dialogue. Maj. Burrows stopped the tape now and then so the actors could be shown their marks. I figured that if I didn't do something stupid like trip and fall on my face that I'd have a good chance of making it through the show without making a fool of myself.

While the Indian dancers were practicing the Entreaty Dance, performed so the spirits would help Black Wolf on his quest, Maj. T showed me where I'd enter and my mark. It was simple enough, just walk in and start talking to Black Wolf. Surely, I couldn't screw that up too badly.

I waited just outside the Council Ring and practiced my lines while the beat of the medicine drum filled the forest. Maj. Burrows started up the tape again and Black Wolf set out on his quest. He stopped for the night and went to sleep. I walked into the Council Ring, trying to feel my part. Black Wolf stirred at my approach and looked at me. I stopped only a few paces from him, gazing into the eyes of Brand. His knowing, mischievous gaze broke my concentration. Brand had the most amazing, sexy eyes. We weren't dressed in costume for practice. Brand and I were both in khaki shorts and our Neeswaugee staff shirts, hardly Native American. It was hard to imagine I was the messenger of the Great Spirit coming to Black Wolf in the dark of night and not just Tyler gazing at sexy, sexy Brand.

The narration played on. It was nearly time for me to speak.

The messenger of the Great Spirit spoke: "Because you are true, strong, and dedicated to the traditions of your people, the Great Spirit has smiled upon you, and has sent me, White Eagle, to help you. Listen to me, Black Wolf. The dangers you face are many. Tomorrow you will come to the Forest of Forgetfulness. The people there are joyous and happy, and will gladly give you what you seek after you have proven yourself to them. They will make you welcome, but do not be deceived, for danger lurks in their kindness. If you are heedless, you will forget your quest, and yourself, and remain in the forest forever. Keep your wits about you. And now, farewell. I shall always be near to help you if you need me."

The messenger from the Great Spirit was swallowed by the clouds of night.

I was going to hook up with Brand after practice! Half way through my speech, Brand gave me a sultry, seductive look. He'd even licked his upper lip with his tongue. No one else could see what he was doing, but I momentarily forgot my lines and even what I was doing standing there in the middle of the Council Ring. The little mischievous grin on Brand's face told me he was tripping me up on purpose. That same grin told me he wanted me again.

I had four pages of script before I appeared again. I went back in and sat on the bleachers and observed the other actors and the dancers. Daniel came over and sat next to me. He glanced at his script from time to time.

"Nervous?" I asked.

"Maybe just a little, but not much. How hard can it be to mouth the words?"

"Harder than it looks."

"You did fine."

"You think so?" I asked. "I felt kind of stupid out there. I just don't know about tomorrow night."

"We'll be in costume for the performance. You'll be amazed at how much that helps."

"You've been in plays?"

"Oh, yeah. When you get into costume, you start becoming the character you're playing. You start to really feel like that person. It's almost as if you aren't *you* anymore."

"I'm not an actor."

"Everyone is an actor. All the world's a stage, Tyler."

"Thank you, William Shakespeare. I was nervous, but it was kind of fun out there."

"Just forget about everything when you're out there. Be the messenger from the Great Spirit. Look at everyone as if that is who you are."

"I can try."

We watched in silence. Daniel gazed at me and smiled reassuringly now and then. Black Wolf successfully retrieved the magic kindling and set out to obtain the black water. Maj. T motioned for Daniel.

I almost cracked up when Daniel spoke, or rather lip synched his lines. The voice of the evil shaman was high pitched and simpering. Daniel's facial expressions perfectly matched. He somehow made the old shaman both menacing and ridiculous at the same time. He was an instant hit. Brand had the largest role, but Daniel obviously had the best.

The first task given to Black Wolf by the evil shaman was to retrieve a sacred plant from high on a hill, avoiding poisonous rattlesnakes that acted as the protectors of the plant. He scaled the steep hill, which was the permanent concrete background of the Council Ring made to look like a natural cliff. There were built-in foot and hand holds, but it was still a strenuous climb. Brand's muscles tensed and flexed as he climbed higher and higher, avoiding the rattlers, until he retrieved the sacred plant from the top. The kids watched with rapt attention, as if Black Wolf was truly in great danger. Black Wolf returned with his prize.

The Evil Shaman said: "What is this? You have retrieved the sacred plant! You must indeed be very brave. But the next test is not so easy..."

I had to bite my hand to keep from laughing. Some of the kids did laugh. That voice...it was just too much. Daniel's performance was awesome. I didn't know it just then, but everyone connected with Indian Lore would be repeating "But the next test is not so easy" for the rest of camp. It became a running gag.

Maj. T took me backstage, right behind the large concrete background that Brand had just scaled. There was a well-worn iron ladder attached to the center of the wall. As T explained what I had to do, I grew a bit anxious. My part was slightly more athletic than I'd anticipated.

I climbed up on the ladder and crouched with my hands gripping the rung just above my head and my knees folded against my chest. I felt a little silly with my butt sticking out, but there wasn't anyone around to see.

I followed the narration. Black Wolf succeeded at the task that was not so easy, but the shaman would not give him the black water as promised and ordered him to be taken away. It was time for my entrance. Tomorrow night, there would be a powder shot so it would look like I appeared in a great flash of fire and smoke.

I launched myself onto the top of the background, using so much force I nearly catapulted myself right off the ledge and into the Council Ring. I regained my balance just in time to keep from taking a header. I stood there and looked down at the shaman and his tribe as if I really was the messenger from the Great Spirit, just as Daniel had advised. He was right. I didn't feel like me anymore. I was the character I was portraying:

The people fell stunned as the messenger from the Great Spirit once more appeared to Black Wolf.

"This old shaman would keep you here forever, setting you to one task after another. You have earned the right to take the black water back to your people. Depart at once!" Black Wolf scooped water from the black spring and hurriedly left the village.

I quickly exited down the steps to the right side while everyone was watching Black Wolf depart. The Council Fire wasn't over, but my part was done.

While one of the dances was going on, Maj. T pulled me to the side and explained the powder shot. A small amount of gun powder would be ignited by someone flipping a switch backstage. When it went off, there would be a large blast of smoke and some flame as well. I'd only be about two feet from the blast, so I had to keep my head down and not launch myself into view until the shot had fired, but I also had to hit my mark before the smoke cleared so it would look like I'd appeared out of thin air. There wasn't any significant danger, but only counselors were allowed to play roles that involved such stunts. I wasn't worried. I thought it made my part extra cool.

We ran through the entire Council Fire a second time. I, for one, needed the practice. I could see why the dialogue was taped. Otherwise, we'd be performing a play after running through it only twice! Less than thirty-six hours would elapse between the time I was handed my script and the performance! Yeah, lip synching was the way to go.

After practice, Daniel and I followed along behind the Indian dancers again. We were both in a good mood. I'd actually had fun onstage and everyone was coming up to Daniel and saying "But the next test is not so easy" in their own imitation of the Evil Shaman's voice.

Brand was at the head of the group. I followed along to Main HQ instead of cutting across the soccer fields to my cabin. I hoped to get a chance to talk to Brand, but he took off so fast when the group broke up that I couldn't wade through the kids to get to him before he'd disappeared. I was hoping to arrange a rendezvous after taps. I needed one.

Everything was beginning to come together for me. I more or less had my cabin under control. I was reasonably sure I wouldn't make a fool of myself in front of the entire camp tomorrow night. I loved teaching Indian Crafts. And, I had what amounted to a summer boyfriend and a smoking hot one at that!

I talked to Lieutenant Baer and the other counselors during milk and cookies—which is when all the kids in the division come up to headquarters for a snack before brushing their teeth and going to bed. Tonight, milk and cookies was this nasty orange drink that comes in a plastic bottle and graham crackers. The drink was nicknamed "Jungle Juice" and it was almost pure sugar. My first taste had been my last. Yuck! Most of the kids liked it, but what do kids know?

I wondered about the wisdom of getting the boys all sugared up right before bedtime, but apparently milk and cookies at taps was a tradition. A lot of things were done at Neeswaugee simply because "we did it that way last year." I could see the military mentality at work.

I got the boys settled in at taps with some difficulty. I turned off the lights and immediately began reading *The Hobbit*. Like most nights, I had to stop once or twice to silently demand a talkative boy get quiet, but this night was a dream compared to my first. I was glad I'd stuck it out. I would have missed out on so much if I'd ran screaming from Neeswaugee as I'd been tempted to do after that first day with my little monsters.

I returned to my quarters after I finished the chapter. It felt so good just to be by myself for a while. Being a counselor was like being a popular kid at school, or at least I guessed since I'd never actually been popular. Everyone noticed me. Most everyone said "hi." I felt like I was on public view twenty-four/seven. It was fun, but I relished those few minutes of the day when no one could see me and I could be alone with my thoughts.

I made myself some hot tea with my electric tea kettle and sat down to spend some time on the Enterprise. I hung out with Kirk, Spock, Scotty, and the others for a whole chapter then put my book to the side. I quietly left my cabin and headed up toward the D&B.

There was no light in Brand's quarters. He probably wasn't asleep since it was only about 11 p.m. so he was most likely down by headquarters or in town. I wandered down to Main HQ hoping I could catch him.

Brand wasn't on the bleachers or the benches out front. I went in, but there was no sign of him inside either. He'd probably gone into town, so I could forget finding him tonight. I was disappointed to say the least, but I decided I might as well catch up on some sleep since I obviously wasn't getting any tonight. It was too bad because I *really* needed some!

I walked back outside and toward the Dining Hall. As I was walking up the steep path toward the Nature Center/Museum, I thought I spotted a shock of blond hair in the moonlight disappearing into the night just over the crest of the first hole on the golf course. I quickened my pace. Maybe Brand was out for a stroll and I was about to get lucky. Then again, maybe I was just seeing things or maybe it was someone else with blond hair. It wouldn't hurt to check it out in any case.

By the time I passed the Nature Center and hurried to the top of the first hole on the golf course, I just barely caught sight of the blond disappearing into the wooded area off to the right. I thought for a minute I saw someone else, too, but I couldn't be sure in the dim light. I hurried on, knowing for sure that I hadn't imagined whomever it was I was following.

Once I hit the shadows under the trees, I was screwed. There was no way to spot anyone in there. I thought about calling out, but we weren't that far from camp and what if it wasn't Brand?

I thought I heard rustling up ahead, so I moved cautiously forward. I thought momentarily of bears, but there hadn't been a wild bear in Indiana for 150 years. The only dangers I had to face were the possibilities of getting a limb in the face, wading through poison ivy or poison oak, or tripping over a fallen log.

I couldn't hear the rustling sound anymore. Likely as not, it was a raccoon that had sensed my presence and was now staying in place to avoid detection. I stood in the shadows for a few minutes, deciding if I should turn back or keep searching. If it was Brand I'd spotted I *really* wanted to catch up to him. I didn't know if it was him, though. He wasn't the only blond counselor on the staff.

I was about to give it up when I heard rustling again, louder this time. I could make out voices, too. I couldn't make out what they were saying. I was following not one person, but two. I began to hope it wasn't Brand I'd seen. I thought about turning back, but the voyeur in me urged me forward. I was doubly careful to make no sound now. I thought I caught movement in the moonlight that filtered down through the trees ahead. Yeah, two people were up there. My eyes were adjusting to the darkness, but before I could make the two figures out clearly as I heard a male voice.

"Dude, stop! It hurts."

I experienced a bit of déjà vu. What the hell was going on? I crept a little closer.

"You know you want it."

I froze. It was Brand's voice.

"No, man. Stop!"

I recognized the other voice now too. I worked with him in Indian Crafts. He was a Division 6 counselor, Lt. Cody. I had noticed his sexy body when he was coming out of the showers.

"Stop, man!"

"Easy, easy. Just hang in there. This is going to feel better than anything you've ever felt in your life."

I clenched my fists in anger and pain. Tears began to roll down my cheeks.

I watched Brand's naked butt move up and down. The counselor beneath him grunted and whimpered. I'd seen more than enough. I turned to go and, of course, stepped on a branch that snapped loud enough to give me away.

Brand jerked his head around and speared me with his eyes. Just my luck, I was standing in a patch of moonlight that filtered down through the trees.

"What's that?" asked Lt. Cody.

"It's *nothing*," Brand said. He began thrusting again even as he continued staring into my eyes. The smirk on his face was like a dagger in my heart.

"Dude, it hurts!"

"Shut up! You know you want it. Why else did you come out here with me?"

I stood there for a moment, indecisive. Should I let Brand do to Cody what he'd done to me? Could I stop Brand? He was a lot stronger than me. Perhaps Cody and I together...but...would Cody welcome my interference?

Cody moaned.

"Yeah, you like it? Don't you? Tell me you like it."

"Oh, yes!"

That made up my mind. Lt. Cody wanted to be there.

Brand looked back at me once more. Tears streamed down my cheeks as I turned and crept away. So much for the intimate moments I'd shared with Brand being special. I felt like my heart had been ripped out and torn to shreds.

Once clear of the trees, my tears flowed more freely. I was so stupid! I thought Brand and I had something special going. I'd given up my virginity to him. I thought that meant something.

"It's *nothing.*"

Brand's words echoed in my mind, as did his gleaming eyes. Those eyes could be so sexy, but when he'd turned them on me in the darkness, they were the eyes of a predator, frightening and dismissive. They'd communicated something that tore into my heart. I was nothing to him. I was just another fuck. I bet I wasn't his first, either. I began to worry again about doing it without a rubber. How many guys had he seduced before me? How many had he taken somewhere private and... Lt. Cody's words and whimpers were like a replay of the night Brand had taken my virginity. Was it some kind of game to him? Did he get off on seeing just how many guys he could seduce into giving it up? Did he carve a notch in his headboard for every cherry he popped? I was so stupid! There was no telling how many guys he'd had.

I walked slowly back to my cabin. I forced myself to stop crying. I didn't want anyone asking me questions. I didn't want to talk about it.

Back in my quarters, I lay on my back and stared at the rafters far overhead. I'd let Brand play me for a fool. I'd been sucked in by his sexy body and handsome face. He'd used me and I'd let him.

I really liked him.

Tears rolled down my cheeks and I wiped them away. Most of this was my own fault—maybe all of it. Brand had never promised to be my boyfriend. He'd never said he wasn't going to get with someone else. I had wanted him and wanted him bad. I got more than I bargained for, but I did get what I wanted, at least physically. Brand hadn't lied to me. Had he mislead me? Perhaps, but I had the feeling that I mislead myself even more. Maybe I just wasn't thinking at all.

Once again you've seen what you wanted to see, instead of what was really there. Good job, Perseus.

I thought of Justin. It had only been a couple years, but the pain was still with me. We'd been such great friends. I'd grown to love him. We were so close I thought he loved me too. He did love me, but not the way I wanted him to love me, not the way I thought he did. Learning the truth had nearly destroyed me. This was just the same mistake all over again. I hadn't had time to fall in love with Brand yet. At least I'd been spared that pain.

I cried a little, then I cleared my mind as best I could and closed my eyes. The best way to deal with a bad day was simply to end it. I fell asleep and did not awaken until my alarm went off the next morning.

Bloomington, Indiana
Thursday, June 30, 2009

I hadn't told Tyler I was gay yet, but I never announced it to anyone, just as I didn't announce thousands of details about myself. My sexual orientation mattered, but then there were countless things about me that mattered, some less, some more, and I never made it a point to announce any of them. I didn't hide that I was gay anymore than I hid my fondness for pineapple on pizza or my love of the *Peanuts* comic strip. If it came up in conversation or became especially significant, I revealed it.

Tyler already knew of my fondness for antiques, hot tea, and fantasy novels by writers such as Tolkien and Lewis. He'd seen my collection of *Star Trek* novels. He'd no doubt noticed I owned quite a few cacti, too. My sexual orientation had yet to come up. There was, of course, the possibility that my sexual orientation would make Tyler uncomfortable in a way my hot tea, novels, and cacti did not.

My attraction to males was significant simply because it was significant to many people. A recent visit to Camp Neeswaugee had illustrated that point all too well. I'd run into some of my old campers who were now counselors. One of them, who had previously been excited to speak with me during my visits, was rather cool when I spoke to him. It was the first time I'd seen him since adding him as a friend on Facebook. I made no attempt to hide the fact I was gay on my Facebook profile. There was no rainbow flag there, but anyone who paid attention could easily figure it out. No doubt the former camper who had given me a cool reception did not like the fact his old counselor was gay. He didn't mention it. He wasn't hostile or unkind, but at first he'd barely spoken to me and when he did speak to me later, he was polite and nothing more. His reaction saddened me, but that's life.

I'd tell Tyler I was gay when he asked or when it became important. I suppose it was important now in a way. I had been attracted to him when I'd seen him mowing the lawn shirtless. I found him attractive, period. I had no attention of acting on that attraction, however, so I saw no need to tell Tyler I was into guys.

Then again, I wasn't so sure. I sensed danger in my relationship with Tyler. I liked him a little too much and anticipated his visits a little too eagerly. Most of that came from the fact that I enjoyed his company. He was rather pleasant to look at and I found him charming, but it was our conversations that I truly enjoyed. I loved his enthusiasm and his genuine interest in my interests. I would have seriously considered him as boyfriend material if he hadn't been so very young. Age is just a number, but there was twenty years separating us. It didn't matter. I had no intention of pursuing any relationship with Tyler other then friendship. Still, I knew I had to be on guard against my own emotions. I did not have the emotional control of the other Mr. Spock, the one with the pointed ears.

I was seeking out other friendships and some romantic possibilities, too. Both searches were progressing slowly, but then I'd moved to Bloomington only recently. Finding a boyfriend, especially, would take time. A relationship like that had to develop out of friendship. It couldn't be planned. All one could do is keep an eye out for possibilities.

Causal sexual relationships were easier to find, especially since I lived so close to IU. Most college boys were sexually active and IU had more than its share of gay and bi boys. I had a fondness for younger guys. As soon as I had the time, I intended to seek out one of the IU guys for some mutual pleasure. That too would help me to think of Tyler only in platonic terms.

Even without college boys to sate my appetite, I was quite capable of controlling myself. I lacked such control when younger, but control is an advantage of age.

I tried to put the whole topic out of my mind when Tyler came over to begin work at three. I was pleased to see him, but not eager to tell him I wanted to move a couple of pieces of furniture around in the living room, again. He gave me a long suffering look, but that was the sum of his comment on my tendency to arrange and rearrange. He probably thought my rearranging would never end, but when I finally achieved the right look, my furniture would likely stay in place for years.

"What's our next task?" Tyler asked when the living room rearranging was finished, for the time being at least.

"Shopping. You're going to help me pick out a rug."

Shopping? Trying to tip the boy off that you're gay?

"Not that I mind, but do you really need me to help you pick out a rug? You seem like the kind of guy who is good at decorating."

Is Tyler trying to tell me something?

"I not only have to pick out a rug; I have to carry it. I definitely need your help with that. I'm quite lazy when you get to know me."

"Lazy guys don't have a Bowflex in their bedroom."

"Who says I use it?" I teased.

"Well, I haven't seen any clothes hanging on it and I can tell by looking at you that you use it. You don't get a body like that pecking at a keyboard."

Was Tyler flirting? Yeah right, just keep on fantasizing old man.

"Okay, I use it, but I'm still lazy in many ways. You'll see."

"I'll believe it when I see it, not before. So where are we shopping for this rug?"

"T.J. Maxx. It's one of my favorite stores. There's one on the west side, near Lowes and Bed, Bath, and Beyond. Come on."

Tyler and I hopped in the roadster. The west side, like just about everything in Bloomington, was a short drive away. That's one of the reasons I'd returned to my home town; that, the museums, the IU boys, the wide variety of unusual restaurants, the college town atmosphere, and did I mention the IU boys?

"I've never been in this place," Tyler said, as he climbed out of the roadster less than fifteen minutes later.

"I see your education is lacking. Everyone should know about T.J. Maxx."

"Oookaaay," Tyler said, smiling.

We walked past the perfumes, shoes, and women's clothing to the rear of the store. Here were located household items of every description, from bedding to kitchen items to small pieces of furniture. I stopped in the gourmet food aisle first.

"I thought we were looking for a rug."

"We are, but I check for tea every time I visit. T.J. Maxx is where I get my best teas."

"Oh, so now I know one of your secrets," Tyler said.

"Only one of them; there are plenty more."

"You're not secretly Batman, are you?"

"I thought about applying for the job, but I'm afraid of heights."

Tyler laughed.

"The problem with T.J. Maxx is that finding what you want is a rather hit and miss proposition," I explained. "It's a high-end clearance store of sorts so what is here one visit may well not be the next. Oh, Scottish Breakfast tea! I've been waiting on this!"

"I've never seen anyone get quite so excited about tea."

"Writers are strange beings, Tyler, you know that. Besides, I was down to my last tin! I haven't found any of this in months. I was facing a tea emergency!"

"I hate to tell you this, but I don't think there can be such a thing as a tea emergency," Tyler said.

"Sacrilege!"

Tyler laughed.

I gathered up all six tins and placed them in my cart.

"Okay, now onto the rugs."

There was a large table near the furniture where area rugs were laid out.

"Oh, you mean a huge rug," Tyler said.

"Yeah, I'm looking for one about 5 by 8. Something with deep red or some blue or both."

"This one has nice colors."

I ran my hand over it.

"Yeah, but it's made with synthetic fibers. I'm looking for one made of cotton, wool, or a mix of both. Here's one. It's the wrong color, but feel the difference."

"The other one is scratchy compared to this."

"A lot of people don't care about the feel since it is a rug, but the rugs made out of natural fibers tend to be better made as well. Oh, here's one."

I uncovered a rug with an oriental design of vines and leaves with a predominantly deep red background, accented with tan, greens, and medium blues. I pulled up the corner to read the tag.

"This one is hand tufted, which means it's made by hand."

"Whoa, it's $150!"

"That's not a bad price at all for a rug like this. In most stores, it would cost three times that, which is why I shop here. So, what do you think of this rug for the living room?"

"I think it will look great on the hardwood floor and the red looks like it will match with that old red table you have."

"I think this is the one. Now is when you become truly useful. Help me dig this thing out."

It took a few minutes to dig down to the rug I wanted. With Tyler's help, I rolled up the rug and placed it across the shopping cart. Minutes later, we stuck the rug in the open rumble-seat.

"So, you've shown me your secret shopping place," Tyler said. "What are some of your other secrets?"

"Oh, no. Revealing one of my secrets in a day is quite enough."

"So, do I get to discover another tomorrow?"

"No promises."

Once back home, Tyler helped me lug the rug inside, unroll it, and position it.

"Good choice," Tyler said, once we had the rug placed. "It creates another room within a room, like we did with the braided rug. It gives this area a comfy feel, like when I'm all snuggly in my bed under my fuzzy blanket."

"I see you have an appreciation for simple things."

"I like to sit up in bed and read. Dad says I'm just lazy, but he's only kidding."

"It sounds like you get along well with your dad."

"Oh, he's the best! In a lot of ways, we're more like friends than father and son, although I still have to come home when he says and take out the garbage. Have you had any kids?"

"Hundreds."

Tyler looked totally confused.

"I was a camp counselor for several years. I never had any children of my own, but those boys were like my own kids. I still keep in touch with some of them."

"That's cool. I might be a camp counselor after I graduate. I think it would be fun."

"It was, but it was a lot of work too. I was exhausted most nights, especially in my later years there. It's one thing to keep up with ten-year-olds when you're seventeen. It's quite another when you're thirty."

"Wow, you were a counselor for a long time."

"Yes, beware. I tried it out for one summer and I kept going back. It's kind of addictive. The same could happen to you someday."

"Do you miss it?"

"Yes, but it's also a matter of 'been there, done that.' The faces change, but camp life remains more or less the same. When I began to grow tired of it, I knew it was time to give it up."

"I really think I'd like to do it. I bet it would be a blast!"

"It is, but as I said, it's a lot of work and there can be pain and heartaches too."

Tyler looked at me with a question in his eyes, but I did not elaborate.

"Okay, all this work has made me hungry," I said.

"We moved three pieces of furniture and went shopping. You call that work?"

"Yes. We writers live by a different standard. That was not only work, but hard work."

"You should try mowing your lawn sometime."

"Oh, no. I hired a sucker...I mean a young guy...to do that for me."

"Very funny."

"So, how about you? Hungry?"

"I'm always hungry."

"Great. I'll take you out to eat."

"I feel a little guilty letting you do that."

"Consider it a fringe benefit of working for me. Besides, I enjoy your company. I get tired of eating alone."

"You don't have anyone...special to spend time with?"

I noticed Tyler didn't say "girlfriend." Was he fishing for information or just being cautious? If he was being cautious, did that mean he suspected I might be gay?

"No. Meeting someone special takes time and I just moved back to Bloomington."

"That's true."

"I spotted a place on Kirkwood I thought looked interesting, the Irish Lion. It's near Chase Bank."

"I've never been in there."

"Then it will be a new experience for both of us."

Tyler and I walked out to the roadster and climbed in. I drove downtown and we were lucky enough to score a parking spot near the restaurant. Parking was sometimes a real problem in Bloomington, but I loved this town.

"I don't know if I'm allowed in here," Tyler said as we entered. He'd caught sight of the old-fashioned bar lined with bottles of liquor.

"We won't be eating in the bar," I said.

The long, narrow bar area was separated from a raised dining area by only a wooden banister. There was an additional dining area upstairs. I loved the dark, polished wood, Victorian trim, and stained glass windows. I really felt as if I was inside an Irish pub.

Our host led us upstairs. He seated us at a table toward the back, near the railing that looked down upon part of the restaurant below. I gazed up at the tin ceiling.

"This building is really old," I said.

"It was built in 1882 as a tavern," said our host. "Here are your menus. Your server will be with you shortly."

"This place reminds me a little of your house," Tyler said.

I browsed the menu and had a hard time deciding.

"Oh, I love Chicken Kiev," Tyler said.

"So order it," I said. "I think I'm going to try the coddle."

"The what?"

"Look under soups and stews. It's a stew with potatoes, bacon, sausage, and onions. It says here it's typical Dublin pub food supposed to prevent a hangover."

"Plan on getting drunk? Does this mean I get to drive home?"

"Not a chance. I don't drink."

"Too bad. I want to drive your roadster."

"Maybe someday."

Our server arrived and we ordered.

"If the food is any good, and I suspect it will be, I'll have to add this to my list of restaurants," I said.

"You don't cook much, do you?"

"It's hardly worth it for one person. I sometimes make a crock-pot of chili in the winter and I make killer French toast, but I prefer to leave cooking to the professionals."

"You mean high school students like me who grill burgers at Hardees?"

"Exactly."

"Here are your drinks and some soda bread and butter for the two of you," our server said, setting down our drinks.

"What's soda bread?" Tyler asked me when our server had gone.

"There's one way to find out."

We each took a slice and buttered it. I tasted mine. It reminded me of sourdough bread, but had a slight taste of soda. It was delicious.

"This is great stuff," Tyler said.

"I agree."

"So, you write, but you don't cook, what are your hobbies...besides *Star Trek* and collecting antiques?"

"I think you just about covered everything," I said. "I love going to museums. I love movies, reading, and going on long walks. Hmm, I'm starting to sound like a personals ad. I like planting a few flowers, but mainly in pots. Actual gardening is too much work. I love eating out, but you know that already. I like traveling. I love historic sites. I love staying in nice hotels. I like sitting and talking to people. How about you?"

"I like some of the same things, really. I'm a skater. I love music, especially musicals, but I'm into all kinds. I love to read and hang out with friends. That's me, I guess."

"This will be your senior year in high school?"

"Yeah."

"High school is an interesting time of life, but what comes after is even more interesting."

"Better, I hope."

"Almost certainly. You know, I haven't attended a single high school reunion? I thought about it, but... I had some good friends back then, but I lost touch with them right after high school. I'm sure they're spread all over and probably don't bother with the reunions either."

"Maybe you should go to the next one."

"Maybe, but that's a part of my life I'm not sure I want to revisit."

"Was high school tough for you?"

"No. Well, no tougher than it was for anyone else, I guess. It's just...I have some painful memories. I think everyone does."

Tyler nodded and didn't pry. I was glad. I didn't want to explain why I'd lost touch with my high school friends. It was a long story and would have revealed too much.

Our food arrived. I'd ordered my coddle in a bread bowl, which was exactly that, a bowl made out of bread. The top of a rounded loaf had been cut out, the inside removed, filled with coddle, and then the top was replaced. The coddle was steaming hot, so I tore off a bit of the lid and tasted it.

"How is it?" Tyler asked.

"Delicious."

Tyler cut into his Chicken Kiev and melted butter poured out. I laughed.

"What?"

"I was just remembering one of the kids at camp. We had Chicken Kiev once. He cut into his and yelled 'There's stuff in mine!'"

Tyler laughed.

"Kids can be so funny. We took a bunch of them on a field trip once. We toured the Indy 500 museum and the Indianapolis Zoo. On the way back, we stopped at McDonalds. When we returned to camp, I heard someone ask one of the kids if he'd had a good time and he said, 'Yes! We went to McDonalds!'"

Tyler grinned.

Celtic music played in the background. That, combined with our surroundings and the traditional Irish food, made me feel as if I actually was in Ireland. Tyler and I ate, talked, and laughed. I hadn't had such an enjoyable evening out in a good long time.

Camp Neeswaugee
Saturday, June 30, 1989

I felt a little better the next morning. I thought about Brand as I took my shower and got ready for my day. I was pissed off at him, but there was plenty of blame to go around. My unrealistic expectations were mostly at fault. Brand was far from innocent and I felt used, but I knew I'd let him use me. Part of me was still drawn to him. He was so handsome, and that body...damn. I shook my head and tried to force Brand from my thoughts. I had a very busy day ahead of me, classes, divisional games, and then the Council Fire. Somewhere in there, I needed to work on my lines. I could just keep repeating "rutabagas and cabbages" like T said if I got into a pinch, but I wanted to do my best and being prepared would set me more at ease.

Brand grinned at me when our paths crossed near the end of breakfast. He looked self-satisfied, arrogant, and mischievous, but he seemed to be flirting with me as well. Was he or was I just seeing something else that wasn't there? I didn't smile back. I wasn't going to let him play me for a fool, not again.

Indian Craft classes were a welcome distraction. I tried to forget about Brand and my Council Fire performance and just live in the moment. I didn't want to let the bad ruin the good. I wouldn't call the Council Fire bad, but I was nervous about it, so it was best to put it out of my mind.

Lt. Cody was a reminder of the night before. He hadn't seen me and I'd seen only his bare butt, but I'd recognized his voice. He gave no indication that he knew I was around when he and Brand were getting it on, but I couldn't get the image out of my mind. Part of me was jealous, as if he'd stolen my boyfriend, but Brand wasn't my boyfriend and I seriously doubted Brand had told Lt. Cody about me. I momentarily wondered if I shouldn't warn him about Brand, but the deed was done. Brand had already seduced him. Besides, for all I knew Lt. Cody was perfectly okay with casual sex. Maybe he and Brand had been hooking up since the very beginning of camp. It was none of my business anyway.

It was difficult to maintain the easy, joking relationship I'd had with Lt. Cody when a part of me wanted to punch him in the face, but I did my best. If he suspected anything was up, he didn't let on.

At lunch and supper, we didn't have to eat with our kids unless we were on duty. I often did, but it was nice to get away from them sometimes. I went directly to the mess hall after my period off and sat with Maj. T and Maj. Burrows. I hadn't counted on Brand showing up, but I guess that made sense because he was a part of the Indian Lore Department, too. He gave me a smirk when he sat down, but I tried to ignore him. That became a good deal easier when Daniel joined us.

"So, how are the parts coming, guys?" T asked Daniel and me.

"I'll have it all down by tonight," Daniel said.

"I hope to have it all down by tonight. I just hope I don't catapult myself over the wall and into the ring."

"Just try to land on your feet if you do," T said, with a hint of teasing in his voice. I really liked T. He'd been working in Camp Neeswaugee forever. I was in the presence of a legend.

I was uncomfortable sitting so close to Brand. I had this irrational fear he was going to tell the whole table what had happened between us in the woods. I also couldn't get the image of him doing Lt. Cody out of my mind. The sex scene kept playing in my mind.

I tried to focus on the others seated at the table, but even that made me uncomfortable. Brand knew I was having trouble looking him in the eyes. Whenever I looked at him, he smirked at me. I wanted to punch him in the face. A part of me was still drawn to him. He was so damned sexy! I tried to push him out of my mind, but there was no getting rid of Brand.

***

In the afternoon, I coached my first divisional baseball game. There were two differences between a divisional game and a cabin game. The divisional teams were made up of boys from different cabins while cabin teams included everyone in a particular cabin. The idea of me coaching baseball was fairly ridiculous, but I'd come up with a batting order that seemed decent and assigned positions based on what the boys claimed they could do. I knew the claims might not live up to reality, but it was only a game and it was better than guessing blindly. The best thing about divisional baseball was the second difference. We had an umpire. That meant I didn't have to call balls and strikes. Yes!

It became obvious in the very first inning that Jay Heyerdal more than lived up to his claim of "I'm a pretty good pitcher." He was incredible! Not only could he pitch like a miniature pro, but he could catch anything that came near him. I ended up with some other good players, but Jay was the star. What especially impressed me about him is how he encouraged the boys on the team who didn't do so well. Most of the jocks at my high school viewed those who lacked athletic talent with disdain, but Jay did everything he could to make boys who struck out or missed an easy catch feel better about themselves.

By the end of the fifth inning, we were up by 11-4. I'd like to claim it was due to my superior coaching abilities, but that would be an absolute lie. I was a good coach in that I encouraged my kids, tried to help them do better, and didn't scream at them for mistakes, but I was almost completely lacking in what are usually considered coaching abilities. No, my kids were just that good. Even the least talented weren't all that bad and the best, well, I'd never have that kind of athletic ability!

The umpire was positioned not behind the catcher, but just behind and to the right of the pitcher. I think this was so he could watch the bases as well as call balls and strikes, but the positioning became significant when the other team was at bat in the sixth inning. One of the boys on the opposing team made an incredible hit that streaked right toward the umpire's nose at warp speed. The ball was moving so fast I didn't even know what had happened until it was over, but I saw Jay, my pitcher, whip his glove in front of the umpire's face. A fraction of a second later, there was a loud smack as the ball hit Jay's glove. He'd caught the ball half a second before it would have smashed into the umpire's nose. The poor guy didn't even realize his danger until it was over. I didn't even want to think about what would've happened to his face if it hadn't been for Jay. He would've had a broken nose at the very least. We had one grateful umpire after that.

We won the game 14-5. Our score could have been much higher, but we took it easy on the other team. I was proud of my boys for considering the feelings of the Division 3 boys we were playing. The boys shouted and laughed all the way back to the division. The win made me look good in front of the other counselors, which was rather funny since I had less to do with the victory than anyone.

The Indian dancers ate early so they could prepare for the Council Fire. I departed with the boys from Division 4 who were performing that night. Daniel and the Division 6 Indian dancers joined us at our table. Daniel was as friendly as ever and enthusiastic about the evening's performance. A few of the kids came up and said, "But the next test is not so easy" in their imitation of the old shaman's voice.

"I bet you're going to get tired of that," I said.

"Eventually," Daniel laughed.

The food was extra good at supper. It was "make your own taco" night. Neeswaugee had pretty good food, with an occasional notable exception. I don't even want to talk about the roast beef au jus. I loved the tacos, though. I made mine with extra sour cream.

There was a certain pre-show excitement in the air that I'd never experienced before. Despite my nervousness, I was glad T had roped me into performing. I had neither the talent nor the outgoing personality to perform in the productions at my high school, so this was probably my only chance to experience life upon the stage.

Daniel and I skipped the roll call at the bleachers since we, unlike the kids, were responsible for getting ourselves to the Council Ring. We lingered in the Dining Hall for a while eating vanilla pudding. I hadn't spotted Brand at supper and I didn't particularly want to see him so I was more than happy to avoid him.

Daniel and I walked back to the Council Ring together. He had his lines down, so he'd offered to help out backstage before the show. I was still memorizing my part. I was definitely not a natural when it came to acting. Daniel went off to help Maj. Burrows, and I walked up the path behind the Council Ring, script in hand, trying to memorize my lines. I read a line, repeated it in my head several times, and then went onto the

111

next. As I walked, I slowly put the lines together until I was repeating whole paragraphs in my head. Unfortunately, I had to keep looking at the script, but I was getting it down.

I realized after a while that I was following the same path that Brand and I had used not too many nights before. I was even near the spot where Brand had led me off the path and into the deeper wood. I forced the events of that night from my mind. I didn't have time to waste thinking about what Brand had done to me. I'd had mixed emotions about the events of that night even before I'd learned I was nothing more than another of his summer conquests. Now...well, I just wasn't going to think about it. The messenger from the Great Spirit had lines to learn.

I walked and memorized dialogue until I thought I had it down. When I arrived back at the Council Ring, most of the kids were sitting around on benches backstage, already in costume with makeup on their faces. Makeup was applied to make the too-white faces more of a reddish tan so the audience could more easily believe they were watching the Potawatomi. Some might have objected to the use of makeup, but I was part Native American myself and I didn't find it objectionable, so I didn't really see why others would. The Council Fires definitely weren't a put-down. The whole Indian Lore program was rather respectful of Native Americans.

Maj. T directed me to the back of the costume shed and showed me my costume, a white buckskin shirt and breeches with beautiful beadwork. I was almost afraid to wear it because it looked like it belonged in a museum, but I knew the costumes had been used in shows over and over for decades.

That's something I loved about being a member of the Indian Lore Department—the nostalgia and the sense of history. There had been an Indian Lore Department for about as long as there had been a Camp Neeswaugee. Since the camp was founded in 1912, that was quite a long time! The original Indian Lore staff had been composed of actual Native Americans. Not half-bloods or mixed-bloods like me, but truly the real thing. Even now, the dedication to Native American cultures was strong. There were even real eagle feathers on a few of the costumes. The feathers were treated with great care. It wasn't even legal to own an eagle feather now, since eagles were an endangered species. The Indian Lore Department had possessed the feathers since the 1920s or before, so it was legal for us to have them. They were irreplaceable and treated with reverence.

I looked into a small mirror while I wiped makeup onto my face, neck, and hands with a small sponge. Only those parts of my skin not covered by the costume needed to be made up. I had less need of the makeup than most. I tanned easily, perhaps thanks to my Native American ancestry, and I'd been out in the sun a lot, so I was far from the pale white of many of the kids. My hair was another matter. My normally brown hair had bleached out in the sun. A wig would cover my hair, however, so there were no worries there. The makeup didn't feel as nasty as I'd feared. Once it dried I hardly knew it was there.

I stripped down to the black shorts I was wearing and put on my costume. Next came moccasins, a wig, and headband. When I next glanced in the mirror, I was transformed. I wasn't Lt. Perseus anymore. I was the messenger from the Great Spirit. Daniel was right. The costume made me feel as if I was the character.

I went over my lines one final time and then put my script away. If I didn't have my lines down by now I never would. I walked back to the benches where all the kids were sitting. A couple of kids from my own cabin were there, but I barely recognized them. Everyone looked different all done up.

I recognized Brand more easily than the others. He even looked hot in costume! He wasn't wearing a shirt and the muscles of his torso rippled with his slightest movement. Before I could stop myself, I had a little fantasy about Brand in costume and...but enough of that. I spotted Daniel and walked over to him. He looked much older with his gray wig and ragged old clothing. Where my costume was impressive, his looked like it should have been tossed. I guess I lucked out by getting my part instead of his. Then again, he did have that cool "But the next test is not so easy" line.

Maj. Burrows called for everyone to get quiet because the campers and visitors were gathering to take their seats in the Council Ring. Soon, the slow beat of the medicine drum began, which meant the divisions were slowly filing into the ring. A few minutes later, three quick and loud drumbeats signaled for everyone in the Council Ring to sit down.

The first actors and dancers were moved into place, leaving far fewer of us sitting on the benches backstage. The tape began playing, sounding much louder over the sound system than it had coming from the small tape player. The story began and Black Wolf began his quest.

I took up my position outside the Council Ring well before it was time for me to go on. Then, the moment came. In my mind, I wasn't Tyler anymore. I was the messenger from the Great Spirit. The spotlight hit me as I walked into the Council Ring, brilliantly illuminating my white buckskin costume. Brand gazed at me with smug, mischievous eyes as I mouthed my lines, only he wasn't Brand anymore. He was Black Wolf. Before I knew it my first scene was over and I was back outside the Council Ring. My heart was racing. I shook my head, feeling as if I'd just awakened from a dream. For a few moments, it had all been real.

I had some time to spare before my next scene so I watched part of the show from outside the bleachers. I made sure I had a good view when Daniel delivered his "But the next test is not so easy" line. It got a laugh from the crowd, even though it wasn't meant to be funny.

I took up my position for my second and last scene with time to spare. It was a good deal more difficult getting into place this time, because now the backdrop and all the lights were in place. I had to carefully edge my way along the wall towards the ladder to avoid casting shadows above. I didn't want my arms to give out so I climbed up the ladder and hung there like a monkey only about thirty seconds before my entrance.

I heard and felt the powder shot as it ignited on cue. The audience gasped. I vaulted up a few moments too soon and for a couple of seconds I was way too close to the burning gunpowder. Pain seared my arms and other areas of exposed skin and I thought I might actually be on fire. I stayed in character, however, and ordered Black Wolf to gather up the black water he needed and escape before the spell I'd thrown on the Evil Shaman and his villagers wore off.

Once again backstage, I examined myself to make sure I hadn't been burned. I had escaped damage.

As the Council Fire continued, I entered the costume shed, pulled off my wig, headband, and buckskin clothing and slowly

114

transformed from the Messenger of the Great Spirit to just plain Tyler. When I was once again dressed in my uniform, the only evidence that I'd been in the Council Fire was my makeup. I'd have to wait until I got back to camp to get it off. Capt. Chadwick, who drummed for the Council Fires, told me the best way to remove makeup was simply to wash it off in the shower.

The Council Fire ended. Brand took the Indian dancers back to camp and I stayed back to help Maj. Burrows take down the large shields that decorated the Council Ring, put away props, and just basically help out so everyone could go home. That done, I hurried back to my cabin.

My kids were excited that I'd been in the Council Fire and treated me like a celebrity. I got a taste of what it felt like to be famous. Was this my fifteen minutes of fame? If so, it was good enough.

I read my boys to sleep, then got out of my now stinky uniform and into my robe. I walked up to the officer's latrine in my flip-flops, disrobed, and took a shower. The water refreshed me and I was delighted to get the makeup off.

I dressed in a fresh uniform and walked out into the night. I was too pumped from the Council Fire to sleep yet. I was also thinking about Brand again. All the same thoughts rolled through my mind. I wished I could just stop thinking them. It was like being forced to watch a rerun over and over. Why couldn't I get him out of my head?

Because, despite everything, you still want him bad.

I walked across the soccer field under moonlight and starlight. It was so quiet I could hear the waves of Lake Potawatomi in the distance. I could see the moonlight glinting off the water. I thought about changing course for a walk along the lake, but something drew me toward the path that led up to the Council Ring. It was almost too dark to see under the trees, but I knew the path well enough to keep from wandering into the woods.

Camp had been a much different experience than I was expecting. I never dreamed I'd get it on with a hunky guy like Brand. I never dreamed I'd lose my virginity or that I'd catch the guy I thought of as my boyfriend cheating on me. A lot of other things took me by surprise, too, like how I actually liked the military aspects of the camp and how much I cared for my boys.

I didn't exactly arrive expecting to hate the kids in my cabin, but I never realized I'd feel almost as if they were my own sons. I wasn't disappointed that camp hadn't been what I'd expected. Mostly, it was better than I'd anticipated. I still wasn't quite sure how I felt about Brand. I didn't like him, but...he confused the hell out of me!

I walked into the darkened Council Ring. I could still smell the wood smoke, although the fires had burned out. Some magic lingered in this place. It was said that the Native Americans had danced in this place, just as we did today. Perhaps it was true.

"Couldn't sleep?"

I gasped and turned quickly. I hadn't realized anyone was there. It was Brand.

"What are you doing here?"

"I could ask you the same," he said.

"No. I couldn't sleep."

"Me either."

Even his voice was seductive, but I was still too hurt to be lured in.

"So. Out with it," Brand said.

"Out with what?"

"Oh, please. You've been playing the role of wronged lover since last night. Half the time you won't look at me and when you do, you look either pissed off or jealous."

"I didn't expect to find you with someone else."

"I never said we were exclusive, Tyler."

"I know that."

"Then, what's your problem?"

"I just...I just thought there was more between us."

"It's just sex, Tyler. It's just something that feels good. It did feel good, didn't it?"

"Yes, mostly."

"Even when it hurt, there was something hot about it, wasn't there?"

"Maybe."

"Tell me the truth, Tyler. 'Maybe' isn't an answer. You were turned on when I took you, weren't you?"

"You shouldn't have done that."

"I did it because I knew you wanted it."

"I didn't want it."

"Liar."

My lower lip trembled. I bit it.

"I bet you want it again right now," Brand said. He stepped a little closer.

"No."

"You're lying again, Tyler. I know you want me. I knew you wanted me the moment I set eyes on you. It took me all of ten minutes to seduce you, so don't tell me you didn't want me."

"I wanted you."

"Yeah, you wanted me and you wanted me to take you in the woods. You could have fought a lot harder when I stuck it in you. I even gave you an out, but when it came right down to it, you didn't tell me to stop, did you?"

I shook my head.

"Would you have stopped?"

Brand grinned. "That you'll never know, but even now the thought that I might not have stopped is turning you on. The danger excites you. I know you're pissed off at me and I'm sure I've hurt your little homo feelings, but I'd bet anything you've fantasized about doing it with me again. A part of you is hoping I'll jump on you and take you by force right here and right now. You want me, don't you? You want me to grab you and do to you what I did the other night in woods."

"No."

"You can lie to me, Tyler, but you can't lie to yourself."

Brand closed the distance between us. He leaned over and whispered something in my ear. I blushed, but I was powerfully turned on. Brand stepped back again and gazed into my eyes.

"So, I'll ask you again. Do you want me, Tyler?"

"Yes!"

I couldn't believe I wanted him, but I did. How could Brand have such power over me?

"That's all I wanted to hear."

Brand turned and began to walk away.

"But..." I began. Brand turned and looked at me. His eyes were arrogant and hateful.

"I thought we were going to..." I began.

"I've already had you," Brand said. "I've already had you and Lt. Cody is much hotter."

"Then why did you just..."

My words faltered as I read his smug expression. The color drained from my face.

"I wanted to hear you say the words. I wanted to make it impossible for you to deny to yourself that after everything, you'd still be my little bitch. Goodbye, faggot."

Brand laughed at me, turned his back, and walked away. I felt as if I'd just been punched in the gut. My lower lip trembled and a sob escaped from my lips. I stifled the anguished cry that erupted despite all I did to keep it in. I didn't want Brand to hear me. I didn't want him to know how much he'd hurt me. I growled in pain and frustration. Anger welled up inside me. I launched myself at him.

"I fucking hate you!" I screamed.

Brand turned just as I leaped on him. I jammed my fist into his cheek. It was the only good punch I got in. Brand punched me in the stomach, then the face, and before I knew it, I was on my back with Brand holding me down. He pulled his fist back and slugged me in the face again. I moaned in agony. I thought he was going to keep right on hitting me, but he just stared into my eyes.

"You really think you can hurt me, you pathetic little faggot? You hit like a fucking girl. I should fuck you up for jumping on me like that."

Brand pulled his fist back and I cowered.

"Beg me not to beat your ass."

"Please, don't," I said.

"I said beg!"

"Please, don't hurt me. I'm sorry. Just please don't..."

I began crying. I was totally humiliated. Brand climbed off me.

"God, you're pathetic. I don't know why I ever wanted you. You're such a pussy."

Brand kicked me in the side and left me moaning on the forest floor. I curled into a ball and sobbed.

When I was able, I pulled myself up, sat down on the wooden bleachers, and buried my face in my hands. The physical pain was only the beginning. I hurt so bad inside just then that I wanted to die. I'd *really* liked Brand. I could've walked on air when he took an interest in me, and when he kissed me...it was the stuff of dreams. Brand was so handsome and his body so sexy, so muscular and defined. He was a sexual fantasy come true. I felt like a fool for falling for him and yet who wouldn't have? Who could have resisted *him*?

I knew now I was nothing more than a toy to Brand; a boy for him to seduce, use, laugh at, and discard. I probably wasn't the first and wouldn't be the last either. He'd used me and then humiliated me. I'd humiliated myself. Why was I willing to have sex with him again? What was I thinking jumping on him like that? Then, when he hit me, I couldn't take it. I'd begged for mercy just like he told me to. I *was* a pussy.

Brand had left me with nothing. I couldn't even tell myself I'd turned away from him in the end. Despite everything, I'd been willing to go back to him. Even as I'd stood there trembling in fear of what he might do, a part of me was so powerfully aroused I didn't care how much it would hurt. I just wanted him again.

How could anyone be so cruel? He'd seduced and tempted me just so he could reject me. He'd made me want him and he'd made me say it out loud, just so he could humiliate me. Now, every time he looked at me, we'd both know he'd used me and I'd come crawling back for more. I couldn't even pretend I had the control and self-respect to turn away from him after he'd treated me like his bitch. I growled in frustration. I hated him!

I wasn't going to sit in the Council Ring crying all night. I got up, dusted off the seat of my shorts, and limped back toward camp. I felt like my heart had been ripped out and stomped on, but what was there to do but go on? Life was filled with pain. At the moment, pain, both emotional and physical, was about all I could feel. I wasn't quite sure which was worse.

I felt like I'd never be happy again, but happiness was out there somewhere. I'd been happy before. I'd been in pain before. Both were temporary states. Pain was something to be endured. Happiness was something to be enjoyed. I felt like my life was in ruins, but I knew that wasn't true. There was still a lot of good left, and now it was more important than ever to hold onto the things that brought me pleasure. The humiliation of Brand kicking my ass so effortlessly added to my unhappiness. Looking into his eyes tomorrow would be unpleasant, but at least there were no witnesses.

I walked back to my cabin, undressed, and climbed into my little bed. I closed my eyes and focused on the coolness of the night air, the softness of the sheets, and the sounds of insects singing their songs outside. I just lay there, breathed, and listened until I fell asleep.

***

A sense of deep sadness and pain permeated me the next morning as I went about getting ready for my day. The black eye that greeted me when I peered into the mirror didn't make me feel any better. I wasn't about to wallow in sadness and self-pity, however. The only way to escape from my funk was to go on with my life and grab what little bits of happiness came my way. A breakfast of donuts with rainbow sprinkles was a start. Reading my *Star Trek* novel for a few minutes between breakfast and Chapel helped, too. It's not like I banished sadness from my life, but when you're feeling miserable any little bit of happiness helps.

The boys asked about my black eye, of course. My bruised face was the first thing they noticed upon awakening. I told them a partial truth. I said I'd been in a fight. I didn't tell them it only lasted about five seconds, or that I got my ass kicked, or that I'd submitted to Brand like a pansy. I didn't tell them I'd fought with Brand, but when he showed up in the Dining Hall with similar bruises on his face, it didn't take the kids long to figure things out. At least that's what I thought until I began to hear the rumors that Lt. Elwolf and I had fought off a bear during the night. I had no idea how that rumor got started, especially since outside of a zoo there probably wasn't a bear within two hundred miles of camp. The rumor was sure a lot more comfortable than the truth, however.

It was a difficult morning. Brand's eyes had met mine only once and briefly, but they were smug. I wanted to punch him in the face again, but I knew how that would play out. I think what upset me the most of all is that I was still hot for him. I hated him, but after everything, part of me still wanted him. How stupid is that?

After Chapel and P.I., the boys went out to play tetherball, ping-pong, basketball, and soccer. There were no classes on Sunday, so I walked outside and sat on the cabin steps in the cool morning air. I felt desolate and alone despite all the activity around me.

"Are you okay, Lieutenant?" Steve asked as he came out and joined me on the steps.

"I will be, sooner or later."

"Girl trouble?" he asked.

"Something like that."

"Boy trouble?"

I jerked my head around and gaped at Steve in surprise, a stupid move on my part because my reaction made it impossible to deny the truth. My face paled. No. I did not need this.

"It's okay. I won't tell anyone. My older brother's gay. It's cool."

"I...um...I really can't talk to you about this."

"Pah-leeze!! Don't tell me you're like all the other adults. Get near the topic of sex and they freak out."

"Well, we're not supposed to talk to you about anything remotely involving sex."

"Oh, like it's a big secret! Does everyone over eighteen think kids are just stupid or what?"

"I'm not over eighteen so I wouldn't know."

"So, I'm right, aren't I? Problems with your boyfriend?"

"I got dumped."

"By Lieutenant Elwolf?"

My mouth dropped open in complete and utter shock. I might as well have shouted "yes!"

"How did you..."

"You're soooo obvious, Lieutenant, but maybe just to me. When Lt. Elwolf is around, you get the same look my brother does when he spots a guy he's hot for—and I've seen you guys together."

I controlled my reaction this time. There is no way Steve could have seen us making out or...anything else.

"Steve..."

"Don't worry. I won't tell anyone. That would not be cool. Forget about him, Lieutenant. He's an asshole."

I laughed. It felt good.

"What makes you say that?"

"Because I heard Miss Singleton talking to Miss Tess about him during golf class when they thought I wasn't listening. Lt. Elwolf was dating Miss Vickers, but he was cheating on her with Miss Clancy and he was a real dick when Miss Vickers called him on it. That makes him an asshole, plus he was dating you at the same time so he's a major asshole, especially if he was a dick like he was with Miss Vickers when he dumped you."

"You know way too much," I said.

"Kids always know everything. Don't tell me you've forgotten that already."

"Maybe I have."

"You guys fought, didn't you? I mean *really* fought. You've both got black eyes."

"Yeah."

"You are better off without him, Lieutenant. He's hot, but he's still an asshole and he's violent. You don't need a guy like that. You don't need a guy who is going to hit you. Forget about him and find yourself a nice guy."

Great, now I was getting advice on my love-life from a nine-year-old. The thing was, it sounded like good advice.

"Oo-kaay, we really need to change the topic."

"Yeah. Yeah. Whatever. Want me to kick Lt. Elwolf in the nuts for you? He can't hit me back."

I was very tempted to say "yes."

"No, Steve, but thanks for offering."

"Any time. I'll see you later, Lieutenant. I hope you get to feeling better."

"Thanks."

"Oh, and you should really go out with Lt. Keegan. He *really* likes you. It's soooo obvious. Now, he's a nice guy."

Steve left me sitting there stunned. That last part about Daniel...could it be true? Steve was right about everything else. He'd seen right though me—that was for sure. He was plugged in to camp life. That was certain, too. Daniel did pay a lot of attention to me. He was always nice to me, but then he was always nice to everyone so that didn't mean much. He did seek me out often, but we'd met at the very first orientation meeting so maybe I was just a friendly face in a sea of strangers. Camp had been going on for more than a week now, though, and surely Daniel had made a lot of friends. So was he still hanging out with me because he was interested in me or was I just one of many friends?

Daniel? Gay? Perhaps. I hadn't detected any interest on his part, but then I'd been pretty much obsessed with Brand. I'd had eyes only for him. I sighed. Why couldn't things just be easy?

Enough thinking about Daniel. I wasn't even sure I was interested in getting with another guy. My experience with Brand had left me reluctant to take another risk. Surely, there couldn't be two Brands around, but I didn't want to take any chances. I needed some time to heal. For now, I just wanted to lose myself in camp life, be a counselor, and work with my kids. I wanted to have the summer I'd planned. I didn't even want to think about guys. Camp life was more than enough. Sometimes, it was too much.

Camp counseling sounds like a cushy job. What could be easier than playing with kids all day, right? If that's what you believe, then you've obviously never been a camp counselor. I'm almost positive anyone who has kids of their own knows better as well. I'm not saying being a camp counselor isn't fun. Sometimes, it's a blast! Often, I can't believe I'm actually getting paid to eat lunch, play Capture the Flag, and watch movies. There is definitely a downside, like coaching soccer when it's ninety-five degrees, trying to control sixty screaming kids at a track meet, breaking up fights, and cleaning up puke. There is also the exhaustion. Every morning, weekends included, I get up about 6:15 a.m. and never get to bed before 11:00 p.m. I'm sometimes so tired I walk around like a zombie. Camp counseling is not for the weak.

The hectic pace of camp helped me to keep my mind off Brand and Daniel. I didn't want to think about either of them, although for entirely different reasons. I did think about them, of course, but at least I was able to focus on other things most of the time.

Brand made it difficult not to think about him. Where before he'd subtly flirted with me, now he treated me with contempt. I wanted to smack that smug look right off his face, but, of course, I didn't dare. I didn't need the added humiliation of getting my ass kicked in front of witnesses. There was absolutely nothing I could do about what he'd done to me or the way he was now being such a jerk now. What made it worse was that Brand knew and enjoyed every second of my frustration. He was a sadistic bastard.

My life didn't get easier as the days passed. I swear I saw Brand everywhere! Okay, I guess I didn't see him any more often than before, but it seemed like it. Before everything went bad between us the merest glimpse of him was a thrill. Now, each encounter was an opportunity for just a little more humiliation to be added to the heap. Brand didn't even have to do anything. The mere sight of him was a reminder of how I'd been used and humiliated.

I tried to avoid Daniel, too. I couldn't help but keep thinking about what Steve had told me. He'd been on the mark about everything else, but it seemed pretty stupid to take advice about my love life from a nine-year-old. The real reason I was avoiding Daniel is that I liked him a lot. Steve made me think about Daniel. No matter how hard I fought it, I couldn't help but get my hopes up a little. What if Daniel really did like me, *that way*? I hadn't noticed him when I'd been blinded by Brand's beauty. *Idiot*. Now that Brand had been revealed as a dick, I began to notice that Daniel was pretty cute in his own way. He didn't have Brand's muscles or his Abercrombie & Fitch model face, but his slim body was kind of sexy. He wasn't at all the kind of guy who immediately caught the eye, but when I took the time to really notice him, he was attractive. Adding to the physical side was his personality. Like I've mentioned before, Daniel was nice to everyone. His kids loved him. I'd never heard him say anything nasty about anyone. I'd been stupid not to notice him before, but like the fool I was I'd been too busy drooling over Brand.

I was afraid of Daniel now—afraid he was straight and I'd make a fool of myself by hitting on him—afraid he was gay but that I was all wrong about him and he'd hurt me just like Brand—afraid that I'd be too obvious if I was around him. If a nine-year-old could figure out I was gay, I obviously wasn't nearly as sly as I'd thought. I did not want to be known as the camp homo.

This summer was supposed to be about trying something new—not about a summer fling. Okay, a summer fling was a new thing for me, but that's not the kind of new thing I'd planned. I needed to just stop thinking about Daniel. I'd taken a risk with Brand and look how that had worked out. It was time to forget about guys and concentrate on camp.

Good luck with that, Perseus.

Sometimes I hated the little voice in my head.

***

Despite my problems, life went on. Keeping busy helped me not to think about Brand and Daniel so much. There was no easier place to keep busy than Camp Neeswaugee. Sometimes, I felt like I was on the move twenty-four hours a day. There was always time for some mischief, though.

I slipped into Main HQ once more during the night and made use of the typewriters and photocopy machine. The next morning when I returned to HQ to check my mailbox, counselors were reading the latest memo from the illusive Maj. P.

Excessive Latrine Use:

By Order Of: Maj. P, Director W.S.A.
(Neeswaugee Security Agency)

It has come to our attention that some staff members have been making excessive use of the latrine facilities. To insure fair and equal time for all we ask that each counselor use the facilities only twice per day, for a period of no greater than three minutes, using the following schedule:

Last names beginning with A-E   8:00 a.m.

F-H   9:00 a.m.

I-M   10:00 a.m.

N-R   11:00 a.m.

S-Z   noon

The schedule repeats in the same order beginning at 1 p.m.

All toilet stalls will be locked and can be opened only by voice identification. Each staff member is required to stop by headquarters and provide two voice samples: one in a normal tone of voice, the second under duress.

Surveillance equipment has been placed in all latrines to insure compliance with the new latrine use rules. After two and one half minutes have passed, you will hear a warning tone. At three minutes the latrine alarm will sound, the toilet paper will retract, and you will have ten seconds to exit the toilet area. If anyone fails to leave within ten seconds, their photo will be taken and posted at Headquarters. Anyone who has their photo posted three or more times per week will be barred from use of the latrine facilities for the following week.

My latest memo was a hit. I derived a certain pleasure from being the unknown perpetrator. There was a lot of speculation about who was writing the memos, but I seriously doubted anyone expected quiet and unassuming Lt. Perseus of Division 4.

Bloomington, Indiana
Saturday, July 4, 2009

"Are you sure I'm not monopolizing your time?" I asked Tyler as we walked toward the football stadium. "Wouldn't you rather be at a Fourth of July party somewhere?"

"Believe me, I'd much rather be here with you. I don't feel comfortable hanging out with the college crowd and parties with guys my age...so not fun. All the popular guys and girls are too stuck up to talk to anyone, even if you can get invited to one of their parties. The jocks down beers until they puke and the cops usually show up because of the noise, under-aged drinking, or both. I would much rather be watching fireworks with you, especially with Dad out of town. We usually watch them together."

"When does he get back?"

"In a couple days."

"If you need anything while he's gone, you know where I live. Oh God, I'm sorry. I'm treating you like you're twelve. Sometimes, the camp counselor in me comes out."

"No, it's cool. I like the idea of having a backup dad for when my dad is out of town."

I mussed Tyler's hair and he grinned. He looked so much like Daniel just then.

There was a huge crowd at the stadium, and we were running late. That was Tyler's fault, not mine. He showed up at my house quite late because he couldn't get his hair quite right. Was I ever like that at his age? I feared so.

Our tardiness worked to our advantage. We arrived only five minutes before the fireworks began. Despite the great number of people, the huge stadium had ample room. We had no trouble finding a seat and since we were there to view a fireworks display and not a football game, our location didn't much matter.

We craned our necks to view the vibrant explosions of red, green, purple, blue, and white light. There were fountains of sparks, deafening bangs, and umbrellas and spheres of intense light. Firecrackers popped nearer at hand. The faces of the crowd were alternately tinged with red, green, and every other color of the rainbow.

As I sat there, I remembered watching fireworks in this very stadium when I was Tyler's age. I remembered, too, other fireworks displays in other places. There was the Fourth of July when I sat on the hill by Cabin 34 with a lone camper. I talked him through his homesickness while we watched explosions of color over Lake Potawatomi and listened to the distant "ohhs" and "ahhs" coming from the stands in front of the Riding Hall. There were several Fourths when I sat with the boys of Cabin 34 on the Riding Hall terrace. Later, there was the Fourth when I sat with Division 6 as its new Division Commander. I wondered what Daniel would have thought that first summer if he knew that someday, years in the future, I'd be running Division 6.

An especially deafening explosion drew my mind back into the present. I gazed at the seventeen-year-old boy sitting beside me, the boy who bore the name that was once and forever mine, the boy who looked so very much like my long ago love. Flashes of light played across his handsome features. When he turned and smiled at me, it was as if Daniel had returned to me across all the long years. I wondered where Daniel was now and if he thought of me from time to time. You can rest assured it was not the first time I'd wondered such a thing. I knew it would not be the last.

The fireworks display was incredible. Just when we thought it was finished, there was more. One explosion of light and sound followed the next until there seemed no end.

I was someone who enjoyed solitude. I was often the most content sitting alone in a comfortable chair with a cup of hot tea and a good book. I also loved being part of a crowd, sharing an experience, feeling a sense of community with strangers who were not truly strangers after all. Someone had once written that a stranger was only a friend one hadn't met yet. That frame of mind alone made the world a better place. I sat now with Tyler and hundreds of friends I had not yet met. I was content.

The grand finale truly lived up to its name. There were explosions of blue, red, purple, and green light everywhere. There was so much to see I couldn't begin to see it all. Fireworks were truly magical.

"Wasn't that incredible!" Tyler said as we followed the crowd out of the stadium. "Let's go back to your place and have a wild party! We can watch a movie and eat junk food!"

I laughed.

"Not a bad idea."

Tyler put his arm over my shoulder with the easy familiarity of youth. His scent was a mixture of cologne and clean sweat. I was drawn to him, but my attraction wasn't overly sexual. There was a trace of such desire there, but the attraction was mostly that that one feels for a good friend. I was attracted by Tyler's youthful exuberance, his easy good humor, and his laughter. As we walked side by side, a part of my mind remembered platonic friendships of my youth while another part envied Tyler's father for having such a wonderful son. There were times I yearned for a son of my own, but at those times I reminded myself I'd been a father to scores of boys back in my camp counselor days. I smiled with pleasant memories.

My selection of junk food was limited, but I had recently picked up honey-roasted peanuts, over-sized Hershey chocolate bars, and a half gallon of butter pecan ice cream. There were soft drinks as well. I generally stuck with diet, but to most people, Coke Zero tasted like the real thing anyway. Tyler didn't complain as we loaded up a tray and carried it into the living room.

Tyler headed for the shelves that housed my DVD collection. I'd recently purchased a big screen TV, but I didn't have cable or even an antenna. I tended to watch everything on DVD. It was a great way to avoid commercials and the news, which I hadn't watched in years.

"Oh yeah! *Twilight*!" Tyler announced.

I was pleased he'd found something he liked. I'd feared he might not care for my taste in TV and films, which ran to BBC comedies, *Frasier*, *Star Trek*, and historical documentaries.

"I'd love to be like Edward," Tyler said.

"You want to be a vampire?"

"Not that part. I just want to be that fast, that strong, and that good looking. I don't think I'd mind being seventeen forever if I could do stuff like him."

130

"I'm sure there's a downside."

"Yeah, there's always a catch, isn't there?"

Tyler plopped down right beside me and we devoured honey roasted peanuts and chocolate while we watched *Twilight*. I was attracted to Edward, but for some reason I found Jasper even sexier. I wondered momentarily if Tyler would be disturbed if he knew I was attracted to the actors on the screen. The younger generation was far more comfortable with differing sexual orientations. They were so much wiser about so many things and yet they could also be cruel.

Tyler and I curled up together on the loveseat. There was an easy familiarity between us. We'd grown comfortable with each other in the short time we'd spent together. I was glad of Tyler's company. Our legs and shoulders touched. Sometimes, Tyler draped his arm over my shoulder. The physical intimacy made me feel comfortable and secure.

Tyler moved onto the butter pecan ice cream, but I'd already slowed down. I hated the feeling of being too full. I almost laughed when Tyler walked back into the living room with the half gallon of ice cream and a spoon. Not using a bowl was such a teen thing to do.

It was past midnight when the movie ended. Tyler yawned. I was tempted to ask if he wanted to stay, but I wasn't sure that was wise.

"Why don't I walk you home?" I asked.

"You don't have to do that."

"I could use a walk. Besides, I'll feel better knowing you've made it home safe."

"You sound like my dad."

"Is that a bad thing?"

"No. Not at all." Tyler smiled at me sleepily.

Tyler lived not far away. We walked only a few blocks before he stopped in front of his home—a charming old place with ivy growing up trellises on the porch and a white picket fence surrounding the yard.

"Have a good night," Tyler said.

Tyler surprised me by hugging me. I hugged him back and then watched as he walked up the path to door, turned the key in the lock, and went inside.

I walked back home with a feeling of contentment.

Camp Neeswaugee
Thursday, July 5, 1989

"I need to escape from my kids."

I looked up from my corn dog, applesauce, salad, and chocolate cake. Daniel grinned at me, but there was a touch of sadness to his smile. I was sitting by myself. The Dining Hall was practically empty since it was not yet time for the first divisions to arrive. One of the advantages of being off-duty was being able to eat early.

"Have a seat."

"Thanks."

I'd been avoiding Daniel for several days, but I knew I couldn't keep it up forever. I definitely didn't want to be rude. To be honest, part of me wanted him to sit with me even though the prospect frightened me.

"So, your boys are getting to you?" I asked.

"They're great for the most part, but I'd just like to talk to someone over eleven for a while."

"I know what you mean, but I'm amazed at some of the kids in my cabin. Günter speaks English, French, Italian, German and Spanish and he's only nine! I've taken three years of French and I can barely say hello."

"Wow, you are bad. I hate to tell you this, but 'hello' is an English word, Tyler. I believe it's 'bonjour' in French."

"Ass."

Daniel laughed.

As if the word had summoned him, Brand appeared with one of his harem. He spotted me, leaned over to his girl of the hour, whispered something, then they both looked toward me and laughed. I could feel my face growing hot. I just stared at the salad bar for a minute.

"Tyler, what's wrong?"

"It's nothing," I lied.

Daniel looked as if he didn't believe me, but he didn't press it.

"Do your kids drive you crazy with questions?" Daniel asked.

"Yeah. It's the worst on movie nights. I swear every one of them asks me what movie we'll be watching even though it's announced to the entire division. I've started just making up titles. Last time, I told them we'd be seeing *The Care Bears Versus Strawberry Shortcake*."

"Oh! I like that! I'm going to start doing that with my kids." Daniel laughed.

"My boys are growing accustomed to my odd sense of humor. I have a tendency to make fake announcements when I'm on full duty."

"Like what?" Daniel asked.

"Like—'Due to unusually heavy indifference, Thursday has been cancelled' or 'The following campers have volunteered for tonight's ten mile run.' After that last one I just pause for several seconds and then go on to the next announcement."

"That's hilarious!"

"Well, I stole the idea from M*A*S*H. It confused the hell out of the kids at first, but they've started asking me when I'll do more."

"Hmm, I'm detecting a mischievous side to your personality. You wouldn't be the one who put the Division 6 sign on the latrine, would you?" Daniel asked.

"Me? Would *I* do something like that? I must admit, the latrine does seem a suitable headquarters for Division 6."

"Hey!"

I laughed. Daniel had actually pulled me out of my bad mood, but it was doomed to return. I looked up to see Brand and his girl heading straight for our table.

"Hey, guys!" Brand said as if he was our best friend. "You know Sheila, right?"

What the hell did he think he was doing?

"Hey, Sheila," Daniel said.

"Aren't you going to say hi, Tyler?" Brand asked. "Oh, that's right. You don't like...I mean, you don't know many girls, do you?"

"Hi, Sheila," I said

There was no reason to be rude to her even if she was with Brand. I thought she'd laughed with Brand at my expense earlier, but that could have just been my own paranoia.

"Are you getting around better, Tyler?" Brand asked. "You were walking funny there for a few days. How's your face? Did you hurt yourself?"

"I'm fine," I said, gritting my teeth. It was bad enough he was taunting me about beating the crap out of me, but I never thought he'd refer to...the other thing.

"So what happened to make you walk that way?" Brand asked.

"I pulled a muscle," I said. "It was just a little muscle, but it still hurt."

Damn, I wanted to jump across the table and punch Brand in the face. I already knew how that would play out, however, so I stayed in my chair.

"Yeah? That's not what I heard, but you know how rumors are around here, true or false, once they get started there's no stopping them."

I could feel myself growing red in the face, or perhaps I should say redder. Sheila laughed and it was quite obvious she was laughing at me this time. There is no way he told her about having sex with me, but I wouldn't have put it past him to tell Sheila I'd bottomed for some other guy, or knowing Brand, for lots of other guys. How could someone so good looking be such a jerk?

Daniel looked confused but also annoyed with Brand and Sheila.

"Only those with no sense at all pay attention to rumors," Daniel said. "I did like the one about you guys fighting off a bear, though."

"Oh, I don't know," Brand said. "There's a lot of truth to most rumors. They can ruin a reputation. Personally, I wouldn't even want to sit with someone if nasty rumors were going around about him. You might want to think about that, Daniel."

"What do you mean?" Daniel asked.

"I'm sure you can figure it out."

Brand grinned at me with a smug look on his face. I fought to keep him from getting to me, but my lower lip trembled. I was about to lose it. I stood up, turned my back on Brand, Sheila, and Daniel, and walked away without so much as a word.

"Damn, what's up your ass, Perseus?" Brand called after me.

I turned and glared at him for a moment but bit down on my lip so I wouldn't say what I wanted to say. I couldn't without outing myself and Brand knew it. I hated him! I turned on my heel and got the hell out of there.

I was out the back of the Dining Hall and walking across the parking lot before I discovered Daniel had followed me.

"Hey, Tyler. Wait up!"

I paused for a moment to let him catch up although I really wanted to just be alone right then. I walked on as soon as he reached me. I didn't look at him. I couldn't.

"Are you okay, Tyler?"

"Yeah," I said, a little too angrily.

"You're not a very good liar."

I just shook my head.

"Listen, I know this is none of my business so feel free to tell me to back off, but you look like you're really upset about something and...well...I'm here if you want to talk about it. I need to talk about things sometimes and it really sucks when there's no one to listen. I don't understand what was going on back there, but it was clear Brand was being a dick about something."

His sympathetic voice cracked my façade. My lower lip began to tremble again and a sob escaped. Tears streamed down my cheeks.

"Tyler..."

I ran up the hill past the Indian Crafts tent and on to the circle of benches where Indian Dance classes met. I sat down on one of the benches and buried my head in my heads. I lost it. I cried as all the pain inside began to spill out.

I felt a hand caressing my back. He didn't say a word, but Daniel was there.

When my sobs quieted, I just sat there with my hands over my face and my elbows resting on my knees. Daniel kept gently rubbing my back.

"I'm so embarrassed," I said, my voice muffled by my hands.

"Don't be. We all cry sometimes, Tyler. We all get hurt."

I slowly pulled my hands away from my face and sat up. I looked at Daniel. He smiled.

"Want to tell me about it? Whatever you tell me will stay with me. I'm good at keeping secrets."

I gazed at Daniel for a moment.

"I'm gay," I said.

My heart pounded furiously and I felt nervous all over. I'd never told anyone I was gay before. I didn't know how Daniel would react. I needed to tell someone, though. I needed to say it out loud. I'd held it inside so long I felt like I couldn't stand it a second longer. I looked at Daniel with fear in my eyes, but I felt a little better just having said it.

Daniel nodded as if he already knew. I kept going.

"Brand and I had...a relationship, but...it wasn't the same for him as it was for me. I *really* liked him." I paused to fight back a sob.

"You and Brand? Wow," Daniel said.

"Brand...for him I was just...someone to get off with. I thought there was a lot more between us, but I was just fooling myself. I thought that because we...did those things together that it meant something, but it didn't mean anything to him. I should have known better. It couldn't have been more than a summer fling at most and he's always flirting with girls. I'm sure he does a lot more than flirt with them, too. Then, after we'd been together, I saw him with another guy—doing it. I *really* liked him, Daniel. I thought…but he just used me. Then…I don't even want to talk about what happened next."

"Does it have something to do with the bruises on your face?"

My bruises had faded, but in some ways they would be with me forever.

I nodded.

"Brand…I'm so stupid…even after I saw him with that other guy…I let him seduce me again. Only, he didn't even want me. He just wanted me to say I wanted him. When I did, he laughed at me and walked away."

"What an asshole," said Daniel. "I never liked him much, but…damn."

"It gets worse. I was so pissed off and hurt I lost it and jumped him."

"Whoa. You attacked Brand?"

"Yes. He kicked my ass."

"I'm sorry," Daniel said.

"And now…"

Daniel pulled my head to his chest and stroked my hair as I began to cry again. I didn't cry nearly as long this time. In a couple of minutes I sat back up and wiped my eyes.

"I'm such a big baby," I said

"No, you're not. You're hurting inside, Tyler. It hurts when you like someone and they don't like you back, especially when you've been close and you think there's more to it than there is."

I nodded.

"A lot of this is my fault," I said. "Brand didn't promise me anything. I can't even say he cheated on me because he's not my boyfriend, but he's so cruel about it. He keeps rubbing my face in it."

I shook my head. I turned and looked at Daniel.

"I'm sorry, I'm probably freaking you out by talking about how I feel about another guy."

"Do I look freaked out?"

"No."

"Then stop worrying."

I smiled. Being able to tell someone was such a relief.

"I don't know why he has to be so vicious. I know he sat with us just so he could say those things to me. He just kept at me and at me. It's like he's threatening to tell everyone about me and about what he did to me."

I jerked my head toward Daniel. I'd said more than I intended, but then he'd probably think I was talking about the beating, not about...memories of the night Brand took my virginity flooded my mind. Part of me needed to talk about it, but I was afraid.

"It wasn't that bad," I said, stupidly.

Way to go, dumb ass. Just keep digging yourself in a little deeper.

"If what he did to you wasn't so bad, why does it bother you so much?" Daniel asked, almost as if he was a shrink.

I opened my mouth to say it wasn't that bad, but Daniel knew I'd be lying.

"It...I...it's not like he forced me. Well, not really. I...I didn't want it, but..."

"We're not talking about when he beat you up, are we?" Daniel asked.

I shook my head. The color drained from my face.

"It was before that, days before. We went out into the woods and we messed around. It was incredible, but then...things went too far."

I didn't think I could get more embarrassed. I was wrong. I couldn't believe I was talking about this, but it just came spilling out.

"Did you tell him to stop?" Daniel asked. "Did you say 'no'?"

"Yes."

"And he didn't stop?"

"No. He didn't. He just held me down and..."

"If you said "no" and told him to stop, but he didn't, then he forced you, Tyler."

"No, it just...hurt...and I was afraid...Brand said it would feel good when I relaxed and he said he knew I really wanted it."

Why don't you just paint him a picture?

"Tyler...just to make sure we're talking about what I think we're talking about, did Brand...fuck you?"

"Yes."

"Did you guys plan it?"

"No. It just sort of happened. We didn't plan it. Well, I think maybe Brand planned it, but I didn't. Brand just...well, we were...I was giving him head and stuff and he just...started it."

"So, he started it, you said to stop, and he didn't."

"Yes, but I didn't fight him all that hard. I mean, I tried to get away, but I could have fought harder."

"Tyler!"

"What?" I asked, almost afraid of Daniel now.

"Tyler, no means no. He raped you."

"No, it wasn't like that. He didn't attack me."

"Yes, it was like that, Tyler. You didn't want it and he did it anyway. That's rape."

"No. After I'd told him to stop a couple of times, he did kinda stop. He told me that if I really wanted him to stop, he would, but there were no second chances. He said it was now or never. I...I didn't tell him to stop."

I looked away. I knew my face was completely red. I didn't think I'd been so embarrassed in my entire life.

"How can you even look at me?" I said. "You must think I'm some kind of sick pervert for letting him do that to me."

"I'm here to be your friend, not to judge you, Tyler."

I lost it again. I bawled right in front of Daniel once more. He held me again as I sobbed into his chest.

"I'm such...a...fucking baby," I said between sobs.

"You're nothing of the sort, Tyler."

"I'm so embarrassed," I said when I could get the words out.

"We all have secrets, Tyler. We've all done things that would embarrass us if others knew. I appreciate that you trust me enough to share this with me. Most guys wouldn't have the balls. You're not a baby. You're just in pain. Brand hurt you and he's being a sadistic ass about it. I always had my doubts about him, but I never realized he was such a dick! Maybe you should report him," Daniel said.

"For what? Think about it. He didn't actually do anything wrong. I had my chance to tell him to stop and I didn't."

"But he didn't stop when you first told him."

"No, but..." I sighed. How could I explain without saying too much?

"So he forced you?"

"No." I took a deep breath. "Brand did what he did to me because he knew I'd let him. He knew I'd fight it, but he knew a combination of seduction and force would get him what he wanted."

"There's that word 'force' again."

"I'm not saying Brand is a nice guy. I'm not saying what he did was okay. He didn't out and out rape me, though."

I had to pause for several seconds before I could go on. It was so hard to say what I was about to admit to Daniel. I almost didn't, but I needed to talk about it. Daniel was listening and he wasn't reacting with revulsion. I took a deep breath.

"Brand knew that deep down I wanted it. If he hadn't given me the chance to stop, then I'd call it rape, but he did give me that chance and I let him continue. God, this is *so* embarrassing. I'm sitting here telling you I'm a little slut."

"What you're describing is the legal definition of rape and doing it with one guy doesn't make you a slut, Tyler."

"Maybe he did rape me. I don't know. I'm so confused. I know I'm not a slut, but...it's still embarrassing. What if everyone finds out?"

"I seriously doubt Brand is going to tell anyone."

"I think Sheila knows."

"He's just messing with your mind, Tyler. If he tells anyone about you, he'll be telling about himself, too."

"You may be right, but I have the feeling he could twist it around. I wouldn't be surprised at all if he told Sheila he saw me with some other guy. I'm scared, Daniel, what if word gets around about me? I like it here. I'm a good counselor, but if people find out..."

"They're not going to find out."

"They might. Hell, one of my own kids figured out I was gay. He figured out I had something going with Brand, too. What if word does get out? How do you think the parents would react to that? I'd get fired. Everyone will think I'm a pedo. I can just hear it—'Yeah, he loves working at a summer camp with all those little boys...'"

"No one is going to fire you because you're gay."

"They'll have to, Daniel. A lot of people would think I was a monster if they found out I was gay. They'd think all kinds of horrible things and they wouldn't want me near kids. I would never do anything like that, but how could I convince them of that?"

"You're worrying about things that aren't going to happen. Brand is not going to tell anyone about you. He may hint. He may start rumors, but he's not going to outright tell anyone. He's got as much to lose as you. He's not going to say anything for the same reasons you won't tell anyone about him. He knew you'd keep your mouth shut when he went after you," Daniel said.

"Which makes him an even bigger bastard. Maybe you're right. I'm being paranoid. Brand is a dick, but he loves it here as much as I do. He's not going to jeopardize that. Hell, the kids love him, especially his kids. Brand is a bastard, but as much as I hate to admit it, he's also a great counselor."

"Maybe he has a split personality."

I rubbed my forehead with my fingers then looked at Daniel.

"Thanks," I said. "I did need to talk to someone about all this, even though I didn't really want to talk about it."

"I'm sorry all this happened to you, Tyler."

"Me too. I feel so stupid and so used and to have him rub my face in it..." I shook my head. "It's so unfair that someone who is such a dick gets to look like that. Dammit, he's gorgeous."

"Maybe he's such a dick because of the way he looks. Maybe he's not as lucky as you think. Would you want to be like him?" Daniel asked.

"No, I guess not. It's just that he's so good-looking."

"You're pretty good-looking yourself."

"So are you," I said in a far too meaningful tone. Daniel gave me a simple compliment and I start flirting.

You are such a homo, Tyler.

I laughed.

"What?"

"Nothing. Thanks for listening to me."

"What are friends for?"

"We are friends, aren't we?"

"I like to think so."

"Me too."

I paused for a moment to make sure I wanted to say what I was going to say next.

"You know how I said one of my boys had figured out I'm gay?"

"Yes."

"He also said I should look for a nice guy and he recommended you."

I blushed.

"Did he?"

"Yes. He says you're interested in me."

I'm going to die of embarrassment right here on this bench.

"He's a smart kid," Daniel said, gazing into my eyes.

We just sat there looking at each other for several moments. We were so quiet I could hear my own breath. I reached out slowly, expecting Daniel to pull away despite his words. It was too much to hope that he'd like me, *like that*, especially after all I'd just told him. I kept my hand moving forward through sheer force of will. My fingertips grazed Daniel's. I took his hand in mine. Daniel looked into my eyes and smiled at me.

"Maybe we could take a walk along the lake tonight," I said.

"I'd like that."

"Me too."

My heart beat so fast I wondered if Daniel could hear it. I was so excited I felt like I could run faster than the wind. Daniel and I stood and walked back toward our cabins together. We looked at each other now and then and grinned. How could I feel so happy after feeling so miserable only minutes before? Brand didn't seem to matter so much anymore.

I sighed, then smiled when Daniel cut off the path into D6 territory. I walked the short distance to D4 alone with my thoughts. I was beginning to wonder if Steve was right about everything. I also wondered if kids weren't a lot smarter than adults. Steve had figured out I was gay, but he made no assumptions. Then again, he knew what kind of person I was from having lived in the same cabin with me. Still, he gave me a little bit of hope for the future. If he could be understanding and accepting, maybe others could too. To think I'd pegged him as a brat!

When I passed Steve later in the day, he stopped and smiled.

"You look like you're in a much better mood. I bet you got some."

"Steve!"

"Yeah, you did, didn't you? I bet you hooked up with Lt. Keegan."

"I cannot talk to you about this."

"Which means yes!"

"I didn't say that."

"I saw you walking with him earlier. You are sooo obviously a couple now."

"You are jumping to conclusions."

"Haven't you ever heard the saying 'Never try to kid a kid?'"

"We're just friends and even if there was something more there, I couldn't talk to you about it."

"Give me a break. You counselors and your 'secret' lives. You're all so obvious."

"Only to you. I think you're an alien with mind reading abilities."

"You've read too many *Star Trek* books, Lieutenant."

"Not possible."

"I'm glad you're feeling better."

"Thanks, Steve. You're turning out to be not so bad. I almost like you."

"Oh, you like me! You know you do! Who wouldn't? I'm incredible!"

"You're certainly not lacking in self-esteem."

"Later, Lieutenant!"

***

I looked at my watch. It was nearing 10 p.m. I closed *The Hobbit* and told the few boys who were still awake goodnight. I walked into my quarters, put the book away, and sprayed on just a little cologne. I walked back through the cabin to make sure all was well.

"Hey, Lieutenant," Steve whispered.

I walked over to his bunk.

"What?" I asked.

"Have a good time tonight and don't be afraid to kiss him," Steve whispered so that only I could hear.

"Goodnight, Steve," I said. He giggled. I swear the boy was psychic.

I was supposed to meet Daniel where the paths from the Cub area and the Beaver area met just before descending a steep hill than meandered toward the lake. We arrived only moments apart.

"Hey," he said.

"Hey."

As we descended the path we could hear counselors laughing, kids in nearby cabins whispering, and a screen door on one of the latrines slamming shut. These were the sound of camp life.

"Steve is onto us," I said.

"Yeah?"

"He saw us walking together earlier and said we looked like a couple."

"A couple, huh?"

"Yeah."

"It would be a shame to disappoint him."

"Yes, it really would. We have to think of the kids first, of course."

"Of course."

"He also caught me as I was leaving and told me to have fun and not to be afraid to kiss you."

"Good advice, especially the last part."

We were in the tunnel under the highway by then and out of sight. I stopped, leaned in, and pressed my lips to Daniel's. The mere touching of our lips filled me with excitement and passion. I took him in my arms and kissed him more forcefully. Daniel responded with equal intensity. I wanted to just keep on kissing him, but someone would be along sooner or later and we definitely didn't want to get caught. We left the tunnel behind, and followed the path as it led us to Lake Potawatomi.

"You see, Steve was right," Daniel said.

"So far, he's been right about everything. It's scary."

The gentle lapping of waves upon the shore was soothing and romantic. It was not far from this spot where I'd met Brand at the beginning of camp. That had been a fantasy come true, but the fantasy had turned into a bad dream. Would I have better luck the second time around? I was almost certain of it.

The waves reflected the moonlight, making the surface of Potawatomi sparkle like...I was going to say a million shimmering diamonds, but the lake at that moment was far more beautiful than diamonds could ever be. Daniel risked taking my hand as we walked along together. I smiled at him shyly. We left the path where a few trees grew near the shoreline and gazed out at the lake. We just stood, watched the moonlight reflecting off the water, and listened to the waves running along the shore.

"It looks like there's something over by Long Point," Daniel said after a while.

"A boat?"

"No, not a boat. There are no lights, but can't you see it? There's something white over there, dancing on the water."

I peered carefully toward Long Point, at first I saw only moonlight on the water and a few boats in the middle of the lake, but then I caught sight of something. I gasped.

"It's Paukooshuck."

"Who?"

"Paukooshuck. There's a legend about his spirit dancing on the lake."

"Really?"

"Really. It's said that Chief Paukooshuck can be seen dancing on the waters of Lake Potawatomi on some moonlit nights. Seeing him is rare and it's supposed to be very good luck."

I continued peering across the lake as I spoke. I was afraid if I looked away that the spirit would disappear.

"Is this true or are you making it up?"

"Oh, it's true. Maj. T said something about it and I looked it up. Paukooshuck was one of the Potawatomi Chiefs who lived on the shores of Lake Potawatomi long ago. After he died, he was buried on Long Point. People used to see his spirit paddling his canoe across the lake or dancing on the waters. No one has seen him for decades; however, so people think it's just a story."

"What do you believe?"

"Chief Paukooshuck was real. He loved this place. Why wouldn't he return to dance upon the water? Besides, if that isn't Paukooshuck out there, what is dancing on the lake?"

We watched in silence for several long moments more until the dancing figure dimmed and then disappeared. Even after Paukooshuck had gone, we stood there in companionable silence for a few minutes more.

"That was incredible," Daniel said quietly. "I'm glad you were here with me. I wouldn't have known what I was seeing without you. Even before you told me about Paukooshuck, I thought it looked like a person out there dancing on the lake, but I would've just thought I was seeing things. People don't dance on the water."

"No, but spirits do."

"So seeing Paukooshuck is good luck?"

"Very good luck."

"And we saw him together," Daniel said.

I looked at him and grinned.

We walked back to the path and continued along the lake. Soon, we passed the Naval pier where the Academy fleet lay at anchor. Small sailboats of various sizes rocked on the waves, metal clips on the rigging clanging against the masts. In the deepest water at the far end of the pier sat the Frobisher, the Academy's three-masted sailing vessel. It was the largest to ply the inland waters of the U.S. We strolled on past the Naval Building, the swim pier, and the First Class Ring where only First classmen were supposed to enter. Soon, we passed the Memorial Library.

"It looks like a castle," Daniel said.

"It's modeled on one in England. I think it's built 2/3 scale or something like that."

"It's wonderful."

There were more trees here and soon the path climbed a little and ran right next to the lake. On our right, we passed the president's home, which looked like a Swiss Chalet. It was one of the most beautiful homes on the lake. Soon, we walked by the old Kulver Inn. The dining room was closed now and all was dark, but it was a beautiful old place. I sighed.

"What's wrong?" Daniel asked.

"They're going to tear it down."

"What?"

"The Inn."

"Why? Isn't it historic?"

"Yes, I think it was the very first inn built on the lake, in the 1870s."

"Why would they tear it down? It looks like it's in good shape."

"They're building a new library."

"Couldn't they put it somewhere else?"

"Yes. They are tearing down the president's house, too."

"That's a shame."

"Yeah, and the worst of it is they wouldn't even have to tear down the Kulver Inn because the library isn't going to sit where the Inn is, but a little more towards the current library. The Academy doesn't care anything about its own past. I don't understand it."

"The reception in the Inn during orientation was great. I came out on the porch and gazed at the lake while eating cheesecake," Daniel said.

"Yeah, unfortunately that will be the last orientation reception there." I was silent for a moment. "They're destroying The Shak, too. It's connected to the Inn."

"The Shak?"

"Yeah, it's a burger/ice cream shop/hangout place. It's been here since at least the 1920s, but enough of this, I don't want to ruin our time together by thinking about what's going to be done to the Inn. There is always something to worry about, always something bad going on, and life is too short to worry about it all."

"Yeah. I try to just live in the moment and enjoy what I have, like now," Daniel said and smiled.

I grinned back.

"Now is good. Damn, I wish I'd met you before Brand."

"You did, but you were too busy checking him out to notice me."

"I'm really sorry. You must think I'm a shallow bastard."

"No. There is no need to be sorry. You were nice to me, even though you didn't seem to pick up on how much I liked you. As for being shallow, well, Brand is hot enough to be on the cover of a magazine. Who wouldn't be attracted to a guy like that?"

"Are you?"

"Physically, yes. He's gorgeous. He's so cocky, though, so full of himself. I find that very unattractive."

"Wow. I feel like a total idiot. How is it that you can see past his looks so easily, but I was sucked right in?"

"I think it's just that I scout out the situation before I make a move. You dove right in."

"Yeah. I never thought about anything but how he'd look without a shirt."

Daniel laughed.

"I wanted him so bad," I said. "I never thought I'd get him. Brand was like a fantasy. Then, when I actually did get him, it was like a dream come true at first, but like a dream it became twisted and confusing. I got what I wanted, but I really paid the price. It's like all the stories of wishes coming true. There's almost always a nasty catch."

"*Almost* always. We all make mistakes. I'm sorry he hurt you."

"I guess I'm too trusting. I don't get guys like Brand. He knew he was going to dump on me from the very beginning. He wanted to have sex with me, but he wanted to fuck me up even more. It was just a twisted game to him. I think he even knew I had deeper feelings for him. I could never play with someone's feelings like that."

"Which is one of the reasons I like you."

"I'm sorry. I talk about Brand way too much."

"Yes, you do, but I understand."

We walked on past the doomed Kulver Inn to the Faculty Pier and then stepped out onto the pier itself. We walked to the end, took off our shoes and socks, and dangled our feet in the water as we sat side by side. We were alone. Daniel leaned his head against my shoulder. I took his hand and interlaced my fingers with his own.

"I think we're getting along pretty well so far," I said.

"Yeah."

I knew Daniel was smiling, even though I couldn't see his face.

"You'll probably like me less once you get to know me," I teased.

"Try me. Tell me about you."

"Hmm, well, I want to be an archaeologist and I love history. I'm always reading books on ancient history and sometimes on Native American history and legends. I love *Star Trek* and have a big collection of novels, although I don't think I qualify as a Trekker because I don't know all the trivia. Hmm, what else? I love walking. I collect antiques, especially stoneware, Depression glass, and country furniture. Have I turned you off yet?"

"Not a bit, but I have questions."

"Shoot."

"You're seventeen and you collect furniture? How? Where do you put it?"

"I buy it at auctions and I only buy things that are selling pretty cheap. Sometimes, I get lucky. I keep some of it in my room and some of it in my log cabin."

"You own a log cabin?"

"Yeah. I have since I was fifteen. I bought this little piece of land from my uncle. A family friend gave me a log cabin and everyone helped me move it. It was kind of like a giant set of Lincoln logs. The expensive part was putting in a new floor and putting on a new roof. My parents helped with that."

"You really have your own house? That's incredible."

"Well, remember, there is no electricity, no running water, no bathroom. It's pretty much the way it was when it was first built a 150 years or so ago."

"That's still really cool. Now, tell me what stoneware and Depression glass are."

"Stoneware is pottery, made of clay. I mainly collect jars and jugs that were once used to store things, the way we use glass and plastic bottles and jars now. I have some bowls too and a pitcher. Most of it is a hundred years and more old.

"Depression glass is glassware that was made in the 1930s, during the Depression.

It mostly comes in pink and green, although some of it is yellow, clear, and even cobalt blue. I started collecting it when I was about eight years old because it was really cheap. Now, I mainly just collect one pattern called Parrot. It's very rare and pretty expensive, so I can't afford much of it. It's so hard to find that I don't have to worry about the price too much."

"That's really cool. About the only thing I've ever collected are coins."

"Oh, I like coins too. I like a lot of stuff, but I can't collect everything. Believe me, I've tried. I have way too much stuff, so sometimes I set up at flea markets with my parents and sell some of it."

"You must have a lot of money to buy so much stuff."

"No. I just watch and wait and buy when I can get what I want fairly cheap. Then I end up selling some stuff, so I'm really just spending the same money over and over again."

"It never seems to work that way for me. I spend my money and it's gone," Daniel said.

"That's because you're normal and probably spend your money on movies and music. I'm weird and spend my money on old stuff."

"Normal is boring," Daniel said.

"Well, you're not boring."

"I'm also not normal." Daniel leaned in conspiratorially and whispered in my ear. "I even think other boys are sexy."

"No!" I said, pretending astonishment.

Daniel laughed. I loved the sound of his laughter. It rang out over the lake, almost like a song.

"What do you like so much about old stuff?" Daniel asked.

"I like thinking about where something has been and who has used it before. There's a connection to other times, people, and places with old things that isn't there with something new. Like...a couple of years or so ago my parents bought the contents of this old house. It wasn't very big and there wasn't a whole lot of stuff in it, but part of it was a log cabin. We were looking around and I spotted this old bed in what had been a back bedroom, except the roof had collapsed. It was a really cool oak bed, a hundred years old or so. The rain had darkened the headboard in a spot, but it wasn't ruined yet. Mom and Dad let me have it. We took it home, cleaned it up, and now I use it. It's beautiful. It's got these big panels in the headboard and footboard. I like thinking about how it's been used for over a century. Whoever used it before me left it behind and it sat there as the house grew older and the roof collapsed. If I hadn't come along it would have just rotted away, but now it's mine. Maybe someone else will use it after me. It may be around a century after I'm gone. Who knows?"

"That's really interesting."

"I have other stuff that's even older. Not too long ago, I bought an old kitchen work table that has this really old red paint on it. It dates to about 1830 or 1840. I use it in my bedroom. I love the worn red color and sometimes I stop and think that my table has been used since before Lincoln was President. It was actually around during the Civil War. I'd better stop talking about the stuff I collect or I'll bore you into a coma."

"I doubt that."

"So, what about you?"

"I like taking pictures. I've even had a couple published in the local paper. I don't take pictures of just anything and everything. I look for a special shot. I like taking pictures of friends, places I visit, sunsets, animals, flowers, and just whatever interests me. I think I get the same feeling from pictures as you do your antiques. I've been a photographer since I was little and I like looking at pictures I took long ago. It helps me remember things I did before and people who aren't in my life anymore. Sometimes, I'll look at a picture and I'll remember something that I hadn't thought about for years. I just like having a record of people and places, too. Like this summer, someday when I'm old and gray I'll look at the pictures I took and I'll remember the summer when I met this wonderful guy and we took a walk by the lake."

I smiled at Daniel.

"Hmm, maybe I should take some pictures, too."

"Okay, I'll let you use my camera and you can take me antique shopping and help me pick out something old with lots of memories attached to it."

"Deal."

Daniel yawned.

"We'd better get back. I'm exhausted," he said.

"I know the feeling. It's hard keeping up with all those little rug rats. Do you think we were ever like that?"

"Impossible," Daniel said.

I helped Daniel to his feet and we walked back along the lake. The campus was so quiet the only sound came from the waves hitting the shore. I loved the scent of the breeze as it came off the lake, a mixture of fresh spring water and summer. I was so happy just then that none of the unpleasant events of the recent past could touch me. Brand, his smug-knowing looks, and pointed verbal jabs meant nothing to me. Daniel had kissed me and made it all better.

"I really like you," I said. "I mean I *really* like you."

"That's just what I was hoping to hear. Just for that you're getting a special reward when we get to the tunnel. I *really* like you, too."

I can't describe how Daniel's words excited me and I must admit I kept thinking about that special reward all the way back to the tunnel. Once there, Daniel pulled me close, hugged me tight, and kissed me. This time, he slipped his tongue into my mouth and we made out as we rubbed our bodies together. It was sexier than anything Brand and I had done.

When our lips parted, Daniel rubbed his nose against mine, then kissed me lightly once more. We left the darkness of the tunnel, climbed the hill, and stopped briefly where the path split.

"Tomorrow," Daniel said.

"Tomorrow."

A single word could hold such promise.

Bloomington, Indiana
Wednesday, July 8, 2009

I was a little too eager for Tyler to arrive. I never dreamed when he knocked on my door that first day that I'd come to enjoy his company so much. I guess it was opportunity knocking that first day. I'm glad I answered.

It wasn't such an odd way to make a friend. Most of my friendships had begun with chance encounters. It was as if certain people were meant to be together. Some might think a friendship with someone so much younger was odd, but what I cared about when it came to friends was their interests, disposition, and personality. Their age, looks, race, or sex didn't matter.

Tyler arrived right on time, as usual.

"Okay, make me into a great writer!"

"Tyler, I'm a writer, not a miracle worker."

"Yes, Dr. McCoy. You're obviously also not a comedian."

I laughed.

"You recognize subtle *Star Trek* quotes. I like that."

"You call that subtle? More like blatantly obvious."

Tyler crossed his arms and attempted to scowl, but his grin ruined it.

I led Tyler to a table where a pot of tea and two cups & saucers were waiting. I poured us both tea as Tyler took out a notebook.

"Perhaps the most important thing you should understand as a writer, is that you're in control. I'm going to give you some tips and advice. When you take English composition classes your teachers are going to throw a lot of rules at you. It's up to you to decide what works for you. In writing, the rules are meant to be broken. Writing is about communicating ideas and sometimes it's necessary to break the rules to succeed. The rules are there to make communication easier, but sometimes they get in the way."

"What about basic grammar rules? I've had English teachers who think they're sacred."

"Most writers follow the rules of grammar most of the time, but, as I said, rules are meant to be broken. In fact, a grammatically perfect novel would be almost unreadable."

"Why?"

"All languages are constantly evolving and changing. It often takes the rules a while to catch up to actual usage. There are times when following the rules of grammar actually prevents communication. There are grammatically perfect sentences that almost no reader will understand. Grammar rules are the same as any other rule. They are meant to be broken. There are English teachers who might have me killed for saying so, but it's true."

Tyler laughed.

"I promise not to turn you in to the grammar Gestapo," he said.

"I think I'm already on their list."

I took a sip of Irish breakfast and continued.

"One of the biggest mistake beginning writers make is tell their reader what is happening, rather than showing them. For example, I could write *Tyler was so exhausted he didn't think he could finish the race.* The sentence communicates the scene quite well, but I'm merely telling the reader what Tyler is feeling. To show what Tyler is feeling, I could instead write *Tyler's breath came hard and fast, his heart pounded in his chest, and his legs screamed with the effort of pushing toward the finish line.* See the difference? In both sentences, Tyler is about to burn out, but in the second sentence the scene comes alive; the reader can hear Tyler's breath, feel his heart pounding, and his legs aching. Even though I didn't mention it, the reader will likely picture Tyler sweating with the effort of running."

"Yeah, that is much better. I try to do that with my writing, but sometimes I find myself just telling instead of showing."

"I do, too. A writer must also decide when it's best to tell the reader what is happening, rather than show him. If you're writing about something mundane, like a character brushing his teeth, it's best to just tell the reader and then move on. Who really wants to read about someone brushing their teeth? Of course, it's generally best to just skip anything mundane, but sometimes rather ordinary events are key to the story-line."

Tyler nodded and wrote in his notebook.

"Just showing the reader what is happening isn't enough, either. Let's say I'm writing about someone drinking hot cocoa as they sit gazing out a window. To really make the scene alive I have to ask myself some questions and then work the answers into the scene. How does the hot cocoa look, smell, and taste? How hot is the cocoa? Does it burn the tongue? Is the temperature just right? Is it too cool? What's going on outside the window? Is it snowing or raining? Is there music playing in the background? Christmas music? What does the character see outside? Kids playing in the snow? What does the character see inside? Is there a Christmas tree?

"A simple scene like that can go in a lot of directions. The details are extremely important. A story without those details is like an action movie without special effects."

"I've never thought about it like that."

"Just remember to ask yourself not only what the character is doing, but what he's feeling, seeing, tasting, and smelling. Each character should experience a scene just like a real person. Thinking about the senses helps bring a character and a scene alive."

"I think this is really going to help," Tyler said, writing more in his notebook. "I usually focus on what a character sees and feels, but I've never thought about much about what one tastes or smells."

"Another point to keep in mind is choosing the right word. Mark Twain once said that the difference between the almost-right word and the right word is the difference between the lightning bug and the lightning. He was right. For example, if you're writing about a tree, it's okay to use the word "tree," but that's the almost-right word. The right word in this case could be oak or maple or sassafras. The right word tells the reader the type of tree and allows him to picture a lot of details that "tree" doesn't convey. For another example, you could say a character "ran" into a room. That's okay in some scenes, but in others it's the almost-right word. Instead, you could write that the character exploded or zipped or thundered into the room. See the difference?"

"Yeah, but I think it's going to take me a while to learn to actually do that."

"Oh yes, but if you think about it as you are writing, and especially as you're re-writing, it will begin to become a part of your style. You'll also develop a feel for when you want to use a word like "exploded" and when "ran" is the better choice. Remember, no rule is carved in stone.

"Now, did you bring me any samples of your writing?"

"I did, but...I'm a little nervous about letting you read it."

"I'm not going to mark up your work with a red pen, Tyler. I'm just going to offer some suggestions. You're the writer. It's your decision whether or not to use my suggestions."

Tyler scooted closer and pushed another notebook he'd brought with him toward me. I caught the scent of his cologne and stole a glance at him. Tyler was so very attractive and reminded me so much of Daniel. I nearly leaned in and kissed him, but then I reminded myself this was not Daniel and that I didn't want to pursue a romantic or sexual relation with Tyler. I took the notebook and opened it.

"This is a short story I've been working on. I do most of my writing on the computer, but sometimes I like to write in places I can't take my computer."

I read Tyler's story. He watched me nervously until I laughed out loud.

"This line is *really* good," I said. "This whole scene is well set up. Reading it, I feel like I'm there."

Tyler grinned. I kept reading. I stopped here and there to explain how he could make parts of his story really come alive, but his story-line was interesting enough I wanted to just keep reading.

"I miss the characters," I said when I'd finishing reading his story. "That's the mark of good writing in my opinion. Your story is a little choppy; it needs some better transitions. You also need to think about what I told you before. You're missing a lot of opportunities to make your scenes come alive. It's a very well thought out story."

"You're not just saying that?"

158

"Absolutely not. How would lying to you make you a better writer? Your story needs a lot of work. It's a good story now, outside of the few problems I've pointed out, but it could become a great story."

I pulled out some examples of my own work, showing Tyler the difference between my first draft and the final book. We sat, talked writing, and drank hot tea. Tyler yawned. I looked at the clock. I'd lost track of time. Three hours had passed.

"I'm tired," Tyler said.

"Let's go eat. All this thinking makes me hungry and it's past suppertime," I said.

"Now you're talking!"

"What do you feel like this evening?"

"I told you, tired."

"I mean, what do you feel like eating, smartass."

"Hey, you're the writer. You should know to word questions more carefully."

"Around you that's certainly true."

"Hmm, how about Chinese?" Tyler asked. "There's a great place on Third Street near Borders."

"Sounds good."

A few minutes later, I parked the Shay in the parking lot of a strip mall that included the China Buffet, Borders, the Dollar Tree, the Total Tan tanning salon, PC Max, Jimmy John's, and a Mexican restaurant called Casa Brava. Just across the parking lot was Cheeseburgers in Paradise.

I immediately liked the China Buffet upon entering. We were greeted by an older and very friendly Asian woman who made us feel as if we were being invited into her home.

Tyler and I chose the third booth on the far right, not far from the buffet.

"A lot of the college kids eat here," Tyler said. "It's within walking distance of IU, the food is great, it's a buffet, and it's cheap."

I followed Tyler up to the line. There was a wonderful selection. I chose General Tso's Chicken, peanut chicken, Crab

Rangoon, steamed salmon, and a chicken burrito. My last selection seemed a bit out of place for a Chinese restaurant, but I couldn't resist the golden brown shell. I carried my plate back to our booth, then made a quick trip for some Diet Coke.

"I love this peanut chicken. I've never tried it before," I said. "I think I could handle eating here every week. Thank you for introducing me to this place."

"Think of it as a 'thank you' for telling me a few of your writing secrets."

"They aren't exactly secrets, but I hope you can benefit from my experience."

"Oh, I know I can. I have already. Oh! I finished *Prince Caspian.*"

"What did you think?"

"It's my favorite of the Narnia books so far. Those books are too short! I'm glad there are more of them. I really missed Prince Caspian when I finished the book."

"Ah, that is what I consider the mark of a great story. Whenever I miss the characters upon finishing a book, it's a keeper. I give away most books when I've read them, but I have a special place for those I want to revisit."

"Did you really miss the characters in my story?"

"Yes. That, more than anything else, should tell you that you've got talent."

"Thanks. Hey, I have a book recommendation for you."

"You do?"

"Don't act so surprised! I do read, you know."

"What is it then?"

"*Take a Thief* by Mercedes Lackey. One of my friends saw the copy of *The Lion, The Witch, and The Wardrobe* you gave me and he told me about *Take a Thief*. I checked it out of the library and I really like it. It's set in this fantasy world that is kind of like the Middle Ages. It's about this young orphan boy who learns to be a master thief to survive. It keeps getting better and better."

"Uh-oh, now I'll have to add another book to my "to be read" list. I don't think I'll live long enough to finish the list as it is."

"Aww, you have such horrible problems. I pity you. Try being my age and in high school. Thank God, it's summer."

"I was your age and in high school."

"Yeah, I guess so. It's kind of hard to think of older people being my age, especially really old people."

"I'm not eighty yet."

"I don't mean you! You're my dad's age. That's not young, but it's not old, at least not real old."

I laughed.

"I'm just saying...it's easy to picture myself as being nine-years-old, but it's really hard thinking of my dad that age."

"That's easy to explain. You can picture yourself as younger because, quite obviously, you are you. Many of your memories from your past are still with you. When you think about someone else being younger, you don't have access to their memories. To be honest, I don't have many memories of my grade school years, but I remember high school much better."

"What do you remember about grade school?"

"What stands out are the holidays—Christmas decorations, the Valentine's Day parties where we all exchanged cards, and most especially the yearly fall festival, which fell near Halloween."

"What was so special about the fall festival?"

"The atmosphere. It was the only time of the year I was in my school after hours. It seemed so different when it was dark outside. I remember the cool weather, the scent of fall in the air, walking through the leaves on the way in. All the kids wore costumes, just as if they were trick-or-treating. There were carnival-like games run by the parents and teachers. There was a cake walk. I was always very lucky at that for some reason. There was also a white elephant sale."

"What's a cake walk?"

"It's kind of like musical chairs, except there are enough chairs for everyone and they are numbered. Everyone walks around while music plays and then sits down when it stops. A number is drawn and whoever is sitting in that chair wins a cake."

"That sounds easy enough."

"Hence the expression 'It's a cake walk' meaning something is very easy."

"I'm almost afraid to ask, but what's a white elephant sale?"

"It's like a yard sale or garage sale. Everyone brought in junk they didn't need and it was tagged and sold to raise money for the school."

"Maybe that's what started your collecting obsession," Tyler said.

"No, that was entirely the fault of my parents. They took me to auctions when I was little. They bought and sold antiques and junk. I picked it up from them. Don't get me started on collecting, however, or you'll be on your knees begging me to shut up."

We talked and ate, but mostly ate. When I returned to the buffet for more Diet Coke, I discovered hot water and tea bags. I came back to the table with not only my soft drink, but a cup of steeping tea. When I finished my peanut chicken, Crab Rangoon, and everything else, I returned for some ice cream with crushed peanuts and chocolate sauce.

"Hot tea and ice cream, this place has it all," I said.

Tyler had his own cup of tea by that point, although he was working on a second plate of Chinese food.

"Don't forget the vanilla pudding," Tyler said.

"I'll leave that to you. I can only eat so much."

I thoroughly enjoyed Tyler's company. A friend like him would have made my high school years easier to endure. I laughed to myself.

"What?"

"Sometimes, I just think funny things."

Tyler raised his eyebrow in a Spock-like manner. I don't know if it was intentional or not.

I laughed out loud because I did have a friend like him in high school, but he was more than a friend...

I was tempted to stop by Borders after we'd eaten, but I'd only buy something. Besides, I could go there any time.

"I'll drop you off at your house," I said when we were back in the car. "It's the least I can do after exhausting your brain with all that information."

"I think eating too much made me even more tired. Hey, want to meet Dad?"

"Sure and I imagine he wants to meet me."

"Why's that?"

"Because I'm a stranger who is spending a good deal of time with his son."

"Oh, Dad won't worry about that. He trusts my judgment."

"So, you've sensed I'm not a serial killer then?"

"A cereal devourer, I've seen inside your cupboards, but a serial killer, no."

I pulled up in front of Tyler's home in only a few minutes.

"Here we are," Tyler said. "Crap, the car is gone. Dad's not home."

"I'll meet him eventually."

"Yeah, that's true. I just think you guys would hit it off."

"Why is that?"

"Well, you both like me! You obviously have good taste."

"That's something at least."

"Thanks for everything," Tyler said.

"Good night, Tyler."

I drove the short distance home, stuffed and content.

Camp Neeswaugee
Monday, July 9, 1989

"What are you doing, Lieutenant?" Cody asked when he walked into the cabin after lunch, followed closely by Greg and Diego.

"Moving in our new camper."

"We're getting someone new?"

"Sort of."

"Sort of?"

"We're going to play a little joke on everyone else, if you guys can keep a secret. This will only work if we all work together."

Cody grinned.

"What is it?"

"I'll tell everyone at rest period, but if you three want, you can start the rumor that a new boy is coming in today from Norway. Just be subtle about it."

"Subtle?" asked Diego.

"Subtle means not obvious. Don't go out and tell a bunch of people. Just mention it to one, or better yet briefly talk about it where someone can overhear you."

The boys pestered me for more information as I folded and put away clothes in the bins, but I wouldn't tell them anymore until rest period. I knew the minor mystery would drive them crazy and make them more enthusiastic about what I had in mind.

Rest period was only a few minutes away, but by the time it arrived all the boys were quietly sitting on their beds. The mere fact that I didn't have to get them settled down told me word had spread that something was up. I walked out on the front porch for a moment to make sure no boys for other cabins were around, then returned.

"If you guys will cooperate, we can try a little experiment. Everyone has to keep the secret, though, or all will be ruined."

I outlined my plan to make others believe in an imaginary camper. The boys were all for it. They even volunteered to finish putting away Haakon's uniforms and make up his bunk. I had enough extra sheets and blankets and had gathered enough uniforms from lost and found that by the time we were finished, it really looked like a new boy had moved into Cabin 34.

Maj. Wilder was in on it, of course, and in the following hours I clued in the other counselors. Haakon Haakonson was even added to the roll call and from that point on the boys in my cabin answered for him on a rotating basis, always being careful than none of the boys from the other cabins could see them do it. This last task was easier than it sounds. Roll is called while the boys stand at attention, staring straight ahead. Anyone who turned his head to try to get a look at Haakon would be spotted and reprimanded by the Division Leader or duty officer.

The key to our ploy was attention to detail. Haakon was listed on the Point chart posted on the bulletin board in my cabin. Every day I listed his points for passing P.I., writing letters home, and for performing small tasks just as I did for the other boys. His progress in working toward his C was checked off on the C chart. His dress jacket had a name tag, just like all the other boys. I even got onto Haakon for misbehaving inside the cabin when boys from other cabins were near enough to overhear.

I was afraid my kids would blow it by overacting, but they were having too much fun tricking everyone else to ruin it. In only a few hours, the boys in Division 4 believed a new camper had arrived, even though no one had actually seen him.

In the late evening, when the boys had free time, I was approached by one of the kids from Cabin 36 while I was sitting on the steps of my own cabin.

"Lieutenant, where's the new boy at?"

I pointed down toward the soccer field where a huge group of Division 4 and Division 6 boys were playing a pickup game of soccer.

"He's right down there—the blond boy, the slim one. See him?"

That description fit more than one boy in the division.

"Yeah, I see him. I think I saw him at supper, too."

"Probably."

"Thanks, Lieutenant."

I grinned as he left.

By the end of the next day, several boys in Division 4 claimed to have met Haakon. They'd seen him with a nature class as the group walked by, they'd seen him coming out of Main HQ, they'd caught sight of him playing tetherball. Soon, my boys didn't have to pretend Haakon was real. The other boys were doing it for them.

As the days passed, Haakon became an inside joke.

"Guys, you're too loud," I said as I walked into the cabin. "Why can't you be more like Haakon? He never causes any trouble. He always keeps his stuff perfect. He's so quiet it's almost like he isn't really here."

The boys grinned.

"You're just saying that because he's your favorite!" Steve complained. He almost sounded jealous.

"Well, he does pass more inspections than any of you. I think he'll be on the corporal list when the next promotion order comes out."

My kids had a lot of fun with Haakon for the rest of the summer. When camp ended, most of the boys outside of Cabin 34 still believed that among my boys *was* a blond from Norway.

I told Daniel about the creation of Haakon Haakonson the next time we walked along Lake Potawatomi.

"That is so funny! You know, I almost asked you about your new kid? Some of the boys in my cabin were talking about this Division 4 boy from Norway that's supposed to be like a super athlete. According to them, he can do anything."

"So could I if I was a pretend camper."

"I can't believe you've gotten so many people to believe in him."

"Believe in him? Half the boys in my division claim to be friends with him. You know how these kids are. They'll believe anything. They think Lt. Hale in Division 7 is an astronaut."

"Really?"

"Yeah, I helped with that one. A couple of his kids came and asked me if he was really an astronaut. I hadn't heard anything about it, but I told them that Lt. Hale and I had been in the Air Force together and that he went on to become a test pilot and then joined the space program."

"That's too funny."

"My kids have learned not to believe everything I say, but then I make up such outrageous stories they can't possibly be true. I figure it's not lying if a story is too crazy to be real."

"Like what?"

"Like...they were jealous when they found out I went to Dairy Queen while they were at Free Swim, so I told them that terrorists forced me into Dairy Queen at gunpoint and made me order a chocolate shake."

"What did they say to that?"

"They just rolled their eyes, but I stuck to the story as if it was true. I think they like having a weird counselor."

"I'm sure you're not boring."

"Life is too short to be boring. Oh, did I tell you about the monkey bracelet?"

"The monkey bracelet?"

"Miss Tess made it in Indian Crafts. It's actually a beaded wrist-band, like those the Gold Cs make for their Top Notch projects? Anyway, Miss Tess designed one with a monkey on it. She asked me what I thought of it when she finished it and I pretended it was the ugliest wrist-band ever made, although it's actually kind of cool looking. Later, I had kids ask to see it and then pretend they had to run outside and hurl because it was so hideous. It's become a running joke in Indian Crafts. Today, I sealed it in an envelope and wrote a warning on the outside, 'Warning! Do not open under any circumstances! Severe danger of vomiting!'"

"What does Miss Tess think of all this?"

"She pretends to hate me, but she thinks it's funny. It keeps the kids entertained."

"It sounds like you have more fun over there than we do in arts and crafts."

"Arts and craps as we call it. You should request to teach Indian Crafts next trimester. Maj. Burrows says we'll be getting more instructors because Indian Crafts gets really popular when the kids find out what we make."

"I think I will, then we can be together more."

"I'd like that."

Daniel and I passed another couple who were walking along the lake, a male/female couple who were walking so close their shoulders were touching.

"I wish we could be like that," I said.

"You want one of us to be a girl?"

"No, you jerk!" I said laughing. "I wish we could be open about being together. I wish I could hold your hand in public and tell other people about you. I'd like everyone to know I've got a boyfriend who is cute and sweet."

"Boyfriend, huh? I like that."

"Yeah?"

"Yeah, but if you're going to be my boyfriend, there'll be no making out with the lifeguards during free swim," Daniel said.

"I can live with that." I grinned.

Daniel looked around quickly, pulled me to him, and kissed me. We broke our kiss and walked on.

"I wish I could tell everyone about you too, but there is a certain excitement to a clandestine romance. It's very Romeo & Juliet," Daniel said.

"Yeah, we want to be like Romeo & Juliet because things ended up so well for them," I said with a smirk.

"You know what I mean!" I could hear a grin in Daniel's tone.

"Yeah. Did you know that Romeo & Juliet were like...fourteen?" I asked.

"Seriously? In the movies they are always twenty or so."

"That's because everyone in our time freaks out if anyone mentions someone under eighteen having sex. In Shakespeare's day, girls were often married at thirteen; boys were usually older, but not much. A girl our age who wasn't married yet was in danger of becoming an old maid. Of course, people didn't live as long then as they do now."

"That's incredible. How do you know all this stuff?"

"I'm a geek."

"Well, if you're a geek, you're a sexy geek, but I don't think you're a geek."

"You're just saying that to keep me away from those life guards."

Daniel laughed.

***

I would have enjoyed my summer at camp even without Daniel, but with him, well, I just don't think it's possible to describe how wonderful I felt. I'd had crushes on boys before, but my feelings for Daniel were much stronger. Just thinking about him made me happy. I could almost not bear being parted from him, even for a few hours. I didn't know what I was going to do when the summer ended, but I didn't let myself think about it. I'd learned to not let negative thoughts ruin good times.

Brand did his best to make my summer unpleasant. He kept up with his insinuating remarks. Some of his harem whispered when I was around. I was sure he'd made up some nasty stories about me. Why did he have to be such a jerk?

Lt. Cody never once hinted he knew about Brand and me, so I was sure Brand hadn't told him anything. Brand probably wanted Lt. Cody to think he was special. I considered warning Lt. Cody, but I knew that wouldn't end well. He would confront Brand and Brand would convince him I was some kind of psycho stalker he'd rejected. Brand could be very charming when he wished. I was certain Brand would use Lt. Cody and eventually toss him to the side, but the lieutenant was under his spell and there was no breaking it.

I was haunted by what had happened between Brand and me. I had this irrational fear I'd be called into Main HQ and asked to leave camp, but there was no way Brand could out me without incriminating himself. While I was innocent of wrongdoing, he wasn't. Technically, Brand didn't force me, but he took advantage of me; he manipulated me and humiliated me. If anything, Brand should have been afraid I'd turn *him* in. I guess he knew he was safe from that, however. I couldn't turn him in without admitting what had happened, and I wasn't about to do that! I also didn't want to admit to being such a big fool.

I was still thinking way too much about Brand. I forced myself to put him out of my mind and relax as I walked toward Indian Crafts carrying a bead-loom. Maj. Burrows had taught me how to make beaded wrist-bands so I could help the Gold Cs with their top notch projects. I'd made a Sioux rattlesnake design wrist-band for practice, but it was so sad looking I'd cut it up and recycled the glass beads. If Miss Tess had seen it, she would've tormented me mercilessly. My pathetic first attempt was nowhere near as nice as her monkey bracelet. Now, I was making an identical and hopefully much better wrist-band for Daniel. The design featured three red diamonds bordered by black and white bands on a turquoise background bordered by a single row of black beads. It took a long time to make a wrist-band, mainly because the beads were so tiny, but it was fun. I knew Daniel would love his when I gave it to him.

Maj. T caught me before I made it to the Indian Crafts tent and handed me another script. This made the third week in a row I was in a Council Fire. I looked through the script as I walked toward the tent to see how many lines I had to memorize.

"Is that a script?" Miss Tess asked loudly as I drew near Indian Crafts.

"Um...maybe," I said, slipping it behind my back.

Yeah, that's smooth, Perseus. She'll never guess it's a script you're hiding.

"I keep asking for a part, but I never get one. You don't even care and every week they hand you a script and say, 'Here's the lead role!'"

"Um...sorry?"

"I should beat you with the monkey bracelet."

"Fight! Fight!" chanted a few of the kids sitting there waiting for Maj. Burrows to call roll.

"Miss Tess, I think Maj. T doesn't give you a part because you're so beautiful he's afraid no one will watch the kids dancing."

"Okay, you may live...for now," Miss Tess said with a grin.

I knew she didn't really buy my excuse, just like she wasn't really mad at me. It was all just a game, like the monkey bracelet and so much that went on in camp. I guess you could call it performance art. I wasn't kidding about her beauty, though. Even a gay guy like me could recognize she was cute.

I hid my bead loom when I spotted Daniel. He'd transferred to Indian Crafts and only the day before. I didn't want him to see his present until I gave it to him at the end of camp Pow-Wow. Daniel had taken over ojos, while I was overseeing shields and the Gold C top notch projects which were all made on the Indian Crafts porch. Now, I could spend four class periods a day with Daniel! We even had the same period off this trimester. I was very tempted to see if he wanted to fool around in his quarters or mine during our free period, but there just wasn't enough privacy. While it wasn't likely one of the kids would walk in on us, we just couldn't take the risk. The last thing either of us wanted to do was traumatize some boy. Not that we were actually having sex, mind you! The thought had crossed my mind, about a million times, but Daniel and I were moving slowly. The thing was, my slow-moving relationship with Daniel was far sexier than what I'd had with Brand. Daniel was better than Brand in every way. I eagerly anticipated each of our night-time walks along the lake in way I hadn't my encounters with Brand. With Brand there had been intense, sometimes far too intense, sex, but with Daniel there was so much more.

Bloomington, Indiana
Thursday, July 16, 2009

It was nearing noon. I put my computer to sleep and left my work behind for the time being. Some people didn't even consider what I did as work, but writing could leave me tired and my brain fuzzy.

Tyler wasn't coming over today. He hadn't been here the day before either. I missed him more than I should have. My resolve to keep our relationship platonic hadn't wavered, but there were times... Those feelings made me feel guilty, as if I was deceiving Tyler about my intentions. I wasn't deceiving him, because I didn't intend for our relationship to progress beyond friendship, but I still felt that way at times. I also felt a little guilty for not revealing my sexual orientation, but then why should I do so? If I was heterosexual, I wouldn't have felt the need to reveal my heterosexuality. I had thought about telling him, but then that felt like a move toward something more than friendship. Tyler might think I was telling him because I was attracted to him. What if he was gay, too? What if he was attracted to me? I wanted to keep things as they were and how could I do that if Tyler was interested in me as more than a friend? How could I keep from hurting him? The chances that he was gay were slim, but it was a "what if" that bothered me. Then again, maybe he was gay and not attracted to me but could use a gay friend. I'd learned in my youth there were no easy answers, but I sometimes I wished things could be simple.

I decided, not for the first time, just to leave things as they were. If my sexual orientation became pertinent, I'd reveal it. If Tyler asked about past girlfriends, or if I was dating, or something of that nature, I'd tell him the truth. Until then, I just wouldn't bring the topic up. I also wouldn't ask him any questions that would require him to reveal his sexual orientation. I was curious, but if I pried, he might think I was doing so because I was interested in him.

It was time to get out of the house. I walked out to the Shay, hopped in, and headed for the east side. The east side; that made it sound as if Bloomington was some large metropolis. The east side was all of ten minutes from my place, if traffic was bad. I was getting hungry, so I made my way to the China Buffet. I'd become a frequent visitor since Tyler had introduced me to the place.

The booths were full, so I took a table right by the front windows. I enjoyed looking out at what passed for hustle and bustle in Bloomington. I was a creature of habit, so I filled my plate with General Tso's chicken, peanut chicken, salmon, Crab Rangoon, and a chicken burrito. I knew I should make myself try other things, but it was hard to get away from food that was so delicious.

I took my plate back to my table and then made a trip for Diet Coke. Soon, I was seated at my table, enjoying Chinese food. Well, Chinese food and a burrito.

I felt a touch of sadness because Tyler wasn't there. I was perfectly capable of eating alone, but I missed him. I was nostalgic over not only the distant past but over recent enjoyable times, too. I'd even been nostalgic over memories of things I'd done alone. Weird, but that was me.

A couple of college boys walked by, both wearing sleeveless shirts, both well-built, both good-looking. One of them was blond. I'd always had a thing for blonds, although why that didn't change after Brand I have no idea. I guess there was no reason to discard all blonds just because one of them was trouble.

A sense of sadness was upon me, but that's not the negative thing it might seem. I was capable of being sad and happy at the same time. At the moment, I was sad because I missed Tyler, but I was happy because of the good times we'd shared. The sadness was a reminder of the pleasure he'd brought into my life. I don't think most people realized that sadness was usually born from memories of happiness. I did and so I could be both happy and sad at once.

I topped off lunch with ice cream and hot tea. I lingered, enjoying lunch and my surroundings. I saw no reason to hurry. There was no one waiting on me at home, not even a pet. I had given some thought to getting a dog or perhaps a cat, but I remembered all too well how troublesome they could be. A pet was worth the trouble, sure, but I knew how much time and effort went into properly taking care of one. Pets tied one down, too. Right now, I didn't have to feel guilty for taking my time because no little dog or cat was home waiting on me. I was also free to take off for a few days with no worries about who would take care of a pet in my absence. I worked at home, so I'd be around a lot, but I still liked to go out and enjoy myself. I was sure I'd get another dog or cat sometime, but not soon. As much as I loved animals, I wanted the freedom of not having so much as a fish to worry about. My plants were as much responsibility as I wanted for the time being.

After lunch, I headed next door to the Dollar Tree where everything costs, yes; you guessed it, a dollar. The store reminded me of the old dime stores. There were still a few around when I was young, although they were almost a thing of the past and most items cost far more than a dime even then. I picked up some dishwasher detergent, liquid hand soap, and other necessities.

I thought about walking down to Borders, but I controlled myself. If I let myself near Borders or the nearby Barnes & Noble, I was sure to buy another book I didn't have the time to read. I preferred to patronize the little, privately owned bookshops in town anyway. I had a hard enough time keeping myself away from those. Instead, I climbed in the Shay and drove the short distance to College Mall. Other than a small section in Target, there would be no books to tempt me.

I parked near Sears and Applebee's and walked inside. I'm not entirely sure why, but I've always enjoyed walking through malls. I'm not so much into shopping as I am browsing and people-watching. The mall wasn't crowded, which wasn't a surprise since it was in the middle of a weekday in July. While there were summer sessions at IU, the population of Bloomington was far less between mid-May and late-August than it was the reminder of the year.

I walked past the food court with its offerings of Little Tokyo, Luca Pizza di Roma, and more. I purposely averted my gaze when I passed Anthony's Pets. I didn't want to see the puppies on display there for the same reason I didn't get near the humane society except to donate dog or cat food. I knew if I spotted a little puppy or kitten I might well take it home with me. My thoughts were turned from pets when I passed Abercrombie & Fitch with its enormous poster of an incredible sexy, shirtless college boy. I resisted entering. I had more clothes than I needed already.

I wandered through the mall, browsing shop windows, and checking out the few IU boys who were shopping. As I passed the entrance to Target, I spotted something I really wanted, but I doubted he'd let me take him home with me. I snapped a few mental pictures of the sexy blond college boy and continued on my way.

I had to fight myself to keep from entering Yankee Candle. I have a fondness for candles and always keep one burning by my computer as I work. I'd recently hit a candle sale and let's just say that I was stocked up for at least the next year. I needed another candle about as much as I needed more clothes.

I kept thinking about that blond college boy, at least I assumed he was a college boy, as I walked through the mall and as I drove home. It had been a long time since I'd been with anyone. I needed some companionship. Perhaps if I had a physical relationship now and then, mixed with friendship or not, I wouldn't be thinking so much about Tyler. It's not as if I lusted after him every time he was with me. In fact, I thought of him that way very seldom. Now and then, though, I noticed what an attractive young man he was. There was nothing wrong in that, but I wanted to keep our friendship platonic.

I'd never been that talented with meeting guys. I didn't drink and hated bars, so places like Uncle E's were out of the question. I wasn't about to go into College Books. I was sure to meet men there and it was only a few blocks away, but it wasn't my style at all. The name was almost misleading as it was an adult bookstore. It did say "adult" on the sign, but I always wondered if anyone went inside and got a big surprise.

As tawdry as it seemed, the internet seemed like my only option, outside of waiting for a chance meeting. I pulled up an old profile I'd used before, updated it, added a new pic, and signed on.

There were more guys online than I was expecting. I almost signed off, however, because a hookup didn't really fit with my romantic view of life. It's not like I hadn't hooked up to satisfy my sexual needs before. Waiting around for Mr. Right can get lonely. Sometimes, Mr. Right Now can be a good, if temporary, substitute. In other places, I had even made friends through hookups. Perhaps I would in Bloomington, too.

I browsed some profiles but didn't see anyone who interested me that much. I grew bored and switched over to my email. I'd been reading and answering messages for about half an hour when my computer emitted an odd buzz. One of the tabs on my browser was flashing. I clicked on in and discovered I had an email on the hookup site. I'd forgotten I left it on.

The email was simple and straight to the point. It consisted of one word—"looking?"

Did I really want to do this? I clicked on the profile of the sender. He was a good-looking young guy of twenty-three, not blond, but otherwise the equal of the boy I'd checked out in the mall.

It had been a long time. Too long. I had to admit that having such a young and attractive man interested in me boosted my ego. I emailed him back. A few messages later and Brad was on his way over.

He looked as good in person as he did in his profile. We talked a little on the couch and then I leaned in and kissed him. I'd always loved kissing. To me, it was hotter than a lot of what usually came after.

We stayed right there on the couch making out for the longest time, our tongues entwined, our hands exploring. We moved the action to my bedroom, leaving a trail of clothes behind us. I'd almost forgotten how good it felt to bring someone else pleasure. When Brad left an hour later, he had a grin on his face.

I was relaxed in a way I hadn't been in too long. I had the feeling Brad would be back and if not I could likely find someone else. I didn't want to hook up too often, but now and then wouldn't hurt. At the very least it would help me keep my relationship with Tyler platonic.

Camp Neeswaugee
Tuesday, July 18, 1989

Each week at Neeswaugee passed in a flash. The end of camp hurtled toward me. Camp was going to be over before I knew it and I didn't want it to end! Daniel was a big part of that, of course, but even if I'd never met Daniel I would not have wanted my Neeswaugee experience to come to a close.

I was still grinning over the success of my latest memo as I headed to Indian Crafts after P.I. I hadn't heard any talk about it during breakfast, but when I went to check my mail, Daniel was sitting with some other counselors in Main HQ laughing as they read my latest creation.

"I can't believe someone went into such detail. This is hilarious," Daniel said.

Revised Revised Dining Hall Schedule

By Order Of: Maj. P, Director W.S.A.
(Neeswaugee Security Agency)

In order to facilitate a more timely flow during BRC, DRC, and SRC, the following schedule is to be followed starting immediately. In the past unattached staff and staff not on duty have been allowed to eat at their own discretion. This practice is to end <u>immediately</u>! Unattached staff <u>WILL</u> adhere to the follow schedule. There will be <u>NO</u> exceptions. Attached staff not on duty will not be required to eat with their unit and may instead eat with any unit that is a multiple of their own unit. (For this purpose D&B will be considered D8) For example D3 staff may eat with D6 but not D4 or D5. D4 may eat with D6, or D8 (D&B), but not D3, D5, or D7.

BRC

7:10 Platoons 1 and 3 of D3 and 2 and 4 of D6

7:11 Athletic Dir., Nature Dir. and all Academics Staff

7:12 Platoons 1 and 3 of D4 and 2 and 4 of D3

7:13 Platoons 1 and 3 of D6 and 2 and 4 of D4

7:14 Platoons 5 of D3, D4, and D6 and Platoon 1 of D1

7:15 Camp Dir. and all Asst. Camp Dirs.

7:18 Scouting Dir.

7:27 Platoon 2 of D1 and Platoons 3 and 4 of D5

7:29 Platoon 3 of D&B and Platoons 1, 2, and 5 of D5 and D7

7:31 Water Front and Indian Lore Staff

7:32 Program and Asst. Program Dir.

7:35 Platoon 1 of D&B and Platoon 4 of D1

7:36 Platoons 1 and 5 of C1 and C2 and Platoon 4 of D&B

7:37 All previously unnamed unattached staff

7:38 Platoon 2 of D7 and Platoons 2, 3, and 4 of C1

7:39 Platoon 3 of C2 and 7

7:40 Platoon 4 of C2

DRC

The schedule for DRC shall be the same as BRC, but with the schedule inverted AND with 12 replacing 7 in the scheduled times.

SRC

The schedule for SRC shall be the same as BRC, but during PM rather than AM hours.

A drive through service for golf carts will be introduced by July 22. This will consist of a "McDonald's" type drive-through window to be placed at the rear of the mess hall. Until that time, golf carts may not be driven into the dining hall unless the driver spends an average of four hours per day sitting in the golf cart and doing nothing else. Attached staff are, of course, excluded from the drive through service as they are not allowed to use golf carts under ANY circumstances. Cars will NOT be allowed to make use of the drive through service and bikes are similarly excluded. Skateboards are eligible at the discretion of the camp director.

Those wishing to use the salad bar ONLY may enter the dining hall five minutes before or after their appointed time, but are not to deviate a greater amount of time, such as ten or fifteen minutes before the assigned time.

What really made my latest fake memo a success was when our Scouting Director stomped away from the mailboxes.

"I can't believe I've been assigned a meal time!"

I very nearly lost it when I caught sight of his enraged expression. It took a supreme effort not to laugh.

"Major, did you read the back...about the drive-through service for golf carts? If the front didn't tip you off that this is a fake memo, the back definitely should," Daniel said.

Our Scouting Director read the back and started laughing. I left Main HQ before I could give any hint that I was the illusive memo writer.

When I entered the Indian Crafts tent, a few of the kids were giving Josh, one of the D&B boys, a hard time. I never allowed any of the kids to get picked on, but something unusual was going on. Some of the boys harassing Josh were his own friends. I was about to say something when I noted the white button pinned to his shirt. It read "Master Dancer Candidate. Not Speaking."

I remembered the Master Dancer plaque hanging in the Indian Lore cabin. It was signed by dozens of boys who had been inducted into the Master Dancer Society. I'd asked about the society and was told that each summer, no more than twelve boys were initiated. It was a huge honor and only the best of the Indian Dancers could hope to have a chance at getting in. Each candidate had to endure an entire day without speaking. Then, there was an initiation ceremony that night, but it was wrapped in secrecy.

"I heard they make you swim Beaver Pond at night," one of the Division 5 boys said, speaking of the initiation.

"Last year, each of the guys woke up somewhere on campus and they didn't know how they got there. One of them woke up over at Eppley Auditorium, another on the Parade Field, and another one on the swim pier," another boy said.

"That's just stupid," another said. "There is no way they could carry guys around campus without them waking up."

"I heard it's true," yet another boy said. "I also heard they have to endure some kind of torture with fire."

The D&B boy wearing the button looked a little nervous but also like he enjoyed the attention.

"Is it true that if you say one word you're out?" one of the Division 1 boys asked. "Is it, Josh? Come on, tell me!"

"Yeah, tell us, Josh!" another of the boys demanded.

The boys surrounded Josh, trying to make him talk. They begin pushing him back and forth.

"Hey! Knock it off!" I said. "You're not allowed to touch him. If you make him talk by shoving him around, it doesn't count."

I made up that last part, but as a member of the Indian Lore staff, my words carried weight. Josh looked at me gratefully.

"I think you were given that button by mistake, Josh," I said. "I've seen you dance."

"Ohhhhh," said a few of the kids.

Josh crossed his arms glared at me. He had a frightening glare for a thirteen-year-old. I grinned, then so did Josh. He knew I was just giving him a hard time.

"You're in for a long day, Josh," I said.

He sighed.

"Congratulations on being chosen."

I reached out and shook his hand.

"Just think, by this time tomorrow you'll be a Master Dancer, assuming you survive the initiation," I said.

Josh started to speak but stopped himself. He punched the table with his fist in frustration.

"Yeah, it's going to be a long day," I said, then laughed.

I spotted a few other Master Dancer candidates throughout the day. Each was being harassed by campers and sometimes staff. It was all in fun, but I imagined the candidates just wanted to go and hide somewhere. I didn't know if I could handle not speaking for an entire day. I had a feeling I'd be ready to scream after a couple of hours of not talking.

Some of the kids inevitably went too far in trying to get the Master Dancer candidates to talk. After supper, I walked up the hill toward my cabin to find Josh, the D&B boy from my first period class, cornered by two larger guys from Division 7. One of them had pushed him up against a cabin and neither looked friendly. I was just about to intervene when a loud voice cut through the air.

"Hey! Get off him NOW!"

The Division 7 boys jerked back and looked as if they might wet their pants. I would too if Brand was bearing down on me with fury in his eyes. The tone of his voice scared even me.

"If I catch either of you guys giving Josh or anyone else trouble again, you'll be very sorry. Do I make myself clear?"

"Y-y-y-ses, sir!"

"Yes, sir!"

The boys took off. Brand spoke to Josh in a much softer tone.

"Are you okay, Josh?"

Josh nodded.

"Let me know if anyone gives you trouble. I'm very proud of you for being selected. I nominated you myself."

Josh smiled. Brand truly was a good counselor. It was hard to believe that someone so good with kids could be such a total jerk to guys his own age.

Josh departed. Brand noticed me watching. He walked over to me.

"Still drooling over me, Tyler? Oh wait, we both know you are."

Brand laughed at me.

"Just leave me alone."

"Come on, Tyler, maybe I'll give you another chance if you beg for it. You know you want it."

"Even if I was willing to beg, you'd just throw it in my face."

"Which is the only reason you're not begging for it."

"No! Do you really think I'm interested in you after what you did to me? After the way you've been treating me, and all those girls?"

"I think you dream about it at night. No, I know you dream about it."

I balled my hands into fists, but hitting Brand would've been suicide. Even so, it would almost have been worth it.

"You're such a pussy," Brand said. "You are so lucky I fucked you. That will be the highlight of your life."

Brand turned and walked away. I wanted to jump on him. I wanted to shout at him. Instead, I tried to calm myself. He was a jerk. What he said didn't matter. I thought of Daniel and I began to feel much happier.

***

The Pow Wow took place the next Monday evening, the last week of camp. Those staff members who had helped with the Council Fires and also about a hundred of the kids who had performed were invited. I went back to the Council Ring early and helped set up. As the time for the Pow Wow grew near, I volunteered to help Maj. Burrows grill hamburgers and buffalo burgers. We covered two huge grills with beef and buffalo patties, burger patties that is, and for the next hour or so, the grills required our constant attention. I only lost one patty when it slipped down into the red hot coals.

Daniel waited for me so we could eat together after the kids had passed through the line. Brand was also around, of course, but he was easy enough to ignore in the crowd. My nemesis gave Daniel and me a knowing look, as he had more than once during the summer. Since he knew I was a homo, it probably wasn't too hard to guess Daniel and I were a couple. Brand had tried to make my life miserable with his knowing looks and innuendo, but Daniel was my armor against his attacks. With Daniel in my life, Brand couldn't harm me.

Most of the kids had already moved to the Council Ring when Daniel and I began to fill our plates with watermelon, corn on the cob, potato chips, and buffalo burgers. We were able to eat together in relative peace. As we sat at one of the tables backstage, the medicine drum began to beat. Part of the Pow Wow was a dance competition for the kids. There were some pretty good prizes for the top dancers, like trophies and moccasins. One nice thing about the dance competition was that Brand was a judge. He'd be too busy to bother us or be an ass.

"I can't believe camp is almost over," I said.

"Yeah. I think time actually passes more quickly here."

"Maybe Neeswaugee is located on a temporal distortion."

"You and your *Star Trek*," Daniel said grinning.

"I'm going to really miss this place, but most of all I'm going to miss you."

I was in danger of getting way too emotional, so I tried to control myself. The last thing I wanted to do was cry.

"I'm going to miss you, too," Daniel said. "We can keep in touch, you know, and there's always next year."

"It won't be the same. I hope I can come back, but I can't stand the idea of not seeing you for all those months."

"Maybe we can get together before next summer. Where do you live anyway?"

"Bloomington," I said.

"Indiana? Illinois? Minnesota? There is more than one Bloomington, you know."

"Indiana. There are others, but Bloomington, Indiana is the only one that counts."

Daniel laughed. He seemed far happier than he should have at that moment. I was a little hurt that he was taking our upcoming separation so lightly.

"You know, I never realized until now that we never talked about where we're from. We've talked about almost everything else, but that!"

"Yeah. Where are you from? Let me guess, California, New Mexico...With my luck you're probably from about as far away as possible."

"Oh, your luck is a lot better than you think."

Daniel was grinning so broadly my heart began to race. What if he was actually close enough we could meet before next summer? What if he lived in Fort Wayne or even Indianapolis? Indy was only an hour from Bloomington.

"How much better?"

"A lot. A whole lot."

"Where do you live? Tell me!"

"Well, it kind of depends on how you look at it."

"Come on, tell me!"

I felt like a kid waiting for Christmas morning.

"What's it worth to you?" he taunted.

"I'll do *anything* you want, just tell me."

"Anything, huh?" Daniel said suggestively. The tone of his voice was so seductive just then that my mind raced with possibilities, and almost all of them involved nudity.

"Anything."

"Well, technically, I'm from Virginia."

"Technically?"

"Yeah, that's where I've lived most of my life."

"But?"

"My parents moved over the summer, so we don't live in Virginia anymore. I knew when I came here I'd never be going back to my old hometown."

"So where will you live now?"

I was incredibly impatient to get the answer.

"My dad is a university professor. He was offered a new position, so he'll be teaching at..."

Daniel paused for an agonizingly long time.

"Come on! Tell me!"

"Indiana University in Bloomington."

"Oh, my God! Are you *serious*? You're going to live in Bloomington? Please tell me you're serious. This would be way too cruel for a joke."

"I'm serious."

"Yes!" I shouted. I grabbed Daniel and hugged him before I realized what I was doing. A couple of kids on their way back to the port-a-potties gave me an odd look, but I didn't care.

"What high school will you be attending?"

"North."

"I go to North! Oh my God!"

I hugged Daniel again. He grinned from ear to ear.

"I can't believe this!" I said. "This is like something out of a novel."

"No way," Daniel said. "This would be far too big of a coincidence for a novel. No one would ever believe it. This kind of thing can only happen in real life."

"This is so incredible. Why did we never ask each other where we live before? I've been trying not to think about being separated from you. I get so sad thinking of parting I just about cry. Okay, I'll admit it; I actually have cried thinking about it."

"Me too."

"If I'd only known...but this is the best!"

"Definitely."

Brand was walking back to use the restroom just then.

"What's the best," he asked me. "Is your pimp giving you a raise or did you get a new dildo?"

I just shot Brand a look, but Daniel stood up.

"Why don't you just shut up, Brand?" my boyfriend said.

"Are you two fags gonna make me?"

I stood up too. I felt like I was standing on a grade school playground being taunted by a bully, but this was a good deal scarier.

"What did you say?" Daniel said, moving toward Brand.

"Daniel, let it go," I said as I put my hand on his shoulder.

I was terrified Daniel would get hurt. Brand could easily beat us both to a pulp.

"You heard what I said, faggot. You're Tyler's new butt buddy, aren't you? Tyler loves it up the ass. Do you pound him good?"

"Shut up!" Daniel yelled. Thankfully, no kids were around and there was too much noise from the friendship dance going on in the ring for anyone to hear.

"Are you gonna make me, fag?" Brand said as he got right in Daniel's face.

"Daniel, don't," I pleaded, while at the same time moving in. If Brand went for Daniel, I had every intention of jumping in to protect my boyfriend.

"I know what you did to Tyler," Daniel snarled. "You should be locked up."

"He was begging for it," Brand said.

"Liar."

"You'd better be careful going near Tyler's ass. He's probably taken it up the ass from half the guys in camp. Just remember. I had him first."

Brands smirk was so insufferable I was ready to slug him myself. I didn't have the chance. Daniel dropped him. My boyfriend moved so fast I didn't even know what he'd done until Brand crashed to the ground clutching his balls. Daniel had kneed him in the nuts with all his strength.

Daniel leaned down and whispered something to Brand. I never could get Daniel to tell me what he said, but it must have really been something because Brand never gave me a bit of trouble after that. Daniel and I threw away our trash and joined the others in the Council Ring.

We sat and watched the dancers as they competed. By now, I was familiar with steps like the busted bunny (which was one of the easiest), the canoe step, free-style, and double-action (one of the most difficult). I could do most of the steps.

I had taught Shane, one of the boys in my cabin, the busted bunny. He was taking Indian Dancing at the time and just wasn't getting it. His real problem was that he was self-conscious, but a little practice with me helped him get over that. He'd turned into a rather good dancer. I hoped he'd place tonight, but competition was tough. There were only three places for each of the groups—cubs, beavers, butterflies, and cardinals. It would be extremely difficult for him to come out as one of the top three cubs.

In between the competition there were giveaways. At the beginning of the Pow Wow, anyone who wanted to present a gift to someone else placed it in a large decorated box with the name of the recipient and the presenter. The only rule was that the gift had to be handmade and preferably of Native American design. A huge number of such gifts were made in Indian Crafts.

After several gifts had been given out, those who presented and received the gifts danced in a large group in the Council Ring. Daniel and I were both invited to drum during one of these dances. I should probably explain that being asked to drum is a huge honor and Maj. T himself invited us. Six of us stood around the huge medicine drum. We were not expert drummers, of course, but the beat for the busted bunny was pretty simple, basically a bump-bump, bump-bump, bump-bump. It took only seconds for everyone to get into sync. Daniel and I grinned as we drummed. It was one of those rare moments in my life when I was truly happy.

There were also a few friendship dances between the dance competitions. These started out with one boy and one girl. They danced together for a few beats, then the drummer stopped and the boy and the girl picked out a friend to join them. After a bit more dancing, each of these went and picked a friend. The group of dancers quickly grew from two to four to eight to sixteen until everyone in the stands was a part of the dance. It was not at all unusual for boys to dance with boys or girls with girls, so Daniel and I could actually dance together without anyone thinking anything about it!

After the competitions ended some two hours or more later, the scores given out by the judges were tallied and the winners announced. Shane won third place, which was incredible for a boy who had nearly dropped out of Indian Dance class.

After the awards were presented, everyone exited the Council Ring taking a small chip of wood from a large wooden bowl as they departed. We gathered in a huge circle just outside the Council Ring. At one edge of the circle the Council Fire blazed.

Maj. T spoke a few words about our summer of Indian dancing and Council Fires. I wish I could remember everything he said because he talked about friendship, memories, and how each of us would always be a part of Neeswaugee and the Council Fire program. He ended with part of a speech I remembered from one of the Council Fires, mainly because I'd preformed that part myself. "May the peace of the forest, the calm of the hills, and the stillness of the lake be with you tonight and always."

Maj. T's speech left my eyes a little watery. A few of the kids were quietly crying. Most of these were Gold Cs who would not be back again, unless they someday returned as counselors. I was a little sorry I'd never attended summer camp, but not much. I wasn't the kind of boy who would have enjoyed Neeswaugee. Things were much better as they are. Perhaps I was a good counselor because I understood those kids who didn't fit in so well. I sometimes had the feeling that I was made differently so that I could better understand and help others who were different too. In the end, most of us *were* different. It was just more obvious with some than with others.

The circle began to move clockwise and each of us tossed our chip into the fire as we passed. When the fire burned out and the ashes cooled, a few would be gathered and added to those from all the past Council Fires. In that way, all the long years mingled together.

After the kids departed, the staff remained behind and exchanged gifts in the costume shed. Most of our gifts weren't handmade and edible goodies were a favorite. Daniel and I agreed to exchange our gifts to each other in private.

When everyone went their separate ways, Daniel and I lingered. Soon, we were alone in the darkened Council Ring. Only the moonlight provided us with illumination. The soft, blue-white light made our surroundings magical.

We sat side by side on one of the bleachers. I pulled the wrist-band I'd made for Daniel out of my pocket, took his hand, and tied it in place around his wrist. The colors were muted in the moonlight, but the diamond pattern could still be made out.

"It's beautiful," Daniel said.

Then, he giggled. I had no idea why until he pulled out an identical wrist-band and tied it around my wrist.

"How?" I asked.

"I saw you working on this one," Daniel said, pointing to the beaded band on his wrist. "You were so secretive and so careful not to let me see it that I suspected you were making it for me. So, between classes, I copied your pattern, and then I made one in my cabin. I thought it would be really cool if we had matching wrist-bands. You aren't mad, are you?"

"Only at myself for not being more careful. Actually, not even at myself because I *really* love us having matching wrist-bands. It's like...exchanging rings."

Daniel nodded, then he leaned in and kissed me. We sat right there in the Council Ring and made out under the stars. As much as I loved Camp Neeswaugee, I felt as if my whole summer had been about meeting Daniel. It was if we were destined to meet. I hoped we'd be together forever, but no matter what, I intended to enjoy what we had right at this very moment.

We must have made out for half an hour. It was getting very late and camp was not yet over. Daniel took my hand and together we walked down the hill and followed the path that led through the woods and finally back into camp. I kissed Daniel goodnight in the darkness under the trees.

***

On Wednesday morning another of my memos made the rounds. I'd slipped into Main HQ the night before after reading my boys to sleep and walking along the lake with Daniel. Lt. Baer joined my table at breakfast. He had a copy of the memo with him. He read it out loud:

Counselor Buddy System
To Be Implemented Immediately!

By Order Of: Maj. P, Director W.S.A. (Neeswaugee Security Agency)

Safety is the number one priority at Camp Neeswaugee, therefore we are instituting a counselor buddy system to insure the safely our most valuable resource, the cabin counselor. As of now, this system will be implemented on a voluntary basis, but we strongly encourage all counselors to participate.

Goal:

The goal of the buddy system is to provide a safety check, similar to that used on the Neeswaugee Swim Pier. This buddy check is intended to insure that every counselor is alive and well, and has not fallen victim to accident, illness (i.e. laying in his/her bunk with bubonic plague without anyone even knowing about it), or a certain blond who is suspected of spreading venereal disease among both male and female members of the staff.

Implementation:

Each counselor who wishes to participate in the buddy system will turn in his/her name and unit number to the Chief Safety Officer of Camp Neeswaugee. Each counselor will be paired with a buddy, based on unit affiliation. If no other counselor is available within the unit, the counselor will be paired with a counselor in an adjacent unit. Counselors may also request a buddy and that buddy need not be a member of the same unit, although this is preferable. It is not necessary that the counselor be paired with the same buddy for all check-in times. A counselor can request a different buddy for each check in time, if so desired. All requests will be fulfilled if at all possible.

Schedule:

Each pair of buddies will be expected to check in with each other at the following times. It is not necessary for Buddy A to check in with Buddy B **_AND_** Buddy B check in with Buddy A. It will be sufficient if Buddy A checks in with Buddy B **_OR_** Buddy B checks in with Buddy A.

Buddy Check Times:

BRC

Mid-Way through 3 CP

DRC

Rest Period

Games/Swim

Showers

SRC

Beginning of Evening Activities

End of Evening Activities

Taps

2 a.m.

4 a.m.

Buddies need not check in with each other at the scheduled shower time, but may, instead, check in at whatever time they chose to shower. Buddies will not be required to shower at the same time, nor will it be necessary for each buddy to check in with the other during the time that each buddy showers. It will sufficient for one buddy to check in with the other while one or the other buddy is showering. Buddies are encouraged, however, to check in with each other during the shower time of each buddy, as this provides an extra measure of safety.

Identification:

Each pair of buddies will be provided with a unique set of paired wrist-bands that will be color coded and inscribed with a serial number. Specific colors will be available on a first-come, first-served basis. The available colors will include, but will not be limited to: red, blue, green, yellow, white, black, violet, puce, pink, purple, vermilion, and turquoise. Requests for additional colors will be honored if practicable.

We hope that all counselors will elect to participate in this program. We feel that the buddy system will provide an extra measure of safety to ensure that all counselors are alive and well and not lying in a ditch dead somewhere.

"I can't believe someone goes to so much trouble writing these," Lt. Baer said, laughing. "Whoever the perpetrator is, he's gotten the convoluted language of the real memos down pat."

I grinned, then laughed. It was all I could do to keep myself from taking credit, but then I so much enjoyed everyone wondering about the elusive memo writer of Camp Neeswaugee.

***

The rest of the week passed in a blur. Classes, final awards, the wrestling tournament, camp play, the final track meet, and so much more were all squeezed into those last days. I was sad Neeswaugee was drawing to an end, but my sadness would have been far deeper if I was saying goodbye to Daniel along with so many others. I couldn't believe my good luck. What were the odds he'd move to Bloomington right after we met?

Still, I felt a great deal of sadness when the last Indian Crafts class had been taught, the last P.I. given, and the last night of reading to my boys was done. I even felt a tug as we played our last softball and soccer games.

Camp Neeswaugee
Friday, July 28, 1989

All too soon it was Friday, the last full day of camp. My morning was spent making sure the boys packed up all their stuff, which wasn't easy because a good many of them were in the final swim meet that morning. Daniel stole a few moments away from his remaining campers to talk a little with me before lunch. He was carrying my latest creation.

"Is that the new one?" Lt. Baer asked. "I didn't check my mailbox this morning, but I heard some of the guys talking about it."

"Yeah, listen to this," Daniel said. He began reading as we sat on the steps of Cabin 34.

Final Camp Orders and Notes:
Maj. P, Director W.S.A.
(Neeswaugee Security Agency)

1) Before final parade, all units must arrive at the dining hall simultaneously (please ignore the Revised Revised Dining Hall Schedule).

2) You are not a real Major or Colonel, so get over yourself. Real military officers laugh at you.

3) Never ever under any circumstances should any staff member never ever wear a hat. If I see anyone ever wear a hat, I have been known to confiscate them and burn them so they cannot contaminate our camp. Hats are the devil's spawn and illegal contraband. They undermine everything I am trying to accomplish here.

4) All staff must be asleep in bed before putting the campers to bed.

5) Because counselors are grossly overpaid, we have decided to fund an extensive security force rather than pay you more money.

6) Kids getting hypothermia is okay so long as the aquatics staff gets an accurate half mile swim count.

7) Girls and boys are not allowed to associate with each other.

8) Your salary is inversely proportional to the difficultly of your job.

9) Summer camp helps finance winter school, so we have zero budget for you.

10) You must sign out if you plan to leave camp at night. We want to know where you are going, who you're with, how much you're going to spend, what you're going to buy, how much action you get, how was he/she, what pick-up lines you used.

11) We will send the SWAT team to your cabin if you forget to sign back in by order of girl's director.

12) Laundry department reserves the right to take your clothes for their own use...then charge you for the missing items at the end of the year.

13) The D&B reserves the right to change the cadence during parade to work to their advantage.

14) Dump trucks will be entering camp to make sure no one is asleep at midnight.

15) Large quantities of sugar must be served to the kids just before bedtime.

16) These rules are subject to change depending on what your daddy does for a living.

17) We are concerned of your whereabouts at 12:30am. You may however be anywhere you want between 6:50am and taps.

18) Counselors are to be treated like campers. Counselors are not to be trusted or given credit for anything.

19) There will be a meeting held approximately one half hour prior to parade to determine which divisions/wings will win the marching banner for the summer.

20) Counselors, please help keep the dining hall clean. We have installed large fans that

blow food off trays to insure that your job is not
too easy.

Both Daniel and Lt. Baer were laughing as Daniel read the memo. I was grinning.

"No one has ever figured out who has been sending these memos," Daniel said.

"I know," Lt. Baer said.

I tried not to look guilty or concerned. Lt. Baer turned to me.

"It was you."

"Me?" I asked feigning surprised.

"Yeah, you. I saw you stuffing them in the mailboxes one night."

"It was you!" Daniel said.

I nodded.

"You are a legend, Perseus. At least you will be when I finish telling everyone the truth. I think the time has come," Lt. Baer said.

Lt. Baer left Daniel and me to ourselves.

"I can't believe you are the nefarious memo writer," he said.

I just grinned.

It didn't take long for Lt. Baer to spread the word. For the rest of camp, counselors, kids, and even parents were congratulating me.

After lunch, more awards were given out and more packing completed. Parents began to arrive and carry away trunks filled with belongings and memories.

At 3 p.m., it was time for the final Garrison Parade. Division 4, along with all the others, waited under the trees near the lake until it was nearly time for the parade, then the Division leaders called out "Forward, March!" and the boys moved out in somewhat straight columns and rows. Division 4 hadn't made a bad showing on the parade field this summer, but the final parade was only taken half-seriously. Still, the boys did a rather good job marching, considering their age.

Once the boys were in place on the field, I withdrew to the stand with most of the other counselors. Capt. Fitch was our Military Officer, so the division was solely his problem now.

I watched from the stands as the Regimental and Battalion Commanders went through the routine that had played out on that parade field for nearly a hundred years. Then, the divisions began to march past the reviewing line. This was it. This was the last time that the Division 4 of 1989 would be together as a unit.

After the parade, I met up with the division near the lake and walked back with them to Division 4. The boys were dismissed and some disappeared with their parents almost instantly. Trunks and laundry bags were carried to cars and one by one the boys departed. Some, mainly those flying out to other countries and far off corners of the U.S., would not depart until the next day, but within an hour, most were gone.

Steve was the last of my boys to leave on Friday. He joined me as I sat on the front steps of Cabin 34.

"All packed?" I asked.

"Yeah." Steve paused. "Thanks for being such a cool counselor this summer. I know I gave you a lot of crap, but I had a blast."

I laughed.

"You're welcome. You did give me a lot of crap, but I think you're my favorite, after Haakon, of course."

Steve punched me in the shoulder, hard.

"I hope you'll come back next year," Steve said.

"I have a feeling I'll come back for a lot of summers. There's something special about this place."

"Yeah. It's too bad you don't live in Cincinnati. You'd make a really cool boyfriend for my brother. He's seventeen."

"Is he cute?" I asked, teasing Steve.

"Of course! He's my brother. How could he not be?"

I rolled my eyes and Steve giggled.

"Seriously, you'd be a lot better than that guy Kevin was dating when I left for camp. He's on Kevin's wrestling team so he's really muscular, but he's soooo stupid it's not even funny."

"Is he blond?"

"Yes! He actually thinks *Cheers*, *Rosanne*, and the *Golden Girls* are real. Seriously!"

"Okay, that is stupid."

"I don't know what my brother sees in him. Kevin is really smart and they have nothing in common. The sex must be incredible."

I grew uncomfortable at the mention of the word "sex." Steve noticed.

"Camp is over, lieutenant. Relax."

"It's not quite over. Even if it was, I don't go around discussing sex with nine-year-olds."

"Maybe you should. You might learn something."

I shook my head. Steve would never change.

"So...not that I'm asking about sex, but how are things with you and Lt. Keegan?"

I grinned.

"That good, huh?"

"Well, as I think you know, I live in Bloomington. Daniel's parents just moved there. We'll be attending the same high school."

"So, he's your boyfriend."

I nodded.

"I'm happy for you, lieutenant. You deserve a nice guy like Lt. Keegan, especially after that asshole, Lt. Elwolf. You should have let me kick him in the nuts for you."

"Actually, Daniel, Lt. Keegan that is, did."

"He did?"

"Yeah, Lt. Elwolf was saying some very nasty things backstage at the Pow Wow and Daniel dropped him with a knee to the nuts. He also leaned down and whispered something to him. I don't know what and he won't tell me, but Lt. Elwolf has avoided me ever since."

Steve laughed.

"I like Lt. Keegan even better now! I didn't know he was a bad ass," Steve said. He turned and looked at me.

"You *really* like him, don't you?"

"Yeah, I do. You were right about him."

"I'm always right!"

"Uh-huh."

Steve's parents pulled up. I'd met them briefly when they came to take Steve out on permit but hadn't really spoken to them. A guy my age climbed out of the car too. He had to be Kevin, Steve's older brother. Damn, he was hot!

"Thank you for taking good care of Steve this summer, Lieutenant. I hope he wasn't too much trouble."

"He can be a little trouble, but he's a good kid. I've really enjoyed having him in my cabin this summer."

"Lt. Perseus says he's coming back next year. I want to be in his cabin again," Steve said.

Steve's mom smiled at me.

I helped carry Steve's trunk and bags to his car. I couldn't help but check out his brother as I did so. He was wearing a tank top and he was ripped! He could have given Brand a run for his money when it came to looks. Steve caught me ogling his brother and grinned. He walked over to Kevin and whispered something to him. I was afraid I knew what it was. Kevin looked at me and smiled.

Steve's parents climbed back in their car. Kevin gave me a wink just before he slipped in the back seat. Steve walked over to me and gave me a hug.

"My brother thinks you're hot," he said.

"About half as hot as he is," I said.

"I'll tell him you said that. If things don't work out with you and Lt. Keegan, maybe Kevin can be a counselor next year and you guys can hook up."

I buried my face in my hands for a moment. I knew I was turning red.

"Goodbye, Steve. I'll miss you."

"I'll miss you, too, lieutenant, and I'll miss embarrassing you."

"Come on, squirt! I'm hungry!" Kevin yelled.

Steve gave me another quick hug and then climbed in the car. In moments, he was gone.

With Steve's departure, I had only two boys left in my cabin. There were only eleven in the entire division where once there had been sixty.

All the boys were moved into my cabin for the night, because it was the closest to Division 4 Headquarters. It wasn't the same, though. Out of my boys only Günter and Diego remained. Even though Fernando and Armando lived in Mexico, their parents had come to take them home and so they weren't staying the night. My pretend camper, Haakon, had gone home too. I'd packed up his stuff that morning as the boys were packing up their belongings. It was amazing how many people outside of my cabin still believed we'd had a blond camper from Norway in camp this summer. I grinned when I thought about it.

None of the counselors could leave the campus, but Daniel and I still managed a romantic walk by Lake Potawatomi. We stopped under the trees near the softball fields and gazed out over the lake.

"I can't believe it's all but over," I said.

"Yeah. At the beginning, I felt like there was so much time ahead. About the end of the 4th week, I felt like I'd been here forever, but as the end neared, I felt like I'd just started."

"Exactly. Think you'll come back next summer?" I asked.

"I hope so, but who knows what I'll be doing after high school? I haven't even picked a college yet."

"I want to come back," I said. "I came here just to see if I could do it, but I love this place. I want to keep coming back for as long as I can."

"Then make it happen," Daniel said. "You can be the next Maj. T."

"I actually miss my kids. That first night with them, I thought I'd made a huge mistake in coming here. I just wanted to go home."

"That bad, huh?"

"They were little monsters. Thank God for the advice Maj. T gave me and for *The Hobbit*."

Daniel laughed.

"Did you read them the whole book?"

"Most of it. The last week of camp I told them part of the story from memory to move it along. I read them the last chapter the final night we were all in the cabin. It's going to feel so weird to be responsible only for myself! I wonder if this is what being a parent is like? How does anyone do it?"

"Most parents don't have a dozen kids," Daniel said. "We also have the advantage of sending them home after six weeks, and we get paid."

"Yeah, I'm not used to making so much money! I know the pay isn't that great here, but I usually make about nothing so this seems like a lot."

Daniel gazed at me for a moment.

"I'm glad our goodbye tomorrow is only temporary. I couldn't stand not seeing you for months."

"I gave you my phone number and address, right?" I asked.

"Yep."

"You'd better call me by Monday or I'll be hunting for you at school!"

Daniel laughed.

"I'll call. I figured I'll be wiped out by the time I get home tomorrow, but I'll call you by Sunday afternoon. We can go grab something to eat or whatever."

"That sounds great."

We were alone for the moment, so I leaned over and kissed Daniel on the lips. He smiled so sweetly when our lips parted I couldn't help but hug him close. This is what it felt like to be in love.

***

By 10 a.m. the next morning, the last of my kids were gone. There were still three boys in the division, but they weren't mine.

I spent the morning packing my stuff into boxes and loading it in my car which I'd parked just up the hill from Cabin 34.

I experienced the weirdest sensation as I was carrying boxes to my car. I felt like I should just now be moving in instead of moving out. I really felt like camp should be beginning instead of ending.

Daniel and I had lunch with some of the other counselors and the very last of the kids in camp. The Dining Hall, like all of Neeswaugee, felt empty with so many of us gone. A certain magic still lingered, however, and I think it always will. The magic is strongest when everyone is in camp, but I think I'd still feel it even if I came here in the dead of winter. Some places are like that. The Earth never forgets what happened in a special place like Neeswaugee.

Daniel's parents came for him soon after lunch. I would have driven him to Bloomington, but his parents were eager to show him his new home and we thought it best to keep our relationship secret. We said goodbye in my cabin. We kissed each other, hugged, and then Daniel kissed me on the forehead. I grinned.

Sadness momentarily overwhelmed me as Daniel left my cabin and walked up the hill, but I reminded myself that this wasn't the permanent goodbye it would've been if Daniel lived far away. I'd see him very soon. I smiled.

I carried the very last of my belongings up to my car and then returned to Cabin 34 for a final goodbye. The cabin was empty and silent now. My footsteps echoed on the wooden floor. I looked around at the bunks, remembering which boy slept where. I missed them all and especially Steve, whom I'd thought such a brat at the beginning. I gazed up at the cabin plaque we'd made near the very end of camp. There, on a large wooden board, was our cabin photo. At the top it read, "Cabin 34 Lt. Perseus. 1989." Below was the photo of my boys and me, standing on the cabin steps. All around and below the photo were the signatures of myself and all the boys. There were other plaques nailed to walls overhead, some dating back twenty years. I wondered if our plaque would still be here twenty years from now and where we'd all be.

I took a last look around, turned, and walked out of my cabin. I climbed the hill and walked to my car. I drove through

Division 6 and down the hill past the Nature Center, the Dining Hall, then on past the Indian Crafts tent and the Indian Lore cabin. I passed the huge Camp Neeswaugee sign and then turned onto the highway and headed for home.

Bloomington, Indiana
Wednesday, July 29, 2009

Had my first summer at Camp Neeswaugee really been twenty years ago? Damn, I was getting old. I didn't feel old or even look old, but...twenty years? What surprised me the most about my ponderings of my summer camp days was the vividness of my memories. When I thought about that first summer I could not only see Cabin 34 in my mind, I could smell the scent of old wood, and hear the voices of my campers. I could hear the beat of the medicine drum and feel the vibration caused by an entire division marching in unison. I could feel the breeze coming off Lake Potawatomi and hear the plaintive call of taps. My summer camp days were over, but moments from those days was stored in my mind.

Of course, most of those memories didn't extend back twenty years. That first summer was the first of many. Steve returned in the summer of 1990 and 1991 and then went on into the Beavers and even into Winter School. He ended up graduating from the Academy. Later, he returned to Neeswaugee as one of my counselors when I was the Division Commander of Division 6. Shane, who I'd taught the busted bunny, came back in later years as an Indian Dance instructor. Diego returned, but as a counselor across the road in the Naval program. It was odd working side by side with young men I'd known as boys, but it was a good odd. After his first week as a counselor, Steve came to me and told me he was so sorry for being such a brat when he was in my cabin. Only now did he truly understand how difficult he'd made my life. I could only smile at the memories of the nine-year-old boy who'd once mooned me and flipped me off. Steve quickly became one of my best counselors. He was especially good with boys who resembled himself at that age.

A knock on my door interrupted my mental journey into the past. I opened the door to find Tyler, dressed in black running shorts and a black tank top. He was quite sweaty.

"Did you run here?" I asked.

"Yeah.

"In this humidity? Are you insane?"

"Why does everyone keep asking me that?" Tyler said with a grin. "So what are you up to?"

"I was just sitting and thinking about the past."

"Is that what old guys do for fun?"

"Just for that I'm going to mislead you so your writing will get worse and worse."

"I take it back! I take it back!"

"I forgive you, this time."

We seated ourselves at the table, but this time I served iced tea. Hot tea is the last thing Tyler needed after his run.

During this session, I spent most of the time reading more of Tyler's material and offering suggestions. I enjoyed being a mentor to him.

I tried to keep my mind on writing as we sat there, but his tank top was revealing and I found myself attracted to him I endeavored to enjoy his youthful beauty as I would a fine painting or beautiful flowers, but my efforts weren't entirely successful.

"Hungry?" I asked, after we'd been at it for over two hours.

"Oh, yeah!"

"Why don't we order a pizza?"

"Sounds great."

"Pepperoni?"

"Perfect."

"I'll order. Want to watch a movie?"

"Sure."

"Go see if I have one you might want to watch and I'll order."

I made the call and then walked into the living room.

"How about *Lords of Dogtown*?" Tyler asked.

"Sure. I haven't watched it in a long time. In fact, I've seen it only once. I really should just rent movies instead of buying them."

"Yeah, but this way you don't have to go out when you want one."

"True."

"Mind if I take a shower? I still feel sweaty."

"Go ahead; everything you'll need is in the bathroom."

"Thanks."

I busied myself in the kitchen while Tyler showered. He was once again wearing his tank top when he walked into the kitchen. His hair was damp and sticking out everywhere.

"All we need now is pizza," I said.

We walked into the living room. I slipped the DVD into the player and turned on the 47" TV and my Bose sound system. I'd previously watched movies only on my laptop, but one of my first purchases after moving to Bloomington was a home theatre system.

Tyler joined me on the couch, sitting so close our legs were touching. I wondered if Tyler was interested in me as more than a friend. Sometimes, I could almost swear... While the prospect was exciting, I hoped not. The age difference didn't bother me much, but something inside told me it just wouldn't be right. I'd learned to trust my instincts. I truly hoped he wasn't interested in me. I didn't want to hurt him.

We lost ourselves in the world of skater boys until the pizza arrived. I hit pause, paid the cute, college-age delivery boy, and carried the pizza into the kitchen. We put large slices on our plates and traded iced tea for Coke Zero. Soon, we were back in front of the big screen.

After we'd stuffed ourselves, Tyler leaned up against me. He even rested his head on my shoulder. He gave no indication of ulterior motives, however. I put my arm around him, also without an ulterior motive. It felt nice, like snuggling with a puppy. I sat there and watched the movie completely content.

Tyler sat up and stretched when the movie ended. He looked at his watch.

"I'd better get going. I'm doing some yard work tomorrow for this sadistic guy so I need to rest."

"Just be glad I've finished rearranging the furniture."

"Thank God."

Tyler stood.

"Thanks for the pizza. See you tomorrow."

"Have a good night."

I cleaned up the plates and glasses after Tyler left, feeling content but also sad at his absence. I'd quickly grown accustomed to his frequent visits. I hadn't missed someone like that in a long time. I turned my thoughts back to Daniel and our first meeting after Neeswaugee...

Bloomington, Indiana
Sunday, July 30, 1989

I walked to the Taco Bell on North Walnut, which was a very short distance from my home. I was filled with excitement and some anxiety. Some little part of me feared Daniel wouldn't be there and that my time with him had been nothing but a dream. Such a thought was completely illogical, of course, especially since he'd called not an hour before and asked me to meet him.

I entered and looked around. Daniel waved to me from a booth. I grinned as he stood and walked over to me. He was wearing black running shorts and a white sleeveless shirt with some kind of Japanese Starburst design that looked like something Ralph Macchio might wear in *The Karate Kid*. Daniel had nice arms. Mmm.

I gave him a quick hug. Two guys could do that in Bloomington without getting their asses kicked. I kept the hug brief, however, in case any guys from school were watching. Bloomington was generally progressive, but that didn't mean it was wise to be out in high school. Some of the IU boys could get by with P.D.A. (public display of affection), but high school was another world.

Daniel and I walked up to the counter and each ordered a couple of soft-shell tacos and a drink. We were soon sitting across from each other in a booth.

"I can't believe you're really here."

"Would I stand you up?" Daniel asked.

"I just mean it's almost too good to be true that you've moved to Bloomington."

"I'm so glad IU got to Dad before USC although at the time I was wishing it was the other way around. I guess fate was looking out for me."

"It's so weird seeing you out of uniform."

"Hey, I wasn't wearing a staff shirt when we said goodbye yesterday morning."

208

"True."

"You look sexy in that polo shirt. Purple is your color."

"Not too preppy?" I asked.

"It's just the right amount of preppy on you."

"It's going to be so cool going to the same school," I said.

"I'm relieved I won't be completely surrounded by strangers."

"I'll introduce you to my friends, then you'll know a few people at least. I'll show you around, too. It's not that hard to navigate North, but I got lost a few times my first day."

"So, do your friends know about you?" Daniel asked.

"That I'm a homo? No. They may suspect, but they don't know. I'm a private person, the kind who doesn't talk about relationships. I think my friends would be okay with me being gay, but I don't want to get into it with them. Besides, the fewer people who know, the better. I don't want to be known as the school fag."

"Are there any out guys at North?"

"No one has actually announced they're gay. There are a handful of guys most people think are queer, but no one is sure about them."

"So, if we kissed each other at school..."

"We'd be the talk of the school and we'd be in for some harassment."

"Would we get our asses kicked?"

"Maybe, maybe not. I'd just as soon avoid being out at school. It's not really the potential harassment or even a beat down that I want to avoid most. I just don't want everyone knowing my business. I like to keep my personal life private. I don't want to be the subject of gossip. There's so much drama at school. It's like some big soap opera and I definitely don't want to be one of the stars."

"And being out would make you one of the stars."

"Oh yeah, we're talking lead role for sure."

"Okay, I can live with that. I'm pretty open about who and what I am, but I don't mind keeping things quiet. I'm not going to lie to my friends, though. I think those closest to both of us should know the truth about us."

"Yeah, okay. Like I said, my closest friends probably suspect. They may even have me figured out. Now that I have a cute and sexy boyfriend..."

"What's that?"

"Now that I have a cute and sexy boyfriend..."

Daniel grinned.

"I like that word, boyfriend."

"Me, too," I said.

"Okay, go on."

"I want to tell my friends all about you and I can't exactly do that without coming out to them. I don't have to tell them right away, do I? I want to kind of...ease into it...wait for the right time."

"I didn't say you have to call them up now. I just meant that I don't want to feel like I'm lying to my friends."

"Yeah, I've kind of felt bad for not telling them, but then it's mostly my private business. It's never really come up. If one of them out and out asked me, I don't think I would have lied."

"I understand."

"I'm a little nervous about telling them and a little frightened, too. Not that I think any of my friends will turn their back on me, but I've just never told anyone something that private about myself."

"I'll be right there with you if you want," Daniel said.

"Thanks."

We both grinned. I noticed I did a lot more grinning when I was with Daniel.

"Do you miss your boys?" Daniel asked.

"Yes and no. I miss being around them, but I don't miss the daily struggle of keeping them in line. I definitely don't miss them knocking on my door every five seconds. It felt so good to get home, close my door, and not have anyone bother me or yell 'lieutenant.' "

"I know exactly what you mean. It feels like of weird being responsible only for myself. When I was getting ready to come meet you, I had the oddest feeling I should be rounding up my boys to come with me."

"That would have been a nasty surprise—walking in to find you and your boys waiting on me."

"Yeah!" Daniel laughed. "I thought I was still in my cabin when I woke up this morning. I panicked for a second because I thought I'd overslept and I didn't know what was going on, then I saw that I was in my own room. Even that confused me because I'm not used to my new room yet. I guess it will take a while to transition back into home life, especially since I don't know my house too well."

"I'd like to go back next year if I can," I said. "I had a great summer for the most part. The beginning was rocky, but it was a lot of fun."

"Yeah, hard work, but fun."

"Of course, not all of it was fun...getting up a little after 6 a.m. almost every day..." I said.

"Turning on the shower to discover there's no hot water left..."

"Walking into the Dining Hall to find roast beef *au juice* waiting..."

"Changing sheets after a boy wets the bed..."

"Enduring mandatory fun during orientation..."

"Freezing your ass off walking to the showers on cold mornings..."

"Mistaking mayonnaise for vanilla pudding..."

"You did that?" Daniel asked.

"Oh, yeah. It looked just the same! I put a big spoonful in my mouth and...yuck!"

"Did you ever drink the chunky milk?" Daniel asked.

"No. I don't drink milk. I just use it on my cereal. I did pour out some chunks once. Nasty."

"I almost took a slug of chunky milk, but someone called out a chunky milk alert and I checked mine. I think I would have hurled if I'd drank it."

"Ah, fond camp memories," I said.

"I wouldn't trade this past summer for anything, chunky milk and all," Daniel said.

"Me either, although I would erase Brand."

"If only we could."

"I don't get how anyone can be that good with kids but be such a total ass. Maybe he has a split personality."

"Who knows?"

"I wish I'd never noticed him and had paid attention to you from the start."

"How could you not notice Brand? Yes, he's a total dick, but damn he's hot. He'll probably end up as a model or something."

"I was hoping his fate was to become a poorly paid porn star."

Daniel laughed.

"A power bottom in prison scenes."

Daniel laughed harder.

"I wish you'd never paid attention to him, too, especially because of what he did to you, but things happen as they happen."

"Maybe it had to happen that way. I ended up with you, so Brand was a small price to pay."

Daniel grinned at me again. This time, he reached across the table and held my hand for a moment.

"Let's go for a walk," Daniel said once we'd finished our tacos. "We can walk around campus."

We refilled out drinks and walked out into the afternoon sunlight. We followed 7th Street toward IU, which was only a few blocks away. We crossed over Indiana Avenue, which always reminded me of the Monopoly game, and entered IU territory.

"There's one of the main common areas," I said, pointing to a large grassy area to our right. "A lot of IU boys play Frisbee shirtless there when it's hot."

"Mmm, shirtless college boys. Maybe we should bring a picnic and watch."

"Yeah, I like the scenery here when it's warm."

"Campus seems kind of empty."

"It is right now. There are summer courses, but there are way more students for the fall and spring semesters. They won't start arriving until mid-August. Campus, and all of Bloomington, is much more crowded then."

"Cool."

"Pretty much all the houses on the other side of the street are IU offices of one kind or another. Up on the right is the Memorial Union. It's the largest student union in the U.S. There's even a hotel and fast food places inside. It has a Burger King! We'll check it out sometime, but I want to show you other stuff today."

"What's that?" Daniel asked, pointing across the street as we drew up even with the Memorial Union.

"That's the HPER, Health, Physical Education, and Recreation Complex. There're gyms, a pool, a sauna, locker rooms, and classrooms inside. There is also a bathroom on the lower level where guys hook up."

"Have you ever been?"

"Are you kidding? I'd be way too nervous to go in there. Besides, I think hooking up in a bathroom with some guy I don't know would be gross."

"Yeah."

"But you've been tempted, right?"

"Well...I've thought about it, especially when I'm really horny."

Daniel laughed.

"I'd probably be tempted too."

"So, um...are you experienced?"

"Yeah! I go to the bathroom a lot!"

"That's not what I meant."

"With sex? Not as experienced as you."

My face paled for a moment and Daniel noticed it.

"I didn't mean that in a negative way."

"I'm sorry. I guess...I know you weren't making fun of me or insinuating I'm a slut, but...I guess I'm just kind of sensitive since you know about Brand and me. I feel like a dirty slut because of what happened."

"Tyler, you shouldn't think of what happened like that. He forced you."

"Maybe, but I've got to be honest with myself, at least a part of me wanted it."

"He still forced you and so what if a part of you wanted it? I'll tell you something. If I didn't know Brand was such a First Class Jerk, I would've let him take me out in the woods, too. I might well have done what you did. Don't be so hard on yourself. Sex is natural. We need it, especially at our age."

"I guess. So, answer my question."

"I've received and given hand jobs and I received and gave head once."

"Anyone I know?"

"No. The hand jobs were just messing around when I was thirteen."

"The blow jobs?"

"One of my friends got 'drunk' a couple years ago and wanted to blow me. I returned the favor because I wanted to try it. We never talked about it after it happened."

"So he wasn't really drunk?"

"No, not even close. It was just his excuse for doing it and so he could pretend he didn't remember it. I think it was also so he could tell himself that it didn't count."

"I've done pretty much everything I guess and all of it with Brand."

"Everything?"

"Well, all the usual stuff. There's probably other stuff I don't know about."

"So, what's there?" Daniel asked, pointing to a building on our left just beyond the HPER.

"That's the art museum. Come on."

I led Daniel into the IU Art Museum. We skipped the exhibits on the first floor and headed up the stairs.

"There is a lot to see here, so I usually just look at one part of the museum each time I visit. I want to show you my favorite exhibit and my favorite piece."

"Whoa," Daniel said as we entered the section that contained pieces from ancient Egypt, Greece, and Rome. "I was expecting paintings."

"Those are on the first floor and there are some exceptional pieces there, but I like this exhibit even better."

We wandered among Greek kraters and vases depicting maidens, nude athletes and warriors, and scenes from everyday Greek life. I loved the burnt-orange and black of the glaze on the pottery and marveled at the artistry. It was almost hard to imagine that all these things had been made over 2,000 years ago.

"This is my favorite piece in the entire museum," I said. "It's the Stele of Apolexis."

We stood before a marble gravestone. It was about a foot and a half tall and the bottom was broken off. Carved on the stele was a nude boy holding a small bird in one hand and the handle of a toy cart in the other.

"It's beautiful and kind of...haunting," Daniel said.

"It makes me wonder about Apolexis, what his life was like, how he died. This stele was carved around 400 to 375 B.C. He lived in an entirely different world. There's a whole story behind this stele, but we can only guess at it. All we have left is this fragment of a gravestone and this image of Apolexis."

"I see why this is your favorite piece. It's a gravestone, but it makes me think about life."

Daniel and I wandered among the other pieces in the exhibit then onto the Roman and Egyptian areas. We took our time and gazed at each artifact. We marveled over a small wooden model of a bakery from an Egyptian tomb and an actual sarcophagus lid that once hid a mummy; however, none of the pieces touched us as much as the Stele of Apolexis.

We left the rest of the museum for another day and headed out into the bright sunshine. We turned to the left and continued our tour of IU.

"The next building is the school of fine arts," I said. "Up ahead is the IU Auditorium. On our right is the Lilly Library."

"Looks small for a university library."

"Oh, that's the Wells Library on 10th and Jordan. It's huge. There are other libraries here, too. This is the Lilly Library where rare books are kept. They have old, old books, first editions, and even a Gutenberg Bible."

"Okay, that goes on the list, too."

We walked aimlessly around for a while. Since it was Sunday, most things were closed and the campus was practically deserted. We ended up behind the Memorial Union so I took Daniel to one of my favorite spots on campus. There was a large, wooded area bounded by Wylie, Kirkwood, and Lindley Halls on one side and Maxwell, Bryan, and Swain West on the other sides. It was known as Dunn Woods.

"It's hard to believe we're in the middle of Bloomington," Daniel said once we had walked into the small forest. I can't even see any buildings."

"Yeah, it's one of my favorite places, a forest hidden in IU."

"Thank you for showing me this."

"You would have found it yourself sooner or later."

"Sooner is better. This is my favorite place on campus so far too. We have a lot in common, I think."

"Yes, there's that being attracted to guys thing for starters." I laughed.

"That's only the beginning. Of course, we have our differences, too. I'm not so big into *Star Trek*."

"Sacrilege!" I said with mock indignation.

"I only said I'm not big into it. I didn't say I didn't like it."

"You may live then," I said.

"Great, my boyfriend is a bit psycho."

"Can you be a *bit* psycho? Isn't that like being a little bit pregnant?"

"I'm pretty sure it's not the same and I happen to like your slightly psycho quality."

We stopped and looked at each other. Daniel leaned in. I kissed him and then hugged him to me. His firm body felt so warm and comforting pressed up against me. Daniel slipped his tongue into my mouth and we made out for the longest time. When we pulled apart, we were still isolated in the woods.

We walked back the way we'd come, talking some, but mostly we walked along in silence, taking in the late afternoon warmth and enjoying each other's company. I wanted to do a lot more with Daniel than make out, but I wasn't in a rush. I wanted a lot more than sex from Daniel.

Brand and I had done *everything* by the second time we'd hooked up. I guess we hadn't done everything. I hadn't topped him for one thing. I had a feeling even suggesting it wouldn't have gone over well. Brand had this overly macho thing going on. Who knows what he would've done had I asked? The point is that Brand and I went straight to sex. There was no getting to know each other. No friendship. We just ripped off our clothes and went at it. I guess my experiences with Brand were of limited usefulness when thinking about my relationship with Daniel. It was like comparing night and day. I wanted there to be a lot more between Daniel and me than just getting off, so moving too fast probably wasn't a good idea.

"I never asked, but are you out to your parents?"

"No," Daniel said. "I don't think they'd freak out, but I'm not sure how they would react. Mainly, I just don't want to talk to my parents about my sex life or even about my sexual interests."

"I know what you mean. I don't want to talk about sex with my parents either. I figure I'll tell them eventually and if they asked me point-blank, I don't think I'd lie, but I just don't want to deal with it. I could be out to my friends more easily than I could be out to my parents."

"Same here. I think older people are more prejudiced. I've never heard my mom or dad say anything bad about gays, but I don't know what they'd think about me being a homo," Daniel said.

"Yeah, my parents are the same. I don't know what I'd do if Dad was anti-gay, except keep my mouth shut about being queer."

"Queer is such a funny word. I wonder how it came to be applied to homos. If you think about it, everyone is queer. I mean, some people collect salt & pepper shakers. I think that's kind of queer. I've known guys who memorize baseball statistics like crazy. That's definitely queer. Then there are those who think running long distances is fun. How can you get more queer than that?"

I laughed.

"I'm never going to be bored when you're around. Hey, I'm getting tired of walking. There's someplace I want to show you. Do you like coffee or tea?"

"I like tea. I despise coffee. Well, I like to smell coffee. I just don't want to drink it."

"Same here. There's a place called Soma on Grant Street just off Kirkwood. It has great drinks."

We walked over to Kirkwood and then down the street, passing Nick's English Hut and lots of little shops. We crossed the street just before reaching the Monroe County Public Library and I led Daniel down Grant for a few yards. We stepped down into Soma, which was located on the lower, basement-like level of an old building.

"It's kind of bohemian," Daniel said. "I like it."

There were lots of notices on the walls for meetings, concerts, and other events. There were little tables and chairs, as well as comfortable arm chairs such as one would find in a living room. The menu was written large on one wall in various bright colors.

"This is so cool," Daniel said, watching fish swim around inside what had once been an old television.

We both ordered hot apricot tea and took a seat at one of the little tables where we could talk.

"This is what I love about Bloomington," I said.

"Apricot tea?" Daniel asked.

"No. Little places like this. Bloomington has all sorts of little shops and restaurants that aren't usually found in towns this size. Thanks to Indiana University—there is a lot here that wouldn't be here otherwise."

"Like me," Daniel said.

"Especially you."

I reached across the table and took Daniel's hand. One could do that sort of thing in Soma. It wasn't a gay coffee shop, but it was gay friendly. Perhaps accepting is a better way to describe it. There was a couple all dressed up in punk attire a couple tables away and two girls who I thought might be lesbians seated together at another small table. The few others in Soma looked as if they were probably IU students. Everyone was friendly to everyone else; it was an accepting place.

"So how is it at North High School?" Daniel asked.

"I guess it's a typical high school, although we've always lived in Bloomington so I don't have a way to compare it. There are little cliques. You know: the jocks, the popular crowd, the misfits, the auto shop types, the nerds, the band geeks, the drama queers, the artsy crowd."

"Drama queers?"

"It doesn't mean they're actually gay. It's just a label. Some of the popular kids and even an occasional jock are part of the drama queer crowd. It depends on who's doing the current play. Of course, there are permanent drama queers."

"So what group do you hang with? Let me guess, the auto shop guys?"

"Funny! My friends and I don't really belong to a group. We're kind of artsy in a way, but we're not part of the artsy crowd. We're in-betweens. I guess that makes us boring. None of us are much involved with school activities. Occasionally, one of us might do a play or an art show, but that's about it."

"So what makes you guys artsy?"

"Shane likes to draw, but he's not involved with art club and only takes basic art classes. Lizzie writes lyrics for songs, but she never lets anyone see them. She's an odd one, Lizzie is, but she's cool. Then there's Jonah. He's a year younger than the rest of us and he'll only be a junior this year. He's the most artsy. He's a poet. The last of our little group is Thor and he's not artsy at all."

"Thor? Is that his real name?"

"Yeah. His dad is a literature professor at IU. The name fits him. You'll see when you meet him. He's kind of short, but built, kind of looks like a body builder. He doesn't do sports, though, other than the weightlifting club. The wrestling and football coaches have begged him to join their teams, but he's not interested."

"I'm looking forward to meeting them. They sound like an interesting group."

"Oh, they're interesting, that's for sure. Lizzie can be very strange at times. She'll say off the wall stuff that has nothing to do what we're talking about. Some of the kids at school call her Lizzie Borden, after the supposed ax murderer from the nineteenth century. Lizzie wouldn't hurt any living creature, though. She loves cats and anything related to cats."

"What about the others?"

"Shane is really tall, like 6'4", and he hunches over all the time like he's trying not to be so tall. He's mostly reserved, shy, and quiet, but then sometimes not. I guess it depends on his mood. He seems very withdrawn and sad sometimes.

"Jonah is really friendly. He likes everyone. He's really cute. A lot of his poetry is very dark, but then he writes about flowers and spring. He's not brooding. That's more a Shane thing.

"Thor, well, he's strong. His personality, I mean, as well as his body. I don't mean he's overbearing or dominant. He's just...strong. It's like he can push his way through anything. He's not cocky or conceited or overconfident. He's just totally sure of himself. He's handsome, but in an intimidating way. He doesn't bully anyone, but when he looks at you it's kind of scary. He's a nice guy, but he's not all that outwardly friendly."

"What about you?"

"What about me?"

"How would you describe yourself?" Daniel asked.

"Well, I'm incredibly good looking and I have an awesome body. Everyone wants to be me."

"Uh-huh, now how would you *really* describe yourself?"

"I'm quiet. I like to read. I like to write. I like to laugh. That's about me."

"If I didn't already know you, I'd want to meet you."

"Thanks."

Daniel and I smiled at each other. I couldn't wait to introduce him to my friends, but I had a feeling it would mean coming out to them—soon. I didn't think I could hide my feelings for Daniel from them and I wanted to tell them all about him! I was pretty sure I was in love.

"Um, this is really bad timing, but I have some bad news," Daniel said.

"What?"

"Mom and Dad are dragging me to Vermont for a two week vacation. Tomorrow."

"Oh," I said, my mood plummeting. "You just moved here. A vacation now?"

"Mom and Dad moved over the summer while I was gone. They've been here almost a month. They waited until I returned so I could come with them. We're staying in this old colonial inn called The Stratford. I am kind of excited, but I'd much rather stay here with you."

I smiled.

"I can't tell them I don't want to go. I kind of do want to go, but mostly I can't disappoint them."

"I understand."

"I feel guilty for wanting to go."

"You shouldn't. Staying in an old inn sounds like fun. I'm disappointed, yeah, but...we'll have plenty of time together when you get back."

I wondered if I was trying to convince him or me that I was okay with his leaving for two weeks. Part of me wanted to scream or beg him not to go, but that was childish.

"I thought about telling you first thing, but I thought that might ruin our day."

"No, this is best. I've had a great day and it's a reminder of what it will be like when you return. Things like this are going to come up. You'd better call me first thing when you return."

"You can count on it. I'll send you a postcard too."

I nodded.

We lingered in Soma, talking and even laughing. I was bummed out Daniel would be gone for two whole weeks, but I wasn't going to let that spoil our time together. Besides, he would be coming back and then we'd be together again. I could just have easily been sitting there alone, missing him, knowing I wouldn't see him for months, or possibly never again. Put in perspective, two weeks was nothing.

Daniel gave me a kiss right there in Soma and then walked me home. Despite the bad news I was happy. Maybe I'd even work up the courage to tell Lizzie about Daniel somewhere in the next two weeks. As much as I feared coming out, I was bursting to tell someone about him!

Bloomington, Indiana
Saturday, August 15, 2009

Tyler led me into Soma, a coffee shop near the library downtown. I hadn't been inside in years, not since I'd moved away from Bloomington. How many times had I hung out with Daniel in Soma? I couldn't even count.

"Something wrong?" Tyler asked.

"Oh, no. It's just been a long time since I've been here. I don't think it's changed."

"Ah, and I thought I was showing you something new."

"Someone else beat you to that long ago, but thanks for reintroducing me to Soma."

"I keep forgetting you grew up here."

"Must be all that furniture you helped me move. All that reorganization has confused your mind."

"Don't remind me."

I felt a sense of *déjà vu* as Tyler and I ordered hot English Breakfast tea and took a seat at a very familiar table.

"School starts in a week," Tyler said.

"Excited or upset?"

"A little of both. This was probably my last free summer. From here on out I'll be going to school, working, or both during the summers."

"Maybe not. I sat out almost every summer when I went to college. I took this little three week intensive session one summer, mainly to get speech out of the way."

"You didn't like giving speeches?"

"I hated it. It made me so nervous to get up alone in front of a group I was practically shaking."

"That's hard to imagine. You seem so confident."

"Well, that was years ago and before I took that speech class. We presented in front of the class so often that, after a while, nervousness became too much of a bother. Now, I could give a talk during half-time at the Super Bowl without batting an eye."

Tyler laughed.

"I also went to school in England for a summer. I studied archaeology."

"Where did you go?"

"Have you ever watched *The Haunting*?"

"Yeah."

"That's where I went to school. The movie was filmed at Harlaxton, which is near Grantham. I spent a summer there helping to excavate a Roman road and touring the country."

"That sounds awesome!"

"It was. I've loved England ever since. It also turned my love of tea into an obsession."

"I guess there is hope for me then."

"You'll survive. I loved college. It was completely different from high school. I never cared much for high school. I've never even bothered to attend a reunion. Most of the people I knew in high school just aren't important me. I...I haven't even kept in touch with those who were my close friends."

"Did you have a bad high school experience?"

"It wasn't bad. It was just...there. I was bored with most of the classes and the whole thing seemed like a waste of time. When I left high school, it was like shutting a door behind me. I've never been interested in going back and seeing what became of everyone. Don't get me wrong. I had a lot of good times and a few very good friends in high school. I had as much fun as possible. It's just that none of it really mattered to me, except my closest friends."

"I would have thought you'd be all nostalgic about high school. You're so into history and antiques and nostalgia I had you pegged as one of those guys who went to every reunion and kept in touch with everyone."

"Perhaps if I'd been a star on the football team or something I would be more nostalgic. High school would have been my glory days. My life is much better now, with an exception or two, so I'd rather dwell on the present instead of the past. I do like nostalgia, but I don't live in the past. I just bring bits of the past into the present. To me the past, present, and future is all one anyway."

"I don't know if I'll go to reunions either, but I have a few friends I want to keep after high school."

"Then you should. People slip away from you if you're not careful. Friendships can end without any big breakup. A lot of people just drift away until you completely lose track of them."

"I don't want the summer to end, but I am looking forward to my senior year," Tyler said.

"It is best to enjoy things as you go along. Too many people rush through their lives. They can't enjoy any of it because they are so eager to get to what's next."

"Not me. I'm perfectly content to enjoy my last week of summer vacation. School will start soon enough."

"Life is a lot more enjoyable with that attitude. I have things I anticipate with great eagerness, but I'm all about enjoying everything I can right as it's happening. If I don't enjoy now, what's the point? Now is always the most important time. Now is eternal."

"You sound like my dad."

"He sounds very wise."

Tyler laughed and threw a waded up sweetener packet at me.

"Dad said that people who rush through their lives are really just rushing to the end and the end is death. Who wants to hurry on to that?"

Tyler told me about some of his friends, their quirks, and what he liked about them. I was curious if he had a girlfriend or a boyfriend, or someone he was interested in, but I didn't want to ask and he gave no hint. Was his silence on the topic because he liked guys and didn't know how I'd react or was he just a very private person?

We exited Soma to be greeted by a brilliant summer's day. We'd walked instead of driving. I enjoyed strolling along by Tyler's side. He was wearing cargo shorts and a black tank top. He was a very attractive young man. Of course, I was reaching an age where youth itself was attractive. I never realized when I was young that my very youth was an attractive quality.

I lost myself in the beauty of the trees, the warmth of the sun, and the brightly colored flowers peeking out from window boxes and small gardens. A shirtless and rather well-built college boy ran past. Tyler checked him out, but I couldn't tell if his interest indicated sexual attraction or merely one guy sizing himself up against another. I was too busy watching Tyler to check out the young college hottie myself, but I wondered how Tyler would react if he noticed me giving such a guy a look of sexual interest.

I thought about the IU boy I'd had over the night before. He was the second I'd hooked up with since moving to Bloomington. He'd only stayed a half hour, but what a half hour it had been. Guys his age were so casual about sex. In fact, what we'd done didn't even count as sex to him. It was just "messing around" as he put it. If there was no insertion, it didn't count as sex. Oral counted as sex for me, but then these younger guys still considered themselves straight if they only received and didn't give head. The rules had changed. I grinned, then admonished myself for hooking up with a boy nearly twenty years younger than myself. Then again, why shouldn't I?

"What are you grinning about? You look like you're up to something," Tyler said.

"You'll never know."

"What is it? Come on."

"Nope. I'm not talking."

"You're just a little bit evil, aren't you?"

"More than you know."

We walked along, mostly in silence. Tyler looked at me now then with a mischievous grin. It was almost as if he guessed what I'd been up to the night before, but that was ridiculous.

In less than half an hour, we were walking up the sidewalk toward my home.

226

"I've been working on a new story I want you to check out," Tyler said as soon as we were inside.

"Great. I've enjoyed reading your work so far," I said.

"You aren't just saying that, are you?"

"Believe me, if I didn't like it I'd say so. Remember what I said about the beach scene in your last story?"

"You said it was dull and lifeless and I needed to bring it alive."

"Exactly. I don't hesitate to criticize. *That* should tell you that my compliments are sincere."

We spent the next hour working on Tyler's latest tale and his regrettable beach scene from his last story. As we sat there at the table, talking and drinking hot blackberry tea, the years melted away and I felt as if I was with Daniel again...

Bloomington, Indiana
Tuesday, August 15, 1989

Daniel called me the moment he returned from his vacation. He was too wiped out to come see me, but we made plans for getting together the very next day. His "I missed you *so* much" almost made up for our time apart.

The two weeks Daniel was gone felt more like two months. I hate to admit this, but I marked off the days until he returned on my calendar. I was truly pathetic. I hung out with my friends, talked way too much about Daniel, and tried to work up the courage to tell Lizzie that I was a homo. I couldn't quite manage it. The only reason I wanted to come out to my friends is so I could tell them all about Daniel. As it was, I talked about him enough they were probably beginning to wonder. I had to practically stuff my fist in my mouth to shut myself up.

All the waiting for Daniel to return paid off. When he came over the next day, both my parents were gone. I hadn't actually planned it, but I grabbed him as soon as he walked in the door and shoved my tongue in his mouth. We stood there making out for a good ten minutes. When we pulled apart, I was so worked up I felt like a wild beast.

"Nice place," Daniel said and grinned.

"This is the couch," I said, falling down upon it and pulling Daniel down on top of me. I grabbed his head and kissed him again.

We made out for a good twenty minutes on the couch. I was kind of embarrassed when I felt myself getting stiff but then I noticed Daniel's shorts were straining too. I wanted to pull his shirt off but I didn't want to move too fast.

"I like the couch," Daniel said with a grin when we ceased kissing.

We sat up and held hands. I reached out and brushed his hair back from his face.

"I'm *so* glad you're back. Tell me about your trip."

"The inn was beautiful and the innkeepers were awesome. They had this caretaker who'd been there his whole life, just well...taking care of the place. He was funny, even when he wasn't trying to be. I took a lot of walks. I wish we could have taken the trip in the autumn. The leaves would've been so beautiful then. Well, they were anyway, but I've always been fond of fall colors."

"Sounds awesome. Thanks for the post card you sent. The inn was beautiful."

"I wish you could have been there with me, but that could have been a little awkward. My parents would probably have caught us making out."

Daniel laughed.

"I can barely keep myself from kissing you again right now."

"So why fight it?" Daniel said.

I leaned in and kissed him. How had I ever survived without this?

I took Daniel on a tour of the house. I was tempted to kiss him in each and every room, but our kisses tended to go on for minute after minute so it would've been a long, long tour.

The last room on the tour was mine. Daniel looked around at the photos, posters, and furnishings as if he was examining exhibits in the Museum of Tyler. He paused in front of my bookshelves, mostly filled with Star Trek novels and then gazed at the *Star Trek IV* movie poster on the wall.

"*Star Trek.* What a surprise," he said.

I arched my eyebrow as Spock would, not knowing if Daniel would get it or not.

"Aren't you going to say *fascinating*?"

Yeah, he got it. I grinned.

"We read this in school," he said, gazing at *The Outsiders* poster on another wall.

"I read the book after the movie came out. I love Ponyboy."

"Yeah, he's a cool character. That him?" Daniel asked, pointing to C. Thomas Howell on the poster.

"Yeah. Sexy, isn't he?"

"I could make out with him, although I'd rather make out with you."

Oh, how I liked this boy.

"So you've never seen the movie?"

"No."

"Your education is seriously lacking," I said. "We'll have to do something about that."

"You have a lot of movie posters," Daniel said, moving to the next poster. "I've never heard of this one."

"Oh, you have to see it. *Breaking Away* was filmed in Bloomington."

"Really?"

"Yeah. Wanna watch it? I have it on tape."

"Sure."

We went downstairs. Before we put the tape in, I led Daniel into the kitchen.

"I'll make popcorn. You get the drinks ready. The glasses are in that cabinet."

We busied ourselves about the kitchen. I had this little daydream about Daniel and me having our own place someday. We'd live together as a couple.

"What?" he asked when he noticed my smile.

"I'm just happy you're here," I said, grinning more broadly than ever.

Daniel hugged me.

We carried a big bowl of popcorn and the drinks into the living room. I popped the tape in and *Breaking Away* began to play.

Daniel snuggled in beside me. I put my arm around his shoulders. We watched the movie and ate popcorn. I was completely and utterly content.

"I've walked by that house," I said when Dave, the main character who is obsessed with bicycle racing, came out of his home. "It's down on the corner of Lincoln and Dodds. I'll show you sometime."

Mostly, I just let Daniel watch the movie, but I pointed out some familiar Bloomington landmarks, too.

"Hey, we were just there a couple weeks ago," Daniel said, pointing to the screen later in the film.

"Yeah, that's over by the Memorial Union and the HPER."

"The street that goes to the art museum and the Lilly Library, right?"

"Yep."

We were both really into the film, so we didn't talk much while it was playing. I paused the tape during one of the scenes at the Little 500, walked over to the screen, and pointed.

"Recognize that kid in the crowd?" I asked.

Daniel got up, walked over to the TV, and peered at the screen.

"Should I?"

"That's me."

"Oh my God! You are in this movie?"

"A lot of people from Bloomington were used as extras. I was seven, I think, so I'm not surprised you didn't recognize me."

"You were cute."

I smiled. We returned to the couch and watched the rest of the film.

"That movie was really cool," Daniel said. "I can't believe Dennis Quad and all those other actors were here in Bloomington. I can't believe you were in it! Hey, did you get to meet any of them?"

"I met Dennis Christopher briefly. He was Dave in the movie. He was really nice to me."

"Did they film the race in that big Stadium on the north side of campus?" Daniel asked.

"No, they filmed it in the old stadium. It was torn down right after that."

"That sucks."

"Yeah, but most of the places where they filmed are still here. We should watch the movie again when you are more acquainted with Bloomington. I get a weird feeling watching it sometimes because there are so many places in it I recognize."

"It's really cool it was filmed here."

"Well, it's based on a true story. Way back in 1962 the Phi Kappa Psi team won the Little 500. One of the riders, David Blasé, rode more than half of the 200 laps himself and he was the one who crossed the finish line. He actually appears in the movie. Remember the radio announcer? That was him. The guy who wrote the movie, Steve Tesich, was another member of the team."

"How do you know all this stuff?"

"I looked it up and I asked around. I love the movie and I love history."

"Thinking about becoming a bicycle racer?"

"That would be a big NO. It would require way too much effort of the physical variety."

Daniel laughed.

"Hey, we still have plenty of daylight left. Why don't we walk over to campus and I'll point out some of the places where the movie was filmed."

"If walking doesn't require too much effort for you," Daniel teased.

"I think I can handle it."

"Sounds good, but let's go in about half an hour instead of now."

"Why?" I asked.

"This is why," Daniel said, pushing me onto my back on the couch. He pressed his lips against mine and we began to make out.

I forgot all about our *Breaking Away* tour as Daniel's tongue slid along mine. We kissed slowly at first. His lips were so soft, his tongue so silky. Kissing Daniel made me feel closer to him, connected to him. Making out with him felt more intimate than anything Brand and I had ever done. Brand had even been inside me, but there was no closeness, no connection, no love.

232

I began to breathe harder. I pressed myself against Daniel. I knew he could feel my arousal, just as I could feel his. I rubbed against him harder as my tongue probed deeper into his mouth. I tugged at his shorts and then stopped myself. I pulled away and leaned back on the couch, panting.

"Why did you stop?" Daniel asked.

"I was about to go too far. I wanted...I wanted to rip your clothes off."

"Who says I would have objected?"

There was that mischievous grin again.

I leaned over and kissed Daniel again. I was so powerfully attracted to him I don't think I could have stopped myself if I'd tried. I let my hands roam over the outside of his shirt, feeling the contours of his chest through the material. I ran my hands lower. I even touched him *there* and he was hard.

I began to breathe harder again. Conscious thought left me. I pulled on the waistband of Daniel's shorts. Soon, his shorts and boxers were down around his ankles. I reached out and grasped him. I began to do to him what I'd so often done to myself. I lost myself in Daniel's physical reactions to my efforts. I loved making him feel so very good.

"Tyler, I'm gonna...I'm gonna..."

Daniel moaned. I moved my hand faster and didn't stop until Daniel cried out and then slumped back into the cushions.

"I'd better get you a washcloth so you can clean up," I said, quickly turning so Daniel couldn't see my face.

I returned a minute later and handed Daniel the wet cloth. He wiped up and then looked at me.

"Tyler, what's wrong?" he asked, pulling up his shorts.

I actually felt like I was going to cry. I fought back my tears.

"Tyler?"

"I'm sorry."

"For what?"

I dropped onto the couch and stared straight ahead.

"For moving way too fast. I'm sorry. I didn't mean to...I just...I really wanted to do that, but now you probably think all I want is your dick."

"No! I don't think that, Tyler. That was great! I loved it! It was so hot the way you just did it. It felt so good."

"Practice makes perfect," I said sarcastically.

"Is this about Brand?"

"Yes. No. Maybe. I want us to be about more than sex. I don't want to be like...Brand."

Daniel took my hand.

"Tyler, look at me."

I did as he said.

"We're already about more than just sex. What have we been doing today? Talking, hanging out, and watching a movie. Yeah, we made out and you gave me a hand job but so what? Think about all the time we spent together at camp. We made out there too, but mostly we talked and spent time with each other. Remember that first day here in Bloomington when we met at Taco Bell and you took me to Soma? Remember how long we talked and how we walked around campus? We're already friends, Tyler, close friends, boyfriends. There is way more to us than sex, but there's nothing wrong with sex."

Daniel leaned over and kissed me lightly on the lips.

"We're okay, Tyler," he said.

He kissed me again.

"I've never felt this close to a guy before," I said.

Daniel kissed me once more.

"I'm in love with you, Tyler Perseus."

"I love you too, Daniel."

He kissed me more deeply. I kissed him back and felt instantly aroused again. Daniel pushed up my shirt and kissed my stomach. I couldn't believe that felt so sexy!

Daniel didn't stop there. He pulled down my shorts and my boxers.

"Daniel, are you sure you want to...ohhh."

I leaned back and closed my eyes but then opened them again because I wanted to watch. The sensations were almost too intense to handle. Daniel's hand felt so good as it moved up and down. I panted and moaned.

"Daniel, I'm about to..."

I moaned. Daniel moved his hand faster. I moaned louder and collapsed back into the cushions just as he had.

"I feel so good," I said.

Daniel grinned at me and then kissed me.

"No more guilty thoughts, okay?" he said. "Sex is a part of *us*—just like all the rest."

I nodded. I did feel a lot better. After I'd touched Daniel's cock I'd felt like a dirty slut, but not anymore. I loved him. I wanted to be with him in every way.

"That was intense," I said.

"Now, how about that tour?" Daniel asked. "I was thinking we could ride our bikes. It would be kind of like being in the movie."

"Okay, but no racing."

"I'll run home and get my bike. I'm coming straight back here, okay?"

"I'll be waiting," I said.

I thought about what Daniel had said while I cleaned up and waited for him to return. He was right. We were about a lot more than sex. Other than making out, what we'd just done on the couch was our first sexual experience together.

I needed to forget about what happened with Brand, or at least not let it interfere with my relationship with Daniel. They were completely different kinds of relationships. With Brand, it was just sex, at least for him. He didn't care about me. Daniel did. That made all the difference. Daniel told me he loved me and I knew he meant it. This time, the relationship wasn't a one-way street. Brand had used me, but Daniel cared as much about me as I did him.

I went out to the garage and pulled out my bike. I waited under the shade of a large oak tree for my boyfriend.

My boyfriend. I loved the sound of that!

Daniel soon arrived and we began riding our bikes toward Indiana Avenue.

"We'll skip Assembly Hall on 17th Street since you've seen it before. First, I want to take you to a spot where Dave rode his bike near the very end of the movie. You'll recognize it when we come to it."

We rode along with the wind in our hair. I grinned. I was content as long as I was with Daniel.

"Dave made a very impressive Italian," Daniel said. "I would totally have believed he was from Italy."

"I thought he was really sexy when I met him, Dennis Christopher that is, who played Dave."

"You thought a guy was sexy when you were seven?"

"Yeah, I had crushes on boys then. It wasn't a sexual attraction like now, but...being around certain boys excited me and made me happy. I was kind of overwhelmed meeting a real actor, too."

"I'm jealous, especially after watching the movie."

We turned onto Indiana Avenue and rode south until we reached 10th Street. We headed east. After about three blocks I pointed to the south.

"Down there is the Memorial Union and the HPER that I showed you before."

"Oh yeah, where those IU guys in the movie were driving that Mercedes Convertible and the Cutters were driving backward."

"Yeah."

We sailed past the outdoor track and up to the Wells Library.

"That's the main library I told you about," I said.

"Yeah, that's more the size I was thinking about. Wasn't there a scene just outside the library? I can remember Dave and his dad talking about college."

"It sure looked like a library. I guess it was this one, but I'm not entirely sure. Like I said, IU has several."

We turned on Jordan and pedaled south. We passed the Drama and Theater Center on our right and soon after Daniel spotted the location that was our destination.

"Hey, I remember this! Dave rode his bicycle right down the hill here, right past the circle."

"Yeah, it's the only spot that looks like this in Bloomington. Well, the only spot near IU."

We kept riding, past the Musical Arts Center on our right and then Read Hall on our left. We turned right on 3rd Street after riding between the Music Library and University Apartments West. When we neared the greenhouse at the edge of Jordan Hall, I didn't even have to point it out.

"I remember that greenhouse. Dave raced by it on his bike when he was chasing down Katrina on her scooter. Hmm, raced."

Daniel took off.

"Hey!" I said, then shot after him.

Daniel raced along faster and faster. I struggled to catch up. Finally, I managed it. Daniel grinned and slowed down. We were even with the Delta Delta Delta sorority house.

"Isn't this where Dave was sitting on the steps when he started yelling 'The Italians are coming!'?" Daniel asked.

"Yeah."

"It's really cool seeing all these places that were in a movie."

"We'll skip the courthouse and the corner of North Walnut and Kirkwood right by it. That's where Dave ran the red light. I'll show you the house where Dave lived some other time. It's several more blocks south."

"Maybe we should take up racing. We could get a couple other guys, form a team, and enter the Little 500."

"Are you *serious*?" I asked.

"No."

"Thank goodness. You had me scared for a moment. It will be exhausting enough just pedaling home. I have an idea: let's grab a bite to eat at Jimmy John's."

"Jimmy John's?"

"It's like Subway, only better. Come on."

We turned north on Indiana Avenue, rode to the official entrance to Indiana University, and then turned left on Kirkwood. Jimmy John's was a couple blocks down. It was a small place, with only a few tables, but the sub sandwiches were great and I liked the red, black, and white décor. We parked our bikes outside and walked in.

We browsed the menu on the wall. I ordered an Italian Night Club and Daniel got a Billy Club.

In a very short time we sat down at a small table with our sandwiches and our Cokes.

"You're not going to start speaking with an Italian accent like Dave, are you?" Daniel asked.

I wanted to answer with an Italian accent, but I thought it wise not to attempt it. I'd just make myself look foolish.

"Just because I ordered an Italian Night Club? I don't think so. Besides, I couldn't handle listening to that music Dave was always playing."

"School starts in a few days. I'm going to feel so strange," Daniel said, changing the subject.

"I'll be there. I've already told my friends about you and they're eager to meet you."

"That will make things easier, but moving to a new school is kind of intimidating, especially my senior year. I'm more excited than anything, though. This is my chance to start over."

"Oh, so you had a bad reputation at your old school, huh? You were a bad ass, weren't you?"

"About as much of a bad ass as you." Daniel grinned. "It will just be nice knowing that no one has any preconceived notions about me."

"This is your chance to pretend to be a foreign exchange student or perhaps a spy..."

"I think I'll just stick to being me—much easier!"

"Good choice. I'm rather fond of the real you."

"Have you told any of your friends about us?" Daniel asked.

"Well, no. I tried telling Lizzie while you were gone, but I couldn't make myself do it. It's a lot harder to say the words than I thought it would be and I wasn't anticipating it would be easy."

Daniel nodded.

"I don't want to push you. They are your friends, after all, but I'm hoping they'll become my friends too and I don't want to lie to them."

"I know. I don't want to lie to them, either. I think they may be figuring things out, anyway. I talked about you a lot while you were gone. A whole lot."

"You did, huh?"

"Yeah, I'm so excited about us that my mouth ran wild. I'm pretty sure that Lizzie, at least, is suspicious. I don't know, maybe subconsciously I want to say too much so I won't have to out and out tell them I'm gay. I guess part of me just wants them to figure it out for themselves.

"As for everyone else, I think we should keep us a secret. I don't think there would be serious trouble. I could be wrong, of course, but I think things wouldn't go much beyond verbal abuse. I don't know, though, people get weird when it comes to stuff like this. They're irrational."

"Well, just tell your friends when you're comfortable with it. Until then, we'll keep them in the dark. I'm not going to lie if they ask, however, and I'm not going to pretend I'm interested in girls."

"Fair enough. The same goes for me. I really want to tell them. I'm just scared. It's going to be very difficult to keep them in the dark. I keep wanting to tell *everyone* about you."

Daniel grinned.

"Does this mean no making out at school?"

"Um, no. I mean yes. No making out at school."

"What about head?" Daniel teased

"Definitely no head," I laughed.

"That would shock a few people, wouldn't it?" Daniel said.

"Get us expelled as well. Schools are so touchy about sex in the halls for some reason."

"Yeah, weird," Daniel said.

Daniel and I finished our sandwiches and then we rode around downtown, pointing out spots we remembered from the movie.

"Remember this place?" I asked as we paused in front of Opie Taylor's.

"Should I?"

"It was in the movie."

Daniel studied the restaurant.

"The location seems familiar, but the restaurant..."

"This was the pizza place in the movie."

"Wow, it's changed a lot!"

"Yeah, but the guys were right here, eating pizza out front."

We explored the town square further.

"Stay right here for just a minute," Daniel said as he stopped in front of one of the shops on the square.

"Why?"

"Just stay. I'll be right back."

I shrugged as Daniel disappeared into a shop that looked as if it sold a bit of everything. He returned shortly with a bouquet of purple carnations.

"These are for you," he said.

"I love flowers!" I said. "No one has ever bought me flowers!"

"Until now," Daniel said.

I hugged him and then had to fight the impulse to look around to see if anyone had noticed.

"Thank you," I said, smiling.

"You're welcome."

We rode home. I clutched the bouquet in one hand. I couldn't believe Daniel had brought me flowers! How long had I dreamed about having someone like Daniel in my life? I guess sometimes dreams do come true.

Bloomington, Indiana
Friday, August 21, 2009

A knock at the door ripped me away from the film I was watching, and just at the very end, too. I hit pause and answered the door.

"Oh, hey, Tyler. Come on in."

"What'cha doin'?"

"Watching a movie."

Tyler joined me on the couch.

"*Breaking Away*. That is my dad's favorite movie. He's showed me all the locations in Bloomington used for filming."

"I'm almost to the end, so if you don't mind, let's watch the rest of it."

"No, that's cool. I like it."

I hit the play button; the Little 500 was down to the final lap. I'd watched the movie a few times over the years, but the race always thrilled me, as if I wasn't sure who would win each time.

We watched the last few minutes of the film, then I turned it off.

"So, are you a big *Breaking Away* freak like my dad or is this the first time you've watched it?"

"I'm somewhere in between. I've watched it a few times. I don't qualify as a *Breaking Away* freak. It's not *Star Trek* after all."

Tyler rolled his eyes.

"I'm relieved. Dad even knows *Breaking Away* trivia. It's frightening."

"Yes, that is scary. He should stick to important things, like *Star Trek*. Did you know that Captain Janeway will be born near Bloomington in the future?"

Tyler threw his head back and banged it against the back of the couch in frustration.

"Now you're just making things up," he said when he looked at me once more.

"No, just watch *Voyager*. Captain Janeway said it herself. That's why I returned to Bloomington, you know."

"Huh?"

"I'm here to make sure her great, great, great grandparents meet. Otherwise, the future will be altered."

"O-o-o-k-a-a-y, I'm going to make a call now and some nice men will come with a special jacket for you to wear. They'll take you to a nice, comfy, padded room."

I laughed.

"You're very, very strange sometimes," Tyler said.

"We've been through this. I'm a writer. Of course, I'm strange."

"True. Now, get up and get dressed."

"Why?"

"Because I'm not going to be seen with you while you're wearing those sweat pants. I have a reputation to keep up, you know. I'm taking you out to supper."

"You're taking me?"

"Yes. Happy Birthday."

"How did you know?"

"I searched the internet."

"You know, I once had a private life."

"Yeah, yeah, you can tell me your sad writer story later. Go change, I'm hungry."

I changed into clothes that wouldn't embarrass Tyler, and we walked out to my roadster. He directed me downtown and then told me to turn right on 8th Street.

"It's up on the right," Tyler said.

"Bloomingfoods? I hate to tell you, Tyler, but this is a grocery store."

"It's a market and deli."

"I'm just messing with you. I used to come here when I was your age."

Bloomingfoods was like an old fashioned grocery store. It featured organic and locally grown products as well as a little salad and deli bar with all natural ingredients. Tyler led me to the deli bar and we grabbed plates.

I chose some ziti with sun-dried tomatoes and parmesan, along with cooked apples, and a few large green olives. I also dipped out a small bowl of cream of potato soup made with heavy cream. Tyler built himself a salad with delicious looking greens, croutons, and cheese. We took a seat at one of the small tables near the windows.

"I haven't eaten in here for years," I said. "I've been meaning to come in since I moved back, but it's hard to get around to everything."

"I'm glad I brought you then. I thought it would be different."

"It's wonderful."

"You've been doing a lot for me and I just wanted to say thanks."

"You mean making you slave away in my yard and torturing you by moving my furniture over and over?"

"Nooo. I mean all the other stuff. You don't treat me like a kid, for one thing."

"You're seventeen, not seven."

"Yeah, but you treat me like an adult."

"You are, or at least you're very close."

"I like how you listen to my ideas and my thoughts just like you would any adult."

"It isn't necessary to be an adult to possess wisdom. I learned a lot of things from my kids back in my camp counselor days. They may have taught me more than I taught them."

"I've just never had an adult, except my dad, treat me like you do. I appreciate it."

"It's no more than you deserve. You're intelligent, witty, and perceptive."

"Wow, I am pretty incredible. Aren't I?"

"Don't get too pleased with yourself."

Tyler laughed.

We sat and ate and talked and enjoyed the atmosphere of Bloomingfoods. I almost wished we'd sat at one of the small tables out front, but the atmosphere inside was like that of a small café.

"I love places like this," I said. "This is a wonderful birthday present."

"Well, you definitely didn't need another book."

I smiled.

We took our time and enjoyed ourselves. When we'd finished, Tyler told me to stay put. I sat gazing out the window at passersby.

"Happy Birthday," Tyler said. I looked up. He set a slice of raspberry cheesecake before me and put another at his place.

"You are spending way too much money on me," I said.

"It's okay. I've got this great part-time job. I work for this guy who overpays me so I have plenty of money."

I smiled again.

Once again, I was reminded of Daniel all those years before. We'd even sat at this very same table once, shared supper, and watched everyone walking by. Sometimes, I felt like I'd stepped back in time.

We didn't go straight back home after supper. Instead, Tyler directed me toward IU and had me park near the HPER.

"Where are we going?" I asked. "You're not going to force me to play basketball or take part in some horrible athletic ritual that involves sweating, are you?"

"Do I look like someone who enjoys torture? You'll see where we're going."

Tyler led me past the HPER and around the north side of the building, by Woodlawn Field, where there was an outdoor running track.

"Here we are," Tyler said when we reached the Arboretum.

I'd walked there before, of course, but only during the day. It had grown late enough that the evening shadows were falling. It made the paved walks and open spaces in the Arboretum almost magical, like some kind of Elven garden out of a story.

I had some very sad memories attached to the Arboretum, which is one reason I didn't go there often, but I had plenty of good memories about the green lawns and the trees, too. As always, I focused on the positive.

"It's beautiful," I said.

The Arboretum was a more open area than it sounds, with more grassy areas than trees. It was more park than Arboretum and yet the trees were a focal point. During the day, it could be rather crowded with students passing between the HPER, Wells Library, classrooms, and dorms. The students were only now returning to IU for the fall semester and at this time of the evening there was almost no one about.

The pond in the center of the Arboretum was quiet and still. The tall red clock we walked past enhanced the park-like atmosphere. Tyler and I wandered aimlessly. After a while, we left the paths and walked down to the pond and sat upon the grass near the cattails. It had been in this very place, years before that...but I didn't want to dwell on the past. The most important time was always now.

Tyler sat right beside me and leaned his head against my shoulder. I wrapped my arm around him. Conflicting emotions surged through me. Tyler had become almost like a son to me in many ways and yet...and yet a part of me wanted him to turn his face toward mine and kiss me.

Tyler sighed and I squeezed his shoulder in a one arm hug. I did have feelings for Tyler, but I wasn't quite sure what they were. There was the age difference, too. Then again, what did that matter? Some thought it mattered a great deal, but then someone could always be found to object to anything. I thought of the writer, Christopher Isherwood and the love of his life, artist Don Bachardy. There was a thirty-year age difference between them. Isherwood was older than me when they met and Bachardy was only sixteen. That was back in the middle of the last century! It was a relationship that lasted until Isherwood's death some thirty years later.

I still hadn't figured out if Tyler was drawn toward males, females, or both. Mostly, I just hadn't thought about it, but when I did I was uncertain. My own feelings toward Tyler were conflicted. Maybe I just needed to find myself a boyfriend. I couldn't play with the college boys forever.

Tyler's body felt so warm against mine. I caught the scent of his cologne on the breeze. He stirred and raised his head. He turned to me and smiled. He was so very handsome. I leaned in to press my lips to his but hesitated. I read confusion in Tyler's eyes. I hugged him to me instead, then drew back.

"Thank you for a wonderful birthday," I said, but then I sighed.

"You don't sound like you've had a wonderful birthday."

"I have. It means a lot that you did this for me. It's nice to be remembered."

"But?"

"I'm a little sad and a little lonely."

"Why?"

Should I confide in him? I pondered this for a few moments only.

"It's been a while since I've dated. I don't have anyone special in my life...not special like that."

"Percy...you don't have to answer this, but...do you like guys?" Tyler hesitantly asked me.

There it was. The question.

"Yes," I said.

I waited to see what would happen. I hoped this wouldn't change things between us.

"I kind of figured you did. Some of your artwork and your books...and then I've seen you check out college boys." Tyler grinned.

"Does that bother you?"

"No. I just wanted to know. It's really none of my business, but if you're sad and lonely, it helps to know what sort of someone might interest you."

I very nearly said "someone like you" but that could have been taken quite wrong. Tyler was still a mystery to me. I almost asked him about his sexual orientation, but he'd tell me when he was ready.

"I haven't had many serious relationships. Finding someone is always on the edge of my mind, but I don't think about it much. Most of my boyfriends have been nice, but...not *special*, or at least not special enough."

"Most. That's means there was at least one who was special enough, right?" Tyler asked.

"Yeah, one and only one, but that was a very long time ago."

"You still think about him?"

"All the time."

"Why don't you call him or email him or is he..."

"I don't know where he is. I lost him long ago."

"I think there's a story here. Tell me?"

"I don't know, Tyler."

"Please?"

"It's a rather long story."

"So tell me part of it now. You can tell me more later. It can be like a miniseries."

I laughed.

"I don't know if you'll find it that exciting."

"It doesn't have to be exciting. Everyone loves stories and especially love stories. You did love him, didn't you?"

"I still do," I said, as a single tear slid down my cheek. I don't cry easy and the tear took me by surprise. There was no warning. It just happened. I guess it was the combination of thinking about Daniel while sitting right by the pond where...but I didn't want to think about that just now.

"Wow. He must have really been something."

"Oh, he was."

"Tell me. Please?"

"Let's walk while we talk," I said.

We stood and walked away from the pond. I began telling Tyler my story.

Wait," Tyler said, stopping me. "I thought your name is Percy."

"I go by Percy because that's the name I've written under for years, but my name is actually Tyler."

"Wow, we share a name."

"Yeah. So do you want to hear my story or not?"

"Yes! Go on, Percy... or Tyler." Tyler grinned.

I told Tyler about meeting Daniel, how I'd ignored him at first, about Brand (minus the gory details), about how Daniel was there for me, and how Daniel and I fell in love. Tyler looked most thoughtful at times, almost as if he was going to say something, but he remained silent.

We were back home long before I finished telling Tyler about my first summer at Camp Neeswaugee. I continued the tale while I made us hot Yorkshire tea. Tyler produced a small birthday cake he'd somehow snuck past me when he'd arrived earlier. It was even decorated with roses in my favorite color, purple.

I had some vanilla ice cream in the freezer so we sat and ate birthday cake and ice cream while I told my tale all the way up to the first day of school at Bloomington North back in 1989. Tyler grinned a lot while I was talking, as if he was about to do something sneaky.

"Are you sure you want to hear the rest of this tonight?"

"Oh, yeah. You keep talking. I'll keep eating cake and ice cream. You just think I bought this cake for you. There probably won't be any left when I go home." He grinned.

"Hmm, I think you're getting the better end of this deal. I thought it was *my* birthday."

"Yeah. Yeah. So what happened next?"

North High School—Bloomington, Indiana
Monday, August 21, 1989

"Is this him?" Lizzie asked, gazing at Daniel as he and I walked toward the entrance of the school together. Daniel had met me at my house so he could ride to school with me.

"This is him," I said.

"I'm Lizzie. So, did Tyler say anything mean about me?"

I opened my mouth in mock surprise and put my hand to my chest.

"Me? Saying something mean? About you?"

Lizzie rolled her eyes.

"He, um, said you're one of his best friends and you love cats. I didn't know there was going to be a quiz."

Lizzie grabbed Daniel by the sides of the head. I think he was afraid she was going to kiss him. She pushed his hair back and stared deeply into his eyes. I was glad I'd warned Daniel that Lizzie could be dreadfully strange at times. She stood back. Daniel gazed at her, bewildered.

"I think you have Elven blood in you."

"Elven?"

"Lizzie believes Elves lived here a very, very long time ago," I said.

"Hundreds, perhaps even thousands of centuries ago, but they were here," Lizzie said. "I saw it in a vision."

"Interesting," Daniel said, without a trace of sarcasm. That's something I loved about Daniel. He never wanted to make anyone feel less than positive about themselves.

"Don't think I'll forget that you said I *believe* Elves lived here," she said, giving me a smack on the chest. "I'll see you later, Daniel."

I rubbed my chest where Lizzie had hit me as we went our separate ways.

"I like her," Daniel said.

I could tell from the tone of his voice he meant it.

"She can be rather bizarre at times."

"I like someone who has the courage to talk about Elves to someone she just met."

"Yeah, but as if they were real?"

"Maybe they are," Daniel said.

"You just like the thought of being descended from them," I said.

"Okay, prove to me Elves don't exist."

"I can't do that."

"See?"

"This means nothing. Have *you* ever seen one?"

"No. I've never seen Mexico either, but I'm pretty sure it's there. The point isn't whether Elves exist or not, but that Lizzie believes they did and isn't afraid to say so. I like that."

"You're just a little bit odd, too," I said, smiling.

"And-you-like-that," Daniel said, poking my chest lightly with his finger for emphasis.

"Come on, I'll show you to your locker," I said. "It's very close to mine."

Daniel and I had already received our schedules and locker assignments through the mail a few days before class. His locker, 234, was only a few lockers away from mine, 246.

We both tried out our combinations, just to make sure they worked, then closed our lockers. We'd be receiving our texts in our classes, so we didn't have much to put in our lockers yet.

"Now, I'll direct you to Biology II," I told Daniel as we began to walk down the hallway.

Daniel and I shared classes three out of seven periods, which wasn't bad. First period, we both had Biology II. Fourth period we had English Literature and Composition. Seventh period, which was the last of the day, we both had art history. We were both in Honors Government, but not during the same period. Most importantly, Daniel and I shared our lunch period, which was right after fourth period.

Daniel seemed quite at ease. My presence probably helped some. Even one familiar face in a crowd of strangers can be a relief. I have a feeling Daniel would have gotten along quite well even without me. He was friendly, good looking, and didn't possess any oddities that would make him a target. The fact he had a boyfriend was an oddity, but no one could tell that just by looking at him.

Daniel's looks were a major asset. Not that Daniel was gorgeous, except perhaps to me, but he was good looking and looks are important to high school students. It shouldn't be that way, but people were nicer to you and much less likely to cause you trouble if you are attractive. It was yet another part of the pecking order. I tried to remain aloof from it, but I know others judged me by my looks, too. I couldn't do anything about that, but I wasn't going to base how I treated someone on their looks. Okay, I guess sometimes I was nicer to guys I thought were hot, but I tried to be kind to everyone, regardless of how they looked, how they dressed, or how much money their parents had in the bank.

Biology wasn't my thing and yet it did sound interesting. I have to admit my mind was more on Daniel than it was on receiving my text book and listening to what we'd be discussing in class. It still amazed me that Daniel, formerly Lt. Keegan, was sitting right next to me in North High School!

Daniel and I dropped off our text books after first period. Our next classes were in entirely different parts of the building, so I gave him directions and told him I'd see him fourth period. I wanted to hug him and give him a quick kiss so bad. I actually thought of doing it, but I wasn't quite brave enough. Daniel and I smiled at each other and that was enough.

I had Pre-Calculus/Trigonometry next. Math wasn't my thing either so this was not likely to be one of my favorite classes, but then again I didn't mind math too much. I was glad I had it early in the day, both so I could get it out of the way and so I'd be a little sharper.

Even though Daniel and I didn't share the class, he was still in my thoughts. I knew he was in the building and that we'd be sharing two more classes and lunch together. I'd probably see him in the halls now and then, and he *was* riding with me. Senior year was going to be vastly different from the previous years and it had nothing to do with the fact I was a senior. I hadn't exactly felt alone before, but now I felt connected. Daniel and I *were* a couple. I was half of a pair and not just me anymore. I liked that feeling.

Maybe I was lonely before and just didn't know it. When I thought back to myself in previous years, I seemed lonely compared to now. I definitely didn't know what I was missing. Then again, I didn't feel lonely, at least not much, so I guess I did okay. I guess there was no reason to analyze it. Like everyone, I had my ups and downs, but I was generally happy.

Periods between classes and lunch became far more significant than in the past. It was then that I did, or at least could, see Daniel. The merest sight of him made my chest swell with happiness.

I didn't spot Daniel between second and third period, but I lingered by my locker after third and caught him so I could walk him to our English Literature and Composition class. Once more, we sat beside each other. Daniel brought North High School alive. He made the monochrome world of high school burst into color.

"How was your first morning at North?" I asked as we walked to our lockers after class.

"Great! I got lost on the way to third period, but this jock-type stopped and asked if I needed help. The jocks at my high school were usually jerks, but this one gave me directions."

"I think we have a few jerk jocks here, too, but a lot of them are actually pretty cool. Just don't tell them I said that. Most of them are conceited enough with all those muscles."

"Muscles," Daniel said and gripped my bicep.

I had to fight myself to keep from pulling away. I was too uptight. It wasn't like he'd kissed me, although a part of me wanted him to kiss me soooo bad.

We dropped off our books and headed for the cafeteria. The line wasn't too long, but it didn't matter because Daniel was with me. I could talk to him for hours.

"Burgers, fries, applesauce, carrot sticks, and a no-bake cookie," I said. "This is a promising start."

"Are the burgers good here?"

"They're definitely not Hardee's quality, but then Hardee's doesn't have to prepare hundreds of burgers in an hour or two. When you think about how many meals the cafeteria staff has to prepare, it's kind of amazing we aren't stuck with peanut butter and jelly sandwiches every day."

"Yes, but we have to complain about the food. It's tradition."

I looked around as we came out of the line. Lizzie and Jonah were sitting off in the corner at a round table. We headed in their direction. Lizzie didn't even look up from her book as we arrived, but Jonah smiled.

"Jonah, this is Daniel."

"Tyler has been talking about you non-stop," Jonah said.

Daniel gave me a mischievous grin.

"Tyler told me about you, Jonah. He was right. You are cute."

I could not believe Daniel said that.

"Thanks," Jonah said, with a grin that was on the verge of becoming a laugh.

"So, you're a poet?" Daniel asked.

"Yeah, I like to get my feelings down in words when I can. It helps me figure things out. I just like writing poems, too."

"I'd love to read some sometime, if you'll let me."

"Sure. I'm not secretive about my poems like Lizzie is with her lyrics. She won't let any of us read them. Isn't that right, Lizzie?" Jonah said.

Lizzie completely ignored him, if she heard him at all.

"Lizzie often gets completely immersed in a novel," Jonah said, gazing at the cover of *Pride and Prejudice* which she was reading. "I thought she'd read all the Jane Austen novels, but maybe that's one of her favorites. She's not being rude if she ignores you. She's just being Lizzie."

Shane joined our table. At 6'4", he towered over us all before he sat down, even though he was slightly hunched over, as always. When I introduced him to Daniel, his only response was "hey." Daniel didn't attempt to draw him out. I'd already told him Shane tended to be shy and reserved.

Thor was the last to arrive. Where Shane was the tallest, Thor, along with Lizzie, was the shortest. He stood at 5'9". Daniel's eyes widened when he caught sight of Thor, or more specifically, Thor's body. He had the broadest shoulders in school and his chest...damn. The first time I saw him without a shirt I totally gaped at him. It's a wonder I didn't out myself right then and there. It was our freshman year. Thor had shot me a look, which intimidated the hell out of me, but then any look from Thor was usually intimidating. It's just the way he looked at people.

"Hey, Thor," I said. "This is Daniel."

"'Sup?"

"Nice to meet you," Daniel said, fighting to keep his eyes on Thor's face instead of his chest.

"This is the whole gang," I said to Daniel.

"I'm the most talkative," Jonah said.

"Sometimes we can't shut him up," Thor said.

"Thor doesn't usually say much until he's finished eating," Jonah said.

Thor just stared at Jonah for a moment. If I didn't know Thor, I would have taken his gaze for a death threat, but I doubted he was even mildly annoyed.

Thor had two lunches piled on one tray. That was his usual lunch. I guess it took a lot of fuel for that body.

Daniel and Jonah hit it off. I was almost a little jealous. Jonah's sexual orientation had yet to be revealed and he was definitely cute with that long shaggy brown hair and sexy brown eyes. I'd read some of his poems, but they were unrevealing. A lot of his poetry was very dark, a complete contrast to his personality. From those poems, I'd picture him as an Edgar Allen Poe type who dressed all in black and was always thinking about death. Jonah was nothing like that. If I had to describe him in one word, that word would be "boyish."

"Hey, Thor. We'd really love it if you came out for football this year. We could use you, man."

Thor looked up. One of the North football players was addressing him.

"Not interested," Thor said.

"If you change your mind..." his voice trailed off as Thor scowled at him. He turned and left.

"All the sports teams want Thor," Jonah said.

"It's a waste of time," Thor said.

"I bet you could kick ass in wrestling," Daniel said.

"Probably, but who cares?"

I loved Thor's completely disregard for sports. When Jonah said all the sports teams wanted Thor, it was a vast understatement. They drooled over the possibility of Thor joining him. I had the feeling the captains of the football and wrestling teams would blow Thor if it meant he'd play for North. I'd fantasized about blowing him myself, but that had nothing to do with sports.

Lizzie never spoke a word during lunch, which wasn't unusual. Lizzie had her book reading days and her talking days. She heard every word we said while she was reading. A fact proven now and then by a disapproving arch of her eyebrow if we said something she didn't like.

"You know this is our last year together?" Jonah said. "Next year, I'll be the only one of us left. You'll all have graduated."

"You'll have to find a whole new set of friends," I said.

"It won't be the same."

"Things change," Thor said.

I knew from experience there was a lot of meaning packed into what Thor said. He had a wondrous economy with words. He saw no reason to elaborate. He cut an idea down to the bare bones. He tended to speak in extremely short sentences. Some people thought that was because he was stupid, but thinking Thor was stupid was stupid in itself.

"Flex your bicep," Daniel said to Thor.

The table got quiet. Jonah actually looked frightened. Thor pushed back his sleeve and flexed his bicep for Daniel. It was huge! I'd heard of baseball-sized biceps, but Thor's was more like a softball. Thor's entire arm from his forearm up to his shoulder was knotted with muscle.

"Can I feel it?" Daniel asked.

Thor nodded.

Daniel reached out and grasped Thor's bicep, making me wish I was him. I would never have had the balls to ask.

"Hard as a rock," Daniel said.

Thor shrugged, rolled his sleeve back down, and turned his attention back to his lunch. I noted with some amusement that girls at nearby tables had gawked at Thor's arm, a few guys too. Even Lizzie had looked up from her book long enough to check out Thor's muscles.

Thor's sexual orientation, like Jonah's, was a mystery. He didn't seem particularly interested in either sex. Of course, even if Thor was carrying on a wild affair or taking part in a weekly orgy, he'd never talk about it. None of us would dare ask whether Thor preferred boys or girls. Well, Daniel might.

My friends took right up with my boyfriend. I was relieved. It's not that I feared they wouldn't like him, but my friends were important to me and Daniel...I loved Daniel! If they hadn't gotten along, it would have been awkward.

"You scared me," I told Daniel at the end of lunch period as we walked back to our lockers.

"How?"

"When you asked Thor to flex his bicep and especially when you asked to feel it!"

"What's the big deal about that?"

"Everyone is kind of afraid of Thor."

"Even his friends?"

"Well, we're not exactly afraid of him, but we wouldn't dare to ask to feel his bicep. I was afraid he'd punch you."

"I asked to feel his bicep, not his dick."

"Damn, I want to feel it."

"You want to feel Thor's dick?"

"Yes. I mean, no! I meant his bicep!"

"Too late, Tyler. You answered truthfully the first time. I wouldn't mind getting a feel of Thor's dick or at least a look. You think it's big?"

"Maybe."

256

"You've thought about it. Haven't you?" Daniel asked mischievously. I could feel myself turning red.

"Yes. Now, let's talk about something else."

Daniel laughed.

"You sure you don't want to keep talking about Thor's dick?"

"Yes, especially not here."

"Okay, Jonah's really cute. Think he's gay?"

"I don't know. Maybe. I've never been able to figure him out."

"So, you've thought about it?"

"Sure, I have."

"What about Shane?"

"I don't know about him either. Sexual orientation isn't something we talk about. We don't even talk about sex. Shane is really shy. Thor never says more than a few words. Lizzie is more often than not reading. Only Jonah and I talk a lot and I've never been comfortable talking about my sexual preferences. It's just not the kind of thing that comes up all that often."

"I guess I'll have to liven things up."

"You're not going to tell them about us, are you?"

"Not without your permission," Daniel said. He moved to kiss me, but I jerked back.

"What if someone sees?" I asked.

"Sorry, I wasn't thinking about everyone else just now. Only you. I wanted to kiss my boyfriend."

I smiled.

"You can kiss me all you want after school," I said quietly.

"I'll hold you to that."

I spotted Daniel once in the halls after lunch. He was walking and talking with a couple of girls. He smiled and waved to me and my heart soared. We met at my locker before seventh period and I guided Daniel to our art history class.

Art history was a good close to our school day. I don't think I could have handled Bio II or Pre-Calc after lunch and certainly not last period. I liked my schedule. I couldn't have organized my classes more perfectly, except for having Daniel in more of them, of course.

I could tell I was going to enjoy art history, even though it was going to start at the beginnings of art. When I thought art history, I thought about studying the works of Leonardo Da Vinci or Raphael. I'd never given thought to cave paintings or geometric designs on Mesopotamian pottery. Since I liked history, going back to the early stuff wasn't going to be a problem.

The best part of the day was walking to my car with Daniel. In previous years, I'd gone home alone to my homework. I might read or watch TV or something, but I was mostly alone unless I got together with my friends. We didn't hang out a lot, though, so I'd been alone more often than not. No more. I had Daniel!

"What are you smiling about?" Daniel asked.

"You."

"Good."

We climbed into my car.

"Now, how about that kiss you owe me?"

"Someone might see."

"Live dangerously."

Without allowing myself to think about it, because if I thought about it I'd never have the courage, I leaned over and kissed Daniel. I'd planned on a quick peck, but he deepened the kiss and I didn't have the willpower to pull away. When our lips parted, I looked around, paranoid that we'd been seen. We had not. My heart pounded and my breath came in gasps.

"Welcome to the thrill of risky sex," Daniel said.

"Seriously, what if someone saw us?"

"It wouldn't be the end of the world."

"I really, really don't want to be out my senior year, Daniel. I just don't want to deal with it. In college next year, maybe, but not now."

"I've been thinking about it and I'd like to be out, but I won't push you into anything. I know what it's like not to be ready."

"Thanks, but now I feel guilty, like I'm holding you back."

"Don't feel that way, Tyler. You aren't holding me back. I've just been thinking I'd like to be out. Besides, I could be out without anyone knowing about you."

"I guess that's true. Listen, if you do come out, even if I don't have the courage to come out too, I'll watch out for you. I won't let anyone hurt you if I can stop them."

Daniel smiled at me and that said it all.

I drove Daniel back to my place.

"Are your parents home?" Daniel asked as we walked in the door.

"No, not for an hour at least."

"Good."

Daniel slid my backpack off my shoulder and pressed his lips against mine. I started to protest we should go to my room instead of making out in the living room, but I had no willpower once Daniel began kissing me. He pulled my shirt out of my jeans and ran his hands up under it as he kissed me. I moaned into his mouth.

Daniel walked me backward toward the couch, never taking his lips off mine until he pushed me down onto the cushions. He pushed up my shirt and kissed my stomach and then began loosening my belt.

"Daniel, what are you doing?" I asked.

"What do you think I'm doing?"

Daniel unfastened my belt, unbuttoned my jeans, and pulled down the zipper.

"Daniel. I'm not sure we should..." I said, but my voice was weak and shaky.

Daniel pulled my jeans and my boxers down. Thor's bicep wasn't the only thing hard as a rock.

"Daniel. We shouldn't..." I moaned. Daniel closed his lips around me.

"Daniel. Don't, stop. Daniel! Daniel, I'm going to..."

I lost control. Daniel ignored my warning and kept going until I'd finished. I lay back on the cushions, panting.

"Wow, that was incredible," I said.

"Thank you."

"No, thank you." I grinned. "It felt so good, then I looked down and saw you doing it and...I couldn't hold back."

Daniel hugged me to him.

"I love making you feel good," he said. "I love you."

"I love you, too."

We just sat there and hugged each other for a few minutes.

"What about me making you feel good?" I asked hesitantly.

As much as I wanted to do it, I thought I might die of embarrassment. I know that didn't make sense after Daniel had just given me a blow job, but the thought of...I could feel my face growing red just thinking about it. This was all Brand's fault! I wouldn't be feeling embarrassed if he hadn't made me feel like such a slut. When would I be able to forget about him?

"That can wait until you're ready."

I didn't ask how he could tell I wasn't ready yet. Daniel understood me. I loved him for being patient with me. I loved him for loving me.

"I want to make you feel good, though."

One look at the front of Daniel's jeans told me how badly he needed some relief.

"Well, kiss me then, and make me feel good in a way you're comfortable with."

I smiled.

I leaned over and kissed Daniel. I loved the texture of his lips and tongue. I loved his taste. I loved kissing him.

As I kissed him, I ran my hands up under his shirt and felt his soft skin. I could feel his heart beating in his chest. I ran my hands lower, over his stomach, and down onto his jeans.

Still kissing him, I loosened his belt, unbuttoned his jeans, and pulled down his zipper. Daniel held his hips off the couch as I tugged down his jeans and boxers. I grasped him and stroked him slowly.

I slid my tongue deeper into his mouth. I kept kissing him as I stroked him. Daniel began to make little moans and whimpers and I reveled in giving him such pleasure. I quickened my pace with my hand and kissed him more deeply. The more he moaned, the faster I moved my hand. Daniel arched his back and moaned loudly into my mouth. His entire body convulsed and then calmed. We kept kissing, more and more softly until our lips parted.

"That was incredible," Daniel said.

I grinned and hugged him.

"Is that the bathroom?" Daniel asked, pointing with his head to a door across the living room behind the couch.

I nodded.

"Be right back. I need to clean up."

I sat there on the couch. I didn't feel embarrassed. I felt good about myself and that I'd been able to bring the one I loved so much pleasure. Soon, very soon, I'd bring him even more pleasure. That thought made me grin.

Daniel came back and sat by me on the couch. He took my hand and held it.

"Are you okay?" he asked.

"I'm better than okay. Why do you ask?"

"I was kind of aggressive. I get that way when I'm all worked up, but after Brand...maybe I shouldn't have been so aggressive."

"No. It's okay, really! I like your aggressive side, but..."

"What? Too aggressive? Did I push you into doing too much?"

"No. It's just...I don't want you to think of me as the girl in this relationship."

"I've seen positive proof you're a boy. I'd say nearly seven inches of proof."

"Of course, I *am* a guy. I just don't want you to think of me as the girl. Sometimes, I want to take the lead, too."

"Tyler, I don't think of either of us as the girl, ever. We're both guys. I like that you're sensitive and caring, but I also like that you're masculine and well...a guy. Does this have anything to do with the fact I bought you flowers?"

"I loved the flowers, Daniel. I can't even begin to express how wonderful it made me feel when you bought me flowers. It's just that I want to take care of you, too."

"I want you to take care of me," Daniel said. "I want us to take care of each other. There is no girl in this relationship. We're both the guy. Yeah, I was the aggressive one this time. Other times, you'll be the aggressive one. You already have been. You're always aggressive when we make out."

"I am?"

"Are you kidding me? I love how you go at it when we kiss. I like the soft kisses too, but when we get to making out, you're all over me. I love that! So, you see, you've nothing to worry about."

I smiled.

"I'm sorry if I'm a little dysfunctional. Brand made me feel like the girl when we were together."

"Brand is a jerk and he's a user. He's the one who will suffer the most in the long run. I'm sure he gets plenty of sex, but no one will ever love him. He'll never have what we have right now."

"I sure wouldn't trade places with him, not even for that incredible body."

"Your body is quite incredible enough, Tyler Perseus."

I smiled.

"You make me feel so good, and I'm not just talking about sex."

"Ditto."

North High School—Bloomington, Indiana
Friday, August 25, 1989

"Tyler. Daniel's here." Mom called up the stairs.

"I'll be right down."

I pulled on my red polo and ran my fingers through my damp hair. I checked myself out in the mirror, slipped my wallet into my jeans, and rushed to pull on my shoes.

Daniel was sitting on the couch talking to Mom when I came downstairs. They both turned to look at me.

"Don't you look handsome, Tyler," Mom said.

Daniel's eyes told me he agreed with her.

"Where are you boys going tonight?" Mom asked.

"We're going to see *Indiana Jones and The Last Crusade*," I said.

"Again?"

"Hey, I've only seen it twice."

"At least you're going out. I'm glad he met you, Daniel. Tyler usually just sits home on Friday nights."

"Mom!" I turned to Daniel. "Ready?"

"Yep."

Daniel and I headed for the door.

"Drive safely!"

"Yes, Mom."

I rolled my eyes. Why did she always say that? Did she think I was going to rip through the streets of Bloomington like I was in some kind of drag race?

"I was going to pick you up," I said as Daniel and I walked to my car.

"It was so nice out I wanted to walk. Besides, it gave me a chance to talk to your mom."

"What did you say to her?" I asked, with just a trace of suspicion.

"I told her we're madly in love and had sex on the couch."

I knew he was kidding, but I couldn't help but jerk my head in his direction.

"I told her how you showed me around the school, introduced me to your friends, and have been showing me the sights in Bloomington. Relax, I have met your mom before, you know."

"Yeah, but...I just don't want her finding out about us."

I started the car and headed for College Avenue.

"I think she'd be fine with it."

"Yeah, she'd be fine with finding out her son is a homo."

"Your parents obviously love you. Even I can see that and I've barely been around them."

"I just don't want them to know. Not yet. Maybe not ever."

"Well, I'm not out to my parents either, so I can't criticize, but I'm going to tell my parents sometime. I don't want to go through my whole life with them not truly knowing me."

"I just don't...I don't know. I guess I just don't want to deal with it," I said. "I also don't like the idea of talking to my parents about anything remotely related to sex, especially when I'm talking about sex with another guy."

"Come on, you could tell them how good you are at giving hand jobs."

"Daniel!"

Daniel laughed.

"I understand, Tyler. I understand perfectly. I might as well be you."

I turned right on Kirkwood and headed for the west side.

"I thought Showplace was on 3rd Street," Daniel said.

"It is."

"Then why are you turning on Kirkwood? Isn't Kirkwood the same as 5th Street?"

"For a while. The streets here can get a bit odd. Kirkwood will take us right to 3rd. Trust me, if I drive down to 3rd Street, I'll just have to come back up Rogers to Kirkwood. Otherwise, 3rd turns into this weird one-way street with islands we'd have to drive around. It's the oddest street in Bloomington."

A few minutes later we were parking in the Showplace parking lot. Daniel bought the tickets and I bought us Cokes, Lemonheads, and Reese's Pieces.

"I love Lemonheads!" Daniel said, as we walked away from the concession counter.

"I think you like anything with the word 'head' in it."

Daniel laughed.

"Well, I was thinking we could find a dark place to park after the movie and..."

"Stop or I won't be able to think about anything else," I said.

Daniel had a wicked grin on his face. I loved it.

Showplace had stadium seating and comfortable seats. Daniel and I settled in about half-way up. *Indiana Jones* had been out a few months, so there wasn't a large crowd. Daniel and I leaned in toward each other as the previews began.

We lost ourselves in the movie, but I was still keenly aware of Daniel's presence. Sometimes, I looked over at him, just to reassure myself all this was real. Sometimes, he looked back at me and when he did so he always grinned. We sat shoulder to shoulder and even held hands through some of the film. I wish I could express how holding Daniel's hand made me feel. Comfortable, secure, loved...I felt all these things and so much more.

After the movie, I spotted some guys from school leaving the theatre with their dates. They noticed Daniel and me together. Did they think we were there just as friends or did they think we were "special" friends? I didn't know any of them all that well. They were just guys from some of my classes. I guess it didn't matter what they thought, but I was a little uncomfortable. Then, I became angry with myself for feeling uncomfortable.

"What's wrong?" Daniel asked, as we walked toward the car.

I told him what I was thinking.

"Be patient with yourself, Tyler. Life isn't exactly easy for guys like us... it takes time to get comfortable with who you are."

"Are you? Comfortable with who you are, that is?"

"Mostly. I don't care what the guys from school think. I can't claim to be perfectly at ease with myself, but I'm mostly there."

"Have you always felt like this?"

"No," Daniel said. "At first, I didn't have any problem with being gay. I thought everyone was like that. It was only after I learned that most boys were attracted to girls and not other boys that I began to feel different. Then there was all the name calling, not directed at me, but at others. When you see someone else called a faggot and pushed around, it affects you too, you know? Then, there were church and family groups telling me I was evil. Again, not me specifically, but still *me*. It took me a while to understand that it was those groups and not me that was the problem. I'm not saying those groups are evil, exactly, but they aren't nice people and they aren't telling the truth. I think what I've been getting back to is the way I felt when I thought everyone was like me. I know most guys are attracted to girls, but there are a lot of guys who are attracted to other guys. There always have been and there always will be. If you think about it, gays have always been here. We're meant to be here. If we weren't here, something would be terribly wrong."

"I don't know. I feel like I'm okay. I guess I know I am, it's just that I don't like thinking about everyone knowing. I don't even think I'd mind being called names all that much. The guys who would call me names are jerks anyway so what would it matter? Maybe I just like my privacy. I don't like the way hiding makes me feel about myself, though. It's like I'm doing something wrong. Being in love with you isn't wrong."

Daniel grinned. We were in the car by then. He leaned over and kissed me. I didn't draw back, even though someone might see us. Maybe I was getting a little braver.

"I'm hungry," Daniel said.

"I bet you are," I teased.

"Not for *that*. Well, yeah. I'm always hungry for that, but I meant food."

"I could go for some...food, too. How about Hardee's? It's close."

I turned left onto 3rd Street, drove across the overpass, and then made a left. I pulled into Hardee's and parked the car.

We each paid our own way this time. I bet dating a girl got expensive real fast if the guy paid all the time.

"What?" Daniel asked as we walked away from the counter with our burgers and fries.

"I was just thinking how expensive it must be for guys who date girls if they have to pay for everything."

"*If*? I'm sure they always pay in hopes of getting some." Daniel laughed.

"We have the advantage. We split the cost of dates and we still get some."

"Keep talking like that and I'll attack you in the car."

"Promise?"

"Yes."

I wanted to rush eating and dash out to the car, but I made myself slow down. There was time enough for everything and I enjoyed all my time with Daniel.

I love Hardee's hamburgers. I think it's the red onions. They were so much better than white onions. The fries seemed especially good, too. Dairy Queen also had good burgers, but the service always seemed slow at Dairy Queen, especially the one up by Camp Neeswaugee. During the summer, one of the counselors said that Dairy Queen only had three speeds: slow, very slow, and stop. They did have the best ice cream around. It was worth the wait.

Shane and Thor came in shortly after Daniel and I had claimed a table. I tensed for a moment, but I was just being stupid. So what if Shane and Thor saw us together? They were together and I doubted they were dating. Thor nodded to us and then he and Shane joined us when their food was ready.

"What's up?" Shane said.

"We just watched *Indiana Jones*," Daniel said.

I tensed again. What was wrong with me?

Paranoid much, Perseus?

"Ah, cool. I love when Indiana's dad takes out that Nazi fighter plane by scaring all those seagulls."

Shane was in a more talkative mood than usual, but then sometimes he was that way when he was away from school.

"Yeah, that's awesome," Daniel said, putting his hand on my back. Daniel had moved over to my side of the booth when the guys joined us.

Thor noticed the way Daniel was touching me. I turned a little bit red. I couldn't help it. I could almost see the gears turning in Thor's head. Daniel and I had watched a movie together, now we were eating out, and he was touching me. I glanced at Daniel. He seemed completely unaware that he practically had his arm around me. I resisted the urge to pull away from him. Thor and Shane were my friends. If I couldn't be myself around them, then where could I be me?

I swallowed and looked nervously at Thor. He was gazing at me. I reminded myself that he always looked intimidating, but the color still drained from my cheeks. At least my face wasn't red anymore.

It took a supreme effort on my part, but I scooted a little closer to Daniel. I'm sure that seems like nothing, but it was a major step for me. Daniel looked at me and smiled. I grinned back.

Thor didn't say anything, but then he wouldn't. Maybe he wasn't even thinking what I thought he was thinking. Thor's strength made him frightening. I pitied anyone who ever made him angry.

Shane didn't seem to notice anything out of the ordinary, but then his reactions were about as minimal as Thor's words. I could almost picture his reaction to Daniel and me dating as a Spock-like raising of the eyebrow. I almost laughed out loud as I momentarily pictured Shane with pointed ears. He'd make a good-looking Vulcan.

Thor gave Daniel and me an inquisitive look a couple of times, like he was trying to figure us out, but otherwise we all talked and laughed as if we were sitting in the high school cafeteria. Only Lizzie and Jonah were missing. Despite his intimidating demeanor, Thor did laugh quite a bit. So did Shane, even though he was the reserved, quiet type.

I had a good time with my boyfriend and my friends at Hardee's, but I still breathed a sigh of relief when Daniel and I walked back out to my car. Daniel and I didn't talk about it, but he smiled at me. I know he was pleased I'd moved a little closer to him.

I was thinking more about coming out to my friends. I wasn't ready to do it just yet, but I was giving it a lot of thought. It would be really cool if Daniel and I could do something like we'd just done with Thor and Shane, only with them knowing just how much Daniel and I meant to each other. I'm not sure why I wanted our friends to know about us. Maybe I just wanted someone to be happy for us. I didn't think of Daniel as any kind of trophy, but I wanted to let the whole world know he was my boyfriend.

As I was driving back to the North side of town, Daniel put his hand on my leg and began to rub it.

"Find somewhere dark to park," he said.

That's all it took to get me breathing harder and for something else to get harder too. It took a while to find a spot. There were street lights everywhere! When I finally pulled into a dark parking spot, Daniel made good on his promise and attacked me. His tongue was in my mouth before I could even unfasten my seat-belt.

I was bolder than I had been before. I groped Daniel as we made out and I could feel him throbbing. I surprised myself by ripping my way through his buttons and zippers. My hand went to work, then I leaned over and engulfed Daniel.

"Oh, Tyler!" he moaned.

I hadn't let myself think about it before going down on Daniel. I had to do it without thinking. Otherwise, I would have let embarrassment stop me. I'd wanted to do it so bad so many times. Now, I was finally doing it and if Daniel's moans were any indication, I was good at it.

After a few minutes, Daniel pulled my head up and kissed me passionately. We made out for a while and then he leaned over and took me in his mouth. I leaned back and moaned. I bet straight boys never had it this good!

When I was getting too close to the edge, I pulled Daniel's face up to mine and kissed him some more, then I dove into his lap again. I could tell from his breathing, the way his body tensed, and his moans that Daniel was on the edge. I moved a little faster and he exploded in my mouth. I felt incredibly powerful at the moment. I had made him do that. I had brought him the most intense pleasure possible.

Daniel didn't forget about me when he finished. He pushed me back in the seat and went down on me again. It didn't take long at all before I was moaning too.

I felt such closeness with Daniel after we'd finished that I can't describe it. We'd just shared something incredibly intimate. Some people would say we'd had sex. That was true, as far as it went, but it was more than sex. We'd made love. As much as I enjoyed what Daniel had done for me, what I loved most of all was making him feel so incredibly good. Sex between lovers was a gift both given and received and I loved presents!

"You're really, really good at that," Daniel said.

"Hopefully, there will be more opportunities for me to practice," I said.

"Oh, I'm sure I can provide lots of opportunities."

Daniel leaned over and kissed me on the lips. I pulled back onto the street and drove him home. I was completely and utterly content.

Bloomington, Indiana
Friday, August 21, 2009

"I hope I'm not giving you too much information," I said as I paused in my story-telling to take a sip of tea.

I'd scanned Tyler's face when I'd talked about messing around with Daniel to gauge his reaction. I'd left out the most intimate details, but I could never tell a story half-way and sex was a part of this story.

"Please, if this was a movie it would be rated PG. I've heard more shocking stuff watching the news."

I laughed.

"I didn't want to freak you out with too many sexual details, especially of the boy-on-boy variety."

"This is the 21st Century, you know," Tyler said. "It is hard to imagine you as a horny teenager. You guys went at it!"

"Most teenagers will if given the chance," I said.

"You've got that right."

"Are you sure you're interested in hearing the rest of this? You know all about high school life, I'm sure."

"Well, just hit the highlights. I figure you and Daniel kept going to school, eating lunch with your friends, and making out and messing around. I don't need to hear about that. Tell me something significant. Like, did you ever come out to your friends?"

"Oh yeah, I did, although they pretty much had Daniel and me figured out by then."

"So, how did it happen?"

"It was about a month after school started..."

North High School—Bloomington, Indiana
Friday, September 29, 1989

The bell sounded, ending our lunch period and a very odd period it had been. Thor all but ignored Daniel and me. He was more sullen than usual. Jonah kept stealing glances of us and Shane was quieter than ever. Lizzie was the only one acting normal, normal for Lizzie that is. She was completely engrossed in *The Persian Boy* by Mary Renault. That left Daniel and me to carry the conversation, which was difficult because everyone else at the table was so very quiet. It was as if there was a silence that was not meant to be broken.

I was relieved when the bell rang. I started to stand up, but Lizzie grabbed my wrist. The look she gave me told me to stay put. She glanced over at Daniel and he remained seated, too. Thor scowled at me as he rose. He looked like he was thinking about punching me in the face. Shane left without a word. Jonah smiled at us nervously and then scurried like a little rabbit.

"Alexander the Great was so in love with Hephaestion he nearly lost his mind when Hephaestion died," Lizzie said.

"Okay," I said, quite lost.

"He loved a Persian boy, too. His men didn't approve, but not because he was in love with a boy, but because the boy was Persian."

I was beginning to get an inkling of where Lizzie was headed. Without several years of interpreting Lizzie's bizarre ways I wouldn't have caught on, but this was her way of telling Daniel and me she knew about us.

"How long have you known?" I asked.

I looked over at Daniel. He was still completely lost.

"Since pretty much the first day of school," Lizzie said.

"Known what?" Daniel asked.

"That we're a couple," I said, turning to him.

"Are you okay with it?" I asked.

Lizzie gave me a perplexed look as if she didn't understand what I was saying, but I knew the look on her face actually meant she thought my question was utterly ridiculous.

"Thanks, Lizzie," I said. "I wanted to tell you, but...it's just really personal, you know?"

She looked at Daniel and me and smiled.

"You make a very attractive couple."

"Thanks," we said.

Daniel and I stood.

"Thor wants to see you after school," Lizzie said. "He's not happy about this at all."

"What? Thor knows?"

"We all know."

I swallowed. Thor knew I was a homo and he wasn't happy about it. I was going to get my ass kicked.

"Does he want to see Daniel, too?" I asked, suddenly fearing for the safety of my boyfriend.

"No, just you," Lizzie said. She drifted back into her fictional world as if she'd keep on reading forever.

I walked away from the table feeling as if I was pacing down death row. Daniel was looking at me with a worried expression on his face.

"What do you think it means?" he asked.

"It means Thor is going to kick my ass."

"He's your friend, Tyler."

"Friendships end over things like this. I feared something like this although I really thought my friends would understand. Lizzie is fine with it and I think Jonah is too, but Shane didn't even speak to us and Thor...I am so fucked."

"So don't meet him after school."

"Then what? Hide from him the rest of the school year?"

"I won't let him hurt you," Daniel said.

"Please just stay out of this," I said. "The two of us together are no match for Thor and I don't want to see you get hurt, too."

"I can't just stand by while he beats the crap out of you!"

"You know Thor. He's a minimalist. He'll probably just give me one good punch and it will all be over."

One punch that will rearrange my face permanently.

Daniel looked more worried than I'd ever seen him. He was on the verge of tears.

"I'll talk to him, Daniel. Believe me, if there is any way of getting through this without getting my ass kicked by Thor, I'll find it. He's my friend, or at least he was. That has to count for something."

"You're very brave," Daniel said.

"I don't see what's so brave about facing an inevitable situation. I have to face him sooner or later so it might as well be sooner."

The rest of my school day was not enjoyable. I tried not to think my upcoming showdown with Thor, but how could I not think about it? Showdown. The word made me think of an old western gun fight. No, showdown was not the right word. Thor had muscles bulging out everywhere. When it came to fighting, I was practically unarmed. Massacre would be a better word to describe what was probably going to happen.

I couldn't even properly enjoy last period art history. I mostly sat there watching the clock. I wondered how much getting punched in the face would hurt. Would Thor break my nose? Would Daniel have to take me to the hospital? How many people would be there to watch me get my ass kicked?

Thor hadn't touched me yet, but I was already in pain. Thor and I had never been close. I wasn't sure he was close to anyone. We had been friends for a long time, however. I'd known him when he wasn't a walking mass of muscle. We'd been through some rough times together and we'd had fun together, too. I thought all that meant something, but I guess the fact that I liked guys erased all that.

I knew Thor wasn't afraid of being associated with a homo because Thor wasn't afraid of anything. He didn't care what anyone thought about him. If someone gave him shit, he'd punch them out. He wasn't going to kick my ass to prove to others he wasn't a homo. I almost wished that was the reason.

No, Thor must really hate me now. Losing one of my friends hurt.

After art history, Daniel and I walked first to his locker, then to mine. I read pity, fear, and frustration in my boyfriend's eyes. I knew this was as tough for him as it was for me. I just hoped he didn't get himself hurt. I hoped Thor would just take me out with one swift punch and that would be the end of it. If there was more to it, Daniel would jump on him. I knew Daniel would jump in no matter how much I pleaded with him to stay out of it. I knew what he'd do because that's what I'd do if our situations were reversed.

Daniel put his hand on my shoulder.

"How are you?" he asked.

"Scared to death," I answered truthfully.

I wasn't going to put up a brave front for Daniel. He'd see through it anyway. I *really* did not want to face Thor, but it's something I had to do.

Thor stalked toward us. He scowled. Shit. He was gonna kill me.

"Let's talk outside," he said.

He turned and I followed him. Daniel was at my side. Thor led us to a grassy area far enough away for the departing hoards of students we couldn't be overheard. They'd all come running to watch once he began pummeling me.

Thor stopped and turned. Daniel placed himself squarely between us. I was afraid this would happen.

"You and Tyler have been friends for years. How can you even think about beating him up because he's gay? Some friend you are."

Shit. Daniel was going to get himself killed. Okay, not killed, but hurt. I wanted to say something but I didn't know what to say.

Thor just stared into Daniel.

"This is between him and me," Thor said.

Thor grabbed Daniel by the shoulders, lifted him, and set him down out of the way. I stepped up to Thor to make it more difficult for Daniel to get between us again. Thor stared into my eyes. I trembled but forced myself not to step back. Shit. This was going to hurt.

"Why didn't you trust me enough to tell me?" Thor asked.

I just looked at Thor in a sort of daze.

"We've been friends for a long time, Tyler. Why didn't you ever tell me? Did you think I was too stupid to understand? Did our friendship not mean enough to you for you to share this with me?"

Thor's words slowly cut through the fog of fear and confusion in my mind. Thor was...hurt.

"I...I'm sorry," I said. "I...I never told anyone. I just...it's very personal. I wanted to tell you and the others, but...I never found the courage. I especially wanted to tell you when Daniel and I started dating. He makes me so happy. I'm...sorry. I've never thought you were stupid, Thor. I know better. Our friendship means a great deal to me. Walking out here...I was terrified because I knew you were going to kick my ass, but I was also really *really* hurt because you're my friend and I thought you'd understand..."

"You thought I was going to hit you?"

"Hit me, or worse."

Thor shook his head in disgust.

"You *really* don't know me then, Tyler."

"I'm *really* sorry," I said, on the verge of tears. "It's just that...you don't know what it's like to be afraid that your friends won't be your friends anymore if they find out who you really are." Tears began rolling down my cheeks and sobs escaped despite my efforts to maintain control. "You, and Lizzie, and Shane, and Jonah, mean so much to me. I've always figured you'd understand, but...to take that chance..."

I began crying. Thor did something then I'd never seen him do—ever. He pulled me to him and hugged me. I cried into his massive shoulder.

It took me a little while to get myself under control. When I did, I stepped back.

"I'm sorry, Tyler," Thor said. "I had no idea what it was like for you. Who you sleep with doesn't matter to me. I never stopped to think that you'd be worried about what I'd think of you. I was just hurt because I didn't mean enough to you for you to tell me."

"I would have told you, but I was afraid. I tried to show you and Shane at the Hardee's. I trusted you enough to do that, but you and the others mean so much to me I was afraid to say the words."

"I understand now." Thor grinned. He was extremely handsome when he grinned. "You really came out here with me when you thought I was going to kick your ass?"

I nodded.

"That is brave. I don't know another guy who would have the balls to face me like that." Thor turned to Daniel. "I've never had anyone get in my face the way you just did either. You must really love Tyler."

"I do."

"You guys have balls," Thor said.

I released a huge sigh of relief.

"We're cool, then?" I asked.

"Of course we are. And if anyone gives you guys any trouble, you come to me and I'll take care of them," Thor said. He punched his fist into the palm of his hand with a loud smack. "No one fucks with my friends."

"Thanks, Thor," I said.

Thor walked toward his car. Daniel and I watched him leave.

"That turned out differently than I expected," I said.

"Thank God," Daniel said

"Thank you for trying to protect me, even though I told you *not* to do so."

"I couldn't just let him hurt you, Tyler."

"I know. I feel kind of crummy. I never thought that I might have hurt Thor's feelings."

"Don't be too hard on yourself. You know him a lot better than I do, but I think most people probably don't even realize he has feelings."

"Everyone has feelings."

"Yeah, but Thor is so tough it seems like nothing could get to him."

"That's what I've always thought. Now, I wonder what pain he's hiding under that tough exterior."

"I have a feeling you'll find out. In case you didn't notice, your relationship with him just changed. I think he'll be more likely to talk to you about his problems now. Besides, us gay guys are known for being sensitive."

"You know, I have never seen Thor hug anyone, ever," I said. "That's part of what made me cry so hard. I didn't realize until then how much he cared about me. It felt so good, especially after I'd been so afraid."

"You didn't see the tears in his eyes, did you?" Daniel asked.

"Thor? Thor had tears in his eyes?" I asked, astonished.

"He cares about you a lot, Tyler. You don't hurt for someone else unless you care about them."

"Wow."

Daniel and I walked to my car. We drove to Jiffy Treet on Walnut Street to celebrate. Jiffy Treet had some of the best homemade ice cream around. Daniel and I ordered a banana split and sat at a little table to share it.

"I'm so glad that's over," I said.

"I'm glad Thor didn't rearrange your face."

"I was not looking forward to that."

"Who would?"

I smiled.

"What are you grinning about?" Daniel asked.

"Lizzie and Thor are both cool with me being a homo and having a boyfriend."

Daniel smiled at me.

"I wonder about Jonah and Shane."

"Jonah is okay with it," Daniel said. "I could tell from the way he was looking at us. Shane...I'm not sure."

"Yeah, Shane wouldn't look at us at all. I don't fear any violence from Shane. Of course, I didn't fear any from Thor until Lizzie told me he wanted to talk to me after school. I kind of jumped to conclusions there."

"I thought he was going to kick your ass, too. We just misinterpreted the looks he was shooting us."

"Well, that's all cleared up. I feel even closer to Thor now."

"We also have someone to look out for us," Daniel said. "I can't imagine anyone wanting to cross Thor."

"That makes me feel good, too. I want to fight my own battles, but it never hurts to have a secret weapon."

I drove Daniel home. He kissed me before he left the car. It had been an eventful, tearful, sometimes terrifying day, but now I felt better than I had in a long time.

***

I awakened the next morning with renewed courage. Now that I'd had time to think things over, I realized I *had* been brave the day before. At the time, I was so busy trying to control my fear that I didn't realize how much courage it took to face Thor when I fully expected him to beat the crap out of me. I didn't feel brave at the time. I was trembling too much to feel anything but plain scared. The point is that I went ahead and faced Thor, despite that fear. Someone once told me that was the definition of courage, doing what needed to be done despite the fear. There can be no bravery without fear. Courage is all about conquering fear, not allowing it to keep you from doing what you've got to do.

After Thor, approaching my other friends was easy. Lizzie already knew about Daniel and me, but that still left Jonah and Shane.

***

I spotted Jonah in the hallway between second and third periods. I caught up with him and pulled him into an empty classroom.

"What's up?" he asked.

A little part of me wanted to hesitate, but I pushed that part of myself aside and got straight to the point.

"I just wanted to know if you're cool with me being a homo and having a boyfriend."

"So, it is true? You guys are sooo cute together. I'm so happy for you!"

Jonah hugged me. I'd always wondered about him but could never quite figure him out. His comment that we were cute together made me suspect Daniel and I weren't the only homos at our table.

"So...are you gay, too?" I asked.

"Oh, yeah! I'm so jealous you have a boyfriend. I want one!"

This time, I hugged Jonah.

"I'm sure you'll find one, Jonah."

"So, is this a big secret or..."

"We just want our closest friends to know. Lizzie knows, so does Thor, and now you. I plan on telling Shane later today."

"Was Thor okay with it?"

"Yes. He was hurt I didn't trust him enough to tell him before you guys started figuring it out, but I explained my reasons to him. We're cool."

"He was giving you some nasty looks yesterday," Jonah said. "He didn't seem all that upset when we, Lizzie, Thor, and I, that is, were talking about Daniel and you; how we suspected you were more than friends, but yesterday..."

"Tell me about it. I thought he was going to kick my ass, but everything is cool now."

"I'm glad."

"Have you told Thor you're gay?" I asked.

"No, but I'm going to tell him. I think I'm going to do it today. I have no reason not to tell him now."

"Good. We'd better get to class, but I just wanted to make sure everything is fine between us. Your friendship means a lot to me," I said.

Jonah smiled.

"We're perfect."

I watched for my chance to talk with Shane, but it didn't come until lunch time. Jonah was more friendly than ever, if that's possible. Thor almost smiled at Daniel and me, which was a big emotional display of acceptance for him. Lizzie had her nose stuck in a book, *A Connecticut Yankee in King Arthur's Court* by Mark Twain, but she did glance up and smile now and then. Shane was just as quiet as the day before and seemed even more ill at ease.

I tried to catch Shane's eye when he'd finished eating, but I couldn't get him to look at me. I didn't want the day to end without speaking to him, so I quit waiting for a chance and created one.

"Shane, I need to talk to you," I said.

Shane looked up and gazed at me uncomfortably.

"Come on," I said, standing up with my tray. I indicated with a glance for Daniel to let me handle this alone.

Shane and I dumped our trays and then I led him into the empty band room near the cafeteria. He looked around nervously.

"Shane. I think you, like the others, have figured out about Daniel and me. I hope this doesn't change things between us or at least, I hope we can still be friends."

"So it's true? You're gay?"

"Yes, it's true, and Daniel is my boyfriend."

Shane looked around the band room.

"It makes you uncomfortable, doesn't it?"

"Yeah...I...I'm not prejudiced, but...it's just...strange. I don't understand why two guys would want to...do stuff together like that."

"Can you understand why a girl would be attracted to a guy and want to do stuff with him?"

"Sure."

"Well, when I look at a guy, I'm attracted to him the way a girl would be. It's not exactly the same and I'm not a girl so I can't say for sure, but it's close to the same thing. We've known each other for a long time, Shane. You know what I'm like. I'm not a jock and maybe I'm more sensitive than most guys, but basically I'm a guy. The only difference is that I'm attracted to other guys, a lot like a girl is attracted to a guy. Do you understand?"

"Kind of. Um...so...are you attracted to me?"

Is this what was bothering him? Was he afraid I wanted him?

"You're an attractive guy, Shane, but I'm not attracted to you. We're friends and...I don't know how to explain it but that kind of short circuits any attraction I might have felt. It would feel a little like being hot for my brother. I'm not attracted to *every* guy, just certain guys. You aren't attracted to every girl you see, are you?"

"No."

"I bet you know some attractive girls that you aren't attracted to because you're friends. Am I right?"

"Yeah."

"It's the same thing. You're attractive, but I'm not attracted to you because we're friends. If you're worried that I'm hot for you, don't be. I don't think about you like that. I recognize that you're handsome, but that's as far as it goes."

"Listen, I'm sorry I've been weirded out by this. It's not so much I've been afraid you were attracted to me as much as it is the idea that you like guys. That's just hard for me to understand. I don't know anyone who is gay. Well, I didn't until now. I just never considered that you might be, but then you and Daniel were always hanging out together and you seemed so close. Thor, Lizzie, Jonah, and me kept seeing you guys together everywhere and you seemed...like a couple. It kind of freaked me out. I'm sorry, I...it's just hard for me to understand."

"Are we still friends?" I asked.

"Yeah."

"Then it's okay, Shane. All Daniel and I want is to be your friend. Maybe being around us will help you understand guys like us. We're really no different from other couples, except we're both guys."

"So, you love him?"

"Oh, yes. I love him so much I can't even describe how much. He makes me happy."

"Then I'm happy for you."

"Thanks, Shane."

We walked back into the cafeteria. Lunch period was almost over. Daniel was still sitting at the table with the others. Jonah was watching expectantly. He smiled when I nodded to Daniel. I wondered how Shane would feel when he discovered that Jonah was gay, too. Time would tell.

"Well, that's done," I said as Daniel and I walked back toward our lockers. "All my closest friends know and they're all still my friends."

"What did Shane say?"

"He had trouble grasping the whole concept. I think I made him understand. When I told him I love you, he said he was happy for me."

Daniel smiled.

"I bet you're relieved."

"Yes. I always thought my friends would understand, but there was always a lingering doubt. I'm not sure I even realized how much that hurt until I was talking to Thor about it. All that pain came right to the surface. Now, I feel...free."

Daniel leaned over and gave me a quick kiss on the cheek. It was an extreme risk, but I didn't care.

One Month Later

I clicked the shutter and the Canon AE-1 Program made an odd electronic whir.

"Is it supposed to sound like that?" I asked as I lowered the camera.

"Yeah," Daniel said.

"Is this really all there is to taking a picture?"

We were standing on the IU campus, in front of the Rose Well House, which I'd just photographed.

"Well, I have the camera set on program, so you don't have to worry about all the settings. This camera does a great job so I let it make the decisions most of the time. If I want some kind of special effect or if there is tricky lighting I'll do the settings manually, but for most photos it's as simple as clicking the shutter."

Daniel gazed at the pavilion and the forest beyond.

"This is a beautiful location. I didn't notice it when we walked be here before."

"That's because I didn't take you by the well house. I was saving it for later."

"I remember it from *Breaking Away*," Daniel said, taking a seat on the stone bench in front of the pavilion. I sat beside him.

"Yeah, I left it out of our *Breaking Away* tour by accident. I meant to bring you here, but then I got hungry."

"Always thinking with your stomach," teased Daniel.

"Well, you always think with your...decidedly perceptive intellect."

Daniel punched me in the shoulder.

"Hey, we should ride down and see the *Breaking Away* house today, too," Daniel said.

"We never have done that, have we?"

"No."

"It's taking us a long time to do everything we've planned to do."

"Well, I am finally getting around to teaching you how to take photos. Next it will be your turn to take me antique shopping." Daniel turned his attention to the well house. "Do you know anything about this well house?"

"A little," I said. "I don't know when, but there was a fire at the old campus that destroyed the old College Building. I think that building was pretty much all there was of IU way back then.

Anyway, the two surviving portals or entrances were brought here and used to construct this pavilion over the only cistern on the "new" campus. It's named after Theodore F. Rose who donated the money to build it."

Daniel leaned in and gave me a quick kiss. I smiled at him and took his hand in mine. We could be much more open on the IU campus than at North, or anywhere else for that matter.

"I love it here," Daniel said. "It's so quiet and peaceful, even though we're less than a block from downtown. I love the trees."

"Just wait until the leaves really began to change color."

"We'll have to come back then. It shouldn't be long."

We sat there in silence for a while, holding hands. Only a few college students walked by. If any of them noticed us holding hands, they didn't comment on it.

"Let's ride down to the *Breaking Away* house," Daniel said.

"Okay, but you carry the camera. I don't want to break it."

We walked to our bikes, climbed on, and rode off campus. We hit Lincoln and pedaled our way to the corner of Lincoln and Dodds. There it was, the very house that Dave lived in. It was immediately recognizable as the home used in *Breaking Away*.

We climbed off our bikes. Daniel handed me the camera and I took a few pictures of it.

"This is turning into another *Breaking Away* tour," I said.

"At least this time food hasn't distracted you."

"Yet."

"Okay, I've shown you how to take pictures. It's time for you to take me antique shopping."

"Are you sure?" I asked.

"Of course, I'm sure."

I handed Daniel his camera and we climbed back on our bikes. We headed north for a few blocks, up past the library and Kirkwood to 7th Street. We turned to the west and after a few blocks reached the three story brick building that had once housed a grocery wholesaler at the beginning of the century. We parked our bikes out front and walked up the wooden steps.

"Wow, there's a lot of stuff in here," Daniel said as we entered.

"That's the idea. There's probably more than a hundred booths, all filled with old stuff."

We began browsing through booths, most of them filled with interesting things. There were old hats like they wore in the 1920s, china and glassware from even earlier, paintings, Victorian furniture, stoneware, and all kinds of other stuff.

"It's kind of overwhelming. There are just so many things to look at," Daniel said.

"I kind of scan over it and focus on what most interests me."

"How do you decide what to collect?" Daniel asked.

"It's not a conscious decision. It just happens. How did you decide to collect coins?"

"I just...liked them. One of our neighbors was having a yard sale and he had some old foreign coins. They were really old, like early 1900s, and they were cheap. I thought they were cool so I bought them. Then, I started looking in coin magazines and I ordered a few from dealers."

"That's how you start collecting. You see something you like and it just happens. Oh, here you go," I said, as I spotted a flat case full of coins.

"Oh, wow," Daniel said.

His eyes lit up. I knew that look. I got it when I spotted something I really liked. He looked through the glass at the coins like a kid looking in a candy store window.

"A 1941 D Standing Liberty half dollar, uncirculated," Daniel said while gazing through the glass.

"I think you're about to drool."

"I'd kill to have that coin. I've never even seen an uncirculated Standing Liberty half before. I don't need to be spending $15 on it, though."

Daniel browsed the coins a while and then we moved on. I saw a few things I wanted, but nothing I couldn't live without. I excused myself to go to the bathroom and left Daniel alone for a few minutes. When I returned, we looked through the rest of the mall.

"What the heck is that?" Daniel asked, pointing to a wooden board about a foot long and five inches wide with a bed of spikes in the middle.

"It's a flax hackle."

"It looks more like part of Uncle Fester's bed on the *Addams Family*."

"Way back when people spun their own yarn and thread, they used a flax hackle to straighten out the fibers before spinning the flax. That's where linen comes from."

"How do you know all this stuff?"

"I like old stuff. I read about it. I go to auctions, flea markets, and antique shops with my parents. Mainly, I just kind of pick it up as I go along I guess. I like the stories behind the stuff. Like this flax hackle. It probably used to hang in an old log barn somewhere or a log cabin. Some woman probably spent hours pulling flax through it. I can picture her old-fashioned dress, sheep in a nearby meadow, a little garden of herbs and vegetables, and in the distance a big field of corn."

"You have quite an imagination."

"I like history. When flax hackles were used, the world was like that. When I hold something old in my hands, I can picture where it might have been and who might have used it. I could go into way more detail than I just did, but I think you get the picture."

"That's really cool, Tyler. It's almost like you're a touch telepath."

"Well, I don't see the real past, only my imagined version of it."

"Close enough."

We looked around for a while longer, then left the antique mall. Daniel had been roped into eating out with his parents and we were almost out of time. I stopped when we were a block from his house and climbed off my bike.

"What are we stopping for?" Daniel asked.

"I have something for you."

"Huh?"

I dug into my pocket and pulled out a small bag. I gave it to Daniel. He opened it.

"The coin! The Walking Liberty half dollar! But how, when?"

"I didn't really need to go to the bathroom in the antique mall. I went up front and bought you that coin."

"Tyler, it's too expensive!"

"First, I know how to haggle. I got it for $12. Second, it's worth way more than that to make you happy. You bought me flowers. I bought you a coin."

Daniel hugged me.

"This is too much, but thanks!"

I grinned.

"I'll keep this forever," Daniel said. "Whenever I look at it, I'll remember this day—just like you see pictures of the past in your mind when you hold something antique. Thank you."

Daniel hugged me again.

"You'd better get home or you'll be late," I said.

"I wish I could spend more time with you instead, but I did promise."

"We'll have lots of time, Daniel, maybe the rest of our lives."

Daniel pulled me close to a tree, concealing us as much as possible from prying eyes. He kissed me.

"I love you, Tyler."

"I love you, too."

We climbed back on our bikes and rode to our homes. I smiled all the way.

Bloomington, Indiana
Friday, August 21, 2009

"So, did anyone else ever find out about you and Daniel? Your parents? Kids at school?" Tyler asked.

"My parents never found out about us. We messed around a lot at my house. It's a wonder one of them didn't come home early and catch us going at it. Later, I think they began to catch on to how much Daniel meant to me. They never figured out we were lovers, though, not until I told them years later."

"How did they take it then?"

"They had trouble accepting that I was gay. There was never any question that they loved me. Even when they were struggling to accept the truth, they made sure I knew they loved me. It took them a while, but they grew accustomed to the idea. Now, they just accept it as a part of who I am. If I had to define myself with one word that word wouldn't be "gay." That's just my sexual orientation. It's definitely a part of my life, but it's not my whole life."

"What word would you use to describe yourself?"

"If I was only allowed one word, I would choose 'writer' because it best describes me."

"Did anyone at school find out about you, in addition to your friends?"

"Yes. It was inevitable. We weren't nearly careful enough. You could even say we were careless at times. Like the day I told Jonah and Shane I was gay, Daniel kissed me on the cheek. Straight guys just don't go around kissing each other on the cheek."

"Was there any trouble?"

"Some. As people began to figure us out, Daniel and I were more open, but yet we were low-key. We didn't walk down the halls holding hands or make out in front of my locker or anything like that. We just spent a lot of time together, sat *very* close together whenever possible, hugged sometimes, and on rare occasions, kissed each other on the cheek. We saved the heavier stuff for when we were alone. Our demonstrations of affection weren't for anyone else, just us. If someone saw us, that was okay, but all that mattered to us was each other."

"So you weren't an 'in your face' gay couple."

I laughed.

"No. Our attitude became 'we're gay, deal with it' but we never said that out loud. That was just the way we thought of things. We were just being ourselves and living our own lives."

"How did the kids at school react to you as a gay couple?"

"We were accepted by a lot of them. We were just kind of there. Some weren't very nice about it. We were called all the usual names. I won't say that didn't hurt, because it did, but it was just something we had to deal with. Kids can be cruel and they can be ignorant."

"Was there ever any real trouble?"

"Just once."

"What happened?"

"I'm not sure you want to hear about it."

"Tell me."

"It was after school, not long after Valentine's Day..."

North High School—Bloomington, Indiana
Friday, February 16, 1990

"We need some more masking tape," Daniel said.

"I'll check the art room."

I walked down the hallway, past the dozens of works of art that Daniel and I, along with a few other volunteers, were placing on the walls for the art show that evening. I was beginning to wonder if the extra credit was worth it. I never realized there would be so many drawings and paintings to display. I was enjoying myself, however, mainly because I was with Daniel.

The familiar hallways of North were a little creepy in the half-light. The quiet made me uneasy. A school wasn't supposed to be so quiet. I didn't pay that much attention to the background sounds during the day, but they were notable in their absence. There were no clanging locker doors, no scuffing of shoes on the floors, no talking, no laughing, and no swish of backpacks against clothing. The only sounds were my own footsteps which echoed eerily in the deserted hallways.

The art room was dark, but I flipped on the lights. The room was filled with the scent of oils and temperas. My only art course was art history, so I didn't actually paint or draw, but our class met in the main art room, so I was familiar with the scents. I wished I did have more artistic talent, but at least I could write. That was probably a talent better suited to me anyway.

It didn't take me long to find a couple of rolls of masking tape mixed in with the painting supplies. I grabbed them, shut off the lights, and headed back out into the hall.

The hallway was no longer deserted. I nearly ran into Cody Richey and Brice Treva. They were both football players. Cody had blond hair with long bangs, blue eyes, and a killer body. If he had any inkling about the fantasies I'd had about him, he would have kicked my ass.

I tried to step around them, but Brice got in my way.

"What are *you* doing here?" Brice asked.

"Helping set up the art show," I said, trying to keep the nervousness I felt out of my voice. I wondered what they were doing there, but I thought it best not to ask.

An uncomfortable silence followed. Cody and Brice just stood there staring at me. I moved to get past them, but Brice blocked my path again and this time he also shoved me back.

"I hear you're the school homo," Brice said.

"I've heard more than that," Cody said, but didn't elaborate.

I didn't say anything. I didn't like where this was going. They looked as if they were deciding whether or not to kick my ass.

"I actually saw him kiss his butt-buddy," Brice said. "Gross."

I tried to get around them yet again, but this time Cody shoved me back hard enough that I almost fell. I wondered what my chances were of getting away if I bolted in the other direction. Probably not good, Cody was a running back.

I once more tried to leave, but Cody shoved me up against the wall and held me there with his strong hands gripping my shoulders.

"Did I say you could leave, faggot? Did I?"

I swallowed hard. The tone of his voice indicated I was in for a beat down. He released me, but didn't move back.

"I've never done anything to you," I said. "I don't even know you. Just let me go, okay? I've got work to do. And someone will come looking for me soon."

"Oh! I'm so scared now!" Cody said, then laughed.

I darted to the side, but Brice blocked my escape with his body. I made a futile attempt get past Cody, but he stepped into my path and I collided with his chest.

"Why are you playing hard to get?" Cody asked.

"Huh?"

"You want us, don't you?" Brice said.

"No, but it looks like you want me," I said firmly, even though my voice shook a little.

"I guess faggots are just like girls," Brice said. "Yes means yes and no means yes." Brice and Cody both laughed.

"Tyler?"

I looked over Cody's shoulder.

"Daniel! Get out of here! Find help!" I shouted. "Go!"

Brice turned toward Daniel, but Daniel was already on the move. He sprinted down the hallway, dodged Brice, and leaped onto Cody's back before he could turn around. Brice grabbed for Daniel. I made an ill-conceived dive into Brice's mid-section to stop him. The force of it made him stagger and then fall. Brice landed on his back and my bodyweight knocked the breath out of him. I got in one good punch to his face before he swept me off with one arm.

Cody staggered back and finally managed to dislodge Daniel. My boyfriend sailed back onto the floor. Cody began to turn toward him and I did the only thing I could do, I kicked at his right calf with the sole of my foot. Cody went down, almost on top of me. I scrambled to my feet, but Brice grabbed me and pinned my arms behind my back. I fought against him, but Brice wrapped a forearm around my neck, immobilizing me. I tried to stomp his foot, but he choked me until I couldn't breathe.

Cody grabbed Daniel. I was afraid he'd start beating him, but he twisted Daniel's arm behind his back and pushed him up against the wall.

"I love it when faggots fight, don't you?" Cody asked Brice. "It's so entertaining."

Daniel struggled, but Cody twisted his arm until he cried out in pain and stopped fighting.

"I'm thinking beat-down," Cody said with a smirk.

I struggled against Brice, but there was no way I could break his hold on me.

"Let him go," I said. "Let Daniel go and I'll stay. I won't even try to get away."

"No!" Daniel said.

"Aww, that's so sweet," Cody mocked. "Tyler's offering himself to us so we'll spare his little butt buddy."

"He's my boyfriend," I said. "Not my butt buddy."

"I bet he's the girl for you, though, isn't he?" Cody said. "That's why you're trying to protect him. I bet he takes it up the ass from you."

I turned completely red. I have no idea why I was embarrassed by those jerks while Daniel and I were in serious, serious trouble.

"We've never..." I said.

"You've never fucked him?" Cody asked. "Does that mean you're the bitch?"

"He's never...done that with me," I said.

Cody kept his hold on Daniel but moved closer and looked into my eyes.

"Someone has, though, haven't they?" he said, staring directly into my eyes.

I felt my face grow hot. Cody smiled.

"Yeah, someone has had your ass. Whore." Cody laughed in my face.

Daniel struggled again, but Cody just twisted his arm a little harder. Tears appeared in Daniel's eyes.

"Please," I said. "Please let him go."

Tears began to roll from my eyes. I couldn't bear the thought of them hurting Daniel.

Cody twisted Daniel's arm hard and Daniel cried out in pain.

"Stop it! Don't hurt him! Please," I said, staring straight into Cody's eyes. "Please!"

Daniel drove his heel into the top of Cody's foot. Cody howled and lost his hold on Daniel, who slipped out of his grasp and charged toward Brice. Daniel head butted Brice in the side, which allowed me to stomp Brice's foot.

In moments, we were both free again, but Cody punched me in the face and I staggered backwards. Brice tried to get another hold on me, but I slipped away. Cody was going after Daniel, so I jumped on his back. He staggered but shrugged me off and turned on me. I was laying flat on my back. He drew his fist back and smiled. He leaned over me and that's when I saw my chance. I drew my right knee up to my chest and kicked out into Cody's groin. He cried out in pain and toppled over, holding his balls.

Daniel launched himself at Brice, wildly pummeling him. I jumped on Brice too. Even together, we weren't having an easy time of it, but I don't think Brice was used to fighting guys who stomped feet, pounced on him like a cat, or head butted into his body. The truth was that both Daniel and I were completely inept fighters. We were just doing anything we could think of doing that might get us the hell out of there.

Daniel landed a kick to Brice's nuts and he went down. Cody was struggling up by then and there was murder in his eyes.

Daniel and I were both panting, but this was no time to rest. We bolted. Cody and Brice were after us in a flash, moving much faster that I would've imagined possible after they'd both been kicked where it counts. Daniel and I tore down the hallway, but, even hobbling along as they were, Cody and Brice were gaining on us. We had to outrun them. If they got their hands on us now, we were dead meat.

We ripped around a corner and sped on. We barely avoided a collision with Thor who was approaching from the opposite direction. We actually slid past him before we skidded to a halt on the polished floor.

Cody and Brice were only a couple of seconds behind us. By the time Daniel and I turned, they'd barreled around the corner on a collision course with Thor. Thor held his arms straight out from his sides and clothes-lined both of them. Cody and Brice landed right on their asses.

Daniel and I leaned over on our knees, gasping. I think my heavy breathing was more from fear than exertion. I trembled from head to foot. I'd never been as scared as I was when Cody and Brice started in on me, but then when they went after Daniel...it was ten times worse.

Thor took in the situation without saying a word. He grabbed Cody, who was just beginning to stand up, by the front of the shirt and slammed him into the wall. Cody swallowed hard. He looked more like a frightened rabbit than anything else.

"Tyler and Daniel are off limits," Thor said. "Touch them or harass them and I'll tear you apart. Got it?"

"I got it!" Cody practically shouted.

Thor released Cody and looked at Brice who was still on his ass. Brice held his hands up, palms up, as if trying to both ward off and placate Thor.

"I got it too!" Brice said.

Thor looked at Daniel and me next. I knew his anger wasn't directly toward us but the expression on his face scared the crap out of me.

"They hurt you?" Thor asked.

"Not...a lot," I said.

"But they hurt you?"

I nodded.

Thor turned on Cody and slugged him in the face. He went down hard and just lay on the floor. Brice attempted to bolt, but Thor slugged him in the stomach and he crumpled to the floor. Thor moved toward Brice.

"Thor, don't!" I said. I was afraid he might kill Brice. If the look on his face had been terrifying before, it was murderous now.

Thor looked away from all of us, breathing hard, his fists clenched. I could tell he was trying to get control of himself. Brice squirmed on the floor, holding his stomach, but Cody wasn't moving at all. Thor had knocked him out cold.

Daniel leaned down and smacked Cody on the face a few times. Cody began to stir. Thor was still looking away from everyone, but he was beginning to breathe more normally. Cody slowly sat up, rubbing the side of his head. With a grimace, he crawled over to check on Brice.

Thor turned to face Cody and Brice. They looked up at him in fear. Thor had himself more or less under control, but his face was still a mask of fury.

"If you ever..." he said, glaring at Cody and Brice.

"We won't! I swear!" Cody said.

Cody had tears in his eyes. He was on the verge of bawling.

That was all Thor said. He was a man of few words. He motioned with his head and we followed him, leaving Cody and

Brice lying on the floor. Thor asked us to tell him the whole story and we did, leaving out nothing.

Daniel made me sound heroic for trying to buy his safety. Thor looked impressed. I turned red as a tomato. Truthfully, I didn't offer Cody and Brice anything they didn't already have. I was just hoping they'd be dumb enough to let Daniel go.

"If those fuckers even look at your cross-eyed, tell me," Thor said and smacked his fist into his palm. Daniel and I just nodded. We were intimidated by Thor when his anger wasn't even directed at us.

Daniel and I forgot about the art show. We walked out to my car and climbed in. I felt like a big baby, but as soon as we shut the doors, tears began to roll down my cheeks. I don't know why I lost control when it was all over and there was no way Cody or Brice would dare bother us again, but when I thought of what they were going to do to us...

"You are my hero," Daniel said.

I thought at first he was poking fun at me, but the expression on his face was quite serious. I wiped my cheeks with the back of my hand.

"No, you're my hero for trying to save me."

"No, you're my hero for trying to sacrifice yourself for me."

"No, you're my hero," I said, grinning.

That started us in on a verbal battle that got us both to laughing. For a very long time after that, anytime one of us did the least little thing for the other, the phrase "You're my hero" would be uttered and the none-too-serious argument would start all over again.

Daniel came home with me after our frightening encounter with the football players. We had the place to ourselves. Sex was a temptation, but sometimes just being close was better. I pulled Daniel to me and hugged him. We stood there for the longest time in each other's arms. When we stepped back, I took Daniel by the hand and led him to the couch. We sat side by side. I wrapped my arm around his shoulder and pulled him close.

"Are you okay?" I asked.

He nodded.

"You?"

"Yeah, but I'm still kind of scared. You were really brave for coming to my rescue," I said.

"You aren't going to start the hero argument again, are you?" Daniel asked with a grin.

"No, but what you did was brave."

"My rescue attempt wasn't exactly a success."

"You were brave for trying, regardless of the outcome, and we did escape. I'd call that a success."

"You think we could've outrun Cody and Brice if Thor hadn't clothes-lined them?" Daniel asked.

"I don't know, but I think we were doing exceptionally well for two homos going up against two of the toughest jocks in the school. We actually escaped from them. You have a vicious kick, by the way."

"I'm sure Brice won't forget it for a while," Daniel said.

"At least not for a few hours. It will take that long for his balls to stop hurting."

"Tyler, seriously, you are my hero. I know it sounds clichéd, but I'll never forget what you were willing to do to protect me. You really would have stayed there and let them do whatever they wanted to you."

I nodded.

"That was...brave doesn't even begin to cover it."

"It wasn't that brave," I said. "I just couldn't bear to see them hurt you. Nothing they could have done to me could have possibly been as bad as them hurting you. So, you see, it wasn't that brave. It was just what I had to do to spare us both more pain."

"What about the pain I would have felt knowing what they were doing to you?" Daniel asked. "I would have gone for help, but it would've taken time. I would have gone out of my mind. I understand that seeing me in pain hurts you, but you've got to understand it works both ways. When you're in pain, so am I. So, please, if we get into another spot like that, no self-sacrificing acts. Just stand by my side and we'll face whatever comes together."

I hugged Daniel to me even closer. If I hadn't known we were in love before, I would have then. We were silent for a few minutes. We just sat there, side by side, enjoying the closeness and intimacy.

"What is wrong with guys like that?" Daniel asked finally.

"I don't know. They think we're just fags and that it's okay to do whatever they want to us. It's probably a power trip for them. There are a lot of brutes in the world, particularly in Indiana, people who do things just because they can. They don't care about anyone but themselves. Guys like Cody and Brice call us faggots and talk about how sick we are, but they're the ones who are sick. I'm glad I'm not like that."

"Me too. The thing is, they'll go right on being popular. Everyone will treat them like they're gods."

"We know what they are," I said.

"Scared is what they are right now, I bet," Daniel said with a laugh. "I just about wet my pants when Thor was threatening them and he wasn't even talking to me."

"Same here. Can you even imagine him getting in your face like that? You know he was completely serious."

"Cody and Brice know it too. I don't think they'll ever bother us again."

"Let's stop talking about Cody and Brice. Let's just put them in our past. They're over, just like Brand."

"Except we have to see them at school every day," Daniel pointed out.

"Yes, but they just don't matter. *We're* what's important. *Us.* Those guys may be popular, they may appear to have it all, but they'll never have what we have. They can't. There is no way someone like that can be in love the way we are. You know, I wanted someone special in my life for a long time, but I never even dreamed it could be the way it is with you. I never dreamed someone could mean so much to me, make me so happy, or make me feel so good about myself."

"Ditto," Daniel said.

I leaned over and kissed Daniel on the lips. We just sat there and hugged and kissed. We didn't go any further. We didn't need to or even want to just then.

Bloomington, Indiana
Friday, August 21, 2009

Tyler yawned.

"It's getting late," I said. "I think it's time for you to go home."

Tyler yawned again.

"Can I stay the night? I want to hear more about you and Daniel, but I'm so sleepy."

"If you call your dad and ask if it's okay."

Tyler nodded and walked toward the phone. He was back in seconds.

"It's okay. I knew it would be."

"When do I get to meet your dad?" I asked.

"I think you should meet him soon," Tyler said with a slight grin.

"What?" I asked, suspicious.

"Nothing. I'm just goofy when I'm tired."

"When you're tired?"

"No fair picking on me when I'm sleepy. You can torment me in the morning if you like, while you're telling me more about you and Daniel."

"You're really into this story, aren't you?"

"Well, I have to see how it ends."

"No story ever ends, not really."

"I am too tired to argue."

I guided Tyler to the guest room. Guests were a rarity, but I always kept the room ready with clean sheets and everything else a guest might need. I turned in soon myself. I liked the feeling of Tyler sleeping near. I felt comfortable knowing there was someone else in the house.

In the morning, I made French toast for Tyler and myself, once he got out of bed that is, which was well after ten. I didn't mind. I'd only been up an hour myself.

"This is delicious. Your French toast is as good as my dad's and that's saying something."

"Thanks. I don't cook much, but French toast is one of my specialties."

After breakfast, I put on a kettle of tea while Tyler cleaned away the dishes. Soon, we were sitting with cups of hot Irish Breakfast tea.

"So...what happened with you and Daniel?" Tyler asked. "He isn't here, so something must have happened. If you two loved each other that much, why aren't you still together?"

"It's complicated," I said, hesitant to dredge up old memories that were less than pleasant.

"So, tell me. What happened between you that ended things?"

"In a way, things never ended between us."

"What do you mean?"

"Despite everything and all the years that have passed, I still love him."

"So what happened? Tell me."

Bloomington, Indiana
Sunday, June 3, 1990

High school was over, finally and forever. Graduation had come. Part of me was going to miss it. Part of me was not. Daniel, Shane, Thor, Lizzie, and I posed for group photos; we hugged each other and cried. Daniel and I hugged for an extra long time and I didn't care about the look his mom gave me. Our parents had never found out about us, which was a wonder, but I sometimes had the feeling they suspected we were more than friends.

That suspicion was heightened that very night when Mom and Dad told me they needed to have a serious talk with me. I'm sure my face went pale. My mind jumped to conclusions. They'd figured out I was gay and that Daniel and I were lovers. They were going to try to keep us apart.

My suspicions were completely off, but the bomb my parents dropped on me sent me into a tailspin.

"We're moving next week," Dad said. "I received a job offer I could not pass up."

"What? This happened just today? On my graduation day?"

"No, I received the offer a month ago and your mother and I have been making arrangements."

"And you're just telling me now?!?" I practically shouted.

"We knew this would upset you," Mom said. "We didn't want to ruin your last weeks of high school. It took a lot of arranging to put the move off until after your graduation."

"Don't I get any say in this?"

"Tyler. You're going off to college soon," Mom said.

"If you ever pick a school," Dad interrupted. It was a sore point between us.

"You won't be home that much anyway once you start school," Mom continued.

"All my friends are here and my...everyone I know is here!"

I very nearly said "and my boyfriend" but caught myself just in time.

"Most of your friends will be going off to college, too," Mom said. "You can still keep in touch with them. You might even end up attending the same school. Who knows?"

"That's not very likely. Where are we moving anyway?"

"New Mexico."

"That's like another country!"

"Don't be so dramatic," Dad said. "It is a different climate, but a change might be nice."

I wasn't happy in the least, but it was obvious it was a done deal.

"I don't like this," I said firmly. "I don't want to move."

I thought I was doing an excellent job of controlling myself. I wanted to rant and rave.

"I couldn't pass this job opportunity up, Tyler," Dad said. "It means quite a bit more money, but more importantly I'll finally be in charge of a design team instead of working on one little section of programming."

"Your father has been waiting on a chance like this his whole life, Tyler. Designing software has been his dream since he was your age," Mom said.

"Did they even have computers back then?" I asked.

"Yes, but they were enormous," Dad said.

How could I argue without looking like an insensitive jerk? How could I expect Dad to pass up on whatever he'd been offered because I didn't want to move?

"I need to take a walk," I said.

My parents didn't try to stop me. They knew I was upset— they just had no idea how upset. What about Daniel? What was to become of us?

I couldn't blame my parents. There was no bad guy here. Even though I wished I could've had my say before the decision was made, I doubt it would have changed anything. They were probably right not to tell me until graduation. If I'd known this a month ago, it would have ruined my final weeks with Daniel and my friends.

I walked and I thought. I was glad I hadn't shouted the things I'd wanted to shout at my parents. I was glad I'd controlled myself. They didn't do this to hurt me. They were even right about most of my friends leaving for college. Daniel hadn't decided on a school yet, but Thor, Shane, and Lizzie were all heading off for college in the fall. All too soon, I wouldn't see much of them anyway. The whole thing still sucked.

Daniel. How was he going to take the news? What were we going to do? I felt like we had all the time in the world to make decisions about our future and now that time was up. In a week I'd be gone, so far away that Canada was closer. New Mexico wasn't a foreign country, but it might as well have been. What was in New Mexico anyway? Cacti? Tumbleweed? It was a desert, wasn't it? Were there even trees there? I guess it didn't matter. If Daniel wasn't there, nothing mattered. My anger melted into sadness and pain. How could I even tell Daniel? My life was over.

***

Daniel and I had planned to hang out the next day. For the first time ever, I dreaded seeing him. It wasn't that I didn't want to see my boyfriend. I just didn't want to bring his world crashing down with the news of my impending move. I went out and sat on the front steps a few minutes before Daniel was supposed to arrive. I gazed at the daisies, lavender, and violets in the flower beds. Mom had planted them when I was little and they came up every year all on their own. Next year, I wouldn't be here to see them. I guess I knew things would change someday. I'd just graduated from high school, which was a big change, but even that wasn't quite real to me yet. Part of me felt like I'd be going back in the fall to join Daniel, Thor, Lizzie, Shane, and Jonah for another year at North. Only Jonah would be returning. I wondered what he'd do without the rest of us. I was sure he'd find new friends. Next year was his senior year. Yes, I knew change would come, but it had always seemed like some far distant event. It would only happen later. Now, later had come and I did not care for it at all.

I spotted Daniel walking up the street. I stood and brushed off the seat of my khaki shorts. Daniel was grinning at he approached. He was so happy. Knowing what I had to tell him nearly broke my heart. I tried to smile, but my lower lip quivered and I had to fight back tears.

"What's wrong?" Daniel asked as he stepped toward me. "Did someone die?"

I shook my head and fought back the tears. I motioned for Daniel to walk with me.

"Tyler, what's wrong?"

I didn't want to say it. I didn't want to speak the words. I knew I had to do it, however, and waiting would only make it worse.

"We're moving, to New Mexico, in a week," I said.

Daniel's face fell.

"What? Why? When did you find this out?"

I explained everything. The anguished look on Daniel's face tore into my heart.

"I can't believe you're leaving," Daniel said when I'd given him all the details.

"I can't either, but I have to start packing today."

"I hate this and it's a shock having it happen so suddenly, but I'm kind of glad your parents didn't tell you before. It would have ruined the whole last month," Daniel said.

"Yeah. I was angry that they'd kept it from me, but the more I think about it, the more I think it's best this way. I can't even really be mad at them for moving. This is like my dad's dream job. He's been waiting for this his whole life."

"Well, we have a week," Daniel said. "I'd rather have a week with you than a lifetime with someone else. Let's make the best of it. Then, we'll see what happens. Letters and phone calls won't be the same, but...who knows?"

"Yeah, who knows?"

I felt like our relationship was dying before my eyes. Letters and phone calls. They were no replacement for Daniel's arms around me or his passionate kisses. I wanted to lay by him every night, not think about him from hundreds of miles away.

"Have you decided on a school yet?" Daniel asked.

"You know I haven't."

"Well, maybe we can go to the same school."

"Maybe. I don't know. There's so much to think about. All I know is that I don't want to leave you. I want us to be together."

Daniel hugged me. I felt so safe in his arms. How could I survive without him?

***

The next week passed far too quickly. It was a week filled with sadness and regret and yet Daniel and I made the most of our time together. We were able to forget, for a while, that soon a great distance would separate us, but the knowledge would return to assail us and when we remembered it hurt worse than ever before.

As the day for my departure drew near I grew increasingly desperate to somehow stop the inevitable. I couldn't live without Daniel. I just couldn't. I began thinking about possibilities and wild schemes, most of which were utterly ridiculous, but I knew I had to do something.

The day before our departure, Daniel and I sat on the grass near the pond in the IU Arboretum. My time with him was slipping by so quickly. I wanted to hold onto each passing moment and refuse to let it go.

"Come with me," I said suddenly. It was one of the wild schemes I'd considered.

"Huh?"

"Come with me—to New Mexico," I said.

"I think your parents might object, to say nothing of mine."

"I wish I could hide you in a suitcase and sneak you into my car."

Daniel smiled at me sadly.

"I wish you could too."

"I hate this!" I said.

"Maybe you could stay here," Daniel said.

"I've thought about that, but where would I live? My parents would never allow it. They're trying to hold onto their time with me just like I'm trying to hold onto my time with you."

We sat in silence for a good long time. I plucked blades of grass and twisted them in my finger.

"Leave with me tomorrow," I said.

Daniel gave me a "we already discussed this" look.

"Not with my parents, with *me*."

Now Daniel looked confused.

"My parents have last minute papers to sign tomorrow, something about selling the house. We're leaving for New Mexico at noon. You and I could take off before then, or even tonight."

"Where would we go, Tyler?"

"I don't know. It doesn't matter. I just want to be with you."

"I...I love you, Tyler, but I don't know if I could just leave my family like that...without a word."

"You can leave them a note or call them after we leave. It doesn't mean you'll never see them again. We can go somewhere. I have quite a bit of money saved up, enough to get us started. We can find a place to live and get jobs. Together, we could make it work."

"What about college?"

"We can still go to school. Neither of us has even decided where we want to go. We can pick a school, maybe get campus housing together, and then work our way through college. We can do anything, Daniel, as long as we're together. I don't want to live my life without you. Letters and phone calls aren't going to be enough. I need you with me. I don't care where we are. I'll go anywhere you want. I just want us to be together."

Daniel hugged me.

"I love you so much," he said.

"I love you."

"Let me think about this, okay? This is a huge decision. I want to be with you, but...going off on our own is...intimidating. I don't know if I can leave my parents like that. I want to be with you, but...I wish I could go *and* stay!"

I wanted to plead with Daniel. I wanted to beg him to run away with me. I knew doing so would not be fair. He was being pulled in two directions and I understood that all too well. The thought of leaving my parents was almost too much to bear, but the thought of losing Daniel was even worse. I couldn't lose him! I just couldn't! And yet, leaving my parents would be so very hard. I knew also that running off was very likely an ill-conceived idea. I also knew I was grasping at straws, but what else could we do? I could not, would not, lose Daniel.

"Just think about it," I said. "I won't say any more about it. We'll spend the day together, revisit all our old spots, and make the most of our last hours in Bloomington. Then, tomorrow, meet me here by the pond at 11. I'll be here waiting. If you come, we'll leave together. If not...I'll still love you."

I had tears in my eyes. Daniel did too. I was frightened but hopeful. I knew how hard it would be for him to leave everything he knew behind, but I also knew he loved me with all his heart. I hated forcing such a terrible choice upon him, but it was either that or leave tomorrow for New Mexico with my parents and perhaps never seen Daniel again.

We spent the rest of the day revisiting all the old familiar places. We met up with Thor, Shane, Jonah, and Lizzie for lunch at the China Buffet on East 3rd Street. The goodbyes nearly killed me, but I held onto the hope that tomorrow Daniel and I would be leaving together.

Daniel and I made out in secluded spots on the IU campus, particularly in Dunn Woods, as couples beyond count had doubtless done before. At night, we even made love on the grass in a remote spot, under the moon and the stars. As it grew late, I walked Daniel home and kissed him on his doorstep. There we said "goodbye."

I couldn't sleep that night. There was nothing to do but lie on my bed and wonder about tomorrow. My room was all but empty. Most everything had already been packed up and shipped out. My most necessary belongings were already packed in my car for the trip to New Mexico. I was glad not everything had gone in the big moving van. I'd need my clothes, checkbook, and toiletries if Daniel and I were going to run away together. I lay there and stared at the ceiling. What if Daniel didn't meet me at the pond? What if he did? My last night in my boyhood home was restless and mostly sleepless.

The next morning, I ate a big breakfast. I didn't let on that I might not be there when Mom and Dad were ready to depart. I hated the thought of leaving them wondering. I assuaged my guilt by planning to call them and tell them I was going just before Daniel and I left. They'd try to talk me out of it and when they couldn't they'd try to find me, but I knew I could give them the slip. I didn't want to do that to my parents, but I couldn't lose Daniel!

I stuffed the last of my things into the trunk of my car while Mom and Dad were busy closing up the house for the very last time. I don't know why I was so secretive. I'd been loading stuff into my car for two days. The back seat was crammed full and now so was the trunk. The plan was for me to follow Mom and Dad in their car all the way to New Mexico.

At about fifteen minutes before ten I gave Mom and Dad a hug, told them I loved them, and left for a last drive around town. At least that's what I told them. I think I very nearly gave myself away by being so emotional, but my parents probably just thought I was upset over leaving.

I made the short drive to campus and parked as close as I could to the Arboretum. I was beginning to have doubts even before I got out of the car. I felt unsure of myself as I stepped onto the sidewalk and headed for campus. I felt uneasy and off, like I wasn't doing the right thing, but I couldn't leave Daniel. I loved him too much. I didn't realize leaving Mom and Dad would so hard. I knew it wouldn't be easy, but I was practically in tears. I thought about them standing by the car, waiting for me, just standing and waiting when I was never coming back. When I didn't return they would become impatient, then worried, then frantic. I knew my parents. They would begin imagining all sorts of horrible things. What if I couldn't reach them when I called? The phone was being disconnected today. What if it was already disconnected? If I couldn't tell my parents I was taking off alone, they'd imagine all kinds of horrible things. They'd probably head straight for a payphone and start calling my friends and then finally the hospital looking for me. How could I do this to them?

Before I'd walked to the Arboretum, I decided I'd get word to my parents before I left town one way or another. If our phone had been disconnected, I'd call Lizzie and tell her Daniel and I were running off together. She would understand. I'd ask her to go to my parents and tell them what I'd done. They could call Lizzie and give her their phone number when they settled in. I'd check in with Lizzie so Mom and Dad would know I was okay and then later I'd call them myself. My parents wouldn't like it, but at least they'd know I hadn't been kidnapped.

It was just a couple of minutes before 11 when I sat on the grass near the pond in the Arboretum. The cattails swayed gently in a light breeze. I was going to miss Bloomington. It was a beautiful town and the IU campus was like a big park. No tree could even be cut down on campus without going through a great deal of red tape. I admired a university that cared so much about trees.

Daniel wasn't here. What if he didn't come? What if he decided he couldn't leave his family and his home? Jumping to conclusions was illogical. It was just now 11. He might be a few minutes late. He was walking and he might have some trouble getting away. The minutes crawled by, each seeming like it lasted an hour. At 11:15, there was still no sign of Daniel, but I wasn't giving up hope. At 11:30, he still hadn't arrived. I paced back and forth on the grass and threw bits of wood into the pond. I gazed about me, but no Daniel. At 11:45, tears welled up in my eyes. Daniel was never late. I'd been lying to myself for the better part of an hour, telling myself not to worry, telling myself he'd come. I couldn't lie to myself anymore. If he was coming, he would have been here on time. He wouldn't have made me wait. Still, I lingered in the vain hope that something had held him back and that he'd come running to me at the last minute. I looked at my watch, 11:50. No Daniel. I was supposed to leave with my parents at noon. I couldn't wait any longer, but I did. Each minute passed in slow motion. For a few moments, I thought I saw him walking toward me, but when the figure drew near I saw it was just some college guy. At 11:55, I left the pond and walked toward my car. Tears filled my eyes and ran down my cheeks. I'd really thought Daniel would come with me. I really thought we'd be together, but he wasn't coming. I'd lost the boy that I loved.

Bloomington, Indiana
Saturday, August 22, 2009

Tears rimmed my eyes and Tyler reached across the table and took my hand. I smiled at him, squeezed his hand, and then released it.

"Did you ever see him again?" Tyler asked.

"No. At first I was so hurt I didn't even want to think about him. Of course, I thought about him all the time anyway. Then I was angry, terribly angry. Later, I began to think more clearly. I knew how hard it would have been for me to leave my parents and I understood all too well how hard it was to leave my home. I liked New Mexico. It turned out to be an incredible place to live, but it wasn't Bloomington. I understood, after a time, that Daniel just couldn't leave everything he knew and especially his parents. I couldn't be angry with him for that, at least it wasn't fair to be angry with him. So, I wrote him a letter, but...he never answered."

"Never?"

"No. I waited, but the days passed and I received no answer. I thought that maybe the letter was lost so I wrote him another and another and another. He never wrote me back. Finally, I called."

I paused. It was difficult for me to talk about this even after so many years.

"What happened?"

"His mom answered. She told me he didn't want to talk to me."

"I'm so sorry."

"I was devastated and confused. I didn't understand why he wouldn't answer my letters and why he wouldn't even talk to me. We had been so close. We'd been so much in love and then...he wouldn't even speak to me. No explanation. Nothing. I called a few more times, but his mom or dad always answered and told me Daniel didn't wish to speak to me. Finally, his mom told me to never call again."

"Did you ever find out why he wouldn't talk to you?"

"No. I think I made a big mistake, too. I was so upset and heartbroken that I didn't even want to think about Daniel anymore. I didn't want to hear his name. I should have called Thor, Shane, Lizzie, or Jonah to see if they could find out anything, but it hurt so much to think about him that I never did. In fact, I did something terrible. I was supposed to give my friends my new address and phone number as soon as we found a permanent place to live in New Mexico. I never contacted them. I disappeared from their lives just like Daniel did from mine. I've always regretted that. I just abandoned them as he abandoned me. It was stupid, but I was in pain. I wasn't thinking. I knew, also that they'd surely mention Daniel and I just couldn't bear to think about him.

"I returned to Camp Neeswaugee the next summer. I didn't go the summer my family moved to New Mexico because Daniel and I had planned to spend the whole summer together in Bloomington. By the time I knew that wasn't going to happen it was too late to get a position. I applied early for the next summer and I was back in Camp Neeswaugee again. I thought Daniel might be back in Division 6, but he didn't return. I thought of visiting Bloomington while I was in Indiana, but I never did. There were too many memories there, memories that were painful. I saw no reason to seek Daniel out. If he didn't want to communicate by letter or phone, he wouldn't want to speak to me in person either."

"I'm so sorry that happened to you," Tyler said.

"It tore me apart, but now, looking back, I think the time I had with Daniel was worth the pain. I'd never been in love like that before nor have I since. For a long time, that love was tainted by Daniel's rejection of me, but little by little those bad feelings went away and I'm left with the memory of a time when I was loved."

"Do you think about him sometimes?"

"I don't think a day passes without Daniel entering my thoughts. I often wonder where life took him. I thought about looking for him, but even after all this time I don't think I could take seeing a picture of him with a boyfriend on a facebook page.

I very nearly destroyed the pictures I had of him, but I'm so glad I didn't. I treasure them now."

"Can I see?"

I hesitated.

"Yes, I'll show you, but there's something I should tell you first..."

"What?"

"Daniel looked...a great deal like you. So much so that when you came to my door that first day, I thought you were him for a moment. Of course, I realized that twenty years had passed, but still, the resemblance is uncanny."

I walked to a small antique cabinet and took out a little photo album. I handed it to Tyler. He opened the album and just stared.

"These look like pictures of me," he said.

"And yet they were taken before you were born."

Tyler grinned. He eagerly looked through the photo album, devouring each picture with his eyes.

"You may not want to hear this, but I should come clean about something," I said.

"What?"

"Well, I like you for you. I enjoy your company, but..."

"You've been trying to relive your past with me?"

I smiled. Tyler was both perceptive and intelligent.

"Not exactly. It's just that when I'm with you, sometimes it feels like it's twenty years ago and I'm with Daniel. I feel myself drawn to you. On some occasions I've even been attracted to you and when that happens I know I'm thinking of you as Daniel. I do want you to know that I value you as a friend and not for your resemblance to a memory. As for the attraction...I have no intentions of acting on that. I wouldn't feel right, even if you were interested, because at those times I'm seeing Daniel instead of you. I'm remembering what it was like with him and there's a part of me that longs to be with him, even after all this time. I didn't tell you this before because I feared it would make you uncomfortable."

"I understand and it doesn't make me uncomfortable. I might even be a little flattered, except it's my resemblance to Daniel that attracts you."

I noticed Tyler said nothing that revealed his sexual orientation and that was okay. His sexual orientation didn't matter to me. I liked him as he was.

"I value *your* friendship, Tyler. I look forward to your visits. I enjoy going out with you. You've come to mean a great deal to me. The beginnings of our relationship may be rooted in your resemblance to Daniel—but only the beginnings. I like you for you, not for your resemblance to my first and only real love."

Tyler grinned.

"You mean a lot to me, too," Tyler said. "I can't believe you're willing to spend so much time with me. I like how you don't treat me like a kid."

"Why wouldn't I want to spend time with you? You're intelligent, you have a witty sense of humor, and you're a wonderful companion. If I didn't know you, I'd be looking for someone like you. I think of you as young, but not as a kid. I believe everyone should be treated with kindness and respect. You are young enough to be my son, but I think the contrast makes you even more interesting. I love seeing familiar things through your eyes and I enjoy the new experiences you've brought into my life."

"You remind me a lot of my dad," Tyler said. "He doesn't treat me like a kid either. He never has, even when I *was* a kid. He's always been a lot like a friend, and yet still my dad. You two have got to meet. I know you'll really like each other and he's been alone too long."

There was something in Tyler's last sentence that made me raise an eyebrow.

Tyler's dad is gay? That explained his accepting attitude, but then again the younger generations are wiser about these things than the older.

"Are you trying to set me up with your dad, Tyler?" I asked with a slight smile.

Tyler reddened.

"I know you'll really like each other. You're perfect for each other. I've been thinking that for quite a while and now I'm sure of it. Even before I began to figure out you were gay I was thinking you'd be great for my dad."

"So you've just been hanging out with me so you can play matchmaker," I teased.

"No! But, you've got to meet Dad."

"I'd like to meet him," I said. "If for no other reason than he's your dad. Just don't get your hopes up, Tyler. I can tell you love your dad very much and you want him to be happy, but don't assume we'll hit it off just because we're both gay. Don't expect too much."

"Oh, I know you're a match," Tyler said with a grin.

"Tyler..."

"If it doesn't work out, it's not going to ruin my life. I'll still have you and my dad. I'm sure it will work out, however."

"What makes you so sure?"

"That's my secret."

"You're just a little evil. I like that."

"I know."

"So, are we okay? Even after all I've just told you?" I asked.

"Of course we are," Tyler said. "Thank you for sharing such a personal and private part of your life with me."

Tyler stood and gave me a hug. I hugged him back and smiled.

"You know, Tyler, your dad is lucky having a son like you. I wish...

"What?"

"I wish I had a son like you, too," I said.

Tears actually rimmed my eyes for a few moments. Tyler grinned at me.

Bloomington, Indiana
Sunday, August 23, 2009

I walked up Kirkwood toward the Sample Gates, the entrance to the Old Crescent Area of the IU Campus. Most of the IU campus was beautiful, but this was one of my favorite locations. I crossed Indiana Avenue and then paused to gaze at the gates and the beautiful old buildings beyond. I often walked here, but I did so today with a sense of trepidation. I tried to shake the feeling off, but it persisted. I was on my way to finally meet Tyler's dad. That in itself didn't trouble me. I wanted to meet him and had for some time. I was concerned about Tyler's expectations. We'd grown very close and he loved his dad very much. Tyler had an idea in his head that his dad and I would hit it off. I very much feared he hoped the two of us would develop a romantic relationship. That was far too much to expect of two guys who had never met. I didn't want to see Tyler disappointed.

I would have been more comfortable if I was meeting Tyler and his dad somewhere for a cup of tea or perhaps dinner, but Tyler absolutely insisted I meet his father alone at the old Rose Well House. I knew the location well. It was a small, Gothic-style, open-air pavilion with a tile roof. It was made of limestone and had been built using the two surviving portals from the old campus building. Sometimes, I liked to sit on a bench by the pavilion or on one of the window sills. The pavilion had been used as a location in *Breaking Away*, too.

I walked on. I didn't want to keep Tyler's dad waiting. I pushed my sense of ill-ease to the side. Based on my experience with Tyler, I was sure to get along with his dad. I had a feeling Tyler would be happy as long as his dad and I were on friendly terms. That we could surely manage.

I didn't see anyone near the Rose Well House as I approached, but then I caught sight of someone standing inside. I wondered if Tyler's dad was as uncomfortable meeting like his as I was. At least Tyler had picked a beautiful location and a good place to talk.

I walked to the well house, crossed the portal and stopped. Tyler's dad and I stood there just gazing at each other in dumb silence. Neither of us spoke as the seconds ticked by, but my heart beat faster and I almost felt as if I could cry.

"*Daniel?*" I asked, my voice choking. It wasn't truly a question. I just couldn't believe he was standing there after all these years.

"*Tyler?*" he asked.

I nodded unnecessarily.

"Tyler, my son Tyler that is, said your name is Percy."

"That's my penname. I've gone by Percy for years now. Everyone calls me Percy, except my parents."

"I...I...don't know what to say," Daniel said.

"I don't either," I said, grinning. "I'm just so glad to see you again."

I couldn't help myself. I hugged him. Tears ran down my cheeks. When I released him and looked into his eyes, Daniel's cheeks were wet with tears, too.

I grinned and shook my head.

"Your son is very devious. He *knew*."

"But, how?"

"I've been telling him about you, about us, all those years ago. I had no idea he was your son. He looks so much like you, but...I never thought... That little knowing grin of his makes sense now. Somewhere along the line, he must've figured out I was talking about you. That's why he was so sure we'd hit it off."

"He was very mysterious about this meeting. I thought it odd, but..." Daniel frowned. "Tyler...Percy, why didn't you ever try to contact me in all these years? I waited and waited after you left. Not one phone call. Not one letter. You just...disappeared."

"But...I did write. I did call. I waited for you in the Arboretum by the pond. I waited until the last possible second, but you never came. I wrote you, but never received an answer. I called, but your parents told me you didn't want to talk to me. I kept calling until finally they told me never to call again."

"I can't believe they did that," Daniel said, looking angry.

"Did what?"

"I never saw your letters. They never told me you called. I thought you'd just forgotten me. I thought you didn't care anymore. It broke my heart."

Tears ran Daniel's cheeks and mine, too.

"No. No," I said. "I've never forgotten you. Not a single day has gone by in all these years that I didn't think about you and wonder about you. I've never stopped caring about you, Daniel.

"I hoped you'd return to Camp Neeswaugee that first summer after I moved. I hoped I could talk to you and find out why you didn't answer my letters or take my calls. I hoped we could get back together, but you didn't come. Every summer I looked for you, hoping you'd visit your old summer camp, but you never returned."

"I couldn't go back," Daniel said. "There were too many memories there—memories of you. It would have hurt too much. I had no idea what my parents had done."

"Why didn't you meet me by the pond on the day I left?" I asked. "Why didn't you at least come to say goodbye?"

"Because I was on my way to the hospital."

"What?"

"I did come to meet you, Tyler. I had my backpack stuffed so we could take off together, but I was too busy listening to my Walkman to pay attention crossing the street. I was hit by a car. When you were waiting by the pond, I wasn't even conscious. Only *that* was able to keep me from you."

"I didn't know," I said.

"Of course, you didn't. You couldn't have known. By the time I came to my senses, it was too late, you were gone and I was stuck lying in that hospital bed for days. I planned to join you later if I could, but then I never heard from you. I didn't know how to reach you. Thor, Shane, Jonah, and Lizzie never heard from you either. I kept asking and hoping so I could write or call you, but you never contacted them either."

"I was hurting too much. I just couldn't..."

"I thought maybe you were dead..." Daniel said, then sobbed.

"I'm so sorry," I said. "I'm so *so* sorry."

"It's not your fault. If anyone is to blame it's my parents and maybe that's my fault, too."

"How?"

"There were awkward questions about my backpack. After the accident, my parents opened it. I admitted I was running away with you. I never told them we were lovers, but they weren't stupid. Mom already suspected, I think. She never asked and I never told, but, I think she knew."

"That's why she intercepted my letters and my calls," I said. "To keep me away from you."

"And to keep from losing me."

We just gazed at each other for a few moments.

"We can't change the past," I said.

"No, we can't."

"We're here now and I want to get to know you again," I said. "I know we've both changed, but...I never stopped loving you."

Daniel pulled me to him and hugged me.

"I never stopped loving you either."

Tears ran down my cheeks, but I grinned. When we broke our embrace, I gazed into Daniel's eyes, leaned in, and kissed him. He kissed me back and I felt as if no time had passed at all since we had graduated from high school.

"We have a lot of catching up to do," I said.

Daniel and I walked toward the Sample Gates and then a few blocks down Kirkwood to Soma. We ordered English Breakfast tea and sat at a quiet little table, the same table where Tyler and I had once sat, the same table where Daniel and I had sat when we were teenagers.

"I can't believe you're here," Daniel said. "I can't believe you're Percy DeForest Spock, although that last name is a giveaway. You're still obsessed with *Star Trek,* obviously."

"I'm not obsessed!"

"Please, I bet you've read every *Star Trek* novel out there. I wouldn't be surprised if you've written a few."

"I can't believe you're still in Bloomington. Did you never leave?" I asked.

"Only for college."

"I have to ask this. How did you end up with a son, Daniel? Tyler's wonderful, but...as I recall, you had no interest in girls."

Daniel grinned; it was the grin I remembered from all those years ago.

"Tyler is the result of a favor I did for one of my close friends while I was in college."

"Someone thinks rather highly of himself," I teased.

Daniel shot me a look that said, "Please."

"Lynn wanted a baby very badly, but she didn't want a husband or other entanglements. We were very close and it just seemed natural. The plan was for her to raise the child, but I'd still be a part of his or her life. I wouldn't have any paternal responsibilities, other than loving our child. We discussed it for months and even had legal papers drawn up. The whole thing was ridiculous, of course, but we were young and stupid. Looking back, I almost can't believe we did it, but I'm glad we did because now I have Tyler."

"So what happened?"

"Tyler was born. We were both so very happy. I never thought I'd have a son and there he was, but then, two years later, Lynn developed a brain tumor. Three weeks later she was dead."

"I'm sorry," I said, reaching across the table and squeezing Daniel's hand.

"It was hard losing her. I did love her. It wasn't a romantic love, but I loved her.

"Thanks to Lynn's foresight, there were no legal complications. I was Tyler's father and the papers we'd had drawn up specifically stated I was to have sole custody of Tyler if anything happened to Lynn. Suddenly, she was gone and there I was, a twenty-two-year-old college senior with a two-year-old son. It was rough, but I loved Tyler. Some of my straight buddies were jealous. A two-year-old baby is a chick magnet."

Daniel laughed, then looked at me more seriously.

320

"He's named after you," he said.

I bit my lower lip. I thought I was going to cry.

"He's a wonderful young man. I've thought more than once that if I had a son, I'd want him to be Tyler."

Daniel smiled the proud smile of a father.

"I should have figured out he was your son. He looks almost exactly like you when you were his age. He acts a lot like you, too. The thought crossed my mind, but I dismissed it as ridiculous. I couldn't imagine you with a woman."

"As much as I loved Lynn and as much as I wanted to have a child with her, it was difficult. We did it the old fashioned way and...let's just say it took some creative fantasizing on my part to make it possible."

I nodded.

"When we were actually...doing it, I closed my eyes and imagined I was with you," Daniel said, blushing.

"I'm glad you were up to the task. Tyler and I have become close."

"He's always talking about you. I had no idea it was you, of course, but it's been Percy this and Percy that for weeks. Lately, Tyler has had this knowing look in his eye."

"Very recently, I've been telling him about us," I said. "I told him all about the boy I met at camp, the boy who stole my heart. I don't think I would have told him quite so much if I'd known he was your son. I should have known something was up. I saw that knowing look in his eye, too. Even when I was telling him about the day I waited for you by the pond, he seemed like he was holding back a secret. I bet he was already planning on getting us together."

"He's smart and mischievous," Daniel said.

"Just like his dad."

"I think he hopes we'll pick up where we left off. He's encouraged me before to date," Daniel said.

"It would be a shame to disappoint him," I said.

Daniel smiled.

"Why don't you give your son a call? We'll all go out for pizza. It would be unfair to keep him in suspense."

Daniel nodded and pulled out his cell. I put my hand on his wrist before he punched in Tyler's number.

"Just have him meet you somewhere. Don't tell him I'll be there and don't say anything about meeting me. Just let him wonder."

"You were always just a little bit evil," Daniel said.

He made the call. Half an hour later, Daniel and I were sitting in Mother Bear's Pizza on 3rd Street, waiting for Tyler to arrive.

Tyler walked in. He slowed when he spotted us and then he grinned. He took a seat across from us, smiling and looking back and forth between us.

"So?" he asked.

"So, what?" Daniel asked.

"*Dad!*"

Daniel and I both laughed.

"Come on! You guys are killing me!" Tyler said. "You never thought you'd see each other again and here you are sitting side by side. Say something!"

"Thank you, Tyler," I said.

I took Daniel's hand and squeezed it before releasing it again. I was bursting with happiness.

"What I want to know is how you kept this a secret from both of us," Daniel said. "And, just when did you put it all together?"

"Well, I began to wonder a little when Percy told me about working at a summer camp, especially when he said Camp Neeswaugee. I remembered you telling me about being a camp counselor and I thought you were at Neeswaugee. I almost said something to Percy right then, but I wasn't sure I remembered right and something inside me told me not to say anything. You never talk much about those days, Dad. I didn't have much to go on. I didn't really know for sure until Percy showed me pictures of you guys. I knew that had to be you in the photos. I know how much I look like you did back then and those could have been pictures of me. I also did a little snooping at home and found a few Camp Neeswaugee things. I had no idea you were so wild back then!"

Tyler laughed. Daniel looked at me.

"As I said before, I gave Tyler a few more details than I would have had I known he was your son," I admitted.

"You were a horn dog!' Tyler said.

Tyler looked back and forth between us.

"So? Are you guys going to date? I know it's been twenty years, but you two were crazy for each other, so..."

"I wouldn't mind seeing more of your dad, if he's interested," I said. In answer, Daniel took my hand, squeezed it, and didn't let go.

"I'm sure we've both changed over the years, but you're still Tyler...I mean, Percy. That's going to be confusing. Which should I call you?"

"I think that since you already have a Tyler in your life it might be best to call me Percy," I said.

Daniel looked at his son.

"I never told you this before, Tyler, but you're named after him," Daniel said, pointing to me.

"Wow! That's really cool."

Tyler sat there, grinned, and looked back and forth between us.

"I'm so psyched about this!" Tyler said. "Percy DeForest Spock and my dad. You guys are perfect for each other. I thought that even before I knew you had a history. I thought that as soon as I figured out Percy was gay. Dad, I *really* like Percy, so if you two want to get married or something..."

"My son, the matchmaker," Daniel said.

"You need someone, Dad, and so do you, Percy."

"He's very intelligent. He may be onto something," I said to Daniel.

"So, now that I've solved all the problems with your love lives, how about some pizza?" Tyler asked.

Daniel and I laughed and pulled the menus forward. I hadn't been so happy since...since I was with Daniel before. I squeezed Daniel's hand. Yes, twenty years had passed, but he was the same Daniel. Now that I had him again, I had no intention of letting him go. I looked across the table at Tyler. I was already very fond of him. I'd often regretted not having a son and now I felt as if Tyler was my son, too. I knew I was getting ahead of myself, but I didn't care. I could feel Daniel's love for me in my heart and I knew this time we'd stay together. All the old pain fell away when I'd looked into Daniel's eyes and I was left with only happiness.

After we finished off a large pepperoni, Daniel and I strolled around the IU campus across the street, revisiting all the old familiar places. The only thing different this time was that Tyler was with us. For the first time in a long time, I felt complete. I felt like I'd finally found my family.

Information on Mark's upcoming books can be found at markroeder.com. Those wishing to keep in touch with others who enjoy Mark's novels can join his fan club at http://groups.yahoo.com/group/markaroederfans.

Made in the USA
Columbia, SC
09 July 2025

60537701R00195